PRAISE FOR SUE MARGOLIS'S NOVELS

GUCCI GUCCI COO

"A wickedly prescient novel...Likeable characters and a clever concept make this silly confection a guilty pleasure." —*USA Today*

"It's Margolis's voice that separates *Gucci Gucci Coo* from other entries in the fast-growing chick-and-baby-lit category....Her language...is fresh and original....[This] is a fast, fun read...a great book for any smart girl who has ever had to attend a baby shower." —*Chicago Sun-Times*

"This popular British author keeps turning out fun and witty novels that readers will grab off the shelves....Though her previous books have drawn many *Bridget Jones* comparisons, her writing may become the new standard for the chick-lit genre." —*Booklist*

"If you liked any of Sophie Kinsella's Shopaholic books or Allison Pearson's *I Don't Know How She Does It*, you'll like this British take on pregnancy and motherhood....A fun, entertaining read and a book you'll pass on to friends." —Mamarant.blogs.com

"You'll laugh out loud at Ruby's humorous escapes...and relate to her many misgivings about her life and where it's going. Ms. Margolis's trademark witty, bright writing style shines through. Fun!" —freshfiction.com

"This humorous, personable tale has an added touch of mystery which makes for a fun and enjoyable read....Don't miss *Gucci Gucci Coo*. It's the perfect book for the summer!" —*Romance Reviews Today*

ORIGINAL CYN

"Hilarious...Margolis's silly puns alone are worth the price of the book. Another laugh-out-loud-funny, occasionally clever, and perfectly polished charmer." —*Central Contra Costa Times*

"Delightful...fans will appreciate this look at a lack of ethics in the workplace." —*Midwest Book Review*

"Has something for everyone—humor, good dialogue, hot love scenes, and lots of dilemmas." —*Rendezvous*

"A perfect lunchtime book or, better yet, a book for those days at the beach." —*Romance Reviews Today*

BREAKFAST AT STEPHANIE'S

"With Stephanie, Margolis has produced yet another jazzy cousin to Bridget Jones." —*Publishers Weekly*

"A heartwarming, character-driven tale...a hilariously funny story." —*Romance Reviews Today*

"A comic, breezy winner from popular and sexy Margolis." —*Booklist*

"Rife with female frivolity, punchy one-liners, and sex." —*Kirkus Reviews*

"An engaging tale." —*Pittsburgh Post-Gazette*

APOCALIPSTICK

"Sexy British romp...Margolis's characters have a candor and self-deprecation that lead to furiously funny moments....A riotous, ribald escapade sure to leave readers chuckling to the very end of this saucy adventure." —*USA Today*

"Quick in pace and often very funny." —*Kirkus Reviews*

"Margolis combines light-hearted suspense with sharp English wit...entertaining read." —*Booklist*

"A joyously funny British comedy...There are always great characters in Ms. Margolis's novels. With plenty of romance and passion, *Apocalipstick* is just the ticket for those of us who like the rambunctious, witty humor this comedy provides." —*Romance Reviews Today*

"Rather funny...compelling...brilliant send-ups of high fashion." —*East Bay Express*

"[An] irreverent, sharp-witted look at love and dating." —*Houston Chronicle*

SPIN CYCLE

"This delightful novel is filled with more than a few big laughs." —*Booklist*

"A funny, sexy British romp...Margolis is able to keep the witty one-liners spraying like bullets." —*Library Journal*

"Warm-hearted relationship farce... a nourishing delight."
—*Publishers Weekly*

"Satisfying... a wonderful diversion on an airplane, poolside, or beach." —*Baton Rouge Magazine*

NEUROTICA

"Screamingly funny sex comedy...the perfect novel to take on holiday." —*USA Today*

"Cheeky comic novel—a kind of *Bridget Jones's Diary* for the matrimonial set... Wickedly funny." —*People* (Beach Book of the Week)

"Scenes that literally will make your chin drop with shock before you erupt with laughter... A fast and furiously funny read."
—*Cleveland Plain Dealer*

"Taking up where *Bridget Jones's Diary* took off, this saucy British adventure redefines the lusty woman's search for erotic satisfaction.... Witty and sure... A taut and rambunctious tale exploring the perils and raptures of the pursuit of passion." —*Publishers Weekly*

"Splashy romp... giggles guaranteed." —*New York Daily News*

"A good book to take to the beach, *Neurotica* is fast paced and at times hilarious." —*Boston's Weekly Digest Magazine*

"This raunchy and racy British novel is great fun, and will delight fans of the television show *Absolutely Fabulous*." —*Booklist*

Also by Sue Margolis

Neurotica
Spin Cycle
Apocalipstick
Breakfast at Stephanie's
Original Cyn
Gucci Gucci Coo

Forget Me Knot

Sue Margolis

Bantam Books

Forget Me Knot is a work of fiction. Names, characters, places, and incidents either are the product of the author's imagination or are used fictitiously. Any resemblance to actual persons, living or dead, events, or locales is entirely coincidental.

Published in the United States by Bantam Books, an imprint of The Random House Publishing Group, a Division of Random House, Inc., New York.

BANTAM BOOKS and the rooster colophon are registered trademarks of Random House, Inc.

Library of Congress Cataloging-in-Publication Data
Margolis, Sue.
Forget me knot / Sue Margolis.
p. cm.
ISBN 978-0-385-33900-1 (trade pbk.) — ISBN 978-0-553-90672-1 (ebook)
I. Florists—Fiction. I. Title.
PR6063.A635F67 2009
823'.914—dc22
2009002091

Printed in the United States of America on acid-free paper

www.bantamdell.com

4 6 8 9 7 5 3

Book design by Carol Malcolm Russo

For Avril,
who always takes time to smell the flowers

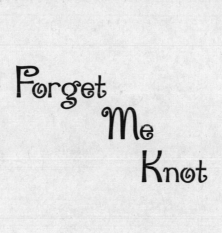

Chapter 1

"HANG ON," SOPH SAID, "you're telling me the corpse had an erection?"

Abby transferred her mobile to the other ear and with her free hand began setting the shop's burglar alarm for the night. "No, it was the dove."

"The *dove* had an erection?"

"Duh. Of course the dove didn't have an erection. It flew into the open coffin, found its way into the old man's trouser pocket and made it *look* like he had an erection."

"But why on earth were there doves flying around the house?"

Abby explained that the dead man, who had been lying in state in the front room of his Croydon semi-detached house, used to make his living as a children's party entertainer. "The doves were part of his magic act. Anyway, just before everybody was due to set off for the cemetery, his wife had the dotty idea of letting the birds out of their cages to say good-bye to their master. My guess is that when he was performing, he hid them in his trouser pocket. Right on cue, one of them headed straight for the clown suit."

"The corpse was wearing a clown suit?"

"Yeah. Red-and-white stripes with gold pom-poms down the front."

"Nice."

Abby stepped onto the pavement and closed the shop door behind her. It was thick plate glass with a stainless-steel handle shaped like a rose in full bloom. Abby was particularly proud of the handle. She'd designed it herself, taking great pains to get every fold, twist and angle of every petal exactly as she wanted it. If you looked carefully—not that anyone ever did, apart from Abby—there was even a tiny metal dewdrop on one of the petals. At first, the design had been meant purely as a business logo. Then she'd had the idea of e-mailing it to one of the cutlery firms in Sheffield and asking if there was any way they could fashion a rose door handle.

Earnshaw & Sons (By Royal Appointment) assured her the commission was well within their capabilities. Six weeks later, the exquisitely crafted tea-rose handle arrived by courier, along with Earnshaw's jaw-dropping bill for three thousand pounds.

In the middle of the door, in opaque lowercase letters, was the name of the shop: "fabulous flowers." Sometimes, when there weren't many people about, Abby would stand with her nose pressed against the window and gaze at the outsize glass vases full of flowers, still not quite able to believe that the shop belonged to her.

"So, how come you were at this funeral in the first place?"

Another question. Soph was forever asking questions. How much did you pay for it? Why did your father need a colonoscopy? How come your uncle went bankrupt? Soph

said all Jews were the same. They were genetically pro-
grammed to interrogate. They liked to take an interest in
other people's lives. It was their way of showing that they
cared. Soph's parents were the same. They even bickered in
question marks.

"Sammy, do you have the time?"

"Tell me something, Faye. Do I look like a clock?"

Abby turned the key in the lock. "I wasn't *at* the funeral
exactly." She explained that Smarty Arty, the deceased children's entertainer, had lived across the street from her parents. "Mum had a soft spot for Smarty Arty and his wife.
The feeling was pretty mutual, and when Mrs. Smarty Arty
found out that Mum and Dad weren't going to be able to
make the funeral, she was really upset. Mum was desperate
to make it up to her, and since the Smarty Arties were
pretty hard up and there was no way Mrs. Smarty Arty
could afford more than a cheap wreath to go on top of the
coffin, Mum insisted on paying for a really beautiful
arrangement, which I put together. When I arrived to deliver it, the old lady invited me in for a cup of tea." A smile
formed on Abby's face as she wondered whether her explanation would satisfy Soph or whether her friend would feel
the need to come back with a couple of supplementary
questions or raise points that, to her mind, still required
clarification. In the end, all Soph said by way of reply was:
"Oh, right."

"Three years I've been running this business," Abby
went on, her tone becoming wistful, "and it's only the second time I've had to do funeral flowers."

"And do you remember the first time?"

Even now, two years later, Abby blushed. "As if I could
forget."

Two orders had come in on the same day. One was from a woman wanting to wish friends good luck with their house move. The other was for funeral flowers. Somehow Abby managed to get the orders mixed up, and the dead person received a bunch of sunflowers containing a card that read: *Congratulations on your new home.*

Her monumental cock-up aside, Abby wasn't surprised that she received so few orders for funeral flowers. After all, Fabulous Flowers was in Islington, an area inhabited almost exclusively by hip, health-conscious and very much alive young professionals. Their floral requirements tended less toward funeral wreaths and more toward hand-tied calla lily bouquets, amaryllis centerpieces and giant zinc containers full of contorted willow to set off their edgy loft spaces.

As Abby carried on chatting to Soph, she pushed on the shop door to check that it was secure. Satisfied that it was, she set off toward the tube station, turning up her jacket collar as she went. The heavens had opened a few hours earlier, and the pavement was full of puddles reflecting light from the streetlamps. She couldn't help noticing the weary irritation on the faces of the commuters as they struggled to dodge the puddles as well as one another.

"Oh, for God's sake," she exclaimed at one point.

"What?" Soph said.

"Bloody car just went by and splashed my stockings." She stopped and began rubbing at her shins, which until now had been encased in grime-free, fresh-out-of-the-packet, nude satin stockings. The rubbing seemed to spread the dirt rather than remove it. Then, to her horror, she noticed there were more splashes on the hem of her brand-new three-hundred-quid Diane von Furstenberg wrap dress. She decided that as soon as she got to the restaurant she would make a quick dash to the ladies' room and have another go with a wet paper towel.

As she set off again, she glanced at her watch. It was after seven. She was cutting it fine if she was going to make it to the restaurant by half past. She couldn't be late. Not tonight of all nights. She attempted to pick up her pace, but it wasn't easy, what with the commuters and the puddles.

If it hadn't been for a mother and her daughter debating until after six about whether a bouquet that contained trailing stephanotis as well as longiflorum lilies might eclipse the daughter's wedding dress, she would have been ready on time. Abby, who had been provided with a photograph of the dress, was tempted to say that nothing short of a bunch of hand-tied asteroids could eclipse the meringue *Gone with the Wind*-inspired creation before her—but she bit her lip.

In the end, she had been left with only three quarters of an hour to get home and get changed. On the plus side, her flat was over the shop, which meant her traveling time was roughly fifteen seconds.

"So, your mum and dad enjoying their cruise?" Soph inquired.

"Er, less of the *c* word, please. This is an *expedition*, remember?" Abby's parents, Jean and Hugh, were on their way to the South Pole. They were going to visit the penguins—on one of those cruises designed to make the middle-aged feel better about being on a cruise by cutting back on cabin size, entertainment and rations and pretending it was really an expedition. A few days ago, they had flown to Buenos Aires, where they had boarded an Irish-owned ship called the *Bantry*. The following day they had set sail for Antarctica.

"Dad phoned and left a message the other night to say things are really looking up. The captain had assured them that he is looking into why the loo in their cabin is shooting waste into the sink and that he'll have it sorted in a couple of days. Meanwhile, every time one of them uses the bathroom, Mum has to give the sink a good going over with her spare face cloth and some Dettol."

"Omigod. But don't they realize they could catch typhoid or cholera from something like this? You need to warn them."

"I'm not sure it's quite that bad—at least not yet—but I texted back to ask them why they hadn't insisted on changing cabins and Dad said they didn't want to make a fuss."

"Only the goyim!"

Abby gave a soft laugh. "What does that mean?"

"It means that only gentiles would rather die than risk making a nuisance of themselves. By now my parents would be radioing air–sea rescue, demanding they send out a helicopter to lift them off the ship. At the same time, they would be preparing to sue their travel agent, the cruise line, the captain and all the ship's staff. They would also have faxed my cousin at the BBC and his brother who works on the *Guardian*."

"Yes, and they would also have had strokes from all the shouting and screaming."

"OK, I admit that is a possibility," Soph said with a chuckle. She paused. "So, getting back to this funeral—what were you doing schlepping wreaths all the way from Islington to Croydon? It must have been a twenty-five-mile round trip. Couldn't you have sent them by courier?"

"I could, but I had to go over to Mum's anyway to water

the plants and pick up my dress for tonight. I splurged on this fabulous jade-green Diane von Furstenberg."

"What was it doing at your mother's?"

"A friend of hers was shortening it for me."

"It needed shortening?"

"Yes."

"The store couldn't do it?"

"Not in time, no." A smile was forming on Abby's face. "Anything else you'd like to know?"

"Oops, sorry, I forgot the eleventh commandment: honor thy gentiles and probe ye not, for lo it is written that they are a private people who liketh to keep themselves to themselves.... God forbid a person should show an interest."

Abby had known *Sophia* Weintraub since their high school days. By the time she was fourteen, Soph was the star of the school debating society. She read the newspaper op-ed columns every day and absorbed political arguments as if they were no more complicated than plots in a daytime soap.

Debates took place in the school hall. Soph was so short that she could barely see over the podium, but this little girl with her tight black curls, puppy fat and braces took on all comers and argued the case for antivivisection, the legalization of drugs or the Israeli withdrawal from the occupied territories with the energy of a terrier with a rat, not to mention a wisdom and eloquence that confounded her teachers. The head of English, who wanted Soph to try for Oxbridge, nicknamed her Portia after the lawyer heroine in Shakespeare's *Merchant of Venice.*

Everybody thought she would go into the law or politics.

In the end she decided not to apply to Oxbridge, on the grounds that it was too elitist. She went to Leeds instead, where she studied politics. After graduating summa cum laude, she was taken on by one of the broadsheet newspapers. She spent a year as a junior reporter before being promoted to parliamentary lobby correspondent. She stuck it out for another eighteen months before confessing she was finding the job distinctly lackluster. And Soph was one of those people who craved luster. In the end she abandoned political journalism and went to work for a major West End PR company. After a couple of years she decided she'd learned all she needed to and left to set up her own company.

Some people didn't take to Soph's interrogatory style and the way she came out and said precisely what was on her mind.

Her outspokenness had never offended Abby, though. If anything it made her jealous.

Chez Crompton, straight talking was unheard of. It led to confrontation. Even the prospect of confrontation made Jean and Hugh anxious. It created waves, which in turn caused arguments and bad feeling. Since Abby's parents didn't have the foggiest idea how to deal with bad feelings—their own or anybody else's—they buried them. The upshot was that they were always jolly, optimistic and looking on the bright side—even when the sink in their cabin kept filling with sewage.

On the rare occasions that a negative emotion overtook her father, he would withdraw to the garden shed to tidy his tools. When Jean felt "a bit miffed," she went in for a spot of vigorous weeding. Or, if it was the right time of year, she would give the Christmas pudding a "good old stir."

By contrast, in the Weintraub household, people were constantly emoting. And what extreme emotions they were. Nobody—in particular Soph's mother, Faye—could grasp the idea that an emotional response should fit the event. It didn't matter if the baker had sold the last marble cake before Faye could get to it or if there had been an earthquake in Pakistan that had killed tens of thousands—she was equally "devastated."

On top of that, everybody was permanently on everybody else's case. "Sammy! How can you put all that saturated fat inside you? Don't come running to me if you drop dead of a heart attack!"

"Mum! For Chrissake, can't you just stop nagging Dad for five minutes?"

"Stop yelling at me! I've got a brisket in the oven!"

"Anyway," Soph said, "the reason I was ringing was to wish you luck for tonight. How you feeling?"

"Bit nervous," Abby replied by way of understatement.

"Abs, listen to me. It's going to be fine. You're a beautiful, intelligent, successful woman. You have absolutely nothing to worry about. Come on—who just came in at number twelve in the Sunday *Times*'s 'Style' section's 'Hundred Hottest Shops'?"

"I did," Abby mumbled.

"Er, didn't quite catch that. Louder, please."

Abby could practically see Soph standing with her hands on her hips. She gave a soft snort. "I did."

"And what did the blurb say about you?"

Abby's face was turning crimson. "C'mon, you know what it said."

"Yes, but maybe you need reminding. It said: *Abby Crompton, the inspiration behind Fabulous Flowers, isn't so much a florist as a supremely gifted floral artist who is capable of turning a simple bunch of flowers into a design statement.* Have I got that right?"

"Near enough."

"OK. And was the *Sunday Times* accolade followed by the *London Evening Standard* naming you London Boutique Retailer of the Year?"

"Yes, and that's all fabulous and wonderful, but as far as tonight is concerned, it's irrelevant. Tonight isn't about my creative and business skills. It's all about me as a person and whether I'll measure up."

"Please. How could you possibly not measure up?"

"By coming from Croydon, for a start." By now Abby was heading down the steps into the tube station. "Look, I've got to go. I'm about to lose my phone signal. Thanks for ringing, though. I really appreciate it. I'll let you know how it goes."

"Make sure you do. Now stop worrying. I promise you, tonight is going to go brilliantly."

THE DOWAGER Lady Penelope Kenwood was Abby's prospective mother-in-law. It had been a month since her son, the Honorable Toby Kenwood, had proposed to Abby and she had said yes. Tonight Toby was introducing Abby to Lady Penelope for the first time. The three of them were having dinner at the Ivy, the exclusive showbiz and media eatery in Covent Garden.

Abby needed to take two escalators at Angel Tube. Difficult as it was in heels, she managed to run down them both. Breathless, she stepped onto the platform just as a train was pulling out of the station. She looked at her watch. By now it was ten past seven. According to the indicator board, there wouldn't be another train for eight minutes. "Sod it," she muttered, plonking herself down on an empty bench.

As she waited for the train, she found her mind going back to the night a week or so after she had accepted Toby's marriage proposal. The two of them had been in her kitchen drinking wine and waiting for the Bolognese sauce to cook.

"You do realize," Toby had said, "that on my mother's death I shall become Lord Kenwood and that, for official purposes at least, you would assume the title of Lady."

Abby, who loved Toby for reasons that had nothing to do with his wealth and status, had laughed off the idea of becoming a *lady*—even if it was only for "official" purposes.

"Can you imagine me, Lady Abby from Croydon? I don't think so. Plus I hate the whole hereditary-peerages thing. People should earn titles, not inherit them. It just props up the class system."

Toby said he adored it when she got on her political high horse. It was one of the reasons he had fallen in love with her. "I agree with you," he said, "but you might change your mind when the time comes. Like it or not, a title gives you influence and, even now, can open a great many doors."

Toby tended not to talk about his mother. In the nine months she had known him, Abby had gleaned little beyond a handful of bullet points. Lady Penelope had been the first woman in her family to go to university rather than to finishing school. She had studied law and later become a highly successful criminal barrister. Her career ended when she married Toby's father. It was she, not he, who'd insisted that her loyalties were now to her husband and that it was only right and proper she give up work in order to breed and help run the Kenwood estate.

Toby described her as: "Horsey, a terrible snob, judgmental, overbearing. Think Margaret Thatcher but a lot less reserved. You can imagine Mother collaring Hitler after a rally and bawling him out for slouching."

"Blimey. So, do I greet her with a kiss or a salute?"

Toby gave a nervous half smile. "You know, I'm still not sure you meeting my mother is such a good idea. She's so bloody scary. She intimidates everybody she comes into contact with. Maybe we should wait a bit longer."

"No way," Abby laughed. "We're engaged. I have to meet her. It's time. Look, after everything you've told me, I'm not going to pretend I won't be nervous, but I'm sure I'll cope."

He smiled. "I know you will. I just want you to be prepared, that's all."

"Oh, I'm nothing if not prepared." She laughed again.

"The way to get into my mother's good book is to get her talking about foxhunting. She's master of the local hunt and loves to show off."

Abby said she didn't mean to be difficult, but she wasn't sure how she felt about feigning an interest in blood sports, which she thought were despicable and should be banned.

Toby groaned. "Come on, Abs, can't you just get off your soapbox for five minutes? Hunting is my mother's life, and wittering on about it keeps her amused. Couldn't you humor her? Just for me? If you lock horns with my mother, all hell will break loose. I promise."

He came over to the stove, where she was stirring the spaghetti sauce, and put his arms round her waist. "Say you won't goad her...please." He started kissing the back of her neck.

"I don't know."

More kisses.

"Oh, all right. If it's going to make her happy. The last thing I want to do is create waves. God, I sound like my mother."

"Good girl." He began opening a bottle of wine. "You know, I haven't hunted for years—not since I moved to London. In some ways I miss it. You really feel at one with the countryside."

"I'm sure the fox feels the same," Abby said, sprinkling a pinch of dried herbs into the meat sauce. "As the hounds tear it apart, you can imagine it thinking, 'This hurts like hell, but, hey, at least I feel at one with the countryside.'"

He ignored the comment. "Plus," he said, grinning, "I look absolutely fabulous—don't you know—in the red coat and cravat."

He was laughing, sending himself up, but Abby was in no doubt that he meant it. Toby looked good in anything, and he knew it. With his tall, lean frame and broad shoulders—not to mention the thick blonde hair, cobalt eyes and patrician jaw—Toby had been put on this earth to wear clothes.

But it wasn't simply his coloring and build that made him look so good in everything he wore. When it came to matters sartorial, Toby had an unfailing instinct about what worked and what didn't.

The first time she'd met him—at a posh charity dinner organized by a friend of Soph's—he was standing at the bar, looking knee-tremblingly magnificent in his evening suit and black tie. Roger Moore in his James Bond prime, she thought. He was drinking what looked like Campari and flirting with three or four braying, hair-flicking Fulham women—all clearly smitten. Abby couldn't help but be smitten, too, but upper-class, Roger Moore look-alikes were way out of her league.

Then, while she was waiting to be served at the bar, an elderly woman bumped into her and managed to spill not one but two glasses of champagne over her brand-new dress. In an instant, Toby was at her side, proffering towels and soda water gleaned from the bartender. He must have spent fifteen minutes helping her get the stains out of her dress. During that time, something clicked between them. So much so that, when dinner was announced, Toby persuaded one of the waiters to squeeze in an extra place at Abby's table. They didn't stop talking all evening. He had her in hysterics, impersonating some of his more outrageous titled relatives—including a duke who kept a urinal behind a screen in his dining room.

They'd still been talking and laughing when he dropped her home at two in the morning.

"But how do you know he's an aristocrat and not one of those posh con men you read about?" Soph had said to Abby the next morning. Soph was petrified that Toby was about to suggest whisking her friend off to some romantic Far East destination and that Abby would wake up one morning minus a kidney.

Abby was determined not to give in to Soph's paranoia by Googling Toby. In the end she didn't have to. The next day, as she was flicking through an old copy of *Tatler* at the nail salon round the corner, she came across a picture of Toby and a couple of male friends attending a birthday bash of some aristocrat she'd never heard of. The picture caption referred to Toby by name.

Over the next few weeks he wooed her with dinners at exclusive eateries. While the rest of the world had to book months in advance, Toby never had a problem getting a table at Le Caprice or Pétrus. During the day he would forward her jokes and cartoons from the Internet. *Thought this would make you laugh. Hope you're having a good day. Missing you. Can't wait until tonight. XXX Toby.* The jokes always did make her laugh.

It wasn't long before small intimacies developed between them. For reasons connected to one particular *Monty Python* sketch they both happened to adore, fruit buns became known as *fruit bats.* The TV remote became the *dibber.* Once, when Abby glanced at a restaurant bill that Toby was about to pay, she gasped, "My God, that's not a bill, it's a full-on *William.*" Toby had burst out laughing and, from then on, they referred to all bills as *Williams.*

As the weeks turned into months, Abby found herself falling in love. It wasn't just Toby's looks, intelligence, sharp wit, attentiveness and generosity that captivated her. There was something else, something that went much deeper and that Abby found irresistible. At thirty-four, Toby was a real grown-up. Abby had dated too many men who, even as they hit their mid-thirties, were still trying to work out what they wanted from life and where they were going. They were frustrated, tormented types who—often for good reason— yearned to give up jobs that gave them no satisfaction and take off round the world on a Harley. They weren't sure if they could commit to a long-term relationship. Marriage, a mortgage and children felt like a trap. One of her old boyfriends went even further and said it felt like "death."

Abby wasn't unsympathetic. She understood their frustrations, but having spent years struggling to build a successful business, she wanted to be with somebody who was as focused and determined as she was. Toby fitted the bill perfectly. He'd had his fill of backpacking and jobs in seedy beach bars in Thailand. Now he wanted to build up his career and settle down.

Toby said it was her humor and feistiness that had stolen his heart.

In the beginning at least, class difference wasn't an issue. Toby made light of his aristocratic roots and so did she. After all, it wasn't as if Toby were some chinless squire who strode around the shires in plus fours, expecting the lower classes to doff their caps. He worked for a living, just like she did. It did occur to her that when she met his family— his mother in particular—they might look down on her because she knew none of the "right" people and hadn't been to posh schools, but she was too much in love to give it much thought. Not only could she stand up for herself, but Toby would never let anybody hurt her.

Jean and Hugh were so intimidated by Toby's status and wealth that it took them a while to relax and get to know him. The first time Abby brought Toby home for dinner, Hugh felt the need to splurge on a thirty-pound bottle of wine. Jean prepared for his visit by having all the carpets, curtains and upholstery cleaned and insisting Hugh drag all Grandma Ginny's long-discarded silver-plated cutlery and tableware down from the attic.

Jean also fretted about whether fish knives and forks were bourgeois and suburban and instructed Hugh not to refer to the living room as the "lounge."

Toby, on the other hand, didn't appear to be remotely ill

at ease. He arrived bearing Maison du Chocolat truffles for
Jean and was in top form all evening. Over predinner
drinks, when Jean prattled on nervously about her garden,
he showed genuine interest and asked questions. Ditto when
Hugh started banging on about the special features on his
new Citroen C4.

"The sat nav comes as standard, of course, but you pay
extra for the speed limiter. What with all the police cameras
around these days, I thought it had to be worth every
penny . . . Now, then, Toby, why don't you try some of Jean's
mushy pea dip? It's rather good."

Jean blushed and tried to cover her embarrassment with
nervous laughter. "Hugh, it's guacamole. I'm always making
it. You love it."

"I do?" Hugh said, his brow knitted in confusion.

"Course you do. I made it the last time your sister Kath
came over, and you practically ate the lot."

"But that must have been ages ago. Kath's been in the
mental hospital for three years."

Jean flushed scarlet. "Another ham and cheese spiral,
Toby, dear?" she trilled.

As Toby's visits became more frequent, Jean and Hugh
started to relax. Jean felt able to make him a cup of tea in an
Ikea mug, and Hugh began serving £6.99 Aussie red with
dinner.

Like Abby, they, too, picked up on Toby's maturity.
"Such a sensible, dependable young man," Abby heard Jean
telling Aunty Gwen on the phone. "Hugh and I think the
world of him. Abby is so lucky. He's perfect for her. Just
perfect."

Jean and Hugh certainly weren't surprised when, after
eight months, Abby and Toby announced their engagement.

Overjoyed, Jean's thoughts turned at once to the wedding reception. "I thought we could put up a tent in the garden," she'd said to Abby on the phone the other day. "We can have sparkling wine and nibbly bits when everybody arrives, followed by a hot and cold buffet. The fishmonger has said he can do me a dozen salmon en croute so long as I give him plenty of notice. And then there's your aunty Gwen's tiramisu. Everybody was raving about it at Uncle Phil's retirement do." She paused. "Look, darling, I know it won't be the kind of grand affair that Toby's mother is used to, but he's such a lovely boy—not at all the snob your dad and I were expecting—and I'm sure his mother's the same and that she'll understand it's the best we can do."

"I'm sure she will," Abby said. "And it all sounds absolutely lovely." She decided not to tell her mum what Toby had said about his mother's personality. Nor was she about to confess to her doubts about whether Lady P would take kindly to her son's wedding reception being held in a tent in a Croydon back garden, where she would be expected to drink Waitrose Fizz and queue up with all the other guests for a plate of Aunty Gwen's tiramisu.

When Abby told Soph that she was going to marry Toby, her friend had hugged and congratulated her and then broken into a chorus of "My Sweet Lord."

AS THE Edgware Road train finally pulled in, Abby stood up and her thoughts returned to her present anxieties. Even though Toby would be there to defend her against Lady Penelope, Abby was certain that tonight's dinner with her ladyship was going to be something akin to being hauled up before her old headmistress, the formidable Miss Raffan. She imagined Lady Penelope catching her using the wrong glass or fork. "Abigail Crompton," she would boom across her vast and noble bosom, "you have let your school down. You have let your house down, but most of all you have let yourself down."

The train doors hissed open and Abby stepped inside. There was barely any standing room, let alone a spare seat. She found some space for her hand on one of the metal poles and felt the train lurch out of the station.

On the bench seat opposite, a young couple with backpacks at their feet were studying an Italian guidebook to London. The young woman's head was resting on her boyfriend's chest. Every so often he would stroke her hair. She kept trying to pronounce names in the book and getting them hopelessly wrong. His English was better than hers and he tried to correct her. She would repeat the names after him, but when she still got them wrong, the two of them would start giggling.

As Abby observed the pair, she felt an unexpected wave of emotion. She couldn't quite put a name to the feeling. It wasn't jealousy exactly, more sadness and disappointment. She couldn't remember the last time she and Toby had been giggly and affectionate together. Not that it was anybody's fault. She worked six days a week at the shop, and Toby put in such long hours at the office that he was permanently exhausted. Corporate lawyers—particularly ones as anxious to make their mark as Toby—couldn't pack up and go home at six. More often than not he was still at his desk at eight or nine in the evening. Usually he would come to her place for supper, but afterward all he wanted to do was watch *Newsnight* and fall into bed.

It wasn't as if Toby hadn't tried to get time off so that the two of them could spend more time together. For half of the eight months they'd been going out, he'd been promising that they would take a romantic break. But every time they got close to booking something, another case would come up or another major deal would be on the verge of collapse, which only he could rescue.

Last month they had finally made it to Paris. By way of apology for all the aborted trips, Toby's law firm had paid and booked them into the Georges Cinq for an entire week.

On the first night, they went to bed early with a bottle of Cristal. Abby lay there in her brand-new La Perla satin negligee, waiting for Toby to ravish her. When he tried but failed to rise to the occasion—despite vigorous and inventive encouragement on her part—they put it down to his exhaustion. "You'll be fine tomorrow, just you see," Abby soothed, stroking his hair. But the following night was no different. Toby said it was like trying to force jelly into a slot machine. Again she held him and comforted him and did her best to convince him that getting anxious would only make the situation worse.

They had just fallen asleep on the second night when the phone rang.

"Leave it," Abby said. "Whoever it is can leave a message."

"No, I must take it," Toby said, reaching out to pick up the receiver. "It could be the office."

It was. A moment later, Toby was looking taut and running his fingers through his hair. "Yep. OK, fine. I'll be there. Leave it to me." He put down the phone and turned back to Abby. "The MSP merger is about to go tits up. I have to go to Brussels tomorrow to try and rescue it."

"Oh, come on, Toby, this was meant to be our romantic break. We really need this time together; surely they can send somebody else."

"No, they can't. This is my case. My responsibility."

She didn't mean to lie there looking sullen, but she couldn't help it.

"Abby, what do you suggest I do, tell my bosses to take a running jump? I am paid a fortune to do this job."

"That doesn't mean they own you."

"You know what, Abs? Actually it does."

In many ways she admired Toby's work ethic. After all, he received money from a family trust fund and had no real need to earn a living. He maintained that the importance of working hard and contributing to the world was something his mother had instilled in him. Apart from the occasional meeting with the managers employed to run the Kenwood estate, his late father had never worked. The man had been a drunk and a gambler. By the time he died of cirrhosis of the liver at age fifty-six, he had boozed and gambled away hundreds of thousands of pounds—not that this had left much more than a slight dent in the family fortune. "Eventually my mother came to despise the pathetic wretch he had turned into," Toby had confided to Abby. "After he died, she became a local magistrate, hospital governor and master of the hunt. She also threw herself into charity work. She worked non-stop, and with my father gone, she became my role model."

Now Toby reached out and took Abby's hand. "Look, I will make this up to you, I promise. I'll make sure I'm back by six tomorrow—seven at the latest." He suggested she spend the day at the Louvre—where she had never been. "And afterward we'll meet up for dinner. I'll book somewhere really special."

She leaned forward and kissed his cheek. "OK. Deal," she said.

The next morning, Abby woke to see Toby standing in front of the mirror.

"Mornin'," she said through a yawn.

"Thank heavens I changed my mind and packed a suit," he said by way of greeting. "I almost didn't. But then I thought it might be nice to wear one if we went out for a posh dinner." He lifted his shirt collar and draped a gray-and-purple-striped silk tie around his neck.

When he'd finished adjusting his tie, Toby came over to the bed to say good-bye. "I'm really sorry things keep turning out like this."

She kissed him and told him it was OK.

"You know what I think?" he said.

"What?" she said from under the covers.

"I think we should get married. That way we can take a month's honeymoon and be sure of no interruptions."

She pushed back the sheets and blankets. "Hang on. You want to get married just to get a holiday?"

"No. I want to get married because I love you. As a bonus, it would be a chance for us to get away. What do you say?"

"That this isn't exactly the most romantic proposal I've ever heard."

"Oh, come on, Abs—we're not romantic types. You'd have hated it if I'd gone down on one knee at the top of the Eiffel Tower."

"I would?"

"Of course. It's the most appalling cliché."

"I suppose ... But you could have proposed tonight over dinner."

"Yes, and I could also have hidden a diamond engagement ring at the bottom of your champagne glass. Tacky or what? Besides, you know you want to choose your own ring. And the firm gets a massive discount at this place in Hatton Garden."

"This proposal is getting more romantic by the second."

He shrugged. "I'm being practical, that's all. No sense in wasting money if you don't have to."

"I guess."

"So, what do you say?" he said, sitting himself down on the bed and taking her hand. "Will you have me?"

She didn't have to think. Even though she would always have to share Toby with the firm, she was in no doubt that he would always love and care for her.

She beamed up at him. "Of course I'll have you, you dope."

"Brilliant! Absolutely wonderful." With that he took her in his arms and kissed her on the lips with such passion that she found herself begging him to come back to bed. "Come on," she giggled, reaching for his belt buckle. "Just for five minutes. I bet you anything you could do it this time."

"Behave." He smiled, gently removing her hand. "I've got to run or I'll miss my train."

He rang her at six to say the meeting was running on and could she change the dinner reservation he'd made from eight to nine. An hour later he was on the phone again to say negotiations had reached a stalemate and he was going to spend the night in Brussels. "Abby, I am so, so sorry. I will make this up to you. Somehow."

"Right," she said, making no attempt to hide her hurt.

"Oh, Abs, don't be like that."

But she couldn't help it.

He stayed in Brussels two more days.

"You know, Toby, this really has got to stop," she said during one of their late-night phone calls. "Not just for me, but for you, as well. They're working you far too hard. You're going to get ill."

"I know. I know. When this case is over I'll talk to one of the partners."

Abby decided not to go home. She wasn't about to give up five nights in a suite at the Georges Cinq. Instead, she played tourist and shopped.

Toby made it back to Paris on the fifth night, full of apologies and promises that he would never allow anything like this to happen again. After presenting her with the biggest bottle of Chanel No. 5 she had ever seen, he announced that he had booked them a table at L'Orangerie. With its three Michelin stars, people waited weeks for a table, but Toby had a friend who worked on the Paris stock exchange and knew the maître d'. The man had managed to pull a few strings.

"So, can you forgive me for treating you so badly?" he asked over dinner.

She took another bite of heavenly, melt-in-the mouth duck confit with orange compote and grinned. "Oh, I think I can probably find a way."

SHE PICKED up the Piccadilly Line at King's Cross. It was only as she sat down and counted the stops to Covent Garden that she remembered—to her horror—that the station had no escalator. Covent Garden station was so deep that it had an elevator. Suddenly her pulse sped up and she started to feel sick. Abby didn't ride in elevators. The last time she had been in one was the summer of 1984.

She had been on holiday in Corfu with her parents. One evening, while Hugh and Jean were having a drink in the bar, Abby and another English girl who was staying at the hotel decided to play in the elevator.

They rode it up and down for twenty minutes or more. Then, without warning, the elevator stopped between floors and the light went out, leaving the two nine-year-olds in complete darkness. Terrified, they screamed for help, but it was several minutes before anybody heard them and an hour on top of that before the elevator engineer managed to get the thing moving again.

From that day on, the fear of being trapped in an elevator had never left Abby. When she told people that she would rather take the stairs to their office on the tenth floor because it was good exercise, they looked at her as if she had a screw loose.

There were stairs at Covent Garden, of course, but since Abby had waited ages for a train at King's Cross, she was now running seriously late. Trudging up all those stairs would add at least another ten minutes.

Her choice was stark. She could give in to her phobia by taking the stairs and thereby suffer the wrath of the fearsome Lady Penelope, or she could close her eyes, hold her breath and do what the rest of the world did and take the elevator.

There was no choice. Lady P's wrath was infinitely preferable to the grizzly, suffocating, heart-stopping panic she would experience the second she set foot in the elevator. Her mind was totally and absolutely made up.

She felt the train slow down and pull into the station. Abby stood up and headed toward the doors. On the other hand, she was desperate to make a good impression on Lady P. If she arrived late, the woman would interpret it as a snub and hold it against her forever. Their relationship would be over before it had begun. It went without saying that Toby would be livid as well and probably wouldn't speak to her for days.

As she thought about taking the elevator, beads of sweat began to break through her foundation. She couldn't do it. She simply couldn't. Then she tried to convince herself that, unlike the rickety contraption in Corfu, the Covent Garden elevator was large, air-conditioned and modern. On top of that, the journey couldn't possibly take more than a few seconds. And she would be surrounded by loads of people.

It didn't matter. There was still no way she was about to set foot in the elevator.

The train doors slid back. Abby got out of the car along with two or three other passengers. She stood on the platform and stared at the sign pointing toward the elevator. Her heart started to race. By now the platform was filling with other people who had gotten off the train. She looked for the sign to the staircase but couldn't see it. The crowd was moving toward the elevator, and she was trapped in the middle. Knees trembling, feeling that she was somehow detached from reality and walking through porridge, she found herself unable to break free. She was aware of her breathing becoming shallow and rapid.

At one point, she stepped aside to let through a party of boisterous French schoolchildren who had been on her train. The kids charged toward the row of elevators. Almost immediately, a set of doors opened and they piled in, along with the other passengers who had been waiting. Abby, her eyes firmly shut to block out the terror, tried to squeeze in, as well, but there wasn't quite enough room. She and another traveler had to get out and wait for the next elevator.

It arrived straightaway. "After you." Her young male companion smiled, gesturing toward the entrance.

Abby hesitated. The impulse to run for the stairs— wherever they might be — was overwhelming.

"Thank you," she said, returning his smile. She stepped into the elevator and waited for the doors to close.

Chapter 2

THE HEAVY STEEL DOORS glided across the elevator
entrance and met silently in the middle. She was locked
in. Forcibly separated from the noise and bustle of the station platforms and, in effect, the outside world, she felt
trapped and utterly powerless. Somehow she resisted the instinct to pound on the doors with her fists and scream to be
let out.

Her heart racing, she closed her eyes and waited for the
elevator to start moving. She tried to reassure herself that in
a few seconds it would all be over. She imagined herself
stepping out into the fresh air, exhilarated at having faced
her fear. She began counting the seconds. One, a hundred,
two, a hundred, three, a hundred...Come on. Move. After
about six seconds, the elevator was still stationary. By now
her heart was beating so hard and fast it felt like it was
about to burst out of her rib cage. She needed air. She took
several long, deep breaths and felt her head start to spin. In
an effort to steady herself, she opened her eyes and placed
the flat of her hand on the elevator wall. Her traveling companion was standing to her left, a couple of feet away. He

had white iPod buds in his ears. His head was jigging vaguely to music, which was reaching Abby as faint, tinny headphone leakage.

A few more seconds passed. The guy glanced at his watch and tutted. Abby caught his eye and smiled.

"I hope there isn't a problem with the elevator," she said, a broad smile disguising her terror.

He offered her an apologetic look to indicate he hadn't heard her and removed his earphones. "Sorry? I didn't catch that."

"I was just wondering why the elevator wasn't moving."

"It's been a bit slow last few times I've used it. It'll get going in a tick." He put his earphones back in his ears.

How long was a tick? she wondered. A few seconds? More? Was it longer than a jiffy? Shorter than two shakes or half a mo? Come to that, how long was half a mo? Clearly it was 50 percent shorter than the full mo, but unless one knew how long the full mo was, it was impossible to calculate the value of half.

As her interest in ticks, shakes and half mos waned, she became aware that another diversion was required to take her mind off her panic.

She found herself focusing on the elevator walls. There were three smallish posters advertising West End shows. *Les Mis* and *Chicago,* she'd seen. She hadn't seen *The Producers.* Soph had taken her parents to see it for their wedding anniversary when the show first came to London. Abby remembered how they hadn't stopped raving about how wonderful it was. That had to have been four or five years ago. It seemed the show was back in town for a second run.

Having finished studying the theater posters, Abby began scrutinizing the rubber-tiled floor. It was relatively clean, she decided, but badly scuffed. Some candy wrappers had gathered in one of the corners. A few inches from her right foot, there was a dirt-encrusted pink bubble-gum pancake. She wondered how often the elevator got cleaned. Once a day, she decided—probably early in the morning, before the tube started running.

When she realized she had extracted all the information she could from the floor, she turned her attention to her traveling companion. It was hard to do this without giving the impression that she was staring, but she managed by keeping her head still and giving him the occasional furtive glance out of the corner of her eye.

He was tall—six foot, give or take—and about her own age. His hair was a dark roast-chestnut brown. He wore it short and spiky, with long, well-tended sideburns. His strong jawline was covered in light stubble, which suited him, she thought. He was wearing a trendy charcoal windbreaker—more expensive-looking and sophisticated than Gap, but edgier than Gant. Most likely Paul Smith, she decided. Underneath he had on dark-blue denim flares. A pair of black Converse completed the outfit. They looked pretty new. Probably got them in the Office sale. She'd seen them in the window, down to twenty-five quid.

What looked like a black beanie hat was sticking out of his jacket pocket. He had the right head shape for a beanie, she decided. So many men didn't. Including—dare she admit it—Toby. Beanies were the only garments he didn't look good in. Of course, she'd never said anything to him. She couldn't possibly hurt his feelings by telling him that his head was too big for them and that whenever he wore one it looked as if there were a giant egg covered in an egg cozy perched on his shoulders.

The inventory of her traveling companion's ensemble complete, Abby's panic soared again.

"What about all that rain this afternoon?" she blurted, catching his eye again. "Talk about torrential."

He removed his earbuds once more and offered her a bemused frown. "I beg your pardon? I missed that."

"The rain. This afternoon. Pretty heavy."

"Er, yes. I guess." The earphones went back in again.

"I got splashed just before. By a car. Got mud all over my stockings. People really should drive more carefully in the rain."

Out came the headphones. "Sorry again," he said, with an awkward smile. "I'm afraid I didn't catch that, either."

"Drivers. Don't you think they should be more considerate in the rain? Just look at my stockings." She raised her foot and showed him her shin. He managed a polite, concerned nod and went back to his music.

Just then the elevator began to climb. Relief surged through Abby like squid ink in water. "Thank you, God," she muttered. "Thank you."

Then, just as she was feeling in her pocket for her train ticket, the elevator began to slow down. The journey was far quicker than she had imagined. She was just beginning to feel foolish about the way she'd panicked, when the elevator stopped with a sudden and violent jerk. It was so fierce that Abby was thrown against her companion. He, in turn, lost his balance and the two of them spent several seconds trying to right themselves and each other.

"You OK?" he said, once they were properly on their feet again. He looked shaken. She noticed his earbuds had come out of his ears and were dangling over the neck of his windbreaker.

"Yes, I'm fine," Abby said, desperate not to let her panic show. "Why haven't the doors opened?"

"Because we're not at ground level. We were only going for a few seconds. It takes longer than that to reach the top."

"You're kidding?" She hadn't meant to sound shrill, but the words just came out that way. "You mean we're stuck?" Abby felt her fists clench and her nails dig into her palms.

"It looks like we could be." He pressed the red emergency button.

"Shouldn't an alarm ring or something?" she heard herself demand.

"You'd have thought so." He jabbed the button a second and third time. Nothing.

"Let me try. Maybe you're not doing it right." In her panic, she shoved him out of the way. His expression was one of mild amusement more than offense—as if to say, "How many ways are there to push a button?"

She pressed her forefinger down hard on the button and left it there. When there was no response, she pressed even harder. By now she was hyperventilating and starting to feel dizzy again. She had to get out of this elevator right now. She was gulping in air, and the dizziness was getting worse. "I think I need to sit down," she announced, voice trembling.

"I thought you might," he said. His voice was kind, concerned. He took her arm and helped her onto the floor. She sat with her back resting against the elevator wall. He crouched beside her. "Here, try this. I did this first-aid course years ago at school, and it really works." He removed a bottle of wine from the smallish, upscale paper bag he'd been holding. "You need to hold the bag over your nose and mouth. Then just breathe in and out slowly. It balances the oxygen and carbon dioxide. It'll make you feel better."

She took the bag and did as he said. Gradually, her head stopped spinning.

"Would I be right in thinking," he said, "that you're not particularly keen on elevators?"

She took the bag off her face. "I got stuck in one when I was a kid. I was there for over an hour in the pitch black. To me it seemed like a week. Ever since, I've been phobic about elevators and being in confined spaces. This is the first time I've been in an elevator for twenty-odd years. I only took it because I was running late." She paused. "Do you think we should try calling for help? Maybe nobody knows we're here."

With that, the elevator started to move up again, but only for a few feet. After a couple of seconds it came to another juddering halt. "Bloody hell! What on earth's going on?" She was aware that she was clutching his hand. Embarrassed, she withdrew it.

He got up, went over to the doors and administered a purposeful thump with his fist. "Hello!" he called out. "Anybody up there?"

Nothing. He hit the doors again. "Can anybody hear me?"

Judging by the silence, nobody could. "We must be too far down for anybody to hear," he said. He turned to face Abby. "Look, try not to panic. The station staff are bound to know the elevator's stuck. I'm sure they'll have us out pretty soon. We just have to be patient."

Abby rubbed her hand across her forehead. She wasn't sure how long she could hold on before she would throw up or pass out. To add to her panic, she suddenly remembered Toby and Lady Penelope. She imagined Toby drumming his fingers on the table, getting more and more wound up the later it got. She took her mobile out of her bag, but there was no signal. "Great. Just great."

"You're meeting people?" he said, sitting down beside her.

"My fiancé and his mother. I've never met her before."

"And you wanted to make a good impression."

She nodded. "Not much chance of that now. What about you? Where are you off to?"

He drew up his legs and rested his hands on his knees. "Friend's birthday party. He's got a flat round the corner. There are loads of people going. He won't notice if I'm late." He paused. "I'm Dan, by the way."

"Abby."

He held out a hand toward her. "Pleased to meet you, Abby."

"You, too," she said, taking his hand and managing a brief smile. Just then the lights began to flicker. Abby tensed and let out a tiny shriek. "Oh, no," she said, her head tilted toward the ceiling lights. "Please don't let the lights go out." Finally the flickering stopped. Abby slapped her chest with relief.

"So, Abby, where do you live?"

"Islington."

"And what do you do?"

"I own a flower shop."

She was pretty sure that Dan was showing an interest only to calm her down and take her mind off her panic. Nevertheless, she was immensely grateful.

He asked her how she had gotten into floristry, and she found herself telling him about her grandfather's garden. "He and my nan owned a bungalow in Brighton. It had over an acre of garden. Granddad seemed to spend his entire life working out there. Every summer when I was a kid, I'd go and stay with them for a week or so. The garden would be bursting with roses, honeysuckle, sweet peas, lilies of the valley. I just fell in love with the scents, the shapes and the colors. Nan used to arrange the flowers for her church. She was really talented and produced these huge, wonderfully dramatic arrangements, which to me seemed just magical. I remember being about three or four and her giving me a chunk of Oasis foam soaked in water. I must have spent hours decorating it with daisies and forget-me-nots I'd found in the garden." She stopped. "Sorry, I'm wittering on."

"You're not. Honestly." His face seemed to display a genuine interest, urging her to continue.

She smiled as she remembered running into her grandmother's kitchen from the garden, bursting with excitement, her tiny hands clutching yet more flowers to stick into the Oasis. "Later on I became a pretty moody teenager. My parents couldn't handle it. Other people's gloom and negativity makes them feel awkward and embarrassed. So, whenever I felt pissed off with the world, I'd go up to my room and arrange dried flowers. I found it comforting. I didn't have the confidence to sell them, so I got my mum to donate them to local tag sales and bazaars. Then I got friendly with the local florist. She lent me books on flower arranging, and if I went in late on a Saturday afternoon, she would give me all the flowers that were past their prime. It wasn't long before I realized I had a talent for flower arranging, just like my gran." She stopped again, fearing she had been giving him the wrong impression. "Oh, God, you must think I was this sad, lonely weirdo with no social life, who spent all her spare time alone in her room arranging flowers. You should know that I did my fair share of going to parties, smoking dope and getting rat-assed on cheap cider."

He was smiling at her. "It's OK. It didn't occur to me you were a sad, lonely weirdo."

"Really?" She thought back to when she'd told Toby about spending hours on end in her room, arranging dried flowers, and how he'd said that had she been his child he would have carted her off to the nearest shrink.

"With me it was diseases," Dan said.

She tilted her head to one side. "How do you mean?"

"From the age of fifteen until I went to university, I used to spend nearly all my Saturday afternoons in the local library looking up illnesses and their symptoms. I had suddenly become aware of my own mortality and that it was possible to die of some pretty horrendous diseases. I decided that forewarned was forearmed."

"But you grew out of it?"

"Eventually, but even when I was at university, the morbid curiosity lingered. I remember forming this band with some mates and insisting we call it Spastic Colon."

She burst out laughing. Afterward, they fell into silence.

"So, how does it feel to be getting married?" he said eventually.

"Exciting, but a bit scary," she said, aware that concentrating on answering his questions really was easing her panic.

"Why scary?"

She shrugged. "Isn't it normal to be scared before you get married? 'Til death do us part is such a long time."

"Even if you've found the right person?"

She couldn't work out why the question had pricked her

and made her feel defensive. "Oh, I've absolutely found the right person," she declared. "No doubt about that. Toby's wonderful. He works hard. He's solid, reliable. I know he'll never let me down." She paused. "God, I've made him sound like a Volvo. I mean, obviously there's more to him than that. Far more. He's handsome, clever, funny."

The lights started to flicker again. Abby felt her body tense.

"There's clearly a problem with the power supply," he said.

"Omigod. Please don't tell me that means the elevator could go plummeting to the bottom of the elevator shaft."

"Abby, you have to calm down. The station staff will sort this out. They're probably waiting for an engineer." His eyes turned to the bottle of wine standing on the floor. "Look, why don't I open this? A drop of alcohol might ease your nerves."

"OK," she said. At this stage she was willing to try anything. "But how are you going to open the bottle?"

He grinned. "Easy." He put his hand into his jacket pocket and produced a Swiss Army knife. "Thirteenth-birthday present," he said. "I've carried it with me ever since. You never know when you might need to scale a fish or take a stone out of a horse's hoof."

She giggled. "Or open bottles of wine to calm crazy phobics trapped in elevators. Toby thinks I should have gotten over my phobia by now. He doesn't say as much, but even though I've worked really hard to overcome it, I think he thinks I'm a bit of a wimp."

"I don't think you're a wimp or crazy. Your elevator phobia is based on an event that scared the hell out of you. Not wanting to repeat it isn't mad, it's perfectly rational."

She was impressed by his analysis, and for a moment or two she felt rather drawn to him. She'd always been of the opinion that emotional insight in a man was rather sexy.

He was standing up now, the bottle between his knees, tugging at the cork. It finally came out with a delicious pop. He passed her the bottle. "Right, get some of that down you."

She didn't need telling twice. It was a delicious fruity red. "Wow, that is yummy." She looked at the label. "Hang on, this is a Chateau Haut Lafitte Grand Cru. I don't know much about wine, but isn't that megaexpensive?"

"Not really," he said, twisting the cork off the corkscrew.

"Yes, it is. I know it is. While I was driving the other day I was listening to this wine program on the radio and Chateau Haut Lafitte was mentioned. I remember the presenter saying that prices start around fifty quid. And you're meant to decant it and filter it. This was your friend's birthday present, wasn't it?"

"OK, it was. Matt's a bit of a wine buff, but he's got loads of the stuff. This bottle is going to a much better cause."

"I don't know what to say. It's absolutely gorgeous. Thank you."

Dan folded the corkscrew back into the body of the Swiss Army knife and put it in his jacket pocket. "My pleasure."

By now he was back on the floor, sitting next to her. She passed the wine bottle to him. "Here, you have some. I haven't eaten since lunchtime, and the alcohol is going straight to my head."

"That's the idea." He smiled, insisting that she drink

some more. When she finally passed him the bottle, she was aware that she'd downed more than half of it.

"Wow, this *is* good," he said. "Anyway, getting back to what you were saying about the elevator plummeting to the bottom of the shaft. I promise you that can't possibly happen."

"How do you know?" Her head was starting to spin again, but this time it was due to the alcohol rather than her hyperventilating.

"I have a degree in engineering, and I happen to know for a fact that all modern elevators are fitted with a... um..." As he groped for the word, his eyes appeared to comb the elevator walls for inspiration. He was hardly going to find the missing word there, she thought. "A Bialystock joint," he announced finally.

"A Bialystock joint? What's that?" Her brow knitted into a frown. She was sure she'd come across this name somewhere, but for the life of her she couldn't remember where.

"The Bialystock joint is possibly one of the most important inventions in twentieth-century engineering. It took over from the Bloom overload breaker. Once you combine it with the Ulla oscillator, you've got a pretty foolproof system. It's why there hasn't been an elevator disaster anywhere in the Western world for over fifty years."

"Is that really true?"

"Absolutely."

"Well, that's certainly reassuring."

By now the alcohol was really starting to kick in. Drinking always made her garrulous. "Did I tell you that Toby's a corporate lawyer?" she said.

"No, I don't think you did."

"He works for this really big West End firm. Of course, they expect complete loyalty and devotion. They work him far too hard, poor thing." He handed her back the bottle and she took a couple more swigs. "He's always exhausted and irritable. But it's not his fault. It's just his workload. He's promised me that once they make him a partner in a few years, things will calm down. At the moment he's at the beginning of his career and he feels that he's got so much to prove."

"I can understand that."

She carried on drinking. "I know our relationship isn't as exciting as it could be, but, given Toby's work situation, that's only to be expected, isn't it?"

Dan gave a noncommittal nod.

"Plus, we've been together nine months. Work issues aside, things generally start to taper off after a few months, don't they?" She put the bottle to her lips again and drank. "When I say 'things taper off,' I mean, you know"—she leaned in toward him and lowered her voice to a conspiratorial whisper—"in the bedroom department."

Dan registered his discomfort by clearing his throat. "Ah...right. I see." More throat-clearing. "I'm not sure... I mean, I really wouldn't know...."

"The truth is," she carried on, well into her alcohol-induced stride by now, "we haven't done it in ages. But that's normal, isn't it? I know they try to convince you in the magazines that everybody's shagging all the time, but everybody knows it's not like that in real life."

"Well, er...I guess...you know...all relationships go through their ups and downs."

"Exactly. And Toby and I are in a bit of a down phase

at the moment. That doesn't mean to say that one of these days, soon, Toby won't be able to get it up again."

He winced. "Oh, God."

"You see, at the moment"—she lowered her voice again—"Toby says that for him it's like trying to get jelly into a letter box."

Dan sprang to his feet. "Tell you what, why don't I try banging on the door again? Maybe somebody will hear this time."

"I mean, you're a man, Dan—ooh, that rhymes—you must have encountered similar problems."

Dan responded by giving the door three quick thumps. "Can anybody hear me? Can anybody hear me?"

Nothing. "I said, can anybody hear me?"

"You have to make a new plan, Stan!"

"Abby, my name's Dan, not Stan. The wine really has gone to your head."

"Of course your name's Dan. Then what am I thinking of?...Oh, I know—it's that old Paul Simon song. How does it go?" With that she started singing. "...slip out the back, Jack...You don't need to be coy, Roy...set yourself free." She paused. "You know, that's what we should do."

"What?"

"Slip out the back, Jack."

"There is no back."

"Of course there's a back." She burst into a fit of giggles and snorted. "Everything gotta have a back."

"Yes, but there isn't a back we can escape out of."

"Ah. Right." Hiccup. "Got-cha."

He bashed the door again. "Hey! Can anybody hear me?"

The reply—albeit faint—came immediately: "Yes, mate,

'ang on. The elevator engineer's just got 'ere. We'll 'ave you out A-S-A-P."

Dan turned to Abby. "There you are. What did I tell you?"

"Hey, Dan, my main man," Abby cried, "gimme five!"

But there was no time to celebrate. At that moment the elevator doors hissed open. Abby and Dan found themselves staring out onto a filthy, soot-covered elevator shaft wall. They both looked up into the blackness. Thirty or forty feet above them, somebody was shining a torch into the shaft.

"All right," another male voice said. "What we want you to do is to keep well inside the elevator while we try to raise it a few more feet."

Abby and Dan stepped back. Because of all the wine she'd had, Abby was a bit wobbly on her feet by now. Dan took her arm to steady her. After a few moments, the elevator mechanism whirred and clanked and slowly they started to climb. It took nearly a minute to move less than ten feet. By now they could see three or four faces staring down at them.

"How many of you in there?" one of the faces said.

"Only two," Dan said.

"OK, that's something."

The mechanism started up again, but this time the elevator didn't move.

"That's it," came the same voice. "This thing isn't moving any farther. Here's what we're going to do. We've got a couple of harnesses attached to a winch. I'm going to throw them down. You two put them on and we'll hoist you up."

Abby turned to Dan. "Wow, we're going to rappel out of this elevator. How cool is that?"

"You mean you're not scared?"

"Me, scared? I have no fear."

"Since when?"

"Since you got me pissed as a pudding."

The two mountaineering harnesses were lowered. Dan helped Abby into hers. "God, this is so exciting," she squealed. "It's like that film *Touching the Void*. This bloke gets stuck at the bottom of a deep crevasse and has to climb out."

Dan put on his own harness. "OK, we're ready," he called out.

"Right you are," the voice from above came back. "Don't do anything. Just hold on to the rope; sit tight while we do the work."

Abby went first. She felt herself rise a few inches. "Geronimo! Wheeee, I'm flying." Her journey was a bit halting and bouncy, and she kept getting bashed against the filthy elevator shaft, but because her panic had been anesthetized by the wine, it wasn't at all unpleasant.

A few moments later she was sitting on the ground, removing black cobwebs from her face, surrounded by relieved London Transport staff, paramedics and the police rescue team that had winched her to safety. Somebody in a blue London Transport cap was helping her off with her harness. "You all right, miss? I've sent somebody to fetch you a nice cup of sweet tea."

The chap clearly hadn't noticed Abby's ear-to-ear grin. She was more than all right. She was giddy with excitement. "Wow, talk about an adrenaline rush. That was amazing. Usually I get claustrophobic in tight spaces. I cannot believe I just rappelled nearly forty feet up an elevator shaft in the pitch black."

Even though she still felt pretty sloshed from the wine, she wasn't so far gone as to forget Toby. She immediately started rooting around in her bag for her phone. She had to ring him to explain what had happened and let him know she was safe. As she picked up her phone, she noticed that she had six missed calls. She decided that listening to the messages would only waste time. She knew they would be from Toby, who, having been irritated by her lateness, would now be frantic with worry. It was far more important that she speak to him right away and put his mind at rest.

This time her phone had plenty of signal, but when she dialed, the number just kept ringing and eventually went to voice mail. She decided there was probably so much noise in the restaurant that he couldn't hear his phone.

By now Dan was at her side, still in his harness. "You sounded like you were enjoying yourself back there," he said.

"It was totally fantastic," she said, letting out a loud hiccup. "I mean, truly amazing."

The same London Transport man helped Dan off with his harness. Then two paramedics in green overalls came over and suggested Abby and Dan should go to the hospital to be checked out. It was a struggle—particularly as they were convinced that Abby's high spirits were due to a head injury—but eventually Abby and Dan managed to convince the paramedics that they were both fine.

After Abby and Dan had offered their profuse thanks to the paramedics and the police rescue team, another London Transport person arrived with two mugs of tea. She ushered them into the station office and sat them down. As Abby sipped the sweet, treacle-colored brew, she could feel herself beginning to sober up.

"Don't hold me to this," she said, becoming thoughtful,

"but I think I may have conquered my phobia. I've been trapped twice in elevators and survived. Suddenly it feels like there's nothing left to fear."

"That's amazing," Dan said. "I'm really impressed."

"Not half as impressed as I am by the way you helped me," she smiled. "You were brilliant down there. I would have totally lost it if it hadn't been for you keeping me talking. I can't tell you how grateful I am. Thank you. I'm sorry if I bored on."

"You didn't."

"Really?"

"I promise."

They sat drinking their tea. "By the way," she said eventually, "your face is covered in soot." She took a clean handkerchief from her jacket pocket and began wiping his face. "You look like a panda," she giggled as some clean skin emerged around his eyes.

He told her not to worry and that he'd have a shower when he got to his friend Matt's apartment. She told him to hang on to the handkerchief anyway.

"Actually, I think you might want to keep it," he said.

She ran her hand over her cheek. "Oh, God," she said, looking down at the black coating, "I'm going to turn up at the Ivy looking like one of those dancing chimney sweeps in *Mary Poppins*."

"Yes, but on you it looks good," he laughed.

Underneath the soot, she was blushing.

"Right," she said, "I'd better get going." She looked at her watch. It was just after nine-thirty. She had been due to meet Toby and his mother at the Ivy more than two hours ago. She assumed they had gone ahead with dinner without her and would still be there.

"Although I'm not sure the doorman at the Ivy is going to let me in looking like this." Even if her face didn't look too bad now, there was still the question of the massive patch of soot on her jacket. On top of that, her stockings, already grubby from the soaking she'd received earlier, were now full of holes.

"I'm sure they'll let you in once you explain."

"Hope so." She held out a hand for him to shake. "Thanks again for keeping me sane," she said.

"Anytime." He smiled, taking her hand in his. "And good luck with the wedding."

"Thanks."

She headed down Long Acre. Her pace was brisk, occasionally breaking into a run. She was desperate to get to the restaurant before Toby and Lady Penelope left. She couldn't run for very long, though. Her high heels made it impossible.

She'd gone a few hundred yards when it struck her that she knew virtually nothing about the man who had so skillfully prevented her from turning into a hysterical, carpet-chewing loon. She didn't know his last name, what he did for a living or where he lived.

How rude of her to have said good-bye without at least getting his address so that she could send him a bottle of something to say thank you for his kindness.

By now she was a few yards from the restaurant. As she broke into a trot again, a memory of something she had said in the elevator came flooding back. She felt her face flush. While she was drunk, she'd told Dan about her relationship with Toby. She'd revealed details. Intimate, personal details. Her pace slowed to a walk as she remembered telling him how they hardly ever did it. Then the phrase *try-*

ing to force jelly into a letter box leaped into her mind. Abby was horrified that she could have displayed such crassness, such lack of discretion, not to mention such disloyalty to Toby. Abby was so full of embarrassment that she could feel her pancreas turning scarlet.

"Omigod," she heard herself blurt out, "a perfect stranger is *au fait* with my fiancé's penis." A couple of passing teenage girls, dressed up to the nines, heard the remark and burst into giggles. Suddenly her regret that she and Dan hadn't exchanged addresses or phone numbers turned to immense gratitude. At least this way she wouldn't have to face the humiliation of seeing him or speaking to him ever again.

Chapter 3

ONCE ABBY HAD EXPLAINED about being trapped in the elevator, the restaurant doorman and maître d' couldn't have been kinder. The maître d' directed her toward Toby's table and said that a very large brandy—strictly on the house—was on its way. The last thing Abby felt like was more alcohol, but she didn't want to appear ungrateful by refusing.

Abby headed toward the table. The restaurant was packed, and a couple of times she had to stand to one side to let a frazzled, plate-laden waiter get past.

At first she didn't notice Toby coming toward her. "Omigod, Abby," he called out. "Sweetheart. Where have you been? I've been worried sick." As soon as she saw him, she quickened her pace. His arms were open to receive her.

"Oh, thank goodness you're still here," she said, virtually throwing herself at him. His eyes immediately went to the lapels of his gray Dunhill suit jacket.

"Abby, you're covered in soot."

"I know. Sorry. Oh, God, it's all over your suit." She pulled away.

"It's fine, really. Not to worry." He began flicking his lapels. "So, come on, you still haven't told me what happened."

"Omigod, it was so scary. You won't believe it. The elevator broke down at Covent Garden tube, and a police rescue team had to winch me and this other chap up the elevator shaft." The relief at seeing him, combined with the adrenaline still in her body, caused the words to tumble out of her in an excited, breathless stream.

"Bloody hell! You sure you're not hurt?"

"I'm fine. I tried to phone you, but we were so far down, there was no signal."

"But you never take elevators," he said.

"I know, but I was running late. I knew taking the elevator would save time, and somehow I forced myself to do it. You have no idea how petrified I was."

He kissed her sooty cheek. "I can imagine. You poor, poor thing. Look, I think after what you've been through, we should get you home. I'll explain to Mother—"

"No, I'm all right . . . really. Though heaven knows what she'll think of me in this state. I wiped my face, but there wasn't much else I could do."

He dabbed at the dirt on her shoulder and managed—partially, at least—to suppress a grimace. "Don't worry. Once you've explained, I'm sure she'll understand."

"Your mother must be furious with me for not showing up."

He managed a humorous eye roll. "Don't worry, but suffice it to say, you haven't made the best of impressions."

Toby led her toward the table, flicking and dabbing at his suit as he went. "I have spent the last two hours listening to her grind on about how it's not just manners but punctuality that maketh the man."

Abby put her grimy hand in his. "Poor you. I'm sorry. I did try phoning you again as soon as I was out of the elevator, but all I got was your voice mail."

"It must have been when I went to the loo. I left my phone on the table."

"Didn't your mother hear it?"

"Her hearing's not so good these days." By now they were almost at the table. "OK, remember, when Mother gets onto the subject of hunting, just go along with everything she says. Do not start challenging her."

"Toby, stop panicking." She gave his hand a reassuring squeeze. "I promise I won't let you down."

The Dowager Lady Kenwood was seventyish, thick of waist and ample of bosom—exactly as Abby had envisaged. She was wearing a nondescript maroon velvet dress, which made her look like a giant pincushion. Save for a wonkily applied slash of scarlet lipstick, she wasn't wearing a scrap of makeup. Her fine silver hair was drawn into an untidy chignon held in place by two large combs and a mass of pins. As she stood up to greet the soot-dredged Abby, her disapproving smile revealed a perfect set of yellowy-beige teeth, which clashed spectacularly with her red lips.

"Mother, I'd like you to meet Abby," Toby announced, fiddling uneasily with the gold signet ring on his pinky.

Lady Penelope was looking Abby up and down. "Good grief, child," she boomed, "whatever happened to you?"

"I'm afraid the elevator broke down at Covent Garden," Toby volunteered nervously, "and Abby had to be rescued."

"Do be quiet, Toby. I'm sure the girl is perfectly capable of answering for herself. And for goodness sake, wipe the soot off your nose."

Toby instantly reached into his pocket and pulled out a handkerchief.

"I'm so sorry I'm late, Lady Penelope," Abby ventured. "And forgive my appearance. The police rescue team had to winch me up the elevator shaft, and it was pretty filthy."

"How awfully tiresome. Still, you survived in one piece. That's the main thing. I like a girl with gumption."

This was tenderness of a sort, Abby decided. It came as a relief to discover that the woman wasn't quite the dragon Toby had painted.

Her ladyship sat down and patted the seat next to her. "I need you on my right. M' left ear's next to damn useless these days."

Abby sat down and Toby followed. Abby noticed that there were two empty coffee cups and an untouched plate of petits fours on the table. "You know," Lady Penelope continued, "my mother wasn't much older than you when she got caught up in the Siege of Mafeking. Saw all sorts out there. Didn't do her the remotest harm. Quite the opposite, in fact. She was a tough old bird, I can tell you. So, Annie, why don't you tell me a bit about yourself."

"Actually, Mother," Toby broke in tentatively, "it's Abby."

"Abby?" Lady Penelope barked. "But I'm sure you told me her name's Annie." She turned to face Abby. "So, which is it? Come on, out with it. Make up your mind."

"I'm Abby. Always have been."

"Surname?"

"I'm sorry?"

"Your surname. I take it you do have one."

"Yes, it's Crompton."

"Crompton. Ah, that would be the Dorset Cromptons, I presume."

Abby did some nervous throat-clearing. "No, the... er...the Croydon Cromptons, actually."

"Croy-don?" Lady Bracknell in *The Importance of Being Earnest* couldn't have uttered the name with more disdain.

At this point Toby leaped in: "Yes, but didn't you say you thought you might be distantly related to the Dorset Cromptons?"

"I don't think so."

"I'm sure you did."

Abby shot Toby a thin-lipped smile. "No, really, I didn't."

Toby glared back at Abby, who decided to see his glare and raise him a couple of eyebrows. Toby then turned to his mother: "I'm afraid Abby's memory has a tendency to let her down on occasion."

"What?" Abby came back, her voice high with indignation. "I have absolutely no problem with—"

"No engagement ring, I see," Lady Penelope broke in.

"Er, no," Abby said. "We haven't quite got round to buying one. Toby's been absolutely snowed under at work."

Lady Penelope turned to her son. "Don't leave it too long. The girl will think you're not serious."

"Oh, don't worry," Abby said, smiling across at Toby. "I know he's serious."

"So, tell me, Abby, do you hunt?"

"Actually, no, I don't." Toby was looking at her as if to say: "Careful, now. Watch your step."

"Why ever not? Healthy, strapping filly like you should hunt." Several strands of gray hair had fallen from Lady Penelope's untidy chignon and were hanging around her face. She made a couple of feeble attempts to pin them back but gave up when the hair refused to stay put.

"The problem is," Toby broke in, "that Abby doesn't ride. But she's definitely thinking of learning...aren't you, Abby?"

"I am?"

"Yes." Toby was nodding vigorously at her, begging her to follow his lead. "Don't you remember we talked about getting you riding lessons?"

"If you say so."

"Excellent," beamed her ladyship. "We'll have you riding to hounds in no time. I'm master of m' local hunt, you know."

"Yes, Toby did mention it. So, you're a bit of an enthusiast, then?"

"Careful," Toby mouthed.

"I'll say. It's excellent sport, not to mention jolly good exercise. And you meet so many people from so many walks of life. I've met surgeons, lawyers, politicians—all sorts. Toby, I insist you bring Annie to our next hunt ball."

"Mother, it's Abby."

"Oh, do shut up, Toby. This constant hairsplitting is most frightfully tedious."

Toby made no attempt to point out that calling somebody by the correct name rather than the incorrect one—particularly when that someone was his fiancée—most definitely wasn't splitting hairs. Instead, he turned pink with embarrassment.

Abby couldn't believe the change she was seeing in Toby now that he was with his mother. The woman undermined him constantly, and he made no attempt to stand up to her. It was astonishing. The confident, highly articulate hotshot

city lawyer Abby knew and loved had suddenly been reduced to a toadying, weak-kneed wimp.

On the one hand, she felt sorry for him. If at the age of
thirty-four he was still petrified of his mother, heaven only
knew what terror the women must have instilled in him
when he was a child. On the other hand, Abby couldn't help
feeling massive disappointment that a grown man could allow his mother to dominate him in this way.

A waiter arrived with Abby's brandy. She thanked him,
but she still didn't fancy it. What she did feel like, though,
was food. It was only now that she realized how ravenous
she was. She looked up at the waiter. "You know, I could
murder a fat, juicy steak and a mountain of fries." The
waiter assured her it was no problem.

"I'm sure Abby would love to come to the hunt ball,"
Toby said as the waiter took his leave. "Wouldn't you,
Abby?"

"Well, things tend to get pretty busy at work..."
Another kick under the table from Toby. "Yes...er, absolutely. Of course, I'd love to come."

"Jolly good. Jolly good. Toby can teach you to dance the
Gay Gordons. He's particularly good at it."

Toby flushed hunting scarlet.

"So, Annie, tell me—what do your people do?"

"My people?"

"Your parents, girl. Your parents."

"Oh, right. They travel quite a bit, but they don't do a
lot, really."

"Ah, landowners, are they?" Lady Penelope said, apparently forgetting that landed gentry were pretty thin on the
ground in Croydon. "How many acres do they have? What
is it? Arable? Grazing?"

"Well, they've got a hundred-foot back garden, which isn't bad for Croydon, and the grass must be pretty tasty, because from time to time next door's rabbit burrows under the fence and munches at the lawn."

"Really?" The expression on Lady Penelope's face was giving every impression that she was in physical pain.

"And where did you go to school?"

"Manor Park."

"Really? I don't think I've heard of it."

"You wouldn't have. It's just the local—"

"Girls' public day school," Toby piped up.

"And Toby tells me you went to Oxford."

"Well, not actually Oxford. It was Oxford College of Art and Design. I did a degree in textile design."

"I see." Lady Penelope raised a disapproving eyebrow at Toby. In return, he offered her a weak, apologetic smile.

"And what do you do for a living?"

"I have my own flower shop."

"How utterly enchanting." Lady Penelope's smile was taut and thin-lipped. "Toby, you didn't tell me we were about to have a regular Eliza Doolittle joining the family."

At this point, Abby's steak arrived. "So, Annie," Lady Penelope said as Abby began stacking chips on her fork. "I take it that you are in excellent health?"

Abby was taken aback by the question. "As far as I know."

"Ovaries and whatnot all in working order?"

Abby almost choked on her chips. "I believe so."

"You see, Toby is an only child. He is also the last male in the Kenwood line. We rather need a boy to carry on the family name and inherit the estate. So I would suggest that you get yourself checked out as a matter of urgency."

There was so much Abby wanted to say that she didn't know where to start. Would Lady Penelope put pressure on Toby to walk away from their relationship if she did have some kind of fertility problem? And what would his mother do if he refused? Cut him out of her will? And why wasn't she suggesting that he take a fertility test? And suppose they only produced girls? Not that any of this was relevant, because there was no way Abby was about to get her ovaries tested purely to pander to Lady Penelope's outrageous demands.

Abby opened her mouth to tell her precisely that, but Toby got there first. "I'll make sure she sees a specialist, Mother."

Abby swung round to face Toby. "You'll do what?" she hissed.

"Jolly good," Lady Penelope boomed, shoving a lock of wispy gray hair back into her chignon. "You know, Annie, I can't tell you how pleased I am that you're not one of these fearful antihunting types."

There was a pause that seemed to go on forever. Toby was visibly holding his breath. Lady Penelope was fighting with her hair, which refused to stay put. Abby was struggling with her emotions. She was aware that she had promised Toby that she wouldn't reveal her true position on hunting, but she was so cross with him for not sticking up for her—particularly over the fertility-test issue—that she couldn't help herself.

"Actually, I am," Abby said.

"Jesus H. Christ," Toby murmured, head in hands.

"You see, to be quite honest, Lady Penelope, I find the idea of hunting foxes—or any animal, come to that—quite barbaric. It's one thing to exterminate vermin humanely. It's quite another to put on silly costumes and chase a fox across country until it collapses from heart failure. Foxhunting turns killing animals into a ritualized social event, which has everything to do with snobbery and class and nothing to do with concern for the countryside."

Toby's head remained in his hands. "I told you what she was like," he muttered under his breath. "Now look what you've done. You simply couldn't leave it alone, could you?"

By now Abby was on a roll. "The law to ban hunting clearly isn't working, and something needs to be done to enforce it. And as for those chinless, upper-class twits who run the Countryside Alliance . . ."

Lady Penelope looked temporarily vacant—as if she had been shot but her brain had yet to register the fact. Abby watched as she calmly put down her coffee cup and dabbed her lips with her napkin. Then, just as her ladyship seemed about to open her mouth and shower Abby with a cascade of vitriol, her face broke into something approaching a smile. "What you are saying is the kind of liberal twaddle, claptrap and balderdash put out by hunt protesters and the left-wing media. It is the kind of subversive propaganda that, left unchecked, will rip at the heart and soul of the British countryside and ultimately destroy it. Nevertheless, we live in a democracy and I would defend to the death your right to have your say."

"You would?" Abby was stunned by her ladyship's response—as was Toby, who had removed his head from his hands and was blinking in disbelief.

"Certainly." Lady Penelope turned to Toby. "She's a spirited young filly, I'll give her that. Spouts a cartload of balderdash, of course, but I think I might be able to break her given time. Now then, it's late and I'm rather tired. I think I should be getting home. Toby, I would be grateful if you'd go outside and flag down a cab."

Ever the obedient son, Toby got up and made his way to the door.

"Goodness, Lady Penelope," Abby said, "surely you're not driving back to Gloucestershire tonight."

"Of course not. I keep a pied-à-terre in town." Her look of haughty surprise clearly said: "Doesn't everybody?"

"Oh, yes. Toby mentioned you owned a London flat."

Lady Penelope extended her hand toward Abby and smiled. "Good-bye, my dear," she said. Abby reached out and took her future mother-in-law's hand. "Toby must bring you to Kenwood one weekend so that I can verse you in the ways of the countryside. I swear I'll have you hunting yet." With that, Lady Penelope picked up her patent-leather handbag and lumbered away from the table.

THEY HEADED toward the multistory parking lot in Chinatown, where Toby had left his car. Neither of them spoke, but their mutual anger was almost palpable. Abby was the first to break the silence.

"I cannot believe you agreed to me taking a fertility test just to please your mother. How could you do that without even asking me? The two of you sat there discussing me as if I weren't even there."

"And how could you take on my mother like that? I told you not to and you disobeyed me."

"I *disobeyed* you? When did I start having to obey you?"

"I'm sorry. I didn't mean that. It's just that you took one hell of a risk, that's all. You could have wrecked everything. As it happens, I think she rather liked you." He paused.

"Look, I only agreed to you taking the fertility test to shut her up. Of course we won't do it. We'll lie, say you've taken it and that the results came back fine."

She bridled. "You can tell your mother what you like, but if she asks me straight out if I've taken the test, I will tell her the truth. You might be prepared to let her walk all over you, but I'm not."

"Clearly," he said with a bitter laugh.

"What's that supposed to mean?"

"OK, you really want to know?"

"Of course."

"It means," he said, "that I'm jealous. I'm jealous that you were able to stand up to her and I can't."

"But why can't you? She'd have far more respect for you if you did. From what I can see, she seems to thrive on conflict. So what if she shouts? Shout back."

"I've tried; I can't. I know this sounds pretty pathetic, but I'm still desperate for her approval. I've spent my life trying to please her, hoping that one day she'll tell me she's proud of me. The fact is that whatever I achieve, whatever I do, it's never enough."

"I can understand that," she said, allowing her voice to soften.

"And there's something else."

"What?"

"She holds the trump card."

"Meaning?"

"Meaning that the one time I tried to stand up to her, she threatened to cut me out of her will."

"So what? Bloody hell, Toby, you earn a fortune as it is. Surely your self-respect is more important than any amount of money."

They were a few paces from the car. He took out his keys and hit the remote. The lock clicked open. "Abby, let me explain something to you. We're not talking a piddling few hundred grand here. The manor house alone is worth ten million. Then there is the rest of the Kenwood estate, with its farms and houses. There's also a vatload of cash. By rights it should have come directly to me when my father died, but he left it all to my mother so that she would be provided for in her lifetime. I don't blame him for that, but after the way she's treated me, I am not about to let her come between me and my inheritance. And don't tell me you wouldn't get a kick out of being lady of the manor."

His final remark quite literally stopped Abby in her tracks. "I can't believe you just said that. If you imagine for one minute that I'll be prancing round the estate in my green wellies and a Barbour jacket, hosting gymkhanas and dispensing patronage and largesse to the lower orders, then you clearly don't know me."

"That's what you say now," he said.

"Toby, please don't patronize me."

"I'm not patronizing you. I just think you'll change, that's all. Money has that effect on people."

"Believe me. I will not change. Nor will I sit back and watch you let your mother behave toward you the way she does."

He shrugged. "Suit yourself, but I really don't give a damn how she treats me. Not if I'm going to benefit in the end."

"I don't believe you. If you don't give a damn about your relationship with your mother, why are you still looking for her approval?"

Toby didn't reply. Her remark had clearly floored him.

There was silence while they got in the car and he started the engine. He followed the tight, snaking route to ground level, then handed over a twenty-pound note at the barrier and waited for his change—such as it was.

"And why did you keep trying to convince your mother that I'm posh? I can't help feeling that you're just as much of a snob as she is."

He turned on her. "I'm not a snob."

"Then what was all that stuff about the Dorset Cromptons and pretending I went to a private school?"

"I was trying to tell her what she wanted to hear, that's all."

Abby shook her head. "This has to stop. For both of our sakes."

He let out a long, slow breath. "OK, you're right. I do have to sort out my relationship with Mother. It's been a long time coming. Maybe I should get some counseling or something. That's what people do, don't they, when they've got problems?" He shook his head. "The idea of spilling one's guts to a perfect stranger is just so...so un-British. And God only knows how I'm going to fit it in with everything else I've got on my plate. Can you just bear to give me some time?"

There was a beseeching, almost childlike expression on his face. "Of course I can," she said. "And I think seeing a counselor is a brilliant idea. Try not to panic. It'll be fine. Promise." She reached over and kissed his cheek.

He said he wouldn't stay at her flat that night, as she needed her sleep and he had to be up at the crack to catch the early shuttle to Edinburgh.

"That's OK," she said, realizing that she had rather wanted him to stay over. After all the trauma and drama of the last few hours, she could have done with feeling his arms around her tonight.

She couldn't work out if he was genuinely concerned about not disturbing her or whether he was simply trying to avoid having sex. He'd spent weeks assuring her that things would get better, but they hadn't. It had occurred to her several times that his lack of desire might be due to more than stress and overwork. Now the issue was really starting to play on her mind. She knew she had to confront it, but so far she'd chickened out for fear of hurting him. Now, maybe because of the adrenaline still in her system or the fact that she was still emotionally charged up after the row they'd been having, she couldn't let it go.

"Toby, I need to ask you something."

"What?"

"Well, I can't help wondering whether our lack of love-making is somehow my fault." She needed to ease into this. She couldn't come straight out with it and accuse him of being gay.

"*Your* fault? How do you work that out?"

"Well, am I doing something wrong in bed? Maybe you don't find me sexy."

"Abby, of course I find you sexy. You're a beautiful woman. Any man would find you sexy. And, no, you're not doing anything remotely wrong."

"Then why do I get the feeling that it's not me you want? Sometimes I think you'd rather be with somebody else."

"Hang on, are you saying I'm cheating on you?"

"Are you?"

"God, no!"

"So if there's nobody else, then..."

"Abby, what are you trying to say?"

"I'm saying, could it be that maybe...just maybe you don't like women."

He burst out laughing. "You think I'm gay?"

"Well, it did occur to me."

"So, you think because I dress well and occasionally have difficulty getting it up that I must be—"

"It's not occasionally. It's all the time."

"Whatever. Christ, Abby, that is such a narrow-minded, knee-jerk reaction. I'm surprised at you, I really am."

"So, you're not, then?"

"OK, read my lips. I, Toby Kenwood, am not, never have been and never will be gay."

"It's just that we haven't done it in so long...."

"Abby, I get tired, that's all. It's as simple as that. I know it's hard on you and it makes you feel neglected, but I will do something about it. It occurred to me that maybe my testosterone level is down from working all these hours. Perhaps I should think about getting a blood test or something."

"OK. Sounds like a good idea. So, you promise you'll do that?"

"Promise."

For several minutes, they didn't say very much. As they hit Euston Road, Abby noticed a billboard for *The Producers*. There were zany line drawings of the three main characters: Max Bialystock, Leo Bloom and a vampy blonde called Ulla.

Abby started to giggle quietly to herself as she remembered the poster in the elevator advertising *The Producers* and realized that the names had clearly been Dan's inspiration for the Bialystock joint, the Bloom overload breaker and the Ulla oscillator.

"What's so funny?" Toby asked.

"Oh, nothing. Just something on a poster I found amusing. It's not important."

Chapter 4

AFTER A SHOWER AND a mug of warm milk, Abby went to bed and slept so deeply that she didn't hear her alarm the next morning. At a quarter to nine, her mobile finally woke her. Still drowsy, she reached out from under the duvet and fumbled for the phone, which she'd left charging on the bedside table. She assumed it was Toby phoning to check that she'd slept and was suffering no aftereffects from the elevator fiasco.

"Helloo?...Abby?...Mum here," Jean boomed, as if she were on a walkie-talkie in a war zone. Abby felt a momentary pang of disappointment when she realized it was her mother calling rather than Toby. "I'm...on...the...ship's satellite phone. Can...you...hear...me?"

"Loud and clear." Abby winced, moving the phone away from her ear. "There's no need to shout."

"Sorry, dear." Jean lowered her voice. "This any better?"

"Much."

"I'm not dragging you away from something important, am I?" This was how Jean began most of her phone calls to Abby. From the moment Fabulous Flowers took off, she seemed to develop an image of Abby as this wheeler-dealer, hotshot businesswoman who led such a high-octane existence that she couldn't be disturbed—even by her own mother.

If there was one thing Abby wished she could change about her mother, it was her lack of self-esteem. Jean had been brought up in a strict, God-fearing family with a sweet but weak mother and a thunderous, table-banging, lay-preacher father who would frequently address his wife and small children on eternal damnation and the fires of hell that awaited sinners and nonbelievers. Grandpa Enoch had died years ago—when Abby was a baby—but the fear he had instilled in Jean, although much diminished, hadn't gone away entirely. She still couldn't have her highlights done without feeling she was a harlot. The other legacy that Enoch had left his daughter was her inability to confront or challenge others.

It was no surprise to Abby that Jean had married the gentle Hugh. They had met at work. Hugh worked for the local council, in the planning department, inspecting house extensions. Jean was a typist in the same department. Unlike Enoch, Hugh was soft-spoken and kind. When it came to Jean, he was her most ardent supporter and admirer. They never went out without him telling her how lovely she looked. They never sat down to a meal she'd cooked without him telling her how tasty it was.

Hugh was also an agnostic—although he took care never to mention this to his father-in-law.

Once Abby had started school, Hugh encouraged Jean to take a part-time job—not because they needed the money, but because he thought it would help build her self-confidence. Jean never did. Having been at home for six years, what little confidence she'd acquired when she worked for the council was gone.

Abby remembered classmates coming to tea after school. A few of these girls had mothers who went out to work. Some were professional women—lawyers, doctors, teachers.

Jean would serve up her homemade shepherd's pie and make wistful comments like: "You must be so proud of your mum" or "I bet you want to grow up to be just like her."

Usually the children shrugged. Abby knew—because they told her—that they hated being met by the au pair when they got back from school.

As Abby got older, she began to understand the inadequacy her mother was feeling and needed to reassure her. Time and again she would hug Jean and tell her she was the best mother in the whole wide world. "You're always waiting for me when I get home. You always come to assemblies and plays and you make real food for tea, not fish fingers."

Jean would return the hug and thank Abby for being so appreciative, but there was always this faraway look on Jean's face. It was as if part of her was aching to climb to the top diving board and jump off but the rest of her was petrified that she might not surface again.

Abby lay on her side, phone pressed to her ear. "No, Mum, of course you're not disturbing me," she said kindly, "and even if you were, it wouldn't matter. Actually, I'm still in bed."

"Oh, my goodness, I didn't wake you, did I?"

"Yes, but you did me a favor," she said, glancing at the clock and seeing that it was nearly nine. "Somehow I managed to sleep through my alarm." She decided not to

mention the elevator incident. Jean would only get into a
flap and suggest that Abby may have sustained some as yet
asymptomatic injury and insist she go to the hospital to get
herself checked out.

"So, Mum, why are you calling? Is everything OK?"

"Oh, yes, fine. Bit choppy through the Drake Passage
last night. Your dad threw up most of his boeuf en daube
and half a bottle of chardonnay. And the lavatory situation
is still a bit iffy. All the cabins seem to be affected. The
gangways were awash with smelly water this morning, so it
was quite literally all hands on deck with buckets and disin-
fectant. Still, mustn't grumble. We're managing to keep our
chins up. As they say, worse things happen at sea."

"But you are at sea."

"Oh, dear," Jean giggled, "so we are."

"Mum, I'm really worried about what's happening. I
mean, you could get really ill if this leaking sewage thing
isn't fixed."

"Please stop worrying. Everything's under control. Dad
and I have gotten rather pally with this solicitor chappy—
lovely wife, very elegant, image of the Duchess of Kent,
owns an artsy-crafty gift ship in Brockenhurst.... Anyway,
Gerald—that's the solicitor—suggested we get up a peti-
tion to present to the captain."

"Saying what—that if he doesn't get the problem fixed,
you will be forced to instruct counsel and, in the fullness of
time, pursue a claim for damages in the county court?
That's bound to have him quaking in his boots. Mum,
something needs to be done right away. This is serious."

"We all know that, so the passengers are pulling together. In fact, there's a real camaraderie built up. You know,
Dunkirk spirit and all that. We're pooling our baby wipes

and bottles of Dettol. Now, the reason I rang was to remind you that it's your aunty Gwen's birthday the day after
tomorrow, and I thought you might like to send her a card
and a nice Il Divo CD. Or you could get her a sweater or a
bottle of that Body Shop white musk scent she likes."

Abby had completely forgotten her aunt's birthday. She
said she would pop out at lunchtime and buy a card and
present.

"Look, Mum, I have to go. It's past nine and I need to
go downstairs and open the shop. But please promise me
you'll get this problem sorted. You and Dad need to take
some direct action for once and stand up for yourselves."

"We will, dear. Now stop fussing—ooh, before you go.
Aren't you meant to be having dinner with Lady Penelope
this week?"

"Actually, it was last night."

"How did it go? I bet she was lovely. Is she very beautiful? I've always imagined her as very elegant and chic, with a
perfect figure—a bit like Princess Grace of Monaco."

"Well, she's certainly got a figure," Abby said, grinning
to herself.

"And she's nice?"

"She's a real character," Abby said—ever the diplomat.
There seemed little point in furnishing Jean with a descrip-
tion of Lady P's personality, as it would only leave her anxious and frightened. "Look, I really do have to open the
shop," Abby said. "I'll tell you all about last night when you
get home."

AFTER ABBY hung up, she lay in bed, aware that all she
wanted to do was go back to sleep. On top of that, her head

was filled with a dull ache. She wasn't surprised. Getting trapped in the elevator had been traumatic, to say the least, and she was probably still in shock.

She knew she had to get up, but for the moment her body wasn't inclined to move. Instead, she lay gazing up at the ceiling, reliving the desperate panic and claustrophobia she'd felt when she realized she was trapped in the elevator. Then she remembered her elation at being rescued and her certainty that her phobia had disappeared.

She felt herself flush with embarrassment as once again she recalled telling Dan about Toby's inability to perform in the bedroom. On the upside, though, she was unlikely to ever meet him again. She imagined how much more excruciating it would be, waking up this morning knowing that she had revealed her most intimate secrets to a boss or work colleague—somebody she would have to face again in a few hours.

Finally she remembered Toby's behavior in the restaurant. Even though he had apologized and she'd forgiven him, she realized that she was still cross with him for not supporting her. Hearing him try to convince his mother that she was one of the Dorset Cromptons had made her feel small and socially inferior. And as for his agreeing to her taking a fertility test, part of her was still struggling to believe she had heard him correctly. On the other hand, she had been massively disloyal to him while she was in the elevator—though admittedly while drunk and in the throes of a massive panic attack. Then, to cap it all, she had ended the evening by accusing him of being gay.

She decided to ring him to say hi and let him know she was OK. She tried his direct line at work but got his voice mail. When she tried his mobile and the same happened, she decided to leave a message. "Hi, Toby, it's me. Just to say I'm fine and that I'm sorry I got so cross with you last night. I'm sorry about the other thing, too. It had been on my mind, that's all, and I thought we should discuss it. Hope you weren't too upset. OK, let me know if you're coming to mine for dinner tonight and I'll get something in. Bye. Love you."

She glanced at the clock again. It was half past nine and the shop opened at ten. She absolutely had to get up. She allowed herself a few more glorious seconds of being horizontal before kicking back the duvet, sitting up and swinging her legs onto the floor.

Once she was fully vertical, she threw on yesterday's work jeans and one of the long-sleeved T-shirts she always wore in the shop. Next came her denim jacket and the violet cashmere pashmina that Toby had bought her and that she always wore as a scarf, tied round her neck. The shop had to be kept cool for the flowers. During the cold months, like now—particularly with the shop door constantly opening and closing—she was always frozen.

She was on her way to the bathroom to brush her teeth when she heard a key in the shop door. It was Martin Scoredaisy. "Hiya," she called downstairs. "Sorry—I'm running late. I'll be down in a sec with coffee."

Martin Scoredaisy was Abby's assistant. He had been with her almost a year. Until then she had run the shop alone. Now she couldn't imagine how she had managed without him. Before coming to Fabulous Flowers, Martin had worked at Carnation Nation, up the road.

Of course, Scoredaisy wasn't his real surname. Martin's actual surname was Roberts, but back home in Liverpool, his mates had nicknamed him Scoredaisy on the grounds that it seemed an appropriate epithet for a gay florist named Martin.

From the outset, Martin had insisted that Abby call him Scoredaisy. At first she'd felt shy using his nickname. After all, nicknames assumed a degree of intimacy, and she was his employer, not his friend. Then, as they grew closer and actually became friends, she started to feel more at ease with it. Soon she was so comfortable with the name that she even took to calling him Scozza for short. These days she counted Martin among her closest friends. She loathed the term *fag hag*, but there really was a great deal to be said for having a gay best friend. Like most gay men, Martin came with an added bonus. He possessed a sensitive feminine side. This meant that he could talk about his emotions and feelings, cook the best ever mushroom risotto, as well as deliver a stinging discourse on the sartorial imprudence of wearing Miu Miu past twenty-five. He frequently did all three at the same time, although it has to be said that when it came to expressing emotions and feelings, more often than not the focus of Martin's passionate outpouring was himself.

When she had finished brushing her teeth, Abby went into the kitchen and took two clean mugs out of the dishwasher. She put a teaspoon of instant coffee in both—regular for herself, decaf for Martin Scoredaisy. Whenever they wanted to make coffee, they had to come upstairs to the flat. There was a storeroom at the back of the shop, but no kitchen. The truth was there wasn't much of a kitchen in Abby's flat. The real estate agent's blurb had described it as a galley kitchen. In fact, it was nothing more than a row of—admittedly new—Ikea kitchen units at one end of the living room cum dining room. The arrangement was great

for entertaining, because she could cook and chat to her
guests at the same time. The downside was she had to keep
the kitchen area spotlessly clean and tidy. For Abby, there
was nothing worse than sitting watching TV while being
able to see—not to mention smell—stacks of unwashed
dishes and rubbish overflowing the waste bin.

The living area was sizable—over three hundred square
feet—with a high ceiling and plaster coving. It also had the
original black marble fireplace and tall, wooden-shuttered
windows overlooking Upper Street. The shutters were original, too. She'd painted them white, along with the walls.
She liked plain white walls because in her opinion they provided the best background on which to hang paintings. Not
that she owned a single canvas. Even though the business
was doing well, by the time she reached the end of the
month, she didn't have much cash left over. Apart from
all the usual bills, her money went to rent and paying
Martin—not that he wasn't worth every penny. On top of
that she was also paying back the bank loan she'd gotten to
set up the business. That was costing her a couple of hundred pounds a month.

In theory, the living-room shutters obviated the need
for curtains or blinds, but although they blocked out the
light and offered privacy, they weren't brilliant draft exclud-
ers. In winter they offered no protection against the wind
that rattled through the ancient, ill-fitting sash windows.
Besides that, there were the drafts that whooshed up between the floorboards she had so painstakingly sanded and
covered in white floor paint. If only she'd had the strength
to stick her finger up to style and put down carpet. Keeping
the central heating on max all day was costing her a fortune.
Even then it only took the edge off the cold. Each winter

she promised herself she would go to Habitat and buy a couple of rugs, but she never seemed to get round to it. Then the warm weather would arrive and she would forget. She was aware that much of her time was spent battling the cold, both in the shop and in the flat. Sometimes, when she was lying in bed with her hot-water bottle, bundled up in her flannel PJs and bed socks, she would imagine it was summer and she was in Provence, lazing by the pool on the grounds of a vine-clad farmhouse. If she concentrated, she was able to summon up the fragrance of lavender, jasmine and sweet-scented myrtle.

As she waited for the kettle to boil, she opened the shutters and put her hand to the window. The glass didn't feel quite so icy today. Maybe the northerly wind had changed direction and a warm front was on its way.

She stared out the window onto Upper Street and watched a gaggle of Islington mummies with their baby harnesses and buggies—a few had toddlers in tow—piling into Caffe Nero. Part of Abby longed to be with them, sharing the chatter and gossip. She was thirty-four. It was time to at least start thinking about having a baby. The shop was doing well, and she knew it would be in safe hands if she left Martin in charge for a few months. The only problem was Toby. She had no doubt that he wanted children, but because of the hours he worked she knew he would be a less-than-involved father. This meant that in all but name, she would be a single mother. Parenting was hard enough when there were two parents involved. She didn't want to face it alone. She wanted Toby to be a proper father, not one who got home long after the children were in bed and whose only real contact with them was on weekends and holidays.

Abby let out a long, slow breath. Motherhood would have to wait until Toby was made a partner at the law firm and he could reduce the number of hours he put in. A partnership had been in the cards for ages. Surely it couldn't be long now.

She poured water onto the coffee granules and took the hot mugs downstairs to the shop. This morning the familiar cold damp air that greeted her was heavily perfumed. It was March, and the day before they'd had a delivery of lilac, irises and sweet-scented hyacinths.

The shop was deep and narrow but wide enough to accommodate the large tiered display stand that took pride of place in the middle. It was circular and made of molded shiny white plastic. It looked like a giant, futuristic cake stand, except that instead of cakes it held tall, oblong-shaped glass vases full of flowers.

Along with the lilac, hyacinths and irises, the shop was bursting with other spring flowers. There were orange and gold crown imperials, ranunculus with their dainty tissue-like petals, anemones in clashing reds and fuchsias, guelder roses and French tulips in white, red and deep purple. Of all the spring flowers, Abby liked white tulips best. To her, their simplicity was a reaction to the decorative excess of Christmas. She often took half a dozen up to her flat and arranged them in a clear glass rose bowl. She loved watching the tulip heads move as they craned their necks to catch the light. Then, after a day or so, the flowers would open and the stems would bend and droop and arrange themselves with such exquisite artistry over the edge of the bowl.

The counter was at the back of the shop. Behind it was the small workroom where they made all the floral arrangements and bouquets.

One of the shop walls had been left blank, to give a sense of space. The other was lined with trendy white "floating" shelves. These held displays of candles, vases, fancy metal urns and gift cards.

Martin Scoredaisy was standing in the shop window, his hipster jeans displaying six inches of black Calvin Klein boxers. He was holding a small hand mirror close to his elfin, not-quite-thirty-year-old face, which was covered in its usual fine stubble. She watched him prodding the skin around his eye.

"Hi, Scozza. Gawd, you might have put the heater on. It's freezing in here." Using her elbow, she carefully pushed a pile of purple tissue wrapping paper to one side and put the coffee mugs down on the counter. Then she bent down to flick the switch on the fan heater. It whirred softly, giving out a comforting jet stream of warm air.

"When you stand in the light, you can still see them," Martin said by way of reply.

"See what?"

"My crow's feet. Come over here and tell me they're not still there. That wrinkle filler was totally useless. Five hundred quid those injections cost. I've a good mind to walk in and demand my money back."

She abandoned the warmth of the fan heater and went over to Martin. He presented his face for inspection. She caught a whiff of Hugo Boss Energise. "I can't see anything," she said.

"What do you mean? Look at those lines, they're like crevasses."

She could just about make out a fan of fine laughter lines. "Martin, those are hardly crevasses."

By now he was tugging on his sandy-colored eyebrows, making his eyes bulge.

"I'm wondering about an eye lift. What do you reckon?"

"What I reckon is that you went out carousing last night, ended up coming home alone and you're still feeling depressed."

"Ah, but darling, you know me so well," he said, assuming a deep Noël Coward drawl and waving an imaginary cigarette in a holder. He paused for a second before slipping back into his regular working class Scouse accent. "Do you know I haven't had sex in four months? And don't you dare say, 'No, you hum it and I'll sing along.'"

"I'm sorry, Martin. I know it's hard—"

"That's the point. It's always bloody hard and I've got nowhere to put it. The way I'm going, my genitals are going to wither and die through lack of use." He hoisted up his jeans, and he and Abby headed back to the counter.

"Still, what can you do?" he went on, picking up his mug of coffee. "Get up, curl your eyelashes and seize the day. That's my motto."

Martin Scoredaisy's eyelashes were gorgeous. There wasn't a woman who knew him who didn't covet those dark, lightly scrolled lashes. Only Abby knew they were permed and that, in addition, he curled them with tongs every morning, but he had sworn her to secrecy.

He picked up the worksheet from the counter and read the list of the day's orders.

"OK, we've got another mother and daughter coming in to discuss wedding flowers. Three customers have ordered conterpieces for tonight. I'll make a start on those if you like. . . . By the way, do you think I've got small nipples?" He was already lifting up his skinny ribbed turtleneck. She peered at his chest. "Tell me honestly," he went on. "I only ask because this gorgeous guy I met the other night—absolute spitting image of Naomi Campbell, he was—said he thought they were really small."

Abby looked up. "They're perfectly normal—all three of them."

He slapped her playfully on her arm. "Ooh, you're a cruel woman, Abby Crompton, do you know that?" He pulled down his sweater and went back to his coffee.

"Scozza, can I ask you something really personal?"

"Not if you're just going to make fun of me," he said, pouting and turning his head away.

She smiled. "No, this is serious. Honest. What I don't get is, if this boy was the image of Naomi Campbell, why don't you fancy Naomi Campbell?"

He turned back to face her and shifted his weight so that one hip was jutting out. Then he rested his hand on it, I'm-a-little-teapot style. At the same time he was looking at her as if she had just teamed a Lacroix evening dress with a check Burberry baseball cap and flippers. "OK, I think we need to go back to basics here. The reason I don't fancy Naomi Campbell is because Naomi Campbell doesn't have a penis."

Abby didn't have time to reply, because just then the shop door opened and Soph walked in. The fledgling PR company she ran was just round the corner, and occasionally before work she would pop into the shop for a quick coffee and a chat with Abby and Martin.

"Hi, guys. OK, tell me honestly, am I too short and dumpy for this suit? I can't help thinking that the bright pink makes me look like a five-foot-three jelly bean." Apparently, as a child, Soph was always being told not to worry about her lack of inches and that any day now she would experience a "sudden growth spurt." Between the ages of fourteen and seventeen she gained maybe an inch. By the time she reached eighteen, it was clear that five foot three was as good as it was going to get. These days she had finally been forced to acknowledge that, despite endless diets, her "puppy fat" was simply part of her makeup. The upshot was that when it came to her attitude toward her looks, Soph's air of confidence tended to thin.

Abby rolled her eyes. "Good morning," she said. "I would like to welcome everybody to this inaugural meeting of Body Dysmorphics Anonymous. Soph, meet Scozza. He's worried about facial wrinkles and the size of his nipples. Scozza, meet Soph. Maybe you could reassure her that her stunning dark hair and eyes, not to mention her perfect olive skin, look fabulous against bright pink and that she looks nothing like a jelly bean."

Soph gave a harrumph. "That's easy for you to say, with your size six figure and never-ending legs."

"Then there's the cheekbones," Martin added. "Don't forget the cheekbones. And the brown doe eyes that perfectly accessorize the lustrous, shoulder-length chestnut hair."

"Come on, guys, give me a break," Abby said, an unintentional note of sharpness entering her voice. "I was only trying to help."

Soph and Martin exchanged bemused looks. Then Soph turned to Abby. "You seem tense. I take it last night didn't go so well."

"Actually, it wasn't brilliant."

"Omigod," Martin broke in. "I totally forgot. Of course, you were meeting the dragon. So, c'mon, dish. What's she like?"

"Pretty dragonlike," Abby said with a half laugh, "but she wasn't the problem." She explained about getting stuck in the elevator at Covent Garden.

By the time she had finished telling the tale, Martin looked utterly shamefaced. "And here was me moaning on about me nipples like a centerfold with frostbite. Why didn't you say something?"

"But you never take elevators," Soph broke in. "What on earth made you take one last night?"

Abby explained about running late.

Naturally, Soph's inquiries didn't end there. A barrage of questions followed. Was Abby OK? No, was she *really* OK or just saying she was? Was she sure she didn't need post-traumatic stress counseling? Did she think she should maybe go to the hospital to get herself checked out? Who else was in the elevator? How long was it before the police rescue team arrived? Was she suing London Underground? She wasn't? Why not? Were they going to offer her compensation? Didn't she realize the sum they would offer would be paltry, derisory, an insult and she should see a lawyer now? Toby might not be the best person, because really she needed somebody who specialized in personal-injury claims. She had a friend she could recommend. What did Abby mean, she didn't want to make a fuss? Now she was sounding like Jean and Hugh. She could have died, already.

Martin seemed to sense that Abby was feeling a bit browbeaten.

"So, this guy who was with you in the elevator..." he broke in. "What was he like?"

"Dan? Oh, he was lovely. He immediately sensed I was in a state. He really looked after me."

"I *see*," Soph came back, with a lascivious grin.

"What do you *see*?" Abby laughed. "God, you've got a one-track mind. He got me talking, that's all . . . to calm me down."

"So, what does *Dan* do for a living?"

"I don't know. I didn't ask, but he said something about having a degree in engineering."

"Where does he live?"

"I don't know that, either."

"Is he in a relationship?"

"Dunno. Didn't come up—although I got the feeling he wasn't."

"So, what *did* you talk about?"

Abby shrugged. "This and that. I told him all about how I got into floristry. Actually, we shared a bottle of wine. He'd been on his way to a party and was carrying a bottle of something really classy. Must have cost a fortune, but he insisted on opening it because he thought some wine might help calm me down."

"And did it?"

Abby's face flushed.

"Don't tell me," Soph chuckled. "You got pissed, didn't you?"

"OK, maybe just a bit, but I was in a state and I hadn't eaten."

"So, apart from you getting totally rat-assed, did anything else happen?"

"Not really, no. And I wasn't remotely rat-assed. I was relaxed, that's all."

"What do you mean, *not really*?" Soph paused. Suddenly

her face lit up with excitement. "Omigod, you made a pass at him!"

"Don't be ridiculous! I absolutely did not make a pass at him!"

"Well, something happened. You've got that same guilty look you always have when you're holding something back."

"Look, nothing happened. Stop interrogating me."

"OK, but I know something went on."

Martin was leaning across the counter, his chin propped up on his hand. "Better out than in, that's my motto," he said. "Mark my words, whatever it is will only fester. But it's up to you. We're your friends, and we totally respect your right to privacy and space." He threw Soph a conspiratorial look. "Don't we, Soph?"

"Don't we what?"

"Respect Abby's right to privacy and space."

"God, yeah. Absolutely. You know me, I never pry."

Abby burst out laughing. "Yeah, right."

"All right, so maybe I do," Soph conceded. "But it comes from a good place. You know how much I care about you."

"Plus you can't stand not knowing everything that's going on in my life, because not knowing makes you feel rejected and left out of the loop."

"OK, yeah, well, there is that."

Abby took a deep breath. Soph and Martin would get the story of what happened in the elevator out of her eventually. She might as well tell it now and get the embarrassment over with. "OK, like I said, I hadn't eaten. The wine went to my head and I ended up..." Another breath. "I ended up telling him what we were talking about the other day . . . you know . . . that Toby and I don't do it very much."

"That's nothing," Martin piped up. "I once slept with this pizza delivery guy. All I did was suggest that if he didn't come in thirty minutes it should be free and he punched me."

Abby turned on him. "You don't get it. I told him details. Intimate details. It was the wine that made me do it. I couldn't stop myself."

"Hey, come on, it's not that bad," Martin said. His flippant, jokey manner had disappeared. "So you got drunk," he said gently. "You said a few things you shouldn't have. We've all done it."

"I know, but when I look back I just cringe with embarrassment. I can't believe I said the things I said, and on top of that I was so disloyal to Toby."

"Yes, but you did it when you were tipsy," Soph said. "Not to mention in the middle of a massive panic attack. It doesn't count."

"I'm with Soph on this," Martin added. "She's right. It doesn't count. It's exactly like calories stolen from somebody else's plate or eaten after midnight."

"Yeah, it's exactly like that," Soph said—her expression indicating that it was anything but. "Look," she said, turning back to Abby, "let's get a bit of perspective here: Toby's never going to find out what you said and you're hardly likely to meet this Dan again, so I'd forget it if I were you. There's no harm done. All I would say is that if things are really this bad between you and Toby in the bedroom department, then maybe you should get some couples counseling."

"We don't need counseling," Abby said, shaking her

head. "We've talked about it, and we both agree that the problem comes down to Toby overworking. Things will get better. We just have to wait until the work calms down a bit."

Abby failed to pick up on the looks of concern that passed between Soph and Martin. Over the months, the two of them had become great friends. They could press each other's buttons and wind each other up something rotten. Abby put it down to them both being neurotic and outspoken. But instead of like poles repelling, these two connected.

Once Soph and Martin established that Abby had suffered no physical ill effects, they asked her about how the rest of the evening had gone. Abby didn't say anything about Lady P demanding that Abby take a fertility test and the row she and Toby had had about it afterward. She didn't want to fuel her friends' doubts about the relationship. For the same reason, she didn't mention having confronted Toby about his sexuality. Instead, she decided to change the subject. "So, Soph," she said breezily, "how are things with you?"

Soph lowered herself onto the stool in front of the counter. Her face became one massive grin. "Weeell, I have news."

"Ooh, let me guess," Martin said. "I know—Jennifer Lopez has been run over by a steamroller and is claiming a billion dollars on her ass insurance."

"Guess again."

"They've discovered the eighth dwarf, Horny."

Abby and Soph both laughed at this. "Wrong," Soph said. "My news is that I am seeing somebody."

"You mean as in a man?"

"Yes."

"No!" Abby cried.

"I don't believe it," Martin trilled.

"I'd be grateful if the two of you could look just a bit less surprised. Believe it or not, there are men out there who find short, curly-haired Jewish girls with a body mass index in excess of twenty-five attractive."

"Oh, God, sorry," Abby shot back. "It wasn't that. Of course you're attractive. You're beautiful. It's just that we've been so worried about you because it seemed like you were never going to get over Frank." Until six months ago, a banker named Frank Feldman had been the love of Soph's life. Then, with no warning, he dumped her. By e-mail. A week later, "Frank the Wanker" buggered off to Australia with an Aussie fitness trainer named Rayleen. "But why didn't you say you were seeing somebody?"

Soph offered an apologetic shrug. "Up 'til now I wasn't sure where it was going, and I didn't want to make a fool of myself by blabbing."

"But we're your friends." Abby frowned. "How could you possibly have made a fool of yourself? And it's so un-like you. You talk about everything."

"I know. I didn't mean to shut you out, but believe it or not, I've been feeling a bit vulnerable since the split from Frank. You know me—I don't do vulnerable very well, so I pulled back a bit. Anyway, the point is, we've been out a dozen or so times now and I seriously think he might be the one."

Abby was beaming. "You're kidding."

"Nope. And he is to-tally gorgeous. I cannot believe my luck."

"So is he Jewish?"

Soph giggled. "Who are you? My mother?"

"It's just that I know how important this is to your parents. You're always going on about how much they want you to marry a nice Jewish boy."

"Actually, he's half Jewish. His name is Lamar Silverman."

"Lamar?" Abby said, frowning again. "Isn't that rather an odd name for a Jewish guy?"

"I've told you. He's only half Jewish."

"And what does Lamar Silverman do for a living?" Martin asked.

"He's a doctor."

Abby had her mouth open. "You're going out with a Jewish doctor?"

"No," Soph said, her smile belying her impatience. "I'm going out with a half-Jewish doctor."

"OK. OK. Sorry. But even so. Are you the perfect Jewish daughter or what?"

"Practically perfect," Martin interjected. "He's only half Jewish."

Abby told him to stop splitting hairs and turned back to Soph. "Your parents must be thrilled."

"Actually, they don't know about him yet."

"So," Martin said, "what does he look like, this *half*-Jewish doctor of yours? Is he gorgeous? Will I want to steal him off you?"

"Absolutely," Soph said, laughing. "He's tall, with the most beautiful brown eyes. If I had to describe him, I'd say he's a mixture of Wesley Snipes and David Duchovny."

Abby and Martin frowned in unison and exchanged glances. "Hang on..." Martin said, "if he's a mixture of Wesley Snipes and David Duchovny, that means..."

Abby's eyes widened. "...that the half of Lamar that isn't Jewish is...black....Lamar Silverman is black?"

"Yes. He's half Jewish, half Jamaican."

"Blimey!"

"Oh, come on, Abby, surely you of all people don't have a problem with me going out with a black guy?"

"Me? Don't be daft. Of course I don't have a problem. I'm just trying to get my head round the fact that he's black and he's called Silverman. You know, it's like Whoopi Goldberg being called Goldberg."

"I'm more interested in why she's called Whoopi," Martin mused. "I mean, what kind of parents name their kid after a farting cushion?"

"So, if this relationship is serious," Abby said, "why hasn't Lamar met your parents?"

Soph was shifting uncomfortably on the stool. "I don't want to rush things. I'm thinking sometime in 2020 would be good."

"Oh, come on, Soph, you know full well that your parents aren't racists. They both lost family in the Holocaust. I've heard your dad going on about how he loathes all forms of racism."

Soph was nodding. "I know. They also have nothing against gays, but if they found out I was a lesbian I know they'd struggle with it. On the face of it, they're as liberal as they come, but I might be about to put their views to the test. Suppose they let me down?"

Abby took her friend's hand. "They won't let you down. I promise. I know your mum and dad. They're crazy, they bicker, but they're good people. They are not the types who simply talk the talk."

Soph nodded. "I've always believed that, but a bit of me

is still petrified of bringing Lamar home. Can you understand that?"

"I can," Abby said, "but I really think you're worrying about nothing." She paused. "So, is it OK for us to meet him?"

"Absolutely. I can't wait."

She said that Lamar was taking her to the theater on Friday. She suggested, and it was agreed, that the four of them plus Toby would meet up afterward for a late dinner at Tarantino's in Camden Town.

Just then the shop phone rang and Martin disappeared into the back room to get it. He returned a minute or so later.

"Who was it?" Abby asked.

"That location-finder woman. She wanted to know if it would be OK for her and the film director to come over this afternoon. I said yes. Hope that's OK."

"Sure. No probs." A week or so ago, Abby had received a phone call out of the blue from a woman named Katie Shaw. Katie explained that she was a film location finder and that she was looking for a trendy London florist to feature in a romantic comedy. Apparently she'd walked past Fabulous Flowers a few times and thought it would be perfect. She explained that it was a low-budget movie and that the film company could only pay a minimal fee. On the plus side, though, the shop would appear several times in the film and the makers would retain its name. Even though Abby knew filming would cause an enormous amount of disruption, she thought the end result would be great publicity for her business. She had agreed to the proposition at once, and Katie Shaw promised to ring back to arrange a time when she and the director could come and look at the shop.

As Soph got up to leave, she made Abby promise to call her to let her know how the meeting went. "Oh, by the way, talking of business propositions," Soph went on, "I've just taken on this Japanese client. His name is Takahashi. You probably haven't heard of him, but he's one of these software billionaires. Anyway, his daughter is planning an engagement party next month and I suggested you might do the flowers. Hope you don't mind."

"Mind? Why would I mind? That's fantastic. Wow, Soph, thanks."

"OK, great. Point is that Mr. T has many VIP contacts. I know that if it all works out, he'll put in a good word for you with his friends. Anyway, gotta run. His PA will phone you."

Chapter 5

ABBY SPENT THE MORNING working on three large flower displays for Hugo at Hugo, the Mayfair hair salon. Since her rave review in the Sunday *Times* "Style" section and the piece in the *Evening Standard*, Abby had acquired several upmarket corporate clients. With a bit of luck, she could now add Mr. Takahashi to that list. Even then she wouldn't have quite enough big names on her books to put her on the London florists A list, but she was getting there.

The interior of Hugo at Hugo called for outsize floral displays that made a statement. The salon was made up of several large, high-ceilinged rooms with ornate plaster moldings. Hugo—or, rather, his interior designer—had gone for a rococo feel. To wit, he had filled the place with vast crystal chandeliers and flamboyant French antiques. There were cupids peeing into marble fountains, gold-filigreed chairs covered in cherry velvet, gilt mirrors and heavy silk drapes at the vast bay window.

Martin, who, stylistically speaking, worshipped at the altar of industrial piping and twisted metal, sneered at the interior of Hugo at Hugo and branded it a "drag queen's boudoir." Abby was inclined to agree, but since Hugo was paying her a fortune to fill his distressed-stone urns each week, she didn't grumble.

Since the urns were far too heavy to transport, Abby would arrange each display in a plastic inner container, which she would then deliver to the salon. Today she was putting together a mass of trailing ivy and adding tall stems of flowering cherry. When the three displays were finished, even Martin said they looked magnificent.

By the time she had fought through the traffic, delivered the flowers and got back to Islington, it was nearly lunchtime. She remembered she had to pop out to buy Aunty Gwen's birthday present.

She parked the van and headed back to the shop just to check that no problems had cropped up while she was out.

As she approached the shop, she could see that Martin had been busy. The ready-made hand-tied bouquets they always had standing by for customers in a hurry were sitting on the pavement in zinc containers. Next to them were the hyacinth plants, snowdrops and candle pots. One of the candle pots was particularly stunning. Martin had invented the design, and it had become one of their most popular. Overflowing a galvanized pot was a broad garland of dried red chilies. In the center stood a tall, chunky, creamy-white candle. At Christmas he'd done something almost identical using Brussels sprouts. Martin had such an eye for the quirky. She smiled to herself as she realized how lucky she was to have him.

Her smile vanished the moment she opened the door and heard the raised voices. Martin and his ex-boyfriend, Christian, with whom he had been at loggerheads since their acrimonious split almost a year ago, were fighting again.

"You have absolutely no right to deny me access to Debbie," a red-faced Martin cried, shaking his forefinger at the older man, who was standing on the other side of the counter.

"Don't you start lecturing me about rights," Christian shot back. "You gave up your rights the day you walked out."

"I walked out on you—not Debbie. And how could I have stayed? After what you did."

"For God's sake," Abby hissed, "will the pair of you just put a sock in it."

The two men ignored her and carried on arguing. At one point, Martin, who seemed to be in the middle of making a flower-and-fruit centerpiece, picked up a lime and ran it through with a length of thick florist's wire. He then thrust the fruit's metal tail into a wicker basket full of Oasis. "You promised faithfully that we would have joint custody, and now you've gone back on your word. Have you any idea how Debbie must be grieving? I was listening to this psychotherapist on the telly and she said that parental abandonment causes irreparable trauma. It can be responsible for bed-wetting, inappropriate anger in adult life, eating disorders and phobias."

"I see nothing's changed," Christian snarled. "You still can't put one thought in front of another without reference to Doctor Phil."

"Are you calling me ignorant?"

"You tell me. Despite my best efforts to school you in the high arts, it's you who still thinks Plato invented china.... Anyway, Debbie is staying with me, so you'd better get used to it."

"I will never get used to it. Ever. I'll take you to court if need be."

"Go ahead. I can't wait. Let a court hear how you used to bring Debbie home from custody visits hours after the agreed time, how you didn't cook for her, how you forgot to give her her vitamins, how you used to keep her cooped up all day without any exercise. I shall claim you are an unfit parent and I shall win."

"I was late bringing her back once," Martin cried. "Once—and that's because we were enjoying ourselves too much; I lost track of time. I always cooked for her and I never forgot her pills. You know that."

"Then why did she catch three colds this winter? And when you weren't neglecting her, you were spoiling her. All you did was spoil her. When you weren't spoiling her, you were ignoring her. Whenever she needed you, you were pruning your chest or refurbishing your eyelashes."

"Don't you be the snotty grande dame with me, you pompous old queen. So what if I like to spend time and money on myself? Judging by the state of your pores, a bit of defoliation wouldn't do you any harm."

"That's exfoliation, you ignoramus. Defoliation is what the Americans did in Vietnam with Agent Orange."

"Whatever. It doesn't alter the fact that I have more love in my little finger than you have in all of that dried-up husk you call a body."

"How dare you!" Christian roared. "My body is a temple."

"Yeah—Shirley Temple."

"Bitch."

"Takes one to know one."

"Oh, pluck off."

"Pluck off, yourself," Martin snorted. "Debbie always loved me best, and you can't bear that. You never could."

"OK, that's enough!" Abby cried, striding toward the counter, but the pair ignored her and carried on lobbing insults at each other. "I said," Abby practically roared now, "that is enough." This time both men fell silent. The older man's expression remained belligerent. Martin, on the other hand, looked shamefaced and shaken. He clearly hadn't meant the argument to escalate the way it had. "Are you hell-bent on ruining my reputation and my business? Suppose a customer had come in. If you two want to brawl, you will do it in the street, on your own time."

At that moment the door opened and in loped Debbie Harry—the hugest, furriest, floppiest-of-ear and wettest-of-nose St. Bernard you ever did see. Her cream leather-and-diamanté lead was trailing beside her. "I had her tied up outside the shop," Christian said. "Her lead must have come loose." He turned to the dog and allowed his face to rearrange itself into a smile. "Come here, sweetie," he cooed. "Come on."

Before you could say, "I think, therefore Iams," Martin had leaped over the counter and was hugging and nuzzling Debbie Harry. "Hello, girl. Who's a boo-diful girl, then? Who is? You is. That's who. I have missed you. Have you missed me?" Martin glared at Christian. "Look how her tail's wagging. You can see how glad she is to see me. Have you any idea how much she must have been pining?"

"She has not been pining," Christian spat. "She is fine. Now leave her alone. Debbie and I need to get going."

Martin's expression was pure venom. He was making it perfectly clear he wasn't about to let go of Debbie. Abby shot him a murderous look, as if to say, "Start again and you're fired."

Defeat etched on his face, Martin stood up slowly and tossed Debbie Harry's lead at Christian.

"This isn't over, Christian," Martin snarled as he ruffled the hair on Debbie Harry's head one last time. "Not by a long shot."

"Do your worst. See if I care." Christian bent down and picked up the lead, which had landed at his feet. "Come on, Debs," he said, patting the dog's flank. "Let's go."

This had to be the third time this month that Abby had walked into the shop to find Christian and Martin tearing into each other over who should have custody of Debbie Harry. Their five-year relationship had ended the night Martin came home to find Christian in bed with a drag queen named Tequila Mockingbird.

Christian Sitwell owned Carnation Nation, the florist's shop a couple of blocks farther along Upper Street. Christian had started out as Martin's employer, but it wasn't long before the two became lovers. Abby had never understood the attraction.

First there was the age gap. Christian was over fifty. Martin wasn't yet thirty. Then there was Christian's appearance. Despite his ruddy, drink-generated complexion, he wasn't bad looking. When it came to matters sartorial, though, his look owed more to neatness than style. As far as Abby could tell, Christian lived in fawn or brown cords. Each trouser leg contained an immaculate, knife-edge center crease. Over these he always wore a cashmere turtleneck. He appeared to own dozens—in a variety of colors. The sharp trouser crease was echoed along the sleeves of his sweaters. Today, his color of choice was aubergine.

Completing the outfit was his usual green quilted, sleeveless jacket.

Along with his unfashionable cords and sweaters, Christian also had receding hair, which he was savvy enough to have cut into a crop, but his facial hair was always way too long to be classified as designer stubble. He reminded Abby of a garden gnome who'd had an unfortunate encounter with an army barber.

Martin always said he had never been in love with Christian. Nor had their relationship ever been one of equals. Martin was a working-class lad from Liverpool 8. Christian, like Toby, was the son of wealthy landowners. He didn't really need to work. That being said, it was clear to everybody who knew Christian that running Carnation Nation was far more than a hobby. It was his reason for living—along with Debbie—and it consumed him completely.

"You see, for me London was all about sophistication and glamour," Martin had once explained to Abby. "I was young and I'd just arrived from Liverpool. It's changed a lot now, but until recently the pigeons flew upside down because there was nothing to shit on. Suddenly I'm working for this educated, cultured guy who can teach me about the arts, food, wine, politics. I couldn't believe somebody like Christian was showing an interest in me. Where I come from, they think Siegfried Sassoon is a posh hairdresser's and Iraq is where you keep yer CDs. Christian could be bullying, controlling and unpleasant, but he was a brilliant mentor. I've also seen a caring, loving side to him. He doesn't show it very often, because he thinks it makes him look weak. A few months after we became a couple, I got double pneumonia and was in the hospital for a month.

Christian found somebody to mind the shop so that he could spend each day at the hospital with me. He would sit for hours reading *Harry Potter* aloud. He loathed those books, but he knew I loved them, so he read them just for me. Right now I despise Christian, but part of me will always be grateful to him."

It wasn't just Martin who was constantly at loggerheads with Christian. Abby had issues with him, too. From the moment she'd opened Fabulous Flowers, Christian had made it clear he didn't welcome the competition and had done his best to make life difficult for her. She had no idea why he felt so threatened, since the shop that Fabulous Flowers occupied had been a florist's since the sixties. Christian didn't open Carnation Nation until 1980. Technically, if anybody was trespassing, it was him.

Not that Abby would have pressed that point. She wasn't one to split hairs. Her argument was that Upper Street was a busy shopping street and, even though the shops were only a couple of blocks apart, there was more than ample business to go round.

Christian's business was by no stretch of the imagination unsuccessful. Although his bouquets and floral arrangements weren't nearly as contemporary as Abby's and were less suited to edgy Islington flats and lofts, he maintained a loyal and not inconsiderable client list among the more conservative, middle-aged residents who still lived thereabouts. These people tended to turn their noses up at Abby's—or, rather, Martin's—Christmas centerpieces made of Brussels sprouts in favor of Christian's snowmen topiaries and lavish floral combos of silk roses, wax berries and gold-sprayed pinecones.

Abby knew that, back in the eighties, Christian had

been one of London's top florists. Then, in the mid-to-late nineties, floristry design experienced a grand renaissance and Christian failed to keep up. Suddenly flower arranging, like knitting and cooking, was trendy and cool. Styles of floral design changed almost overnight, but Christian seemed to think that the minimalist displays of birds-of-paradise combined with long grasses would be a one-minute wonder. "The fact that the shop is still called Carnation Nation kinda says it all, really," Martin had once mused to Abby. "I mean, when was the last time you saw a bunch of carnations other than in a supermarket or gas station?"

Martin said that the only reason Christian had refused to move with the times was pigheaded stubbornness. The upshot was that his loyal clients stayed loyal, but he wasn't acquiring new ones. Unlike Abby. The more successful Abby became, the more Christian's anger and loathing increased.

Since Christian was chair of the local retailers' association and had the ear of the local council, he was able to act on his loathing while at the same time disguising it as public duty.

His first attack on Abby came less than three weeks after she opened Fabulous Flowers. Christian put in a complaint to the highways committee, saying that the vans delivering flowers to her shop were causing severe traffic congestion on Upper Street.

In fact, the chap who delivered Abby's flowers parked on a side street and never caused a moment's congestion—unlike the van driver who delivered Christian's flowers. He insisted on parking on the main road and always caused a holdup.

The highways committee took Christian's complaint seriously, and Abby was visited by two council members who took some convincing that Christian had made a "mistake" and that the van delivering her flowers did not cause traffic problems.

Once the council was satisfied that Abby's delivery van wasn't a traffic hazard, Christian tried to convince them that her shop waste was a health hazard. He accused her of dumping piles of rubbish in the alleyway behind the shop and maintained that it was attracting rats. Abby insisted that the rubbish was entirely plant waste, which held no interest for rats. Plus, it was properly wrapped in heavy-duty rubbish bags, which were collected—as Christian knew full well—by the garbagemen every Thursday.

The health inspectors duly descended on the back alley, found a couple of empty take-out containers that had somehow gotten mixed up with the shop rubbish, and Abby was issued an official warning.

In the end, Christian seemed to run out of plausible accusations and the complaints died down. For a few months Christian and Abby managed to get along, although if they came upon each other in the street, Christian would refuse to make eye contact.

Then Christian and Martin broke up. If that wasn't enough, Martin had the audacity to apply for a job as Abby's assistant. From the moment Martin started working at Fabulous Flowers, Christian declared outright war on both of them. He went back on his promise to let Martin have access to Debbie, and at the same time he banged off letters to the council, complaining about Abby's slipping roof tiles, leaking gutters and stinking sewage pipes. The council wrote to Abby demanding she fix said defects. They made it clear that failure to comply could result in the closure of Fabulous Flowers.

Abby couldn't believe that the council was taking Christian's side this time without even bothering to investigate. Then she imagined him marching into the council offices and using his position as chairman of the local retailers' association to intimidate some junior official who wouldn't have dared challenge him.

Abby wrote back to the council, saying there were no defects and, even if there were, they weren't her responsibility since she rented the shop and her flat and any structural problems were the responsibility of the landlord.

The council ignored her letter and carried on demanding she fix the roof, gutters and pipes. Abby tried making contact with the landlord, but he was out of the country. She invited the council to come and inspect the building for themselves, but nobody came. All that came were more letters, which, as time passed, became increasingly intimidating. In the end, Abby simply called in a builder and asked him to provide a written assurance that there were no problems with the building. Naturally, this cost her time, effort and a not inconsiderable amount of money. When the landlord returned from abroad, she tried to get him to reimburse her the money she had paid the builder, but he refused on the grounds that she had no legal obligation to give in to the council and, now that she had, it wasn't his problem. She argued, but in the end she let the matter drop. Loath as she was to admit it, she knew she shouldn't have given in to the council so easily.

Christian and Debbie had almost reached the door when Christian stopped. "Oh, I almost forgot the real reason I came." He had turned round and was looking at

Abby. "I wanted to let you know that the council has received complaints about the amount of pavement space you take up with your bouquets and plant displays. They take complaints like this very seriously, and as chairman of the retailers' association, it's my duty to warn you that you might well face a fine."

"And may I ask who made the complaints?"

"Just members of the public."

"Is that so?" The question carried more freight than an aircraft missile launcher.

Abby then made the point that all the local cafés kept tables and chairs on the pavement, even in the winter, thanks to outdoor heaters. By comparison, her plants and flowers took up hardly any space.

"Yes, but this isn't simply about space. The members of the health-and-safety committee are of the opinion—as am I—that people cannot trip over tables and chairs, which are perfectly visible. They can, on the other hand, trip over plants and buckets full of bouquets, which are at ground level."

"This is utter rubbish and you know it."

"The council doesn't think so. I suggest you remove your display from the pavement forthwith."

Abby said she would do no such thing.

"Suit yourself," Christian said airily. "If you can afford to keep paying the fines, then good luck to you." His attempt at a haughty exit was sabotaged by his having to cajole a stubborn Debbie Harry from the shop. The poor animal couldn't take her eyes off Martin and clearly didn't want to leave him.

"God," Abby muttered. "Just what is his problem?"

Martin shrugged. "Dunno. He never talked much about

his past, but I do know his dad was a violent drunk, which would explain a lot."

By now Martin seemed close to tears—about Debbie Harry rather than Christian's miserable childhood. He wiped his eyes and turned to Abby. "God, Abby, I am so sorry about the ruckus when you came in, but you know how much I love that dog. I adore her. It's breaking my heart not seeing her. And you saw how she looked at me with all that longing in her eyes."

Abby said she did understand and she wasn't without feeling. Nevertheless, she was adamant that today's fiasco should never be repeated.

"If Christian comes into the shop and starts taunting you, you leave him to me. If I'm not here, you simply ignore him or go upstairs to the flat. Are we agreed?"

Martin nodded. "You know, if I don't get shared custody of Debbie, I swear I'm going to dognap her and face the consequences."

"You mustn't do that. Christian will only retaliate, and the whole thing will escalate and get totally out of hand. There has to be another way." They didn't have time to discuss what that way might be, because just then not one but three customers came in. One wanted to place an order. The others required hand-tied bouquets. Abby dealt with the order and one of the bouquets. When she had finished, she told Martin, who was still in the back room putting the finishing touches to the second bouquet, that she was popping out for a few minutes. "I'll be back well before the location finder and the film director get here," she said.

Abby still hadn't bought Aunty Gwen's birthday present. One of her mother's suggestions had been to get her a sweater, so the easiest thing—although perhaps not the

most imaginative—was to go across the road to Swan &
Marshall.

Swan & Marshall—founded in 1887, as their carrier
bags proclaimed in proud gold lettering—had until recently
been the nation's favorite chain store. S&M was as British as
bad teeth, cream teas and rain during Wimbledon fortnight.
Until two or three years ago, practically the entire population shopped there for its socks and knickers. Some people
were so into S&M that they rarely shopped anywhere else.
There was little need, since the store sold everything from
dishwasher tablets to duck à l'orange ready-made meals,
from lacy lingerie to lounge furniture.

Then things started to go wrong. The stores started to
look dowdy. The old-fashioned fluorescent lighting was too
harsh. The beige rubber floor tiles looked positively Soviet.
The clothes were drab and lacking in style and sartorial
oomph. Abby had lost count of the number of times she
had walked into the store looking for a new top or a skirt,
only to be greeted by a rail of long fawn cardigans or gray
car coats.

S&M had lost its edge—big time. Not only were they
failing to attract young, trendy customers but, in the big
cities, sophisticated, fashion-savvy customers of all ages
were deserting the store in droves.

Naturally the newspapers had picked up on what was
happening. Tabloid headlines screamed: "Nation's Knicker
Shop Knackered." The broadsheet banners were more sober
but no less doom-laden: "S&M Share Price Slump,"
"People's Store Reports Another Year of Record Losses."

Both the tabloids and the broadsheets accused the S&M
board of arrogance and complacency. It was clear that the
store bosses had always believed the nation's loyalty to be so

great that there was no need to put so much as an iota of effort into retaining it.

Then, no sooner had the new millennium gotten under way than Gap awoke from its sartorial snooze and upped its act. Exciting middle-market stores like Zara and Mango appeared. Supermarkets started selling affordable fashion that actually looked OK. The country was inundated with cut-price outlets.

People had deserted S&M, but almost nobody took any pleasure in it. Women in particular mourned its decline. They would sigh and remember wistfully how their mothers had taken them there to buy long white school socks or their first bra.

These days, Abby rarely bought clothes at S&M. She did, however, pop in from time to time to buy a sandwich or one of their ready-made meals, which were still excellent. It was always depressing to see how dowdy the store had become. The pain got worse when it came to paying for her sandwich or whatever and the assistant asked if she had a loyalty card. She didn't. She had no reason to feel guilty for this, but she did. It was as much as she could do not to crumble and say: "No, I don't have a card anymore. I'm sorry, but I needed to get away, and, yes, your suspicions are correct, I have been seeing other stores."

Everybody—not just women—had thoughts about how the company could get itself back on its feet. It was public knowledge that every day the chairman of S&M received literally hundreds of letters from concerned, well-meaning people offering advice.

Abby had never actually written a letter to the chairman, but she was in no doubt what she would do to get S&M back on track.

For a start, she would put more women in senior positions. For some reason S&M was run by middle-aged, middle-class men from Middle England, whose style and fashion sense were way off the money.

Then they needed to look at their tailoring. Their clothes were badly cut. People understood that mass-produced suits weren't going to fit like designer ones, but everybody agreed that S&M's tailoring was bad and getting worse. Then there was the color problem. S&M's palette was always just a fraction off. Their colors were almost, but never quite, the shades that were actually in fashion. Somehow S&M's colors always managed to look mass-produced and cheap.

Clotheswise, the company's attempts to cater to the younger market were pretty feeble. It was pretty obvious that their designers, having gone to all the major fashion shows and out onto the streets to see what was hot among twenty- and thirty-somethings, had gotten back to company HQ and decided to enhance the latest fashions with their own unique twist—the embroidered motif.

A couple of times recently, Abby had dared herself to go into a branch of S&M in the hope that the company had upped its act. To her utter surprise and delight, she would pick up what she thought were the perfect pair of black or gray trousers. She would be on the point of rushing up to embrace one of the shop assistants and tell said assistant that, for her part, at least, all was forgiven, when she would turn the trousers over only to discover a pink embroidered rose on a back pocket.

Despite the company's attempts to attract a younger clientele, S&M's target customers were undoubtedly middle-aged men and women from the counties. Abby suspected that fear of alienating these core customers—who she suspected weren't deserting the store in anything like the same numbers as the more-sophisticated city types—was the main reason the bosses at S&M had made no real attempt to update their image.

Abby's mum and Aunty Gwen were perfect examples of the type of customers S&M was desperate to hang on to: conservative, middle-class housewives in their early sixties who had lost confidence in their fashion sense the moment they hit menopause. Poor old Aunty Gwen had also put on weight. Abby could just about remember her as young and slim, with a hand-span waist. These days she looked like a pretty woman whose body had been poured into one belonging to a 1950s district nurse.

Every autumn, Jean, Aunty Gwen and their ilk went to S&M, moved in on the gray lamb's wool cardigans, the tweed A-line skirts and the "practical" navy slacks. They were practical because they contained so much man-made fiber that, after an hour on the fast colored cycle, they would emerge from the washing machine barely wet.

Just before Christmas, Jean would pop into S&M and treat herself to something "seasonal" to wear on Christmas Day. This was usually a loose-fitting scarlet sweater, which she chose because it was comfortable and she "just loved" the "cheery" snowflakes and holly motif on the shoulder.

As Abby looked round the store today, she felt the same sense of frustration and gloom she usually felt. Judging by the clearance-sale array of lackluster attire, it was clear that the bigwigs at S&M were either incapable or for some reason unwilling to put in the effort required to get the company back on track. Their latest move to attract custom was to slash prices. For months now, everything in S&M had been on sale. The huge, blazing 40-percent-off signs only served to make the place look cheap and uninviting. It was clear that, rather than take advice from fashion experts and interior designers, the S&M board preferred to bury its head and surround itself with money men—not one of whom had a creative or imaginative bone in his body.

Then a rail of cashmere cardigans and twin sets caught Abby's eye. One thing that could be said for S&M was that it had always stocked cashmere at an affordable price. And now it was even cheaper. She picked up a twin set in a shade that was heading toward, but not quite making it to, baby blue. Not that it mattered. She knew that Aunty Gwen, bless her, didn't have much of an eye for color and that she would love it.

Realizing she hadn't had lunch—or breakfast, come to that—and feeling a bit light-headed, Abby added a tomato-and-mozzarella wrap and a strawberry yogurt smoothie to her basket and headed for the checkout.

As she walked back into Fabulous Flowers a few minutes later, she noticed that Martin was serving a young woman. Since there were no other customers waiting, she thought she might nip into the back room and quickly eat her sandwich before the location finder and director arrived. Her mouth was already filling with anticipatory juices when Martin looked up and saw her.

"Here's Abby now," Martin said to the customer. "Abby, this is Katie Shaw—you know, the film-location finder."

"Oh, right, yes, of course," Abby said, slightly thrown because she wasn't expecting Katie and the director for at least another half hour. She extended her hand.

"Awfully sorry to be early," Katie said as they shook

hands. Her accent could have cut crystal. "I know turning up early is awfully bad form, but our last appointment canceled on us."

"No problem." Abby smiled. She was busy taking in Katie's untidy, chin-length thatch of overprocessed hair and scruffy cashmere coat covered in dog hair.

"Are you absolutely sure? Because we really wouldn't mind going across the street for a coffee and coming back later."

"I'm completely sure. Really."

"Brill."

Abby had been in Katie's company for less than a minute, but she already had her down as one of those terribly nice, upper-class country girls who had been raised to believe that concern for one's appearance was distinctly bad form and was working merely to fill in time before marrying a chinless merchant banker called Charles or Henry and moving back to Wiltshire to breed and do good works.

"D.J.—he's the director," Katie continued, "shouldn't be long. He's just parking the car." As Katie spoke, Abby detected a faint whiff of tobacco breath.

"There's really no hurry," Abby said. "Look, why don't you take the weight off your feet." Abby reached for a stool and slid it toward Katie.

"You know," Katie said as she sat down, "this shop is so totally spot on for D.J.'s film. The location couldn't be more perfect and it's just the right size. D.J. doesn't want anything too big."

While the three of them chatted and waited for the elusive D.J., Abby asked Martin if he would mind nipping upstairs with her shopping and putting the tomato-and-mozzarella wrap in the fridge. He had just disappeared when the shop door opened.

"Ah, here he is," Katie said. "Finally, the man himself. Abby I'd like you to meet..."

Abby turned toward the door.

"Omigod—Dan!"

Chapter 6

"ABBY! I DON'T BELIEVE it. This is incredible." Dan, who had clearly not picked up on Abby's less-than-welcoming "omigod," was now standing beside her at the counter, smiling and shaking his head in astonishment.

"I know. I mean, wow…amazing or what?" Abby prayed she sounded sufficiently effusive and that she wasn't betraying the shock and embarrassment she was feeling. London had a population of six million people. Until last night she had never met Dan. Then she got trapped in an elevator with him, had a panic attack, got legless and revealed a list of cringe-inducing intimate details about her sex life. Now, less than twenty-four hours later, here she was, face to face with him again. If God was playing a practical joke, He was the only one laughing.

"So you own Fabulous Flowers?"

Abby barely had a chance to nod in the affirmative before Katie broke in.

"Hang on, you two know each other?" she said, her eyes wide with surprise.

"Yes," Abby said, her face still on full beam. "We met last night. We got stuck in an elevator together."

Katie looked at Dan. "Good Lord. This is the woman from the elevator? The one you told me about? Wow! Spooky or what." She started making *whoo-ooo* noises.

Just then a thought seemed to hit Dan. "Hang on, I'm confused," he said to Katie. "I thought you said the shop was owned by a woman named Gabrielle."

"God, Deej," Katie said with a theatrical sigh, "you are so dyslexic with names. I told you it was *Abigail.* Abigail Crompton."

"You did?" Dan carried on looking nonplussed.

"Yes. I even showed you those articles about her in the *Sunday Times* and the *Evening Standard.*"

"Oh, God, yes, of course you did." He turned to Abby. "Boutique Retailer of the Year. Really impressive."

"Plus, Fabulous Flowers was voted twelfth-hottest shop in London," Katie piped up.

Before Abby had a chance to thank Dan, Katie was off again: "D.J. told me all about the pair of you getting stuck in the elevator and having to be rescued. Scary or what?"

Oh, fabulous. What were the odds that Dan, or rather D.J. (what self-respecting male calls himself D.J. past the age of thirteen?), had also told Katie about Abby's sad sex life? Why wouldn't he? By this morning it must have seemed like one huge joke.

"Dan said you became phobic about elevators after you got stuck in one when you were young. Jolly bad luck getting trapped a second time."

"Yes, but Dan was absolutely fantastic. He really looked after me."

By now Martin had come back downstairs and was standing behind the counter. He'd clearly caught enough of the conversation to work out what was going on. "So this is Dan? *The* Dan? The Dan who . . . I mean, this is the one you told all about . . . ? No way! Omigod. How embarrassing is this?" He paused. Clearly realizing he had allowed his mouth to run away with him and that he had dropped an almighty bollock, his face turned scarlet. "Tell me I didn't say all that out loud."

"Actually, you did," Abby muttered through a thin, rictus smile. Finally her gaze shifted toward Dan. "I'd like you to meet Martin, my assistant," she said. The two men shook hands.

Now it was Katie's turn to look confused. "Hang on," she piped up. "I'm totally lost. Why is this embarrassing?"

In an instant it dawned on Abby that she might have misjudged Dan and that it was possible he hadn't spent the morning joking with Katie about her deficient sex life after all. Instead, it was Martin who had blabbed, and now Katie was feeling that she had been left out of the loop. Unless Abby could think fast and explain away Martin's remark, the truth was seconds from coming out. She found herself glancing at Dan and offering him a weak, awkward smile.

Martin's expression had become pinched and taut. "Tell you what," he said, clearly desperate to make himself scarce, "why don't I go into the back and get on with some of these orders."

"Good idea," Abby said.

Martin shuffled off. Abby loved him to bits, but she despaired of how, whenever he got excited, his mouth always seemed to disconnect from his brain.

Katie was still looking puzzled. "Sorry, am I missing something here?"

Abby was at a loss to come up with an explanation.

Dan was rocking on the balls of his feet. "Well, you see . . ."

Abby cringed as she waited for the ax to fall.

"Last night in the elevator," Dan went on, "I developed a rather nasty bout of gas and Abby was incredibly gracious about it."

Wow, Abby thought. How generous was that? Not many people would go to such lengths to spare another person's blushes.

"Eeuuww. Gross." Katie squirmed. "God, Deejster! That's disgusting."

Deejster?

"I really must apologize for my colleague," Katie said to Abby with a roll of her eyes. "With no ventilation, that must have been utterly vile."

"It was no big deal," Abby said, making prolonged eye contact with Dan to indicate her gratitude. "These things happen. Can't be helped. I think we should just forget about it."

"Isn't she just the most frightfully good sport?" Katie said to Dan.

"Definitely." He smiled. "Right. Now that we've cleared the air, as it were, I think maybe it's time we talked about the film." He turned to Abby. "From what I can see, Fabulous Flowers totally fits the bill. I was looking for a trendy urban florist's shop, and this is right on the money." He turned to Katie and congratulated her on her find.

———

THE THREE of them went across the streets to Tinderbox, where they sat discussing the film over cappuccino.

"You know," Abby said to Dan at one point, "I've only just realized I don't know your last name."

He apologized, reached into his jacket pocket and took out a business card.

"Daniel Chipault," she read aloud. "You're French?"

"My parents were born in France, but I was raised here."

She slipped the card into her bag while Dan reiterated what Katie had already told Abby on the phone—that the movie was a low-budget romantic comedy and that they couldn't afford to pay Abby very much for the hire of the shop. Abby said she was happy with that so long as Dan promised that there would be sufficient shots of the shop front to guarantee her a decent advertisement.

"I'm sure we can do that," he said. "Also, as it's March and it's getting light earlier, we can limit filming to early morning, which means you won't have to close the shop. If it does become necessary to film during the day, we will find the money to compensate you for your loss of earnings."

He asked her if she understood what filming would involve. She said she had a pretty good idea. She realized that the place would be crawling with soundmen, cameramen and technicians—not to mention miles of cable and piles of equipment.

"So, tell me about the film. What's it about? Who's in it?"

"Well," he said, "my major coup was managing to persuade Lucinda Wallace to take the lead."

"No! I adore her. She was fabulous in *The Forgotten Hills.* Wasn't she nominated for a BAFTA for best newcomer?"

"She was," Katie said. "We are so unbelievably lucky to have gotten her. She and Dan go way back—known each other since school—so she's agreed to do it as a favor."

Just then Katie's mobile rang.

"Sorry, guys," she said after she'd finished the call, "gotta dash. You'll never believe it, but that was the manager of Soho House. I think he might be up for letting us film one of the party scenes there. He wants to see me in an hour." She stood up and began putting on her coat. She and Dan agreed that she would take the tube and he'd drive back to the office later.

"OK, wish me luck."

They both said they would keep their fingers crossed.

After Katie had gone, Abby asked Dan how he'd raised the money to make the film. He told her how he had remortgaged his flat, convinced friends to invest and managed to convince the National Lottery Fund and the Arts Council to give him some money.

He certainly didn't lack drive, determination or chutzpah. Abby was impressed. She was even more impressed because it seemed that, like her, he'd had no family money to give him a leg up. She remembered how she'd struggled to save the money for the deposit she needed to get Fabulous Flowers off the ground. For four years she'd worked nine to six in a florist's shop and eight to midnight waitressing in Pizza Express.

"So, what's the film about?"

Dan said it was a romantic comedy called *Bouquet*. "It's a modern take on *My Fair Lady*. I spent the last couple of years working on the screenplay."

"Wow, you're the writer and director."

"Yep. I'm also the producer and editor. That's partly

because I'm a control freak." He gave a flicker of a grimace, as if to reassure her that he knew this was one of his faults. "And partly because this project is being made on such a shoestring that we couldn't afford to bring anybody else on board." He drained his coffee cup. "Anyway, Lucinda plays Lisa, a feisty working-class single mother working in a florist's shop. Simon is an aristocrat who falls in love with her."

"Bit like me and Toby," she giggled. "Except I don't have a child."

"And you don't live in a housing project in Peckham.... Anyway, unlike Henry Higgins, Simon doesn't change her so that she can find her place in polite society; she ends up changing him. By the end of the film, it's his values and perceptions, his view of the world that has changed, not hers. Suffice it to say that before we reach that point, they split up for a time and she goes back to her old boyfriend."

"But all the way through, you know it's going to work out for them in the end."

He looked apologetic. "That tends to be how rom-coms work. They're like Greek tragedies. They always follow an identical pattern. You know the routine: man meets woman, usually after some kind of complicated mix-up. They begin a tentative relationship. Something happens to split them up. They either get back together or form new relationships."

"No, I get that—I really do. Everybody adores those plots. You love knowing but not knowing."

He asked her if she fancied another cup of coffee.

"Love one," she said.

As he stood up, she couldn't help noticing how attractive he was. He really did have the warmest brown eyes, and when he smiled, dimples appeared at the corner of his mouth.

Today he was in jeans again, but this time, instead of the windbreaker, he was wearing a white open-necked shirt under a trendy, heavy cotton tailored jacket in a black pin-stripe. The jeans were faded and a bit worn, the jacket slightly crumpled. His look seemed so effortless and un-put-together.

Toby, on the other hand, didn't tolerate creases in the wrong places. His look was impeccable. She had always admired his style, but thinking about it now, she couldn't help thinking that perhaps he looked a bit too perfect. His outfits were so thought out, so self-conscious, as if he'd been styled for one of those TV makeover shows.

Dan came back to the table with a tray of coffee and cake. There were two slices—one chocolate, one lemon drizzle. "God, you read my mind," she said. "I missed breakfast and lunch. I'm absolutely ravenous."

They ended up cutting the cake slices in half so that they each got a piece of lemon cake as well as a piece of the chocolate.

"Before we carry on discussing the film," Abby said, folding cappuccino foam into her coffee, "I just want to thank you for rescuing me back at the shop. It was incredibly gallant."

He smiled. There were the dimples again. "My pleasure," he said.

"I am so embarrassed about last night. I don't know what got into me. Well, actually, I know precisely what got into me—almost an entire bottle of wine. I tend to lose all my inhibitions when I've had a bit to drink. I'm sorry I made such a fool of myself. I hope you weren't too embarrassed."

"Not remotely." He popped a piece of lemon-drizzle cake into his mouth. "Come to think of it, last night's all a bit of a blur and I can barely remember what we talked about." She knew by his mischievous grin that he was fibbing.

"You know," Abby said, "Toby and I... We're really happy together. I don't want you to think—"

"Abby, you don't have to explain anything. Your relationship with Toby is none of my business."

"I know, but I just don't want to give you the wrong impression, that's all."

He nodded. "So, did you get to meet his mother?"

"Oh, yes. She's titled and extremely grand. Very intimidating. She makes Lady Bracknell look like she has self-esteem issues, but I think I can handle her." She took a sip of coffee. "You know, the other thing I felt awful about last night was the way I wittered on about myself and didn't ask anything about you. It was so rude of me."

"No, it wasn't. You were having a major panic attack. Plus, I enjoyed listening to you."

"You did? Even that long, boring story of how I got into floristry?"

"That wasn't boring. It was fascinating. It's always interesting to find somebody who's passionate about something and takes the road less traveled."

She felt herself blush at the compliment. "So, c'mon, tell me a bit about you. I'm assuming you don't actually have a degree in engineering."

He grinned. "What can I say? You found me out. You're right, my degree is actually in English. I guess the Bialystock joint and the Ulla oscillator were a bit of a give-away."

She nodded. "Kind of, but it took me a while to work it out. The penny didn't drop until I saw a poster for *The Producers* on the way home."

"Sorry. I was just trying to reassure you that the elevator wasn't about to plummet to the ground."

"I know, and I'm immensely grateful. So, come on, more about you."

He was starting to look mildly ill at ease. She assumed he was one of those people who disliked being the focus of attention. "What can I tell you? OK—until now I've directed TV drama. Before that, I was a freelance documentaries editor, and before that I was at film school. I am an only child. When I was growing up I had a cat named Gary, who had a black mustache, which made him look the image of Hitler. I have a mild dairy intolerance and a large chicken-pox scar on my left knee. I had my tonsils out when I was six and my appendix when I was fifteen. I try to eat five portions of fruit and veg a day but rarely get beyond two. My favorite piece of music is 'Bohemian Rhapsody,' and my favorite film is *Fargo*. My idea of a perfect night in is sitting in front of the TV, eating Indian takeout and watching *Boston Legal*. I think Denny Crane and Alan Shore are the best comedy duo since Abbott and Costello."

She said she'd seen the ads for *Boston Legal* on the underground but she'd never watched it. "I adore *Fargo*, though. But my favorite film has to be *It's a Wonderful Life*. I put the DVD on every Christmas."

He looked wistful. "God, I haven't watched that film in donkey's years. I'd love to see it again."

"Why don't I lend you the DVD?"

"That'd be great."

She broke off a piece of chocolate cake. As she brought

it to her mouth, she found herself focusing on the attractive fan of smile lines around his eyes. "So are you single?" she blurted. The moment the question left her mouth she turned crimson. "I'm sorry. I don't know why I asked that. Your personal life is absolutely none of my business."

"That's OK." He smiled. "I'm happy to talk about it. My girlfriend and I split up almost a year ago."

"I'm sorry." Her condolences were genuine, but as she offered them she felt her heart take a tiny, almost imperceptible leap of something that felt suspiciously—not to say confusingly—like pleasure.

"Thank you," he said. "I was devastated for a while, but the truth is, the breakup was a long time coming." He explained that he and his girlfriend, Janey, had been together since they were students, but recently they'd both started to change and lead almost separate lives. "It took us ages to admit it. But eventually we reached a point where we realized we weren't making each other happy and we decided to call it a day."

As she watched him pincering up cake crumbs from his plate and rubbing them slowly between his fingers, she could tell he was lost in his thoughts. She searched for something to say that would lighten the atmosphere.

"So, how did you get the nickname D.J.?"

He looked up, his face forming an expression that was half smile, half wince. "Oh, that's just Katie. She gives everybody nicknames. It's how you can tell that she likes you. When she found out my middle name was James, she immediately began calling me D.J. I don't mind, but I do get a bit embarrassed when she refers to me in public as 'the Deejster.' People think that's what I call myself, and they immediately think of me as a prat."

"Oh, I'm sure they don't. I barely noticed when Katie called you Deejster."

"Now you're just being polite." He grinned.

"I'm not. Honest."

They were both laughing. "So," he said, "what's your worst film of the last five years?"

She didn't need to think. "OK, it's not exactly my *worst* film, but I definitely think it's the most overhyped. I know you're going to disagree with me, because absolutely everybody does, but I was less than keen on *Brokeback Mountain*. At the time, everybody accused me of being homophobic, but I'm not. I just found the whole thing utterly tedious."

"I agree."

"You do? You're not just saying that to be polite?"

"Absolutely not. I'm with you on that one. By the time the story reached the 1980s, you just wanted to scream, 'Enough with the breast-beating already. Just get yourselves off to San Francisco and get a life.'"

She laughed. "I know! My thoughts exactly. But, at the time, coming out and saying it felt like committing some sort of heresy."

"But you said it anyway."

She grinned. "I did. And the truth is, it felt great, but I don't find it easy to be the one dissenting voice."

"Why's that?"

She explained how her parents brought her up not to challenge people in public because it might cause offense. "I try not to be like that, but it's not easy. I've still got a long way to go." She sipped some coffee. "So, what's the worst film of the last five years?"

He said that without doubt it had to be Guy Ritchie's *Revolver.*

"It was dire. I walked out—and I was watching it at home."

She was laughing again and realizing how much she was enjoying Dan's company.

Whether it was subconscious guilt that she was enjoying being in the company of a man other than Toby or an awareness that Martin had been looking after the shop on his own nearly all day, something made her look at her watch. It was well after four.

"Please don't think I'm being rude," she said, "but I really ought to be getting back to the shop. Martin has got a load of deliveries to make, and I need to cover for him."

"No problem," Dan said. "Of course you have to get back. Actually, I should be getting going, too. I have another meeting at five." They both stood up and began walking toward the door.

"I'm glad we met again," Dan said. "I've really enjoyed chatting to you—"

"—while I'm calm and sober," she volunteered with a twinkle.

"I wasn't going to say that. In fact, I wasn't about to add a qualifier. I've just enjoyed chatting."

"Me, too," she said, "and thanks again for sparing my blushes earlier."

"You're welcome." He opened the door for her and they stepped into the street. It turned out that his car was parked not far from the shop, so they both set off in the same direction. After a few hundred yards they reached S&M. Abby could never walk past the window without tutting and grimacing. Dan picked up on this.

"I wish I knew why everybody has it in for S&M these days," he said.

Abby laughed. "But how could you not know? The clothes are so dowdy. And just look at that window display. It's trying so hard to be young and funky, but it's so un-edgy. It's more like my aunty Gwen's idea of funky. It just doesn't get your juices going."

She made him look at the mannequins. "See how their jeans are just fractionally too short? And look at the tops. This season's color is teal. But those fabrics are several shades off and look cheap, don't you think?"

He shrugged. "I dunno. What's teal?" he said.

She looked at him to see if he was teasing her. "Hang on, you really don't know?"

"I'm a bloke. How many blokes do you know who could tell you what color teal is?"

"Toby could. Mind you, with him color and style are a bit of an obsession."

Dan was shaking his head. "Sorry, that's something I just don't get. I buy a dozen pairs of socks and underwear once a year—from S&M, as it goes. When it comes to any-thing else, I literally have to force myself into clothes shops. Buying stuff to wear bores me rigid."

She found herself taking another look at the trendy black jacket he was wearing. Maybe he did find clothes shopping a drag, but there was no doubt that he made some pretty good choices.

By now they were at his car. "So," he said, "I'll have that contract drawn up straightaway and get it in the post." He paused. "On second thought, why don't I drop it round and maybe you could lend me that *It's a Wonderful Life* DVD?"

"Perfect," she said.

———

WHEN ABBY got back to the shop, the floor in front of the counter was covered in bouquets and centerpieces, which Martin was waiting to load into the van. "Great, you're back," he said. "I'll be off. Shouldn't be more than an hour."

She asked him how he was feeling about the Christian/ Debbie Harry incident. He shrugged. "I won't give up fighting for her. I know some people think it's daft the way humans bond with animals, but in some way that I can't explain, Debbie and I really connected."

Abby said she didn't think it was at all daft.

"I take it you're ignoring Christian's threats and you're not about to get rid of the pavement display."

"No blinkin' way," Abby said. "If Christian wants a fight, he's got one."

"My nuts in a thoughtshell."

"But we have to stay calm, OK? We both have issues with Christian, and neither of us is going to gain any ground by losing our tempers."

"I know, but he just gets under my skin. I can't help it."

"Scozza, you allow him to press your buttons. That has to stop."

"I know, I know, but it isn't easy." He paused. "Oh, by the way, Mr. Takahashi's personal assistant phoned and left a message on the answering machine."

She looked blank for a moment.

"You know, the Japanese software billionaire Soph mentioned?"

"Right. Yes. I'd totally forgotten."

"His PA is a guy named Ichiro. I have to say, his voice sounded dead sexy. Did I ever tell you I've always had this thing about Asian men? I've left his number on the pad."

"OK, I'll phone him right now."

"And find out if he's gay."

"And how do you suppose I do that? What do I say? 'Oh, by the way, my male assistant has the hots for Asian men and would like to know if you're gay.' Call me over-sensitive, but I think that might just lose me the contract."

"You don't have to ask outright. Just read the signs."

"What signs? Far be it from me to pull rank on a member of an oppressed minority, but I feel the need to remind you that the vast majority of gay men are not remotely effeminate."

"Yeah, yeah. Whatever. Abby, do me a favor, just see if he gives off a vibe."

"OK, if he invites me round to his place to watch *La Cage aux Folles* or happens to drop into the conversation that he always keeps the first day of the Calvin Klein sale circled in his diary, I'll let you know."

ICHIRO SPOKE perfect English with a strong American accent. He explained that Mr. Takahashi's daughter, Mai, had just gotten engaged and was planning a party toward the end of April at her father's house in Knightsbridge. "We've heard nothing but fabulous things about you, Ms. Crompton, and Mr. Takahashi would be honored to have you flower the apartment for the occasion."

Abby said she would be more than happy to take charge of the flowers and explained that in order to get some idea of what was required she would need to take a look around. It was agreed that she should come the following afternoon.

Abby put down the receiver. "He sounds pretty gushy on the phone," she called out to Martin, who was walking out the door with the last couple of bouquets. "And he did invite me to 'flower' the apartment, but that could just be an American thing."

"Yeah, could be."

Martin was of the opinion that since neither of them could decide with any confidence that Ichiro was gay, the only solution was for Abby to meet him and report back.

ABBY PUTTERED about the shop, tidying the counter, removing what she considered to be slightly less-than-fresh stems from the large display vases. There was always a lull during the late afternoon, but she knew that by six the place would be jumping with people wanting bouquets of flowers to take to dinner parties.

This evening it seemed like the whole of Islington was entertaining, and from half past five onward, she had a constant stream of customers. Most people were more than happy to take one of the white orchid plants or ready-made bouquets from the pavement display. Others were more particular and hemmed and hawed—particularly over color combinations. Abby could never understand why people were so conservative when it came to color and why they struggled to appreciate that a purple moth orchid looked stunning against the brilliant orange of a bird-of-paradise.

She had just finished serving her last customer when she received a couple of texts. The first was from Martin, to say the rush-hour traffic was particularly bad and would she mind if he took the van home for the night instead of struggling back to the shop. She replied to say she didn't mind at all. The second message was from Toby: *will be in 4 dinner. Get 2 u around 8.*

It was only then that she realized she'd forgotten to buy any food—apart from her still uneaten tomato-and-mozzarella wrap—while she was in S&M.

Once she'd shut up shop for the night, she popped back to S&M and picked up a couple of tuna steaks, some green beans and a small bag of new potatoes. At the last minute she added a large bar of dark chocolate to her basket. She would make a chocolate mousse.

When she got back to her flat, she put the tuna in the fridge and got together the rest of the ingredients to make the mousse. At the end of a long day, cooking always relaxed her. She poured herself a glass of sauvignon blanc, switched on the early-evening TV news and began separating egg yolks from their whites.

At a quarter past eight, Toby texted her again to say that he was stuck in a meeting and that she shouldn't wait dinner for him as he was going to be at least another couple of hours. Usually she would have ignored his invitation to go ahead and eat and would have waited for him. Tonight she couldn't wait. The only thing she'd eaten all day was two half slices of cake, and she was starving.

In the end Toby didn't roll in until after eleven. She didn't hear his key in the door, because she was fast asleep on the sofa. An edition of *Wife Swap* was playing to itself.

He woke her with a gentle kiss. "Umm, that's nice," she smiled, opening her eyes.

"You look knackered," she said, watching him lay a suit carrier over the back of a dining chair. "Bad day?"

"I've known better." His voice was flat with exhaustion.

"How about a glass of wine?"

"I think I'd prefer a Scotch. I'll get it. You stay there." He loosened his necktie and opened his top shirt button.

"Toby—about yesterday... and that whole gay thing. You're right, it was an ignorant, knee-jerk reaction, and I'm sorry."

"Forget it." He waved a dismissive hand. "I have. Actually, I'm more concerned about how I behaved in the restaurant. I upset you, and I'm sorry, too. Can you forgive me?"

"Well, I have to admit that I was pretty hurt, but, yes... of course I forgive you." Her face broke into a smile.

"Great. So we're OK again." He bent down, kissed her on the lips and then headed into the kitchen.

"By the way," he said, returning with a very large Scotch, "I picked up my new suit today—you know, the one that was being altered."

"Oh, right."

He tugged at the zipper on the suit carrier and walked over to the sofa. "Here, just feel the quality of the cloth." He presented her with a charcoal-colored suit sleeve. "It's pure cashmere."

"Umm, really nice," she said, running her hand over the fabric.

"Nice? Abby, this fabric is beyond 'nice.' It's glorious. And I bought a Paul Smith shirt to go with it." He put the suit carrier back over the chair, opened his briefcase and took out a yellow Selfridges bag. "It's got a thread count of one hundred eighty. Feels like pure silk next to the skin. Just look at the lilac against the charcoal of the suit. Isn't it *the* perfect combo?"

After Abby agreed that it most definitely was, Toby announced he was off to have a shower.

By the time he emerged from the bathroom—one of her giant bath towels tied round his waist, his damp hair all ruffled and sexy—Abby had fried him a tuna steak and cooked a fresh batch of beans and potatoes.

"I don't know what I'd do without you," he said, re-securing the towel round his waist.

"Yes, you do," she grinned. "You'd order takeout every night and get acne and clogged arteries."

He helped himself to cutlery from the kitchen drawer and took the plate of food from her. She joined him at the table and poured them both some wine.

"So, you feeling OK, after what happened in the lift?" Toby said. "I meant to phone you this morning to see how you were, but I left the flat at six and from then on it was pretty full on. I'm sorry."

"Don't worry. I'm fine." She put her wineglass to her lips. "You'll never guess who came into the shop today."

"Who?"

"Well, first Christian came in and had a massive fight with Scozza." Toby knew all about Christian and Martin and the custody battle over Debbie Harry. "Then Christian had another go at me. Apparently my pavement displays are a danger to pedestrians, and he's threatening to report me to the council." She paused. "I wish I knew what his problem was. Martin said he had a rotten childhood, but then, so do millions of people and they don't all turn out to be jerks."

"It's odd," Toby said, "because when I was introduced to him at that retailers' association dinner we went to last month, he seemed pleasant enough."

"Yeah, I saw him sucking up to you. Believe me, he did it only because he's a snob and he knew you were a posh lawyer."

"Yeah, you're probably right." Toby tweezered a tiny bone from his tuna and deposited it on the side of his plate.

"So, anyway, you'll never guess who else came in—only the guy I was trapped in the elevator with. I mean, can you believe a coincidence like that? I was totally knocked out. But it gets even more spooky. It turns out that he's the film director I was telling you about the other day. You know, the one who wants to use Fabulous Flowers in his movie."

"You're kidding?"

"Nope."

"I agree that is pretty amazing. So, how much is this guy paying you for using the shop? I hope you managed to get a decent deal out of him."

"Not much. This is his first feature film and the budget is tiny."

"Yeah, right. That's what he tells you." Toby stabbed a new potato with his fork. "Oh, and speaking of money, we have to think about London Transport and how much we're going to sue them for. I reckon we could get fifty grand out of them easy. Especially if we threaten to go to the press. Just leave the claim to me. I'll handle it."

Abby was shaking her head and smiling. "You know, you and Soph really should go into partnership together. When it comes to money, the pair of you think so much alike. I don't want to sue. I wasn't injured. With the best will in the world, machines break down. The woman from London Transport assured me I'd receive some compensation— enough to replace the clothes I was wearing and pay for a nice dinner. I want to leave it at that."

Toby put down his knife and fork and sat back in his chair. "You are kidding, right? Have you any idea how much you could get out of them for emotional distress alone? That's before we get on to inconvenience and physical injury."

"But I don't have any injuries. I'd be lying if I said I had."

Toby shrugged. "Oh, come on. After being yanked out of that elevator shaft, surely you pulled or twisted something."

She shook her head. "No, I didn't. I'm fine. In fact, I'm more than fine. What happened last night could well have cured my elevator phobia. If anything, I'm grateful, and I don't want to sue."

"You're mad. Do you realize you could be turning down a great deal of money? Thinking about it, fifty grand is the bare minimum we'd get."

"Maybe I am mad, but it's how I feel and I'd like you to respect that."

He shrugged. "I can't force you to do anything against your will."

"And you respect my decision?"

"Of course I don't. It's crass and you will live to regret it."

"Well, at least you can accept it."

He shrugged. "Fine. Whatever."

"Good." She reached across the table and kissed his cheek. "I may be bonkers in your book," she giggled, "but I know that's one of the reasons you love me." She got up and started kissing the back of his neck.

"Please, Abs," he said, shrugging her off. "Not now. I'm trying to eat."

"OK, why don't I have a shower and get ready for bed? I'll meet you under the duvet."

"Good idea," he said. He picked the newspaper up off the table and began scanning the front page.

Ten minutes later she was lying in bed, wearing the same cream silk La Perla nightgown she'd taken on their trip to Paris, her skin positively marinated in Chanel No. 5 body lotion. "I'm way-ting," she called out.

"Yep. Be with you in a bit. Just finishing this article."

It was another fifteen minutes before he appeared.

"Take that towel off," she whispered, holding out her hand toward him. "And come here."

He let the towel drop and got into bed next to her.

"I love you," she said, turning onto her side so that she was looking directly into his eyes.

"I love you, too."

As he began stroking her hair, she snuggled into him. "You know, we really do need to start spending more time together."

Toby instantly pulled away and lay on his back, staring at the ceiling. "Abby, it's late and I've had a long day. Please don't nag."

His response startled her. "I wasn't meaning to nag. I was trying to be loving."

"Well, it didn't sound like it."

She could swear he was trying to pick a fight to get out of having sex. "You're just tense," she said softly. "Come on, how's about I give you a back massage?"

"No, I'm too tired."

"Oh, come on. You'll enjoy it."

"Maybe you're right." He rolled onto his front.

She sat straddling his torso and began digging her thumbs deep into the knots in his shoulders.

"Ooh, that's good. More. More."

"See, all you needed was some help unwinding." She kept working on his back. After a while her hands moved to his buttocks and then to his thighs. When he finally turned over to kiss her, she ran her hand over his stomach. But as her fingers began walking farther south, she encountered no throbbing, rigid yearning, just the limp flopperly-dopperlyness with which she had become so familiar. He took hold of her wrist.

"Abby, I'm really sorry. I'm so tired. I just want to sleep."

She did her best to hide her disappointment. "OK, not to worry. You know, you really ought to see the doctor. Just to check your testosterone level."

"Abby, I promised and I will. But God only knows when I'm going to find the time. And then you want me to see some shrink. Christ this feels like so much pressure."

They lay in bed with their backs to each other. After about ten minutes Toby rolled over toward Abby.

"Abs, you asleep yet?"

"No."

"Me, neither." He asked her if she minded him putting on the TV for a few minutes. "Might relax me." She told him to go ahead. Toby reached for the remote and switched on the small, elderly TV that lived on a table at the end of the bed.

He began channel surfing. "By the way, I forgot to mention some of the chaps and their girlfriends are getting together for dinner Friday night at Feng Wei. We're invited. I said yes. Hope that's OK."

She explained that she'd already arranged for them to meet Soph, Scozza and Soph's new boyfriend for dinner late on Friday evening.

"Can't they come to Feng Wei instead?" Toby said. "I'm sure nobody would mind if they arrived late."

She thought for a moment. "When you say 'chaps,' I presume you mean Guy and the rest?"

"Yes. Why?"

"Oh, Toby, you know how they get when they've had a few. I don't want them telling homophobic jokes in front of Scozza. And what if they upset Lamar?"

"Who's Lamar?"

"Soph's boyfriend. Lamar Silverman. He's half black, half Jewish."

Lamar's ethnicity seemed to bypass Toby. "God, Soph's going out with Lamar Silverman?"

"You know him?"

"I know *of* him. I'm pretty sure I read a profile on him in the *Times* a few weeks ago. Isn't he that doctor who's been attacking baby-formula manufacturers for pushing powdered milk in parts of the Third World where there's no clean water?"

"That's him. He's a real crusader, apparently."

Toby carried on channel surfing until he found a late-night arts program.

"If this doesn't send me to sleep," he said, "nothing will." He looked at Abby. "Now, come here and let me hold you."

She snuggled into him again. "So, will you try to make sure Guy and the others are polite to Scozza and Lamar?"

"Don't worry," he said. "I'll have a word with them. Promise."

Chapter 7

WHEN THE ALARM WENT off at seven-thirty, Toby rolled over in bed and mumbled something to Abby about an early meeting having been canceled and so he was going to have a sleep-in. "Bugger what anybody at the office thinks."

"Good for you," Abby said, leaning over and planting a kiss on his cheek. "It's about time they realized you are not a machine. You go back to sleep."

"Reset the alarm for ten," Toby instructed her from under the duvet. She did as he asked. Then, so as not to disturb him, she quickly gathered up her clothes for the day and got dressed in the living room.

Abby and Martin were in the shop, enjoying their second cup of coffee, when Toby appeared, wearing his new suit and shirt and carrying his briefcase.

"Right, I'm off," he said to Abby.

"Really?" she said, grinning. "You smell fine from here."

Toby rolled his eyes. "Ha-ha," he said, turning to Martin. "Hi, Scoredaisy."

By now Martin was leaning over the counter, peering at Toby. "And yabba dabba doo to you, too. Wow, fabulous suit. Is that cashmere I see before me?"

"Actually, it is." Toby beamed, clearly relishing that Martin had noticed.

Martin moved in on one of Toby's lapels and pincered it between his thumb and forefinger. "Siberian?"

"Mongolian."

"Damn! I knew it! This is far too soft to be Siberian. I wasn't listening to my inner voice."

"OK, for a hundred bonus points, do you want to have a go at guessing the designer?"

Martin leaned back and began stroking his chin. "Hmm. The classic cut screams Armani. But he doesn't usually go in for covered buttons. Do the trousers have a single or double pleat?"

"Single."

"OK, I'm going out on a limb here. I'm going to guess Valentino."

"Right nationality. Wrong designer. It's Fendi."

"Fendi. Of course. The single pleat. The covered buttons. I'm losing my touch."

Toby opened his jacket to reveal his new Paul Smith shirt. "OK, you can redeem yourself by guessing the thread count."

More pincering.

"Easy. Hundred eighty," Martin declared. "You couldn't create that silky texture with less."

"Spot on," Toby cried.

"Am I a genius or am I a genius?"

Abby watched in amused disbelief as the two men high-fived.

Afterward, Martin took a couple of paces back—all the better to peruse Toby's attire. "You know," he said, hand on hip, "you could carry off a handkerchief in the breast pocket."

"Really? You don't think it's aging?"

"I would say yes if you were over forty. But in your early thirties people can see it's an ironic statement."

"OK, maybe I'll take a trawl round Liberty this weekend. I was planning to go tie shopping anyway."

"Look for the Bo Brummel line. It's totally to die for. Not that I can begin to afford it on what your fiancée pays me."

Abby was smiling and shaking her head in mock despair. "Hey, Frasier and Niles, could you please knock it off? The customers are going to think I attract weirdos."

"On the other hand," Toby said, flicking imaginary lint from his lapel, "they might appreciate a master class in style." He stepped forward to give Abby a quick good-bye peck and headed for the door.

"Think lightly poached salmon," Martin called after Toby. "Fab-ulous with your coloring."

"You think? I'll bear it in mind."

Once Toby had left, Abby turned her attention to the dozen or so bunches of lily of the valley that had been delivered an hour ago and had yet to be put in water. As she began trimming the stems with a florist's knife, she couldn't help but gaze in amazement at the perfection of the tiny, creamy bells. At one point she closed her eyes and breathed in the exquisitely sweet perfume. "Reminds me of the first time I was a bridesmaid," she said to Martin. "There was lily of the valley in my bouquet. I'd never smelled it before, and I thought it was the most glorious scent ever. Every time I get a waft of it, I see myself in this pink taffeta dress and ballet shoes."

"Bet you looked dead cute," Martin said.

He had just filled a green plastic watering can with a long narrow spout and was busy topping up the water levels in the vases of flowers. Just then the shop door burst open—startling them both—and Christian appeared, his face taut with fury.

"Christian," Abby began darkly, aware that he was about to launch into another verbal attack on Martin. "I have warned you. I will not have my shop used as a battleground."

Ignoring Abby, Christian strode over to Martin and positioned himself in front of him, inches from his face. "OK, this ends now," Christian snarled, nostrils practically flaring. "If you continue phoning and texting me like this, I will go to the police and have you charged with harassment. Do I make myself clear?"

"And I will phone the police and have you charged with disorderly conduct," Abby barked. "Do I make *my*self clear?"

Yet again Christian ignored her.

Martin refused to be intimidated. "Who the bloody hell do you think you are, coming in here trying to bully me? I've been phoning and texting because I love Debbie just as much as you do and I want a chance to spend time with her." He ran to the window and peered out. "Is she here?"

"Of course she isn't. You have become obsessed and unhinged and I'm not going to risk you dognapping her. You will have nothing to do with that animal. I will get a court order if I have to."

"Don't threaten me," Martin snarled. By now he had pulled himself up to his full five foot nine and a half and was squaring up to Christian.

"I'll do what the hell I like."

"Oh, yeah?"

"Yeah."

"Says who?"

"Says me, that's who."

"Oh, sod off . . . you . . . superannuated queen."

"Sticks and stones will——"

"Oh, for crying out loud," Abby broke in, "the two of you sound like a couple of camp seven-year-olds. I'm not saying this again. If you want to tear strips of each other, go and do it in the street."

"I've said what I came to say," Christian sneered.

"Excellent," Abby replied. "Let me show you to the door."

"That won't be necessary." Christian turned to go but not before bestowing a withering glance upon a container of irises and declaring loftily that they were well past their best. "Oh, by the way, Abby, regarding the matter of your flower and plant containers taking up too much pavement space: you will be receiving a letter from the council ordering you to remove them. I think it would be to your advantage to comply forthwith."

"I think I will decide what is and isn't to my advantage," Abby retorted. "Good-bye, Christian—and, please, don't call again." Abby was aware that her hands had become fists.

"You may depend upon it." With that he took his imperious leave. She watched him step onto the pavement and immediately collide with an elderly woman, almost knocking the poor soul off balance. Abby couldn't hear what was being said, but she could see that Christian had his arm round the woman's shoulders to steady her. Judging by his body language, the way he was leaning in toward her, his brow furrowed with genuine concern, it was clear that he was taking great pains to check that she was in one piece before letting her continue on her way.

"Sometimes you get tiny glimpses of the real man," Martin said, jerking his head toward the window to indicate that he, too, had witnessed the scene with the old lady.

Abby merely shook her head with bemusement.

"Look," Martin said, "I know I should have walked away, but when Christian starts attacking me, I just lose it. I can't help it."

"It's OK. I understand," Abby soothed. "He's starting to have the same effect on me. When he's not tending to old ladies and dogs, that man is poison. Pure poison."

Abby decided they needed a sugar fix to cheer them up, so she popped to the French patisserie a few doors down and bought two pains au chocolat. When she got back, Martin was just finishing serving a customer. He nodded his head toward the counter and two mugs of freshly made coffee.

As they demolished the pains au chocolat and sipped their coffee, Martin seemed subdued.

"Don't let Christian get to you," she said. "Something will sort out. Listen, I know it may sound a bit drastic, not to mention expensive, but have you thought about seeing a lawyer? After all, Debbie Harry is half yours. Surely Christian has no right to stop you from seeing her."

"I had the same thought," Martin said. "Maybe I should make an appointment at the Citizens Advice Bureau." He fell silent.

Abby was wiping pastry crumbs off her lap. "What's the matter? Is there something else you want to talk about?"

He looked to her as if he was plucking up the courage to say something.

"What?" she said gently.

"No, it's nothing."

"Come on. Out with it. I can tell there's something on your mind."

"There isn't. Honest. Forget it."

"God, I hate it when people start something and then leave you hanging."

"What have I started? I haven't said a word."

"I know, but you're thinking something, and if it concerns me, I'd appreciate you telling me what it is."

"God, Abby, you can be so egocentric sometimes. Why do you assume it concerns you?"

"I don't know. For some reason I just get the feeling it does, that's all."

"Well, it doesn't. Now can we just let it drop?" His tone was less than convincing, and she was suddenly certain that whatever was bothering him did concern her.

"Sure." She gave a nonchalant shrug, which was meant to give the impression that she wasn't really bothered, but of course she was. Still wondering what might be troubling Martin and convinced it had something to do with her, Abby went upstairs to get changed. She needed to look smart for her meeting with Mr. Takahashi later on this afternoon, but before that—in just over an hour, to be precise—she was due at Claridge's. One of her clients, the holiday company specializing in upscale cruises, was organizing a huge corporate bash with a Caribbean theme, and they wanted Abby to take care of the flowers.

She spent an hour with the chairman's PA, who was in charge of organizing the event. She loved Abby's ideas of giant vases spilling over with vibrant tropical flowers like lobster-claw heliconia, scorpion orchids and red-hot cattail.

It was only when Abby was in the taxi on her way back to the shop that she started to wonder if her supplier could get the blooms in the quantities she needed and in time for the party, which was scheduled for the beginning of next month.

She was also wondering if she'd quoted a sufficiently high price. Even though the business was doing well, she was as nervous as ever about losing clients through overcharging. The upshot was she tended to be overoptimistic budgetwise. More than once she'd taken on a particularly ambitious project that depended on rare and exotic flowers and had ended up making hardly any profit.

She was just getting off the phone from her supplier as she walked back into the shop. "Fantastic. Seems I got it just about right."

"What?"

"The estimate for the Claridge's do."

Martin nodded. "Great." She picked up on his flat tone and preoccupied look. "Abby, there's something I need to talk to you about."

"Is this the same thing you wanted to talk to me about this morning but chickened out?"

He nodded.

"OK, shoot."

He leaned over the counter and began fiddling with a stray piece of cut stem.

"Come on, Scozza. Whatever it is, just say it. Please."

"All right. Look, you know how over the past months we've become really close."

She nodded.

"And you know I think of you among my closest friends?"

"Ditto."

"And you know how much I love you and how I'd hate to see you get hurt."

"Ditto again. For heaven's sake, what's all this about?"

He let out a long breath. "Look, I know this is absolutely none of my business, but has it occurred to you that Toby could be gay?"

Her defensiveness surprised her. "You're right, Scozz, this is none of your business, but for the record, I have considered the possibility. You may also be surprised to know that I have raised the issue with Toby. He laughed it off, but he was clearly hurt by the suggestion. Like me, you made the classic, shallow assumption that because Toby's really into clothes, he must be gay."

"I don't think it's shallow. There's more to it than that, and you know it. . . ."

But Abby wasn't listening. "He isn't gay. OK? He told me he isn't. And I believe him. Now let it go. I just wish gay men would get over themselves. You do not have the monopoly on dressing well."

"I agree. That's not the point I'm trying to make."

"Then what is?" Her face tightened. "It may have escaped your notice, but Toby and I are engaged—to be married. I think you'll agree the days are long gone when gay men felt the need to marry in order to conceal their homosexuality."

"I'm not sure that's entirely true. There are still plenty of men who for professional or family reasons can't bear to come out." He paused. "Look, I'm trying to see this whole thing with you and Toby in context."

"What context?"

"The context that the two of you don't have sex."

She felt herself bridle. "My sex life has absolutely nothing to do with you."

"What?" He was wide-eyed with astonishment. "But you've made no secret of the fact that you and Toby hardly ever do it."

"OK," she said, reddening because she felt ambushed by the truth, "but there are times when that's up for discussion and this isn't one of them."

"So, you're allowed to bring up the subject, but nobody else is."

"Yes," she said, aware of how unreasonable that sounded.

"Fair enough, but my gaydar very rarely fails me. I thought Toby was gay the first time I met him. I think you need to be aware that he could be lying to you."

Abby suddenly saw red. "He is not lying," she hissed. "How dare you suggest such a thing. God, the way you lot try to recruit, you're as bad as the Salvation Army."

"That's nonsense. *My lot* aren't interested in 'converts.' People are what they are. All I'm saying is that I've got pretty good instincts about who is or isn't gay."

"Oh, right. That's why you're leaving it to me to see if Mr. Takahashi's personal assistant is gay. 'See if he gives off a vibe,' you said. I think that means you trust my gaydar almost as much as yours. In which case I think I'd know if my own fiancé is gay." She paused. "This subject is closed."

"OK, fine. I'm sorry. I shouldn't have said anything. This really is none of my business."

Just then the door opened and a woman customer came in. "You're right. It isn't any of your business," Abby hissed before turning to the woman and smiling a greeting.

RATHER THAN risk getting stuck in traffic, Abby decided to take the tube to Mr. Takahashi's house in Knightsbridge. As she sat on the train trying to read the *Evening Standard*, she realized she was still furious with Martin. He had absolutely no right to interfere in her relationship with Toby. He'd crossed a boundary in their friendship, and it was going to take her a while to get over it.

Toby wasn't gay. He couldn't have made himself clearer on the matter if he'd tried. He was simply an old-fashioned English dandy. Plenty of straight men were. The Sunday supplement "Style" pages were constantly highlighting the growing number of "straight gays" who spent a fortune on beauty products and expensive clothes. And as for his lack of libido, it could well be due to a testosterone deficiency.

On the other hand, if she truly believed Toby when he said he wasn't gay, why was Scozza's suggestion getting her so wound up? Why had she gotten so cross with him? Was it possible that, despite Toby's strenuous denials, she still had her doubts?

Abby got out at Knightsbridge station and began walking along Brompton Road. She passed Harrods on her left and continued on a couple of blocks. Apparently Mr. Takahashi had a house in a brand-new development, somewhere behind Beauchamp Place. While she was walking, she took out her mobile. She would phone Soph and ask her if she thought Toby was gay. She began dialing Soph's direct line at work and then stopped herself. What was she doing? She didn't need Sophie to reassure her that Toby was straight. Toby had said he was and she had to trust him. If she had any nagging doubts, then she needed to confront Toby again.

She put her mobile back in her bag and gave a firm, resolute tug on the zipper.

She reached the gated development, which contained maybe a dozen grand metal-and-glass houses and two apartment buildings. The uniformed guard phoned Ichiro to confirm that Abby was expected and then opened the gate. "OK, miss, Mr. T's flat is the penthouse. Twenty-third floor." He pointed her in the direction of an immense shard of glass a hundred yards or so down the road.

She was overtaken by a wave of nausea. "I thought Mr. Takahashi lived in a house," Abby said, aware that she was sounding childishly indignant.

"No, miss. Penthouse flat."

"You mean, up there?" she said, sounding feeble as well as indignant.

"Yeah. Top floor." The guard was looking at her as if she were either deaf or stupid.

"I see. Right. OK. No problem."

Had her appointment been last week, she would have gone into the building and immediately sought out the fire-escape stairs. Then she would have trudged up all twenty-three flights, arriving at Mr. Takahashi's apartment slick with sweat and in a state of near collapse. Not today.

Her heart racing, she stared at the building. "I can do this. I can do this. I can do this." Slowly, she began to move forward, unaware that the guard was looking at her as if to say: "Gawd. Got a crazy one here."

Eventually she picked up her pace. Soon she was standing in the marble entrance hall, amid brown leather sofas and giant abstract paintings. In front of her were the doors to three elevators. She swallowed hard. Then she headed toward the middle door and pressed the call button. The door opened instantly. She hesitated, sent up a quick prayer for her safe delivery to the twenty-third floor and stepped inside. She hit the relevant button and waited. The glass elevator began to rise. It wasn't particularly fast. In fact, it was a rather elegant ride clearly designed to give the passenger a chance to admire the view. She decided to concentrate on seeing how many landmarks she could spot. She immediately found Big Ben, the London Eye and Canary Wharf. Soon she was pressed against the glass, squinting, as she tried to locate the new Wembley Stadium. She found it just as the bell pinged to indicate that she had reached her destination. She almost didn't want to leave. She hadn't found Battersea Power Station yet.

As she stepped out, she felt a surge of exhilaration. It wasn't quite as intense as the emotion she had felt on leaving the Covent Garden elevator, but it was pretty close. She realized that her elevator phobia really was fading.

Riding in a traditional, closed-in elevator would no doubt present more of a challenge, but she was reminded that every great journey begins with one small step, and for now she was more than happy with how far she had come.

THE MARBLE-and-glass theme continued inside Mr. Takahashi's vast penthouse. Ichiro welcomed her with a flamboyant double kiss. "Abby! How are yeeeeuuww?" His effusive manner suggested that he had known her for years. The accent was pure O.C. Abby never quite knew how to respond when Americans greeted her with "how are you?" Did they really want to hear about the state of one's sinuses or the progress of one's piles? Still, she supposed it was no more vacuous a greeting than the British "how do you do?" to which the correct response was the laughably nonsensical "how do you do?"

"Fine, thanks." Abby smiled, taking Ichiro's outstretched hand.

Ichiro was twenty-something and slim as a reed. Abby was certain that if he turned sideways he would disappear. He was wearing a long black T-shirt over skintight white drainpipe jeans. A wide belt encrusted with multicolored glass gems rested on what passed for his hips. He had a smooth, gamine face and longish, straight hair that had been dyed rich red setter and cut into a trendy, edgy style with a fringe that formed a severe, asymmetric slant. "I am so excited to meet yeeeeuuww," he continued, leading her down a long wide hallway, its walls covered in vibrant, modern abstracts not dissimilar to the ones in the downstairs lobby—probably by the same artist, Abby thought. "And I just know we are going to be able to work together. I felt this instant connection with yeeeeuuww. I can just tell that we're in the same headspace spiritually. I can feel connections between people. It's a Zen thing. Are you picking up on it?"

Abby replied with another smile and a noncommittal "quite possibly."

She almost gasped as Ichiro led her into the magnificent drawing room. It was vast, with a creamy marble tiled floor and matching walls.

"What a stunning room."

"I guess," he said, "but I sometimes wonder if it isn't . . . you know—just a tad beige-a-vu."

"I like it," Abby replied with a soft laugh. At the same time, she was thinking that Ichiro really was as gay as a daisy in May.

She made a beeline for the window, which was a massive expanse of floor-to-ceiling glass.

The views over the city were beyond glorious—although at the back of her mind she could hear her father's voice: "With all this glass, I wouldn't mind seeing this chap's heating bills for a winter quarter."

"Mr. T sends his apologies for not being here to meet you in person, but as I'm sure you'll appreciate, he's a very busy man. He tends not to involve himself in domestic matters, but Sophie has assured him that we're in safe hands leaving the floral art to you."

Ichiro invited her to sit down on one of the giant chocolate leather sofas and then disappeared to fetch them some tea. He came back carrying a tiny wooden slatted tray covered in a black cloth. On it were two white bone-china mugs of green tea and two miniature blueberry tarts, which had been finished off with slivers of bitter chocolate and a net of spun sugar. Abby remarked that they looked far too good to eat.

"I know. Aren't they just divine? Pablo, our pastry chef, is truly gifted. His creations aren't so much food as fine art. What's more, they're wheat-free, gluten-free and less than forty calories a pop." He invited her to sample Pablo's delights.

Abby bit into the tart. She could have easily fit the entire thing into her mouth, but it seemed rude to demolish it in one go. The pastry literally melted in her mouth. The fruit was sharp without being sour.

By now, Ichiro had moved into the center of the room. "You know what, Abby? I've given great thought to this project, and I'd like to share my vision with you." Abby said all ideas were welcome, but added, "But won't Mrs. Takahashi and her daughter be joining us? Mothers and daughters usually have very specific ideas about what they want."

Ichiro explained that Mr. Takahashi was divorced and that his ex-wife lived in Tokyo. Presently, Mai and her fiancé were visiting her and wouldn't be back until just before the party.

"So, organizing the event has pretty much been left to me. With Mrs. T gone, I've become Mr. T's wife." He paused, clearly thinking about what he'd just said. "Omigahd, eeeuuwww. No, not in that way! I'm purely his domestic slave." Another beat. "Anyway," he continued, clearly anxious to bring the conversation back to his artistic vision, "here's my thinking. For a start, I think that clever use of space is vital, don't you?" He was standing arms outstretched, feet carefully placed in second position.

Abby nodded. "Absolutely."

"I don't think we should be filling every spare inch of the room with flowers. I think you make just as much of a statement with the space you don't use."

Again Abby said she couldn't agree more.

"You see, we do connect. I told you so." Ichiro clapped his hands in glee. "Oh, this is so thrilling for me."

Abby asked him if he'd had any thoughts about a color scheme.

"I'm thinking merlot is very now." His feet moved to third position.

"Umm. Maybe."

"You don't think so?" he said thoughtfully. He pulled a nail file from his pocket and started to smooth a jagged edge on his pinkie.

Abby decided it was her turn to share. She said the room was large enough to take a miniature Japanese garden with a scaled-down water feature and a bridge. "And maybe even one of those gloriously gnarled plum trees and a pagoda. Flowerwise, I'd like to go for traditional cherry blossoms. Also, as it's an engagement party, I think we should have lotus flowers, because they symbolize immortality, and peonies, because they're about prosperity."

Ichiro replaced the nail file and joined his hands together, as if in prayer. "Oh, this I love. It's so original."

It was hardly original, Abby thought, but, hey, if Ichiro thought it was original, who was she to contradict him?

Abby was busy making notes and jotting down rough room dimensions on a legal pad when she heard loud footsteps. Ichiro heard them, too, and looked startled, almost to the point of fear.

"It's Mr. T," he hissed.

A short, square, middle-aged Japanese man with a graying mustache and fierce military demeanor strode into the room, looking as if he were about to inspect a regiment of kamikaze pilots. By now Ichiro had assumed a bent, positively geishalike stance. Ignoring Abby, Mr. Takahashi shot Ichiro a ferocious glare and began bawling him out in Japanese. Ichiro responded with a deep bow and words that Abby assumed were a statement of his most profound apologies for whatever crime he had committed. Throughout Ichiro's prolonged telling off, which caused his master's face to turn positively merlot with rage, Ichiro's gaze remained firmly locked on the floor.

When it was over, Abby wasn't sure if Ichiro was going to fall on his nail file or regain his dignity. Somehow he managed to regain his dignity. He raised his head, found his smile and introduced Abby. In an instant, Mr. Takahashi's face lit up. "Ah, Miss Crompton," he said, his speech clipped and breathy. "Welcome." He stepped forward, hand outstretched to greet Abby.

"Kajitsu," Abby said, taking his hand. Whenever she met foreign clients, she liked to greet them in their own language.

"Kajitsu!" Mr. Takahashi responded in delight. He gave a bow, which she returned.

"Mr. Takahashi doesn't speak very much English," Ichiro interjected, "so I will translate."

Abby suggested that Ichiro explain her ideas for the party. Ichiro began, but immediately Mr. Takahashi became irritable and began waving his hand to indicate that he was an important man who had better things to do with his time than discuss floral arrangements. She got the impression from his hand-waving that he had lost something and was blaming Ichiro. While Ichiro scuttled off to find whatever it was that had gone missing, Mr. Takahashi turned his attention back to Abby.

"You like peenis?" Mr. Takahashi inquired.

"I'm sorry?" Abby said, startled and unsure if she'd heard correctly.

"You like peenis? Japanese like peenis. I want beeg peenis. Very beeg peenis."

"I'm sorry, Mr. Takahashi, but I'm not sure what I can do about the size of your—"

"Peenis very big in Jah-pahn."

"Really? I'm afraid I wouldn't know."

"Yes, they very big. Peenis bring—how you say?—prosperity."

"Oh, you mean peonies! Of course. Yes, we are planning to have lots of peonies."

"Very good. We have much peenis at party. Yes?"

"Oh, yes, Mr. Takahashi, I'll make sure there's much penis—I mean, peonies—at the party."

"And other flowers?"

"Yes. Traditional cherry blossoms and lotus flowers."

"Excellent. Excellent."

Just then Ichiro reappeared, carrying a file bulging with papers. He handed it to Mr. Takahashi with an obsequious bow. Mr. Takahashi snatched it and offered poor Ichiro a few more harsh words. Then he turned to Abby, took her hand in his and kissed it. "Good-bye, Miss Crompton," he said, bowing. "We meet again very soon." With that he bowed again and took his leave.

She turned to Ichiro, who still looked a bit shaky. "You OK?"

"I'm fine. That little outburst was nothing," he said. "You want to see Mr. T in a bad mood."

"I do?"

"He gets into these wild, Hitlerian, carpet-chewing rages. But the good thing is they never last long."

Abby knew it was none of her business, but she found herself asking Ichiro why he worked for Mr. Takahashi if he treated him so badly. Ichiro explained that he had two sets of grandparents living in poor areas of rural Japan.

"They're frail and ill. My parents and I give them money, but we're not a wealthy family and it's not enough to support them. As soon as Mr. T found out about them, he started sending them money every month. Deep down he's a good man. He gives millions to charity. I hate being beholden, but what can I do?"

"I really don't know." Abby put her legal pad back in her bag and zipped it. Still at a loss for anything helpful to say, she looked at her watch. "It's been great meeting you, Ichiro," she said, "but I really must get going." She thanked him for the tea and said that she would e-mail him with her estimate.

WHEN SHE got back to the shop, Abby found herself being no more than civil toward Martin. She was still angry with him, so much so that she wasn't about to share the news that she had managed to take another ride in an elevator. She certainly wasn't going to give him the satisfaction of confirming that Ichiro was gay. For what remained of the day, their conversation was confined to work.

Toby rang just as she was closing the shop. "OK, put on something nice, we're going out for dinner."

"Ooh, we are?"

"Yep. I've booked a table at Zafferano's for eight-thirty."

Zaffarano's was one of the best Italian restaurants in London.

"Are we celebrating?"

"Wait and see."

"I'll take that as a yes," she giggled, assuming he had pulled off some major deal at work.

As soon as she got off the phone, she went into the bathroom and turned on the shower. As she undressed, she found herself thinking how unusual it was to hear Toby so buoyed up.

She spent ages thinking about what to wear. Finally she picked out a clingy floral silk dress in raspberry and pale mint. She teamed it with a raspberry cashmere bolero cardigan that tied at the front, emphasizing her bust.

She arrived at the restaurant dead on time. Toby was already there. The moment he saw her, he got to his feet and held his arms open.

After they had kissed hello, he told her how fabulous she looked. She blushed with pleasure.

"This is such a treat," Abby said as they sat down. "Apart from the other night with your mother, we haven't been out for dinner in ages."

"I know. You've had a rough deal these last few months, and it's just my way of saying sorry and how much I love you."

Toby ordered a bottle of champagne.

"So, what are we celebrating?" she asked.

He grinned. "Two things."

"Actually, it might be three," she said, deciding that today's elevator journey was without doubt a cause for celebration. "But you go first."

"OK. Well, first, my boss called me into his office today and told me that I had been made a partner in the firm."

"You have? Oh, Toby, that is such wonderful news!" She got up, threw her arms round him and kissed him. "Oh, sweetie, I am so proud of you. You've worked so hard for this. If anybody deserves to be made partner, you do."

"Thanks, Abs. And you know what? I'm rather proud of me, too. I think by way of celebration, a Porsche might be in order."

"Wow," she said, sitting down again. "So, what's the other thing we're celebrating?"

Just then the waiter arrived with the champagne. They sat in silence while he filled their glasses. After he'd gone, Toby asked her to close her eyes and hold out her left hand.

Abby started to giggle. She was pretty sure she knew what was coming. A moment later Toby was slipping a ring onto her wedding finger.

She opened her eyes and looked down at her hand. The large, square solitaire diamond danced and twinkled in the candlelight.

It was so utterly and uncompromisingly beautiful that for a moment she was speechless. She could feel her eyes filling up.

"I know I should have done this earlier; after all, it's been over a month since I proposed. But my feet have hardly touched the ground these past weeks. Thanks for being patient."

"It doesn't matter. The important thing is that we love each other and we want to spend the rest of our lives together. Toby, this is stunning. I adore it. As usual it's the most perfect choice." She turned the ring on her finger. "Even the fit is perfect. Oh, I do love you." They leaned into the middle of the table and kissed.

"And I love you." Toby raised his champagne glass and Abby did the same. "To us," he said.

"To us."

She was gazing at the ring again. "This diamond is truly exquisite. It must have cost a fortune."

He shrugged and grinned. "Only a small one," he said.

"But when we were in Paris, you said we were going to buy a ring at some discount place in Hatton Garden."

"I changed my mind," he said. "That didn't seem very romantic, and I wanted you to know how much you mean to me." He took a sip of champagne. "Didn't you mention that there was something else we should be celebrating?"

"Yes. I nearly forgot. You'll never guess what. I took another ride in an elevator today. To the—wait for it—twenty-third floor. What do you think of that?"

"Oh, you clever girl. I am so proud of you." He grabbed her hand and squeezed it. "Well done. That is great. Just great."

AFTER DINNER, they went back to Abby's flat. As soon as they got through the door, she took his hand and began leading him toward the bedroom. "The thing is," he said, pulling away his hand, "I've got a mountain of paperwork to deal with. You go ahead. I'll be an hour or so."

Her heart couldn't have sunk any further. Her disappointment must have shown, because he put his hand to her cheek. "Don't worry. I know we need to set more time aside for making love, and we will. I'm on the case. I've found this specialist in Harley Street who's going to give me the once-over, but he's on holiday right now. Things are going to change."

"But you're always saying that, and they never do. There are times, like now, when I just feel so neglected.... Then I get confused and I just don't know what to think."

"Oh, God, Abby, we're not back to this bloody gay thing, are we?"

"No! No, of course we're not." But the truth was—in her mind, at least—they were back to it. She was aware that her stomach was forming a tight knot.

"Good. Look, things will get better. I guarantee. You have to believe me." He pulled her toward him and kissed her.

She swallowed. "I do believe you." The knot in her stomach grew tighter.

"Love you," he said.

"Love you, too."

Chapter 8

AFTER A NIGHT'S SLEEP, Abby's stomach was still in knots. Her inner voice was telling her one thing; Toby, lying beside her, smiling in his sleep, his arms round her waist, told her something completely different. She gazed at her engagement ring. What kind of gay man a) gets engaged—to a woman—and b) spends a fortune buying her a dazzling engagement ring?

Later on, downstairs in the shop, she greeted Martin with a coy smile and an ostentatious wave of her left hand.

He reached for her hand and let out a soft whistle. "So Toby finally got you a ring. Wow, that has to be worth more than me mam's flat in Liverpool."

Abby grinned. "I think you'll agree it's quite a commitment for a gay man."

"I guess," he said, clearly less than convinced.

"Oh, come on, Scozz...don't be like that. Why can't you be pleased for me?"

"I am pleased for you."

"You don't sound it."

"No, I am. Really. I'm sorry, Abby. I shouldn't have said what I did. Forgive me?"

He was saying the words, but Abby knew he was merely going through the motions in order to keep the peace. But she wasn't about to press the point. She didn't want to cause another scene. More than anything, though, she had no wish to stir up her own doubts about Toby. She wanted an end to the sick feelings and knotted stomachs.

"Of course I forgive you." She gave him a hug. "By the way," she said, "I have even more exciting news."

Martin's eyes widened with anticipation. "What?"

She knew how desperate he was to hear her verdict on Ichiro, but she decided to leave him hanging. "You'll never guess what—I took another ride in an elevator yesterday."

She saw how hard he was trying to remain excited. "Wow, Abby. That's fantastic. You really are beating this thing."

"Oh, and there's something else."

"Yes?"

"Ichiro is definitely gay."

Martin's face lit up. "You sure?"

"Believe me, the man is as camp as a row of pink tents."

"And is he pretty?"

"Put him in white face paint, a wig and a kimono and he could have auditioned for *Memoirs of a Geisha.*"

Martin gave a shiver of ecstasy. "OK, you have to work out a way for us to meet."

Abby said that she was bound to need a second look round Mr. Takahashi's apartment before she made a final decision about what flowers to order and that she would take Martin with her.

"Fantastic, but you have to give me plenty of warning. I'll need time to plan what to wear."

DINNER ON Friday at Feng Wei in Chinatown turned out to be a pretty raucous, drunken affair. It didn't help that Toby "didn't quite get round" to speaking to Guy and the others about being on their best behavior. Not that it would have made any difference, Abby decided. Upper-class oafs like Guy Stradbroke didn't take kindly to being told how to behave.

Toby's male friends were nearly all shallow, boorish lawyers and city types. Like Toby, most of them came from aristocratic or upper-class stock. Like him, they drove flashy, expensive cars and owned flats in posh bits of town, while the parental manse was a crumbling pile in the country.

Their Sloaney girlfriends tended to fall into two camps. They were either scruffy, rather jolly types, similar to Katie the location finder, or they were leggy clothes horses with perfect Fulham highlights and plastic, ski-slope noses that had been perfectly constructed for looking down.

Most weekends, one or another of Toby's gang would host a house party at the family home. Sometimes the parents would be there, but more often than not they obliged by being away.

Because Toby usually ended up working at least half the weekend, he and Abby were forced to turn down most house-party invitations. In all the time they had been going out, they had made it to only one—last fall. It was the first time Abby had met Toby's friends.

Guy, who had been Toby's best friend since boarding school, had invited them to his parents' house in Dorset.

Abby had imagined the weekend would be a pretty relaxed affair, until Soph managed to convince her that it would all be very *Brideshead Revisited.* "Bet you anything the men will go out shooting. Oh, and they're bound to get glammed up for dinner. Take a cocktail dress, and remember: diamonds in town, pearls in the country. I picked that up from an episode of *Upstairs, Downstairs.*"

"What are you talking about? First, that show was set before the First World War, and second, nobody under the age of sixty wears pearls."

"I wouldn't be so sure. You know what the upper classes are like. They're sticklers for tradition. Believe me, nothing will have changed."

Broxbourne Manor was situated on the outskirts of an exquisite Dorset village that looked as if it had been freshly transported from a chocolate box lid. There was a winding main street lined with white- and pink-washed thatched cottages. At the bottom, opposite a village green complete with pond and ducks, was an ancient church and a post office selling moth-eaten bread and dusty tins of processed peas. Next door was an oak-beamed pub, complete with log fires and dozing Labradors.

Abby had gotten herself into such a panic about what clothes to take that weekend that she had packed half the contents of her wardrobe. Anxious to look the part, she had also dashed to Harrods to buy a Barbour and a pair of green wellies.

She could have asked Toby what clothes to take, but she hadn't wanted him to think she was unschooled in the sartorial mores of the country-house weekend.

It was after four by the time they'd reached the village. Being late October, the light had all but faded. Then, as they turned a bend in the private, hedge-lined road that led to the house, the grand Elizabethan manor rose out of the dusk, its windows bathed in soft gold light.

Toby parked his Mercedes sports model on the gravel drive alongside several Porsches and Range Rovers. For a moment or two, Abby didn't move. She was too busy looking at the house and taking in the gnarled black-and-white timbers, the red herringbone brickwork and pretty mullioned windows set in yellow stone.

"Wow, it's gorgeous," Abby said, turning to heave her hefty bag from the back of the car. "You half-expect Anne Boleyn to answer the door."

Toby smiled and nodded in agreement. "By the way, leave the luggage. Somebody will deal with it later."

"Sorry," she heard herself say—embarrassed that she didn't know "the form."

Guy turned out to be a prematurely bloated, thin of hair, oafish type with a fondness for loud, Toad of Toad Hall green check tweeds. He greeted Toby with much backslapping and hail-fellow-well-met cheer. It was a few moments before he acknowledged Abby. When he did, he addressed her as "Toby's little lady," before puckering up and planting a limp, slightly damp kiss on each of her cheeks. Then, as they went inside, he ran his hand over her bottom. Had Guy not been a friend of Toby's, she would have turned on him and told him to keep his hands to himself. Instead, she bit her lip.

Setting aside the shabbiness, the overpowering smell of wet dog, and the ancient electric sockets, which looked to Abby as if they had been installed by the first Lord Stradbroke about six hundred years ago, the interior of Broxbourne Manor was just as glorious as the exterior.

There was a dark, oak-paneled entrance hall with a magnificent sweeping staircase. Each of the downstairs rooms had polished wood floors and magnificent Inglenook fireplaces.

Despite there being fires in every room, the house was freezing.

"Ah, clearly Toby's little lady isn't quite *au fait* with the country-house experience," Guy said, after Abby let out an involuntary shiver. "Always brass monkeys in these places. Would cost an arm and a leg to install central heating."

As a result, the Stradbrokes depended on ancient electric-coil fires and fan heaters. The bedrooms, in particular, were Arctic, but Abby and Toby's carved ebony four-poster—in the east wing—was covered in umpteen blankets and a wonderfully thick eiderdown.

Mrs. B, the cheery but much put-upon housekeeper, had even appeared with two hot-water bottles to put in the bed. "Wind is coming in from St. Alban's Head," she announced, pulling back the eiderdown and blankets. "I'll see if I can find you an 'eater, as well."

They had tea in the library, where—to Abby's relief—there was a log fire and an oil-filled radiator, which took the edge off the cold.

People were welcoming enough, but Toby and his friends went way back and the loud conversation was gossipy and full of in-jokes that Abby didn't understand. Since she wasn't able to contribute much, Abby turned her attention to a ginger cat called Asquith and Mrs. B's homemade scones and raspberry jam.

After an hour or so, the women started making noises about having baths before dinner. Guy said he'd had the immersion heater on since lunchtime, but he didn't guarantee there would be enough hot water for everybody. "Some of you girlies might have to take baths together." Guy grinned. "Maybe I could join you. I'd let you play with my duck."

A reed-thin, haughty woman named Tara who had cheekbones that could have sliced paper drew deeply on her cigarette. "Guy, darling, you really are the most disgusting pervert. You're embarrassing poor Abby."

Abby said she wasn't remotely embarrassed. Deciding that she could do with relaxing in a bath, she tipped Asquith off her lap and got up to follow the other women upstairs.

"Oh, please don't go," Tara said. "You and I haven't had a chance to talk."

Until now, Tara had been huddled in a corner gossiping to an equally haughty girlfriend. The girlfriend was now heading upstairs along with the rest of the women.

Abby sat down again, but Asquith, clearly feeling un-welcome, arched his back and padded off toward the door. Meanwhile, Tara made her way to the sofa. She sank into the feather seat cushion and tucked her endless legs under-neath her.

Tara said that she had seen the newspaper write-up about Fabulous Flowers and positively gushed with admiration and compliments. Abby couldn't put a finger on it, but there was something about Tara's manner that seemed insincere and made her feel that the woman's fulsomeness wasn't genuine.

As they spoke, Abby had the distinct impression that Tara was assessing her. Maybe she was being paranoid, but she was convinced that Tara was desperate to find fault—to discover something about Abby that would prove to the others that she didn't "fit in."

The exchange was rapidly turning into an interrogation. Abby looked to see if she could draw somebody else into the conversation to take the pressure off, but by now everyone, including Toby, was poring over Guy's father's latest acquisition, a sixteenth-century map of Wessex.

Abby felt that Tara was hoping for a "wrong" answer, almost as if she was trying to trip her up. Abby's fears were realized when she let slip that she came from Croydon. Tara's eyes positively bulged with delight.

"Hey, everybody," she cried out, "guess what? Abby comes from Croydon. Isn't that simply a hoot?"

"Never heard of it," Guy declared, causing huge levity.

Abby was struck dumb, not only by Tara's bitchiness but by the way everybody else went along with it. She looked for Toby to say something in her defense, but he had disappeared—presumably to the loo.

In the end, all Abby could manage was a thin smile. "I think I'll go and have that bath now," Abby said to Tara, "and then get changed for dinner."

"Changed?" Tara came back.

"Yes, isn't that what everybody's doing?"

"Er . . . oh, yes. Yes. Absolutely."

Abby went upstairs to the tapestry-walled, mullion-windowed bedroom that she and Toby had been allotted. She half-expected to find him there, but she didn't.

The bathroom was a few yards along the corridor and was, of course, freezing. Not even the bathwater could warm it up, since by now several people had had baths and it was no more than lukewarm.

She got back to the room to find that Mrs. B had kept her promise and brought up a fan heater. It was blasting out hot air but fighting a losing battle against the bone-chilling draft rattling through the windows.

Toby still wasn't there, but she knew he had been to the

room to get changed, because his bag was open and his electric razor was on the dressing table. She assumed he'd gone back downstairs.

Abby took time blow-drying her hair and doing her makeup. She dithered for ages about what to wear but finally decided on a slinky gray-blue silk dress. She covered her shoulders with a matching pashmina and prayed there would be a decent fire in the dining room.

When she got downstairs, the dining room was empty. Then she heard the buzz of conversation coming from the kitchen. She followed the sound. As she walked in, she froze. People were sitting at the long farmhouse table, drinking wine and smoking. More to the point, they were all still wearing jeans and layers of woollies.

Everybody, apart from Toby, burst out laughing when they saw Abby in her dress. "Nobody said that Toby's little lady was leaving us," Guy said, his eyes locked on Abby's cleavage. "A dinner date at La Caprice, I assume?"

Abby felt the blush rise from her chest to her face. "Sorry, I just assumed…" Abby turned to Tara. "I thought you said everybody was getting changed."

"Yes, but only in the sense that they were going to find more layers."

Abby realized she could either burst into floods of tears and go tearing upstairs to her bedroom or stand her ground.

She was still undecided when Toby piped up.

"That wasn't funny, Tara. Why can't you pick on somebody your own size for once?"

"Oh, come on, Abby can take a joke, can't you, Abby?"

Abby managed a weak smile and decided that, revenge-wise, she would bide her time. Meanwhile, Toby took off his sweater and put it round Abby's shoulders.

Over dinner—Mrs. B's glorious beef in ale—the men talked sport, specifically rugby and polo. They also got drunk. The women drank only marginally less but smoked more. As before, their conversation was mainly gossip and concerned women in their circle, whom Abby had never met. "You know she's had over thirty lovers," a blonde party planner named India said at one point, referring to an absent friend.

"That's nothing," Tara snorted. "I must have had at least a hundred."

"Gosh," Abby said sweetly, "if you're lucky, they might name an STD after you."

The whole table, with the exception of Tara, burst out laughing. For all her brazenness, she blushed.

It was a minor victory for Abby. Tara's humiliation hadn't come close to Abby's, but at least Abby had shown this woman—not to mention the rest of the group—that she was capable of giving as good as she got. As the weekend wore on, she felt that Toby's friends were starting to warm to her. The problem was, she loathed them all and couldn't have cared less if they liked her or not.

TO ABBY'S profound relief, Tara couldn't make dinner at Feng Wei. Apparently somebody had given her a *gîte* in the Périgord. When Abby heard this, she laughed and said she hoped it wasn't catching.

No sooner had everybody exchanged greetings and sat down than the men started making bets with one another about who could drink the most champagne and stay upright.

Guy seemed to be winning. He was knocking back

Moët as if it were Coke. As usual, the more he drank, the more obnoxious he became. Abby had lost count of how many times he had clicked his fingers at one of the waiters and cried out: "Oy, Chairman Mao, more bubbly over here."

The waiters didn't seem to mind being insulted like this—presumably because the restaurant was making a huge profit on the champagne—but Abby was mortified. Several times she nudged Toby and whispered, "He's your friend, can't you make him behave?" But on each occasion Toby had hissed at her to shut up and accused her of being over-sensitive.

When Guy put his hand on a waitress's bottom and addressed her as "my little prawn cracker," Abby decided she'd had enough. She turned on him and told him to stop being so damn offensive.

"Abby's right, Guy," Toby agreed. "That's enough."

Guy ignored both of them. "OK," he slurred between glugs of champagne, "what do you call a Chinese woman with a food processor on her head? . . . Brenda!"

Toby rolled his eyes while the rest of the men snorted their approval. Somebody let out a long, loud belch.

"OK, I've got another one. How can you tell if your girlfriend's dead?"

"I don't know," the men cried out as one. "How do you know if your girlfriend's dead?"

"The sex is the same, but the dishes pile up."

More hoots and guffaws. Abby glanced at Toby, who was looking distinctly embarrassed. This time the women smiled and exchanged maternal "what do you do with them?" looks.

"Gahd, Guy. You are such a bloody chauvinist," ventured a blonde, horsey-looking girl named Santa, whom

Guy had apparently picked up at the Met Bar the night before.

"Ooh, a dumb blonde who can use words with more than two syllables," Guy came back. "That makes a change."

"Only I'm not dumb," Santa shot back. Then, pausing for effect, she simpered, "And I'm definitely not blonde."

This was met with drunken *wuurrrgh* noises from the men.

"What do you call a smart blonde?" Guy persisted, snorting with laughter. "A golden retriever."

Toby was always telling Abby that she shouldn't be put off by his friends' brashness—and Guy's in particular. He said it was all a front and that they were great chaps when you got to know them. Abby couldn't see it.

By now the blonde jokes were coming thick and fast. Why do blondes wear ponytails? To hide their air valve. Soon, even the women were laughing, albeit reluctantly. What's the mating call of the blonde? "I'm sooo drunk," the girls chorused, giggling.

Abby wasn't so much offended as bored. She couldn't have been more grateful when she spotted Soph and Martin walk in.

While they were handing in their coats at the coat check, she got up and went over to greet them. She established that Soph, Martin and Lamar had come together in Lamar's car, which he was now trying to park.

A few moments later, the door to the restaurant opened again and in walked a tall, handsome man in jeans, sneakers and a rust-colored cashmere V-neck that looked stunning against his dark skin. Lamar was exactly as Soph had described—drop-dead gorgeous and an apparent amalgam of Wesley Snipes and David Duchovny.

"Hi, Abby," Lamar twinkled, taking Abby's hand. "It's great to meet you at last. Soph's always talking about you. She's just been telling me how you got stuck in the elevator at Covent Garden. Must have been terrifying."

Whoa, charming and sensitive as well as gorgeous. Abby wasn't having any difficulty understanding why Soph had fallen for this man.

"It was, but I think it's really got me over my phobia of elevators. I took another ride in one today and I barely flinched."

Soph overheard this. "You're kidding. That's amazing. Good for you. Come on, let's celebrate with a drink. Knowing Toby's lot, they've probably got a vat of champagne on the go."

"Does Elton John wear a toupee?" Abby smiled.

"Actually," Soph said, "I'm not sure he does anymore. Didn't he have some kind of new high-tech transplant thing?"

As Abby led Soph and the others into the restaurant, she warned them that things were a bit raucous at Toby's table. "You don't say," Soph said. She had been out with Abby and Toby and Toby's friends several times and knew what to expect.

As they walked across to the table, Martin whispered in Abby's ear: "Isn't Lamar to die for? I am sooo jealous. Why do all the beautiful ones have girlfriends?"

Introductions were made, extra chairs supplied and more champagne ordered. Straightaway, Martin got chatting to the Sloaney girlfriends. Abby got the impression that somehow Martin's gaydar had sensed possible hostilities from the drunken male camp and, in order to protect himself, he was seeking refuge among the women.

While Soph studied the menu and tried to convince herself that she was entitled to take the occasional night off from her diet and order a portion of deep-fried chili beef, Abby chatted to Lamar about his research into the dangers of formula feeding. "It's not so much an issue in the West, where people understand that bottles have to be sterilized and the water used to make up the milk must be clean, but in the Third World, babies die every day from drinking contaminated milk."

As well as his research and charity work helping to promote breast-feeding in the Third World, he put in a full week at Great Ormond Street Hospital for Children.

She imagined him on the wards, chatting away to sick, frightened children. She could see him telling daft jokes, making faces, going to endless pains to gain their trust.

As they talked, it emerged that Lamar's childhood had been far from easy. "A lot of Jews didn't want to know me because I was black, and blacks rejected me because I was mixed race. For years I just didn't know who I was or where I belonged."

"God, that must have been awful."

Lamar gave a half laugh. "They say what doesn't kill you makes you stronger, and after that, dealing with the middle-class white medical establishment has been a breeze."

Abby was in no doubt that this thoughtful, mild-mannered man would provide the perfect counterweight to Soph's neuroticism. He would be good for her.

At this point Guy piped up again: "So, what's better, to be gay or to be black?"

Abby felt herself cringe. She and Soph exchanged anxious glances.

"Guy, for Chrissake..." Toby hissed.

"Oh, shuddup, Toby. You're such an old woman." Then: "It's better to be black, because at least then you don't have to tell your parents."

Everybody looked at Martin and Lamar, who, to their credit, both managed to laugh.

"So, Lamar," Guy blustered, "do you believe in an intelligent creator, or are some of us, at least, descended from apes?"

Toby turned on him. "Guy, for fuck's sake. That's enough!"

Guy ignored him and grabbed a passing waitress by the wrist. "Hey, gorgeous, fancy coming back to my place?"

Santa, who was meant to be Guy's date, opened her mouth to protest, but Lamar was in there like lightning. "Are you sure there's room for two people under your rock?" His comment cut through the atmosphere like a machete, reducing the table to an embarrassed silence. Then Soph added her two cents' worth: "Guy, you are an ignorant, drunken lout. May your gonads shrivel and die."

A few people tittered, but Guy merely heaved himself out of his seat and announced he was adjourning to the loo because he fancied he might be about to chuck. They all watched as he staggered off.

"So, who'd like to see my engagement ring?" Abby ventured, anxious to alleviate the awkwardness round the table.

"Wow, Toby finally got round to buying you a ring," Soph cried. "About time. So, c'mon, let's see it."

Abby presented her hand for inspection. All the women leaned in and offered the appropriate oohs and aahs.

The men—instantly bored by talk of engagement rings—went back to their drunken banter. Toby disappeared to the loo, while Martin, apparently sensing that

Lamar was feeling a bit left out, began regaling him on the subject of his occasional bouts of gastric reflux.

"God, that is one helluva of a diamond," Soph said, squinting, clearly looking and failing to find any occlusions. "How many carats is it?"

"I don't know."

"What do you mean, you don't know? You have to know for insurance purposes—not to mention divorce purposes. If the two of you split up, you need to know how much you can get for it."

The other women laughed and chorused their agreement.

"Thanks for that, Soph," Abby came back. "It's always good to know that I have a friend who has faith in my ability to sustain a relationship."

Suddenly Abby was aware of Guy standing behind her, swaying. He put a hand on the table to steady himself. "Yeah." *Belch.* "Don't you dare let my mate Toby down—not after the way that bitch Claudia dumped him."

Toby had always been perfectly up front with Abby about his ex, but he'd always maintained that it was he who had ended the relationship.

"No sooner had he put a rock on her finger," Guy carried on, "than she told him to piss right off. Cow."

Abby's brow furrowed. She and Soph exchanged glances. "Toby was engaged?" Soph mouthed.

"No. Guy's confused." Abby turned back to him. "You're drunk, Guy. Toby and Claudia were never engaged."

"Course they were." *Hiccup.* He raised his voice. "Hey, chaps and chapesses, back me up here. Weren't Toby and Claudia engaged?"

Awkward looks were exchanged. Nobody spoke. Finally

one of the blonde girlfriends piped up. "Yeah, I vaguely remember them being engaged, but only for about five minutes."

Guy went back to his seat and started calling for more spareribs. Abby could feel her cheeks burning with embarrassment.

"Well, that was humiliating," she whispered to Soph. She could feel herself getting angry now. It must have shown, because Soph urged her to calm down.

"I am calm," Abby protested. "I need to talk to Toby, that's all. I mean, why the hell didn't he tell me he'd been engaged? It's not like I would have been particularly bothered. I'd just like to have known, that's all."

Soph patted her friend's hand. "I think the two of you need to talk."

Abby nodded. When Toby returned from the men's room, she suggested that maybe it was time to make a move to leave. It was past eleven by now, and since other people round the table were starting to go, Toby raised no objection. They said their good-byes and walked to Toby's car. She insisted on driving, because Toby had drunk far too much champagne. Once again, he didn't argue.

"So," Abby began as she turned the key in the ignition, "why didn't you tell me you and Claudia were engaged?"

He seemed taken aback. "Who told you that?"

"Guy. While you were in the loo he came over and warned me—decent, loyal chap that he is—not to dump you the way Claudia did."

"Look, we were engaged for less than two weeks. And then she broke it off. I didn't tell you because it never seemed important."

"It doesn't matter how long you were engaged. The fact

is, you were engaged. And why didn't you tell me that it was Claudia who ended it?"

"Dunno. Male pride, I guess. Nobody wants to admit they were dumped."

"Not even to me? You know that I would never have judged you or thought less of you." A beat. "And how do you think I felt in the restaurant with all your friends knowing about the engagement and me having no idea?"

"I'm sorry. It must have been awkward."

"Awkward? It was more than awkward. It was humiliating having Guy and the others knowing something so intimate about you that I didn't know."

"Abby, I've said I'm sorry and I really am. It was thoughtless of me not to tell you, and I hate it that Guy embarrassed you the way he did, but can we just forget about it now? Claudia and I are in the past. Meanwhile, we've got our entire future to look forward to. Let's just concentrate on that." He placed a hand on her thigh. "Please."

"All right," she said grudgingly, "but I'm still pissed off. It's not just the Claudia thing . . . Toby, why do you have anything to do with Guy, or the rest of that disgusting rabble, come to that? Their behavior tonight was unforgivable."

"I admit it was pretty bad, and I did my best to get Guy to shut up—"

"Yes, and he called you an old woman."

"How can you take that seriously? He'd had way too much to drink. They all did. None of them knew what they were saying. I know you don't see it, but they're really great chaps underneath. Guy is a very loyal friend, you know. I remember once when we were at school playing rugby and this kid fouled me and almost broke my leg. That night in the dorm, Guy beat him to a pulp."

"Why am I not surprised? Look, pissed or sober, Guy is a racist, sexist bully. I'd really rather have nothing more to do with him or any of them."

"Ooh, hark at you on your high horse."

"If I sound like an ass, I'm sorry," Abby came back. "But it's how I feel."

"Look, if you don't want to see them again, all well and good, but they're my friends. I admit they go over the top, but like I said, deep down they are good-hearted blokes and I have no intention of severing relations."

"Fine." She shrugged.

Neither of them spoke for a minute or two. A strange, unfamiliar sensation was overtaking Abby. She felt a distance between her and Toby that she had never felt before, and it frightened her.

"Oh, by the way," Toby said eventually, "when I gave you the engagement ring the other night, I forgot to give you the box it came in. I don't know if you want it. But it's rather beautiful. The kind of thing that will become a collectors' item one day. I put it in the glove compartment." He leaned forward and pulled on the walnut-veneer panel.

"Ooh, let me see," she said, coming to a stop at a red light.

He opened a velvet drawstring pouch and produced the ring box. It was encrusted with tiny, brightly colored semiprecious stones. "Oh, Toby, this is utterly exquisite," she drooled, taking it from him. "Of course I'd like it. When we were in the restaurant the other night, why on earth didn't you give me the ring in the box?"

He said he'd thought about it, but eventually he had decided it was far more dramatic to produce the ring on its own and slip it on her finger.

Abby opened the lid and ran her index finger over the ruched-satin interior. The lid was also lined with satin. Since they were in a built-up area, the road was brightly lit, which meant Abby could read the name *Moyse Coote.* This was the posh Knightsbridge jeweler that had supplied the ring. Below the name and logo was a gold-embossed heart. Inside this there were two initials. These were quite tiny, and she found herself squinting. Suddenly Abby felt her stomach turn over. "Toby, could you put the interior light on? I want to get a closer look at this."

"Abby, what on earth are you doing? The traffic lights are going to change any second."

"Please, just do it," she said.

He flicked the switch.

A few moments later, the traffic lights changed to green. She handed the ring box back to Toby and pulled away.

"Those aren't our initials," she said.

"What do you mean? I don't know anything about any initials."

"On the inside of the lid—there's a heart and some initials. They aren't ours."

He opened the box. "I don't think I ever looked properly inside."

"Well, maybe you should. Our initials are *A* and *T.* These are *T* and *C.*"

He shrugged. "So, the jeweler gave me the wrong box."

"Oh, for Chrissake, Toby! What do you take me for? I'm not a fool." She took her eyes off the road for a second and turned to look at him. His face was suddenly etched in panic.

Abby felt her fingers tighten around the wheel. "Correct me if I'm wrong, but I'm guessing that when you finished with Claudia, she gave you back your ring. And you kept it, didn't you?"

He didn't reply.

"Didn't you?" She raised her voice.

"So what if I did?"

"And the other night you gave it to me."

"Look, you don't understand," he protested. "If I'd sold it, I'd have gotten only a fraction of what it was worth. Plus, it's a staggeringly beautiful ring."

By now tears were trailing down Abby's face. "Toby, you gave me your ex-fiancée's engagement ring. How could you?"

She pulled into an empty bus stop and jerked on the hand brake. Then she ripped the ring from her finger.

"I don't want it," she said, thrusting it at him.

"But Claudia hardly wore it. We were engaged for twelve bloody days, for Chrissake. Please take it back."

"No! I don't want it."

He shrugged and slipped the ring into his pocket.

"We're engaged," Abby said in little more than a whisper. "For your information, that means you're supposed to love me."

"I do love you."

"Not enough to give me my own ring instead of some other woman's castoff?"

"It's a fifteen-thousand-pound ring," he protested. "It's not a bloody castoff."

"Toby, you're missing the point. This isn't about money.

I'd have been happy with a cheap ring, so long as I knew that it had been chosen by you with love and that it was meant for me and me alone."

They sat in silence. It was Abby who finally broke it. "Why did you and Claudia break up?"

"What's that got to do with anything?"

"I'd like to know. All you've ever said is that it didn't work out."

He shrugged. "It didn't."

"What didn't?"

"I dunno. Stuff."

"Sex?"

"That is none of your damn business," he spat.

He was right, it was none of her business, but she'd come this far, and she couldn't stop now. She felt compelled to press the point. "Did you reject her like you reject me?"

She looked at his face. It was taut, full of silent rage. "OK, this conversation is over."

She opened her mouth to challenge him, but he got in first. "Didn't you hear what I said?"

"Yes, I heard you." He was so angry that she knew it was time to let the subject drop.

A few moments passed before he spoke. "You know what I think?"

"What?"

"I think you're lying about not wanting an expensive ring. You are selfish and spoiled. You know I've got money and you just wanted your own fifteen-thousand-pound rock."

"In which case," she said quietly, "you don't know me. You don't know me at all."

The next thing Abby knew, she was standing on the pavement, tears streaming down her face. She flagged down a black cab. It was only as it slowed beside her that she remembered how much Toby had drunk and that he shouldn't be driving. She began running back to the car, but it was too late. The Mercedes was pulling away with a loud screech of tires.

She felt guilty about letting him drive, but not that guilty. She was too upset. As soon as she got home, she took off her coat and went into the kitchen to pour herself a glass of wine. She'd stuck to Diet Coke all evening—knowing she would probably need to drive Toby home. Now she needed something stronger.

Forgetting that it was well after midnight, she picked up the phone and dialed Soph's number. As the phone rang, it occurred to her she might not be home yet, but finally Soph picked up. For a few seconds all Abby could hear were muffled giggles in the background.

"Hi, it's me," Abby said, feeling embarrassed. "Oh, God, were you and Lamar in the middle of something?"

"Yes, but we hadn't quite reached the point of no return. Whassup? Look, if you've phoned to apologize for Guy's behavior, I'm not listening. It had absolutely nothing to do with you."

"No, it wasn't that. Although I told Toby I think Guy's a total creep and I never want to see him again."

"Good for you. So what's going on? You all right?"

"Not really." She knocked back a mouthful of wine. "Tell me honestly. Do you think I'm selfish and spoiled?"

"Of course I don't think you're selfish and spoiled. Of all the people I know, you are probably the least selfish and spoiled. . . . Abs, please tell me what's going on."

Abby explained.

"Toby gave you this Claudia's ring? No. I don't believe it. Who'd do a thing like that? You have to be kidding."

"Nope. Then he accused me of being spoiled because I said I would have liked a ring of my own."

"What?" Soph was clearly furious. "That is so bloody cruel. What are you going to do?"

"Well, at the moment I feel like ending it."

"I'm not surprised.... Do you want me to come over? We could watch a DVD. It might calm you down."

"No, you've got Lamar there. I'll be fine."

"You sure?"

"I'm sure." Abby flicked some bread crumbs off the kitchen table. "Soph, do you think Toby could be gay?"

Soph's silence said it all.

"The subject's come up more than once, and he always denies it. But I'm getting more and more confused. I just don't know what to believe. From what I can work out, Claudia broke off their engagement because they weren't having sex."

"Oh, God, Abby . . . what can I say?"

"So, you do."

"Do what?"

"Think Toby's gay."

A beat. Then: "Scozz and I have discussed the possibility, yes."

"What?" Abby cried. "The two of you have gossiped about this behind my back?"

"We never *gossiped*. It wasn't like that. We care about you and don't want to see you get hurt."

"But you're my oldest and closest friend. We don't have secrets. You could have said something."

"You're right. I could have. And maybe I wimped out

because I didn't want to upset you and put our friendship at
risk. But I also like to think that I didn't interfere because
neither Toby's sexuality nor your relationship with him is
any of my damn business."

"Scozz doesn't see it that way."

"I know, and that's where he and I differ. He phoned
me to tell me the two of you had a conversation and that it
didn't go very well."

"No, it didn't."

Abby heard her friend draw a deep breath. "Look,"
Soph began, her tone more gentle now, "it doesn't matter
what I think. It doesn't matter what anybody thinks. Your
relationship with Toby is something you have to sort out
for yourself. Whatever you decide, I will always be there to
love and support you."

"Thanks. That means a lot to me. And thanks for listening. Oh, and apologize to Lamar for me. I didn't mean to
spoil your fun."

As Abby put the phone down, she noticed the vase of
white tulips on the kitchen table. The stems had drooped
and the heads were wide open, their petals shiny and
translucent. Two of them had fallen onto the table. Any
other time she wouldn't have hesitated to throw the flowers
in the bin, but tonight she was happy to gaze at the dying
blooms and let them add to her melancholy.

She was still staring at them, tears trailing down her
cheeks, when the phone rang. She looked at the kitchen
clock. It was almost one. The phone ringing after eleven always frightened her. She tended to fear the worst—that
somebody was ill or had had an accident. She felt herself
starting to shake. Oh, God. No. Toby had crashed the car
and this was the hospital phoning to say he was in intensive

care, barely clinging to life. Or worse. Eventually she picked up the receiver.

"Hello, Abby, is that you?" Jean's voice singsonged. "Mum here."

Abby had never felt so relieved to hear the familiar voice.

"Mum! . . . It's you. Oh, thank God. The phone ringing so late scared the life out of me." She paused. Her relief that nothing had happened to Toby turned to fear that her parents had finally succumbed to typhoid or something similar. She felt herself turn cold. "Mum, is everything all right? Is Dad OK?"

"Yes, yes, we're both fine. Sorry to call at this hour, but there's been a problem with the satellite phone. . . . Just to say, there have been some new developments this end, and I thought you should know what's going on before you read about it in the newspapers."

"Read about what in the newspapers?"

"Well, you see, the thing is, the sewage thing is still pretty bad. In fact, it's getting worse. The lower decks are awash with mess and dirty shower water. We're getting no help from the captain. He simply refuses to do anything. We've contacted the cruise line and asked for our money back and for compensation on top. They've agreed to the refund and to bring us home straightaway, but they're refusing to compensate us."

"But that's a complete no-brainer," Abby said. "They'll never get away with that."

"I know, but suing could take years. Anyway, I had this brilliant idea—I've persuaded all the passengers to stage a sit-in."

"A what?"

"A sit-in. You know, like students used to do in the sixties and seventies."

"Sorry, I'm still not with you."

"OK—the ship is on its way back to Argentina. When it reaches Buenos Aires, we will refuse to disembark until a compensation settlement has been agreed upon."

"Oh, brilliant. You're telling me that the lot of you are going to sit in all that filth and put your health at even more risk—all for the sake of a few quid."

"It isn't just a few quid. It could be several thousand quid. And it's the principle. These people took our money without checking that the ship was in an adequate state of repair, and now they're shirking their financial obligation to their customers. They simply cannot be allowed to get away with it."

Abby was shaking her head in disbelief. "And this protest thing is entirely your idea?"

"Yes. I don't know where it came from. All I know is that I've never felt this angry in my life. I could feel this seething...this red-hot rage taking hold of me, and I simply couldn't hold it in. For the first time in my life I knew I couldn't run away. I had to stand up and fight."

Abby couldn't believe what she was hearing. Jean hardly ever got angry. She certainly never seethed. And as for "red-hot rage" motivating her to take up a cause, it was unheard of. Abby simply couldn't get over how fired up her mother seemed. Jean the meek and mild had turned into Jean the revolutionary firebrand.

"We're all busy making banners out of sheets for when the TV cameras arrive."

"TV cameras?"

"You bet. I phoned all the newspapers and the BBC. I think this could be a huge story. We dock in Buenos Aires in a few days, so look out for me. I'll be the one leading everybody in 'We Will Overcome.'"

Just then Hugh came on the phone.

"Hello, poppet—everything all right your end?"

Abby assured him all was well her end.

"Just to say, your mum and I are OK and not to worry. I simply can't believe your mother. I never knew she had such a fighting spirit. You should hear how she's been rallying the troops. I think maybe we've underestimated her and there's more of Grandpa Enoch's zeal in her than anybody imagined."

"Could be," Abby said, preferring to believe that her mother's newfound passion had less to do with Enoch's genes and more to do with finally releasing the long-suppressed anger she felt toward the old bugger.

By now Jean was back on the line.

"Some of the passengers already have the runs, but they're not giving in. We refuse to let these people treat us like this. It's time for ordinary people to rise up, seize the day and let these corporate giants know that the little man cannot be bullied. Power to the people! That's what I say. Things have got to change. You know what, Abby—I have a dream..."

It was all Abby could do not to burst out laughing. "OK, Mum, you and Dad knock 'em dead, but promise me you'll take care of yourselves and of each other and that if you get ill you'll leave the ship."

Silence.

"Mum, speak to me." But the line was dead.

———

THE MOMENT Abby woke up, everything that had happened last night came flooding back. To help her fight back fresh tears, she turned on the radio. It occurred to her that the *Bantry* story might have made the news. She managed to catch the headlines at the beginning of the eight o'clock bulletin, but there was no mention of it. Clearly the media were waiting until the ship docked and the protest got under way.

She went to take a shower. Afterward, while she was getting dressed, the phone rang. It was Toby. He sounded anxious and quite desperate. "Abby, we really need to talk. I made a terrible mistake over the ring, and I want you to know that I'm sorry. What I did was unkind and unthinking."

"I'd agree with that," she said.

"I really think we need to talk," he went on.

She took a few moments to consider this. "OK, you're probably right. We do need to talk."

"Great. The problem is that I have to go to New York this afternoon. Some massive emergency has cropped up, but all being well, I'll be back on Friday. We'll talk then, OK?"

"OK."

"I love you."

She didn't say anything.

"Abby, please say that you love me. I don't want to go away and leave things like this."

Her mouth tried to form the words, but they wouldn't come. Then she found herself thinking about his plane crashing and how she would feel if he died thinking she didn't love him.

"Love you," she heard herself say, but there was no feel-ing behind the words. She felt numb and empty.

AT ABOUT half past nine, Soph popped in on her way to the hairdresser. One Saturday a month she had a cut and blow-dry at TONI&GUY down the road. She arrived a couple of minutes after Martin.

"I just can't get over what Toby did," Soph said, giving her friend a hug. "What was he thinking?"

Martin looked blank, so Soph brought him up to speed.

"Hang on," Martin said to Abby. "You're telling me he gave you the same ring he gave to his ex-fiancée? Geddout..."

Abby shrugged. "It's true. But what you don't know is that this Claudia dumped him because they weren't having sex."

Martin and Soph exchanged knowing glances.

"All in all, Toby and I have some pretty serious talking to do, wouldn't you say?"

Soph squeezed Abby's hand.

"I always liked Toby," Martin said, "but right now I'd like to throttle him with one of his Versace ties."

Abby managed a smile. "That's very sweet of you, Scozza. I appreciate the thought."

"Ooh, it would be my pleasure."

Abby asked if they could change the subject. "I don't want to talk about the Toby situation anymore. It's just too upsetting and I'll only start blubbing." For a few moments nobody could think of anything to say. It was Soph who broke the silence and asked about Jean and Hugh.

"Omigod," Abby said, "you won't believe what's hap-pened."

She told them about the proposed sit-in. Soph, who had known Jean and Hugh since she was a child, couldn't get over it.

"Your parents? Mr. and Mrs. Model Citizen? Well, good for them. It's about time ordinary people stood up for themselves and refused to be bullied by these hoodlums."

"I just hope they don't get ill in the process," Abby said.

Clearly not thinking, Martin said he had watched a TV documentary last week on the ease with which typhoid and cholera bacteria spread.

"Thanks for sharing that," Abby said, and they all sat in glum silence again.

"OK, since we're feeling down," Soph said, "why don't we go the whole hog and talk about my love life?"

Abby frowned. "Oh, God, don't tell me something has happened between you and Lamar—who is a great guy, by the way. I really took to him."

The comment caused Soph to beam with pleasure. "I'm glad. No, nothing has happened between us. It's my parents. My mum phoned yesterday. She's come to the conclusion that since I seem so happy these days, I must be seeing somebody. I made the mistake of confessing that I was indeed seeing somebody, and now she and Dad are insisting that I bring Lamar home for dinner, and I don't know what to do."

Body image and sartorial matters aside, it was almost unheard of for Soph to let her vulnerable side show. Abby could count on the fingers of one hand the number of times her friend had ended a sentence with "and I don't know what to do."

"So, take him home," Martin said. "You're seeing a gorgeous Jewish doctor. Talk about fulfilling every Jewish parent's dream. What's your problem?"

"You know what the problem is."

"That he's black?" Martin said. "But they must know he's black. How many white men are called Lamar?"

"I convinced them it was Hebrew. I said it meant apothecary."

Abby and Martin burst out laughing.

"Well, I'd like to see the two of you come up with something better," Soph said, making a hurt face and folding her arms like a defiant eight-year-old.

"I can't believe they bought it," Abby said, still laughing.

"It was easy. They know hardly any Hebrew, and I pointed out that Lamar sort of rhymes with *Shema,* the Jewish daily prayer."

"But I don't know why you didn't tell them Lamar is black," Abby said. "I've said it before and I'll say it again. Your dad is always going on about how he despises all forms of racism. He told me that, before the war, his father fought the Blackshirts in the East End. On top of that, your parents lost family in the Holocaust. How could they possibly be racist?"

Soph shrugged. "They're not. On the surface, at least. If one of my friends was seeing somebody who was black, they wouldn't have the remotest problem with it. I'm just not sure they are going to feel the same way about me bringing a black guy home."

Martin was leaning against the counter, thinking. "OK, maybe I'm overanalyzing this, but I can't help wondering if you're actually voicing your own doubts and anxieties about having a black boyfriend slash husband and transferring them onto your mum and dad."

Soph bridled visibly. "Are you accusing me of being

racist? How can you say that? If I were, I would never have started going out with Lamar."

"I'm not accusing you of anything," Martin said, straightening. "All I'm saying is that, even as a nonracist, you're bound to be aware of the prejudice that white people with black partners come up against. I'm gay. I know a bit about prejudice. I know how it feels to walk down the street holding a man's hand and see people pointing and sniggering. It's not easy."

Soph became thoughtful. "OK, maybe you're right. If I'm honest, I have been thinking about how I'd feel if we got married and had children and they came up against racial abuse. I don't think I could bear it. It would break my heart." She turned to Abby. "You know me, I'm totally fearless about most things, and now suddenly I'm really scared. And there's something else that frightens me, too. If my parents can't accept Lamar, I would have to choose between them and him, and I know I would choose him."

"Hey, it won't come to that," Abby said. "You're getting this thing totally out of proportion. But you have to tell them—partly for Lamar's sake. It can't be easy knowing that the woman he loves is struggling to tell her parents that he's black."

"You're right," Soph said to Abby. "I'll do it."

"When?" Abby said.

"Soon, I promise."

ABBY SPENT the rest of the morning taking phone orders or serving customers. She was functioning pretty much on automatic pilot. Her thoughts weren't really on work. They were taken up with Toby. About midday, just as she was putting the finishing touches to a spring-flower centerpiece, she heard a familiar voice. "So, how do you fancy going out for lunch to celebrate?"

She looked up. The second she saw Dan's face, her spirits lifted and her face broke into a broad smile. "Hi, this is a nice surprise," she said. "What are we celebrating?"

"I've had the contract drawn up," he said, waving an envelope in the air. "I thought you could sign it and then I'd buy you lunch to seal the deal. And if it's OK with you, we'd like to start filming next week."

"That soon," she said, taking the envelope from him.

He tilted his head to one side. "You seem a bit down," he said. "You OK?"

She made an excuse about orders piling up and not sleeping very well.

"In that case, a good meal is precisely what you need. It'll give you some energy."

"I know, but I'm not sure I'd be very good company today. Also, I'll need to look the contract over before I sign it. So could we take a rain check?"

"Sure. No problem." He paused. "If it would take off some of the pressure, we could delay the filming a week or so..."

"No. Honestly—next week will be fine. I'm just having a rough day, that's all." Suddenly she remembered the *It's a Wonderful Life* DVD. She'd been keeping it under the counter to give him. She reached down.

"For you," she said.

"Oh, wow. That's great. Thanks. I'll enjoy watching it." He slipped the DVD into his jacket pocket.

"I'll sign the contract and put it in the post," she said.

"That'd be great." He was looking awkward, as if he felt he had overstayed his welcome. "Well, I guess I ought to get going."

"Sorry about lunch," she said.

"No problem. Maybe another time."

"Absolutely."

OVER THE next couple of days, she was aware that she wasn't exactly fun to be around. She did nothing but obsess about what was going on between her and Toby. Hurt as she was at having been given a secondhand engagement ring, the issue paled alongside her ongoing doubts—which were rapidly becoming certainties—about Toby's sexuality.

It was the knowing and at the same time not knowing that was causing her such torment. Until she knew for absolute certain whether or not Toby was gay, her future was on hold.

This was one conversation she couldn't wait to be over with. There were times, particularly when the shop was quiet, when the waiting seemed endless and it felt like Friday would never come.

On Thursday night, Abby and Soph were due to have dinner at The Cricketers, a pub in Hampstead where Abby and Toby often ate. It had been ages since the two women had met up for a quiet girly dinner, and Abby was looking forward to it. An evening with Soph would be a break from her constant rumination and introspection.

They had planned to share a taxi to the pub, but in the end Soph called to say that she was caught up in a meeting at work. She promised she would try to get away as soon as possible. Meanwhile, she suggested that Abby go on ahead and wait for her in the bar.

The pub section of The Cricketers was buzzing with thickets of young professionals winding down at the end of the day. She had to fight her way to the bar. Then she waited ages to get served. She ordered a glass of the house red and looked around for a table. Some hopes. In the end she stood at the bar, sipping her wine and people-watching.

When she first noticed Toby, it didn't register that it was actually him. This was Thursday and he wasn't due back until the following day. It had to be his double.

After a couple of seconds, she realized that the man with a male companion sitting at a table in a secluded alcove really was Toby. She was taken aback, but more than that, she was puzzled. Toby had been so anxious to speak to her the moment he got back from New York. Why hadn't he called to say he was home?

Part of her wanted to go over to him and find out what was going on. Instead, the now-familiar gut feeling kept her rooted to the spot. She carried on watching the two men.

Toby was sitting opposite his companion. She couldn't see the other man's face, because he had his back to her. But even from behind, she knew who it was. There was no mistaking the closely cropped hair and mustard-colored turtleneck. It was that vile creep Christian.

Toby appeared to be drinking Campari. She couldn't see Christian's glass. She watched Toby lean in toward him. There seemed to be a great deal of prolonged eye contact— at least on Toby's part. Abby felt her pulse quicken. Then Christian reached out and took Toby's hand and kissed it not once but twice.

There was no gasp from her, no "omigod!" She didn't start to shake or weep. Of course she was shocked—her racing pulse was testament to that—but this came not from the confirmation that Toby was gay but from seeing it with her own eyes. If she'd had to describe her most powerful emotion at that moment, she would have said it was relief.

It was a while before the anger began to rear up inside her. How could Toby have continued to lie to her the way he did? She could hear him now: "I, Toby Kenwood, am not, never have been and never will be gay." The memory of those words made her feel sick. How could he have been so unspeakably cruel, so callous? And on top of the lies, he was cheating on her with Christian. Toby knew how much she loathed him. Suddenly she felt doubly betrayed.

Christian was getting up to leave. Abby looked on as he took his green quilted jacket off the old-fashioned coat stand—which stood to one side of the table—and slipped it over the mustard sweater. Then he pulled Toby toward him and kissed him. On the lips.

She pushed her way through the crowd and headed for Toby's table.

"Toby. Christian." She nodded with faux cheer.

Toby leaped up as if he'd been bitten. Abby could see the color draining from his face. "Abby," he said. "What are you doing here?"

"Waiting for Soph. We're meant to be having dinner here. I won't ask what you've been doing here, because I've had a pretty good view. . . . I take it your meeting in New York finished early."

Toby gave a shamefaced nod. "I'm sorry . . . I should have let you know."

An unmistakable expression of valedictory pleasure

passed over Christian's face, but, to his credit, he said he had another appointment to get to.

Beyond a brief, petrified glance in his direction, Toby barely acknowledged Christian's departure. "Abby, you've got this all wrong."

"Er, I don't think so," Abby shot back. "So, maybe you'd like to explain why we are engaged to be married and at the same time you are having an affair with a man. And with Christian, of all people."

Toby sat down and stared at his drink. When he looked up again, she could see that his eyes were full of remorse. "I'm sorry I lied."

"That's it? 'I'm sorry I lied'? When I confronted you about being gay, you accused me of having—let me get this straight—a narrow-minded, knee-jerk reaction. Have I got that right? Bloody hell, Toby, you made me feel like I was the guilty party. And then I got really confused because I'd stopped trusting what my brain was telling me."

"I know. It was wrong of me. I should have been honest with you."

She burst out laughing at his understatement. "You think? Why, Toby? Why didn't you have the guts to tell me? I cannot believe you were actually planning to marry me. Have you even the remotest idea of how cruel you were being?"

"I was confused."

"Oh, well, that's all right, then. The poor boy was confused. Ah. Did you think we would get married and that I would never find out you were gay? Did it not occur to you that your constant rejection would have become unbearable and that finally the shit would hit the fan?"

"Abby, please sit down. You're shouting and people are looking at us."

"I don't give a damn who's looking. Let them bloody look."

"Come on, let me get you a drink."

"I don't want a drink. I'm too angry to drink."

Finally he persuaded her to sit down.

"You are pathetic," she hissed. "Do you know that? Totally bloody pathetic. Not because you're gay, but because you didn't have the balls to tell me." She was staring at him, her eyes on fire, but he couldn't look at her.

"I know," he said. His voice was barely more than a whisper.

"Presumably you thought that by marrying me you'd convince your mother, your law firm and that racist, homophobic rabble you call friends that you were as straight as a ruler? Meanwhile you could carry on having affairs with men."

"It wasn't that callous. I was in denial. I thought that when we had children, the gay thing would somehow burn itself out. That was stupid and I'm sorry."

She was shaking with fury. "Toby! It may have escaped you, but people need to have sex to make children. What's more, I cannot believe you would have had children purely in order to pander to some absurd fantasy that they might make you straight. Have you any idea how wicked that is?"

"I love you, Abby," was all he said. There appeared to be genuine sorrow in his voice. "I always have. Just not in the way that you want me to love you. Nevertheless, I thought we could muddle through somehow."

"No, Toby. You thought *you* could muddle through. You didn't give a second thought to me or how you were hurting me and any children we might have." She paused. "So how long has this been going on?"

"It started after the retailers' association dinner."

"Well, at least there's one chink of light in all this," she said. "You and I haven't slept together since then, so I can't have caught anything. . . . Christ, Toby, if you had to cheat on me with a man, why did it have to be with Christian of all people? You know that the man has spent years terrorizing and bullying me. He refuses to let Scozza even see Debbie Harry. How could you, Toby? How could you?"

"I couldn't help it. I know he's not conventionally good-looking, but the attraction was instantaneous. It was pretty much love at first sight."

"But you were always working. Even late at night, you never failed to pick up when I phoned the office. When did you find the time to have an affair?"

He looked at her, shamefaced. Clearly he had made time.

"I just don't get what you see in him," Abby went on. "The man is a first-class creep."

Toby was having none of this. "OK, let's get one thing straight. I may have done a terrible thing to you, but I won't have you talking like that about Christian. With me he is kind and affectionate. I admit he has a few anger issues brought about by a miserable childhood, but I'm really helping him work on them."

"Well, bully for you!"

She found herself reaching for Toby's glass and taking a slug of his Campari. "I suppose you could have gotten away with it if I'd been some posh aristocratic girl. That's the way they live, isn't it? They devote themselves to horses and good works and accept that their husbands' infidelities— straight or gay—are par for the course."

He shrugged. "Maybe."

"Deep down—your sexuality aside—class was always an issue with us, wasn't it? Even if you'd been straight, I would never have been good enough, would I? I would always have been the girl from Croydon who never quite fit in with your posh friends. At least Christian has the right pedigree." A beat. "Toby, I need to know—was Christian the only one?"

"Absolutely. All my life I've had only three gay lovers, and the other two were ages before I met you. Abby, please don't hate me."

She pretended to think. "Let's get this straight. You wanted to trap me in a marriage of convenience, but now that I've found out, I shouldn't hate you. Seems reasonable."

"I do love you," he said again.

"Oh, spare me the bleeding heart."

By now there were tears in his eyes. "Abby, I don't want it to end like this. I can't bear the thought of you hating me."

She let out a sigh. Despite herself, she was starting to feel sorry for him. "I don't hate you, Toby," she said, injecting some kindness into her voice. "I'm wounded and outraged by your behavior, but I don't hate you. I understand that you've been struggling with coming out, but by trying to protect yourself you hurt me. At work you're this tough hotshot lawyer, but at the same time you're scared of being judged. You're scared of your colleagues, your friends. You're even scared of your own mother. It's time to grow up, Toby, and find some backbone. Of course people will judge you. Ask Scozza. Speak to anyone who's gay. People find the strength to stand up and be counted. Now you have to do the same."

"I know."

She got up from her chair. "Good-bye, Toby."

Just before she turned away, he managed a forlorn smile.

As she reached the door, she almost collided with Soph, who was coming in.

"What's going on?" Soph said. "Why are you leaving? Hang on, are you crying?"

"Can we talk outside?"

"Sure."

They stepped into the street.

"Abby, speak to me. What on earth has happened?"

"Oh, I just caught Toby snogging a man, that's all."

"What? You're kidding."

"Oh, come on. We both knew Toby was gay."

"Yeah, but still—you don't deserve to see him in action. Oh, sweetie, I'm so sorry." Soph put her arms round her friend and hugged her.

Abby sobbed quietly into Soph's shoulder. "Apparently I was to be part of some quaintly old-fashioned marriage of convenience."

"Bastard," Soph muttered, gently patting Abby's back. "Where is he? I feel inclined to go over and punch his bloody fairy lights out."

Abby found herself smiling. "Oh, I do love you."

"Love you, too," Soph said as they pulled away from their embrace.

"There's no need to say anything to Toby. I left him marinating in remorse. Come on, let's go. I vote we go back to my place, order in a curry and get pissed.

"By the way," Abby said as they started down the street, "you'll never guess who Toby was kissing."

"What? You knew him? God, this gets worse."

"It was Christian."

"Christian? As in Scozza's obnoxious ex?"

"The very same."

Soph grimaced. "How could he? I mean, that man's a malicious pain in the ass."

Abby grinned. "You said it."

Chapter 9

ALONG WITH THE ANGER, hurt and sadness, Abby was also feeling relief. The thought of being married to Toby and all the while nurturing suspicions about his sexuality had filled her with dread. There was a huge sense of having had a lucky escape and that this was something, if not to be celebrated, then certainly to be grateful for.

The following morning, when she told Martin that she'd discovered Toby was gay, there was no "I told you so." He simply put his arm round her and listened.

"I am so sorry," he said finally. "What a bloody awful way to find out. Must have really thrown you for a loop."

"Yeah. Did a bit."

"Coming out is never easy, but to use somebody the way Toby used you...It's so callous."

"There's more," Abby said.

Martin frowned a question.

"OK, I might as well just come right out with it—the man Toby is seeing..."

"Yes?"

"It's Christian."

"Toby and Christian?" Martin said, pulling away. "Oh, c'mon. Don't be daft..."

"It's true. And from what I could tell, Christian seemed mightily pleased with himself."

"*Christian?* Toby's going out with *Christian?* Sorry, I can't get my head round this."

She explained how the pair had met a few months ago at the retailers' association dinner. "According to Toby they got it together soon after that."

"But I thought Toby and I were mates. How could he do this to me? I feel so...so betrayed."

"*You* feel betrayed?"

Martin was so taken up with his own drama that he appeared not to hear Abby's remark. "I thought the two of us had this really deep, meaningful relationship. We were planning to go to the first day of the Yamamoto sale together. Did he tell you that?"

"No, he didn't mention it," Abby said.

"I'm gobsmacked. Totally gobsmacked. He knows how Christian has treated me since we split up. At the very least I thought Toby was on my side."

"Come on, Scozza," she said gently, "I know this is hard, but I'm sure Toby didn't set out to hurt you...the same way he didn't really set out to hurt me."

Despite the early evidence to the contrary, Martin understood that Abby's loss was infinitely greater than his own and insisted she take the rest of the day off. She'd barely slept the night before, so she didn't argue.

While Martin minded the shop, Abby dozed upstairs on the sofa. At one point the phone woke her. It was Soph, checking in to see if she was OK and inviting her over for dinner. "Oh, hon, that's really sweet of you, but I'm not really up to it. I'm just going to order takeout and watch *The X Factor.*"

"You sure?"

"Positive."

"Ring me if you change your mind."

Abby promised she would. "And Soph..."

"What?"

"Thanks for being there."

"C'mon, you don't have to thank me. You're my best friend. Where else should I be?"

The next afternoon, Abby went for a long walk on Hampstead Heath. The walk was meant to help clear her head, but it seemed that everywhere she looked, she was confronted with happy, carefree couples frolicking with children and dogs.

Abby wasn't a jealous soul, but her heart ached for the life she imagined they had. She knew that there wasn't a couple in the world who lived that saccharine-perfect Samantha-and-Darren existence, but for now it pandered to her melancholy to think that they did.

That night she took one of her herbal sleeping pills and, to her surprise and relief, slept for ten hours.

She always looked forward to her Sunday morning sleep-ins, but after everything that had happened, today's was particularly welcome.

At midday she went out and bought all the papers, to see if there was any news from the *Bantry.* There wasn't. She tried to read mind-improving political and environmental pieces, but she couldn't concentrate. In the end she spent the day lying on the sofa, glued to the True Movies channel.

First thing on Monday morning, she got a call from Dan, asking if she'd had a chance to look at the contract yet. "I don't mean to put pressure on you," he said, "but we're on a really tight budget. Until you've formally agreed to us filming in the shop, we can't start renting the equipment we need."

With all that had been going on, she'd completely forgotten the contract. "Dan, please forgive me, but I've had all this personal stuff going on and I just haven't got round to reading it."

"I had no idea." There was real concern in his voice. "You OK?"

"Toby and I broke up."

"I'm so sorry. That's wretched. Look, for what it's worth, I've been through a few breakups and I've got some idea what you're going through. Tell me to mind my own business, but if you ever want a shoulder to cry on—" He broke off. "God, I sound like I'm making a cheap pass, don't I?"

She smiled. "Not at all. It never occurred to me." She told him how much she appreciated the gesture. She knew she wouldn't phone him, though. Even though she always felt comfortable in his company and found him particularly easy to talk to, theirs was a business relationship, and she didn't want to complicate things by adding her personal problems to the mix. On top of that, she'd spent so many hours emoting and unloading to Soph and Martin that she was completely "talked out." Now all she wanted was some time alone to lick her wounds.

AS IT turned out, she didn't have much time for wound-licking. For the next few days, work took over. She was in the middle of organizing flowers for several high-profile spring weddings—two of which were going to be featured in *Hello!* This would be wonderful publicity for the business and she needed to make the bouquets, not to mention the displays in the churches and reception venues, as original and unique as possible.

One of her *Hello!* clients was getting married in Scotland, the other was tying the knot in Gloucestershire. On Tuesday she flew to Edinburgh to look at the tiny thirteenth-century church the bride had chosen, just outside the city. On Thursday she flew back to London and then drove straight to Gloucestershire to see the other church.

At half past eight on Friday morning, she was back at Mr. Takahashi's penthouse. This time, of course, Martin was with her. As they went up in the elevator, Abby was as calm as an afternoon in autumn. Not that Martin noticed or remarked on Abby's demeanor. He was too busy fretting about whether Ichiro would like him. "I don't know why you had to arrange this appointment so early. You know I look like crap first thing. And I came out without curling my eyelashes."

For the umpteenth time, Abby explained that if she'd arranged the meeting later in the day, Martin would have had to stay behind to mind the shop.

"Yes, I know. I'm sorry. Don't think I'm not grateful. I'm just nervous, that's all. So, tell me honestly, are you sure this outfit works? You don't think it's a bit OTT?"

"No, not over the top at all. Not now. . . . Not now that you've lost the bumblebee sunglasses."

"And you think the olive jacket is OK with my skin tone?"

"It's fine."

"Only fine?"

"God, Scozza…"

"OK, what about the shoes?"

Ping.

"We're here," Abby said.

"Yes, but you haven't said what you think about the shoes. Brogues are a real departure for me—particularly with jeans."

"They're great."

"Really?"

"Really."

She was ringing the doorbell. "I don't know why you're so worried about meeting this guy. You've only ever spoken to him on the phone. Has it occurred to you that you might not like him?"

"Impossible. If that man's body is even half as sexy as his voice…" Martin gave a shudder of delight. Then he looked back down at his shoes. "I dunno, maybe I should have played safe and stuck to sneakers."

Ichiro was as effervescent as ever. He greeted Abby with a flamboyant triple kiss. "Abby, it's so wonderful to see yeeeeuuww again."

The moment he noticed Martin, Ichiro's eyes were all over him.

"And who *ever* is this? Wow, Gran'ma, what fabulous English brogues you have on. I simply adore English brogues."

Martin beamed with delight. As they stood in the hallway, Abby made the introductions.

"Martin. Hello. I'm so pleased to meet yeeeeuuww."

Ichiro took Martin's hand in both of his and brought it to his chest. It was clear to Abby that Martin wasn't disappointed by the vision before him. "And I have to say that your shoes are pretty cool, too," he gushed to Ichiro. Suddenly all eyes were focused on Ichiro's feet. He was wearing very flat, pointy leather lace-ups. In cream.

"Aren't they cute?" he said, arranging his feet in first position. "I got them in Rome. The leather is so soft that I can hardly bear to take them off. And they're just so balletic. Don't you think they're balletic?" He went into third and then fourth position.

"Really balletic," Martin trilled.

He led them down the hall. "When I wear them I totally feel this urge to je-tay." Abby was convinced that Ichiro was about to demonstrate his urge by flying through the doorway into the living room, but he didn't. Once they were inside, he invited them to sit down and fetched a tray of green tea.

"So, Martin," Ichiro said, handing out cups, "where are you from?"

And they were off. They were so engrossed in each other—although it was clear that Ichiro was doing most of the talking—that Abby didn't even attempt to interrupt and suggest they get down to work. When the men discovered they both came from poor backgrounds, Abby knew they would be swapping stories for hours.

She took her notebook out of her bag and began wandering around the flat, thinking about where to position her floral displays. She was still set on a traditional Japanese theme, but if she was going to include a water feature, ornamental pagoda and a bridge, she had to think seriously about dimensions and make sure the room wasn't going to look too cluttered, particularly as there would be a bar and buffet table.

After twenty minutes or so, she returned to Martin and Ichiro. "Well, I'm done," she said. "Ichiro, I think maybe I should go over everything with you one more time."

He said he was sure that wouldn't be necessary. "I trust you completely."

Ichiro walked them to the elevator. "Bye, Abby. Speak soon." He kissed her on both cheeks. Then he turned to Martin, took his hand and kissed the back of it. "So good to meet you, Martin," Ichiro said, holding Martin's gaze in his.

As the elevator doors closed, Martin leaned back against the wall and let out a long sigh. "I think I'm in love. Isn't Ichiro just amazing? He's so pretty and so funny and we've got so much in common. Caribbean blue is his favorite color. Caribbean blue's my favorite color. He loves sushi but can't bear sashimi. I love sushi but can't bear sashimi. He puts his boiled eggs in the egg cup pointy end down—"

"—don't tell me; you put your boiled eggs in the egg cup pointy end down." Abby was grinning.

"Now you're making fun of me." Martin pouted, feigning hurt. "I'm just trying to illustrate how alike we are.... You know how it is with some people? We just clicked instantly. We're going to the movies tomorrow night."

WHILE MARTIN drove the van back to Islington, Abby took the tube into the West End. She had an appointment with another corporate client—a director of a hotel chain—in Marble Arch.

It was only as she was leaving that she noticed she had a run in her tights. Had she been on her way home, she wouldn't have bothered to buy another pair and get changed, but since she was seeing a third client after lunch, it was imperative she looked her best. She decided to pop in to S&M on Oxford Street to buy a new pair.

She got changed in the ladies' room. She was out again less than five minutes later and heading for the escalator. As she glanced to her left, toward menswear, she spotted Dan. He was at the cash register.

She changed direction. "Dan! Hi. It's me."

He came toward her, smiling and shaking his head. "It always amazes me," he said, "how in a city this size I'm always bumping into people I know."

"There's probably some obscure law of probability that explains it," she said. "Occam's razor or something."

"I don't think it's Occam's razor. Isn't that about the simplest explanation always being the most likely?"

"Oh, OK, Occam's shaving brush, then. Or Occam's toothpaste."

This made him laugh.

"So," she said, "what have you been buying?"

He held up a blue S&M carrier bag with the characteristic gold lettering. "Socks and underwear. Like I told you, I buy them once a year, and this is that time."

She laughed. "So, you're not filming today?"

"Day off. Our leading lady, Lucinda Wallace, is speaking at some women's charity lunch."

He paused. "You doing anything? Since it's such a lovely day, I was thinking of taking a stroll up to Hyde Park. Why don't you join me? We could get coffee."

Abby said she would love to.

They headed back toward the escalator.

"You know," she said, "I'd love to have a full and frank discussion with the chairman of S&M."

"About what?"

"Easy. The state of their stores." She went through her list: the lackluster displays, the fluorescent lighting, the beige floor tiles. "I just can't understand why they don't up their act. All the stores are the same. They look like something from the old USSR. If it was left to me, I'd rip everything out, take on a big-name interior designer and start again."

"Really?"

"Absolutely."

"Don't you think that might intimidate people—particularly the older customers?"

Abby said she suspected that was what the bosses at S&M thought. For her part, she couldn't see how anybody could possibly be intimidated by an interior that was fresh and modern. "They're just such a bunch of dinosaurs at S&M. I can't help thinking they deserve all they get."

By the time they reached the park, the burden of her discourse had moved from the drab shop interiors to women's fashion—the poor cut, the slightly off-color palette. "Oh, and the motifs. Don't get me started on the motifs. You know what I'd be doing if I was the boss?"

"What?"

"Firing all their hopeless clothes designers and bringing in new ones who actually know something about high street fashion. He needs to get rid of all these money men he surrounds himself with who have convinced him that constant sales and price reductions are the way to go. He should start listening to the customers. They all want the store to modernize. If you want my opinion, S&M ignores their customers at their peril."

"That it?"

"Oh, they need to change the mirrors in the fitting rooms. The ones they've got make you look fat."

"Anything else?" He grinned.

"Nope. I think that's all."

They bought coffee and muffins from one of the park cafés and went to find a bench by the Serpentine.

"By the way," she said, "I still haven't looked over the contract. I'll do it as soon as I get back to the shop and put it straight in the post."

"Don't do that."

"Why not?"

"I was thinking about going ice-skating tonight."

She started to giggle. "You're saying that I shouldn't post the contract because you're planning to go ice-skating tonight? OK, that sounds logical."

"Sorry, I'm not explaining myself. I happened to be passing the rink in Queensway this morning. I haven't been skating since I was a kid and it occurred to me that it might be a laugh."

"Dan, are you asking me to come ice-skating with you?"

"Yes. I know it's a mad idea, but I thought it might cheer you up. Plus you could give me the contract rather than putting it in the post. That way we save time. C'mon. What do you say?"

"I say, I can't skate," she said.

"Well, if it helps, I was always rubbish at it, so we'll both be in good company."

"I don't know. I've got so much to do. I'm behind with all my paperwork. My tax return's late. They're bound to fine me—"

"So do it tomorrow night. If it's this late, another day isn't going to make much difference."

A smile began to form on her face. "You're right. You know what? I'd love to go ice-skating. I shut up shop at six. You could pick me up at half past."

"You're on," he said.

SOPH POPPED in just after five—a few minutes after Abby arrived back from her afternoon meeting. She had a dentist's appointment and had stopped by on her way to find out how Abby was bearing up.

"Oh, you know. I'm getting there."

"And how are things going with Mr. Takahashi?"

"Oh, fine. He has this pretty, übercamp assistant named Ichiro, and I think he and Scozz might be in love."

Soph chuckled. "Good for Scozz. He deserves a bit of fun."

"Talking of fun. I'm going ice-skating tonight. With Dan."

Soph was in no doubt as to the nature of Dan's invitation. "I'm telling you, he's moving in on you."

Abby blushed. "You think?"

"Oh, like it hasn't occurred to you."

"OK, I admit the possibility did cross my mind, but even if you're right and he is interested in me, he's not going to get very far."

"You don't fancy him?"

"I'm not saying that. I have to admit I do find him

attractive, but I'm not one of those women who comes out of one relationship only to glide seamlessly into the next because she can't bear the thought of being alone. I know I need to take time to get over Toby. I'm not ready to get involved with somebody else."

Soph shrugged. "I dunno. I know it isn't the conventional wisdom, but it might be just what you need—you know, somebody who really fancies you. Think how fantastic it would be for your morale."

"Perhaps, but I'm just not ready." Abby decided to change the subject. "So, have you told your parents about Lamar being black?"

"Not as such."

Abby laughed. "What does that mean?"

"It means I still haven't found the right moment. But I will. I'm just so scared that they won't accept him and I'll have to choose between them and Lamar. This whole thing could turn into a complete disaster."

Just then Martin appeared. He'd been out making some deliveries. When he heard that Abby had agreed to go out with Dan, he took the same line as Soph. "A new man in your life is just what you need."

Abby told him what she had told Soph—that she wasn't ready to start dating. "Plus, rebound relationships always end in disaster."

Martin shook his head. "God, when did the pair of you get to be such harbingers of doom? First there's Soph convinced that her parents are going to make her choose between them and Lamar. Now you're convinced that starting a relationship with the gorgeous Dan could only end in disaster."

Soph grinned. "For my part at least, it comes from being Jewish. After five thousand years of pain, misery and persecution, what do you expect? You want a harbinger of joy and delight, be best friends with Big Bird." She looked at her watch and said she had to get going or she would be late for her dentist appointment. "By the way," she said to Martin, "good luck with Mr. T's assistant. Abby tells me he's a real cutie." With that she winked at Martin and headed toward the door.

DAN ARRIVED a few minutes before six-thirty—just as Martin was getting ready to leave. Martin told Dan how he was jazzed at the thought of Fabulous Flowers being used in his film. "Plus I get to meet Lucinda Wallace. I just adore her. She's so unstarry. Always really natural when she's interviewed. Reminds me of Kate Winslet in that respect." He picked up his shoulder bag and lifted the strap over his head. "Anyway, you kids have a fantastic time." He turned to Abby. "See you tomorrow," he whispered. "You can tell me how it all went. I will want details."

With that he said "bye" to Dan and took his leave.

Praying that Dan hadn't heard Martin's last remark, Abby opened her bag, took out the signed contract and handed it to Dan. At the same time she noticed the edgy khaki bomber jacket he was wearing and couldn't help thinking how cute he looked in it. "All seems fine," she said. "So, when do we start shooting?"

He told her that he was aiming toward the middle of the following week.

As Abby flitted about, checking that the back door was

securely locked and gathering up her keys and jacket, Dan wandered round the shop.

"You know, I really love coming here," he said.

"You do? Why?"

"I dunno. It's something about walking in off a noisy city street and entering this very calm, tranquil world full of perfume and color. It's soothing, I guess."

"You wouldn't have said that if you'd been here the other day when Scozza and his ex were screaming at each other." She explained about Debbie Harry and the custody battle.

Dan listened in amused disbelief. "Don't get me wrong, I love animals, but it beats me how two adults could declare war over a dog."

By now Dan had wandered into the middle of the shop and was gazing at the containers of flowers arranged on the circular plinth. "I don't know how you work out what goes with what," he said, carefully removing a bird-of-paradise stem from one of the zinc vases. He moved to the next container and did the same to a long twig of pussy willow. He held this next to the dazzling orange bloom.

Abby wrinkled her nose. "Doesn't work. You're mixing your metaphors." She put down her jacket and bag and went over to him. "Pussy willow says traditional English country house in spring. Birds-of-paradise are bright, angular and much more contemporary. They're also so vibrant they don't really need much else with them, apart from some outsize leaves or tall grass."

She put the pussy willow back in water and took out two more bird-of-paradise stems. "Come over to the counter," she said. Clearly intrigued, he followed her. She found a tall, fairly narrow square glass vase and stood it in front of him. Then she handed him a florist's knife.

"Would I be right in thinking that, like most men, you've never arranged flowers?"

"OK, there was this one time," he said. "I try not to think about it. You have to understand, I was young. I wasn't sure who I was ... and those daffodils were so beautiful ... so seductive. They were just calling out to me."

She bashed him playfully on the arm. "God, why do heterosexual men feel so threatened by the idea of arranging a few flowers?"

"Easy—we think our penises will drop off."

She shook her head and smiled. "Well, I'm going to prove you wrong. You are going to create your very first flower arrangement."

"I am?" he said, frowning. "But shouldn't we be getting to the ice rink?"

"Come on. It'll only take a few minutes."

"O-kay."

"Off you go, then."

He placed the three stems in the vase and stood back. "Quick, simple and effective, I think. Don't you?"

"Well ... first, you haven't used the knife. You need to trim the stems—otherwise they won't take up any water. Second, what you've done is just a tad ..."

"Boring?"

"Let's just say predictable. Try cutting the stems to different heights. That way you make the arrangement more interesting." By now she had located a bunch of not-too-large monstera leaves, which she laid down on the counter, next to the vase. "And these will set it off but without being overpowering."

She meant for him to cut the flower stems in such a way that they would stand in the vase and form an even, downward slant. What he ended up with was one massively tall stem, one a tiny bit shorter and another so short that its head disappeared below the rim of the vase. Finally he picked up the leaves and shoved them behind the stems.

"Ta-da. What do you reckon?"

"Hmm," she said, producing a watering can and filling the vase with water. "Well, it's certainly creative." She tilted her head to one side. "The way the third stem completely disappears is actually rather inventive."

"Really?" He stood back and considered his effort. "No it's not. You're just being kind. It's terrible. I got the heights all wrong. It looks like a gorilla did it."

"No, it doesn't." She paused and felt her mouth twitching with laughter. "All right. Maybe it does—just a bit."

Determined not to be defeated, he got busy with the knife, cutting and recutting the stems, trying to make the arrangement work, but each time he only made it worse. After each hopeless attempt, they would shake with laughter. In the end he had taken so much off the stems that all three flowers had their heads below the rim of the vase.

"Oh, my God," he said, still laughing, "now, that really does look like the work of a gorilla."

She folded her arms. "OK, maybe you shouldn't give up the day job."

THEY DROVE to the indoor ice rink in Queensway in Dan's elderly VW Golf. The backseat was covered in piles of paper and odds and ends of camera equipment. There were a couple of empty Starbucks cups and some sandwich-wrapper remains lying on the floor. "Excuse the mess," he said, as they got in. "We were filming outside last week, and the car became my office."

"Please, don't worry," she said. She wanted to say that she rather liked the shambles. It was such a contrast to the interior of Toby's Mercedes, which was always immaculate. Eating in the car was strictly verboten in case the upholstery got stained, and if he spied so much as a speck of dust on the dashboard he would be right there with one of the anti-static dusters he always kept in the glove compartment. It was impossible to unwrap so much as a toffee without him tensing up.

"So," he said, slowing down at traffic lights, "how are you?"

"Yeah, I'm fine."

"No . . . I mean how are you—*really.*"

She looked down at her hands. "Oh, you know . . . being busy helps."

He nodded. "I know that feeling."

"Dan, please don't take this the wrong way, but would you mind if we didn't talk about Toby and the breakup? I just feel like forgetting it tonight."

She tried to work out why she was holding back. She liked this man. He cared. He was a great listener and she knew she could trust him. But she'd been thinking about what Soph had said about him moving in on her. She couldn't let this happen. Even though she was attracted to Dan, she wasn't remotely ready to start a new relationship. In order to prevent it, she had to set boundaries and keep him at arm's length.

"I completely understand," Dan said. "Of course we don't have to talk about the breakup."

Their eyes met for a few seconds, and she smiled her thanks.

IT TURNED out that Dan was being modest when he said he couldn't skate. In fact, he was rather accomplished on the ice. He had perfect balance and could skate forward and backward, quite fast. Most important, he could stop at will. Abby could do none of these things. At first she clung to the barrier, and no amount of gentle coaxing from Dan could prize her away. Then, when she finally did let go and attempted to put one skate in front of another, she fell backward onto the ice and lay there, arms and legs waving like a marooned beetle.

She was hugely embarrassed by her incompetence. It didn't help that the ice rink was full of dexterous teenagers, speed skating and performing highly complicated maneuvers.

"You must think I'm a complete wimp," she said. "In my defense I have to tell you that my elevator phobia's practically gone. I took the elevator to the twenty-third floor the other day."

"Hey, that's brilliant news. Why didn't you tell me before? The rappelling at Covent Garden really paid off, then." He moved forward, as if he were about to give her a hug. Then suddenly he pulled back. Maybe he didn't want to give the impression that he was making a pass at her. This made her think that maybe Dan wanted nothing more than to be her friend. Perhaps he wasn't moving in on her after all.

Incompetent on the ice as she was, Dan refused to let

her give up. She lost count of how many times she fell over, but after each tumble Dan eased her back onto her feet and tried to demonstrate where she was going wrong. She did her best to copy him but only ended up falling over again.

It must have taken an hour or so, but finally she started to get the measure of it. Soon she was gliding, albeit hesitantly, over the ice.

"Brilliant," Dan cried. He skated over to her and she felt his arm round her waist. "I'll guide you round the rink," he said. "That way you can go a bit faster."

She wasn't sure if she was ready to go faster. "No, I'll fall."

"It's OK, I've got you. I promise I won't let you fall."

As her eyes met his and they exchanged smiles—his urging her on, hers tentative and fearful—she was aware of how much she was enjoying being with this man. As they glided forward, his arm tightened round her waist. She was enjoying that, too.

They began skating round the edge of the rink, away from all the teenage racers. At first they went slowly, keeping well within her comfort zone. Then, after a minute or so, she felt him start to speed up. Panic overtook her.

"Stop! Stop! You're making me go too fast. I'm going to fall."

"No you're not," he soothed. "Just keep concentrating."

But she was too scared to concentrate. Despite his having an arm round her, she could feel herself losing her balance. As she began to wobble, so did Dan. He was unable to save her or himself and they fell backward, landing in a giggling heap of arms, legs and skates.

"Don't say I didn't warn you," Abby laughed, attempting to disentangle herself and sit up.

It wasn't until they were both upright again that they noticed the seats of their jeans were soaked.

"Oh, who cares," Abby said, aware that she hadn't had this much fun in ages. "Come on, let's have another go."

They carried on skating—Abby improving all the time—until they realized they were both starving.

They joined the queue at a falafel stand down the road and ate as they walked back to Dan's car.

They chatted about how the film was going and Abby asked him when he first became interested in filmmaking. He told her how as a kid he'd joined something called the Children's Film Unit. "What began as vague interest soon became an obsession. Every summer we'd go off on location for a couple of weeks and make a full-length feature film. I started off as a runner when I was twelve. By the time I was seventeen I was directing."

"Your parents must have been so proud."

"My mum was. Like you wouldn't believe. My dad died when I was seven."

"Oh, Dan, I'm so sorry."

"Car accident. Took my mum years to get over it. She adored him. Then, when I was twelve, she met somebody and eventually they got married, but up to then she devoted herself to me. I remember her buying me one of those director's chairs for my bedroom. She even had my name printed on the back. When I turned sixteen, my stepfather bought me a posh, albeit secondhand, film camera. It was him who encouraged me to go to film school."

"They sound like lovely people."

"They are. My stepfather's always been a bit of a film buff. Not long after he and Mum got married, he took me to see *2001*. I'll never forget how afterward we went out for a burger and he sat there deconstructing it and explaining what a great film it was."

"And you caught the bug."

"Absolutely. I owe him a great deal."

She asked him if he still missed his father. "I don't really remember much about him. Just the odd thing: I have memories of him coming home from the office and smelling of the cold. I can see him drinking soup. His mouth used to perform this strange chewing action. I remember being tucked up in bed and him reading me *Just William*. Afterward I'd make him look under my bed for robbers. He always went along with it. He never told me I was being stupid—even though my bed was only two inches off the floor."

She sensed the emotion welling up inside him. She didn't want to upset him, so she decided to change the subject.

"By the way, I watched *Boston Legal* the other night. You were right. It's brilliant." She thought for a minute. "I was really worried there'd be nothing left to watch once *Friends* and *Frasier* finished."

"I know what you mean," he laughed. "There's nothing like the panic that sets in when your favorite sitcom is about to end."

"Yeah. It's like: 'Now what do I do on a Thursday night?' I mean, *Frasier* nights were sacred. I'd look forward to it all day. You can't beat being curled up on the sofa with brilliant telly and a takeout curry—"

"Yeah—particularly if there are two of you." His face had gone red and he looked down, clearly embarrassed. She wanted to reassure him that she hadn't taken this the wrong way and that she didn't think he was coming on to her.

This time it was his turn to redirect the conversation. He said he still hadn't gotten round to watching the *It's a Wonderful Life* DVD. She told him not to worry and that she wasn't in a hurry to get it back.

"Tell you what I did watch the other night," he said, "for about the nth time—*The Godfather*."

"Really? I hated that film."

Dan almost choked on his falafel. "I can't believe you just said that."

"Why not? The Corleones are baddies. I didn't care about any of them. There's just nobody to root for, except Diane Keaton. I kept hoping she would eventually see the light and leave Al Pacino. The entire thing bored me."

"I have no idea how you can dismiss one of the greatest films ever made as boring. *The Godfather* is an epic. It's about man and his destiny. It's about family, loyalty, love, violence, betrayal—all the big issues."

"So's *The Sound of Music*. Now, there's a film..."

He started laughing. "I swear, if it's the last thing I do, I am going to make you watch *The Godfather* again. You'll change your mind. I guarantee it."

"Bet I don't."

"We'll see," he said, grinning. He paused. Then: "You know, nobody quite realizes how much general knowledge they acquire from films."

"How d'you mean?"

"Well, if it weren't for movies, you'd never know that all telephone numbers in America begin with five-five-five..."

She was starting to laugh.

"During all police investigations," he continued, "it's

necessary to visit a strip club at least once. If you happen to find yourself being chased through town, you can always take cover in a passing St. Patrick's Day parade—no matter what the time of year. The Eiffel Tower can be seen from any window in Paris. If you decide to go dancing in the street, everybody you bump into will know all the steps..."

"You know, you really have a way of cheering me up."

He turned to look at her. "That was the whole point of tonight," he said.

"Well, it certainly worked. I've had a really great time."

By now they had reached Dan's car. They chatted and laughed all the way back to Upper Street.

"Thanks again for a lovely evening," she said, as they pulled up outside the shop.

"I had a great time, too." He smiled. "Abby?"

"Yes."

"Would you like to have dinner sometime?"

Of course she wanted to have dinner with him. But if she said yes, she risked their friendship turning into something more serious. She could feel herself starting to panic as she thought about him becoming her rebound man and how it was all going to end in disaster. "Oh, Dan, I don't know. It's so soon after Toby, and I'm not really sure that I'm ready to start dating."

"Look, it'd just be dinner. No strings. No pressure. Let's just see how it goes and take it from there."

She sat, dithering. Then she heard a voice, apparently her own, saying she would love to have dinner with him.

"Fantastic."

"When?"

"Tomorrow?"

"Tomorrow?"

"Too soon?"

Her face broke into a smile. "No, tomorrow would be great. I'll look forward to it." With that, she opened the car door and stepped onto the pavement.

"I'll pick you up at eight," he called after her.

Chapter 10

"SO, YOU REALLY LIKE him, then?" Soph said, her voice brimming with excitement. "Did he kiss you? Where's he taking you? What are you going to wear? Are you going to sleep with him?"

Having answered with one yes, a no, two don't knows and one definitely not, Abby said she needed to get off the phone because Martin was on his own downstairs and she'd only popped up to the flat to make coffee and quickly tell Soph her news.

But Soph's interrogation wasn't over. "So what happened? Yesterday you said you weren't ready to start a new relationship."

"This isn't a relationship. Dan is simply taking me out for dinner. No strings. No pressure. At least that's what he told me and it's what I keep telling myself. But I get the feeling he really likes me. And I really like him. On the other hand, I can't stop thinking that I'm going to end up getting hurt."

"I know," Soph said gently, "and most people in your shoes would feel the same. Yes, you might get hurt—but you might not. This could turn into a wonderful romance. Life is all about taking risks. That's how we grow and learn."

"That, of course, is why you didn't hesitate to tell your parents about Lamar."

"That's different."

"How?"

"I'm Jewish. Jews don't take risks. We're too busy watching out for anti-semites."

ABBY TOOK the mugs of coffee down to the shop and placed them on the counter. "What on earth is this?" Martin said, his face forming an exaggerated grimace.

"Coffee. What's the matter? It's no different from what I usually make."

"No, not the coffee." He tapped the glass vase containing Dan's attempt at a flower arrangement. "This."

Abby laughed. "Dan did it. I persuaded him to have a go at flower arranging. It's his first attempt."

"And his last, I hope." Martin picked up the vase and said he would toss the flowers. "No, don't," she said, taking it back. "I want to keep them." She was aware of sounding all girly and soppy, but she couldn't help it. Martin rolled his eyes—with humor and affection rather than disdain.

"Somebody's falling in love," he singsonged.

"Oh, behave. I've known the man five minutes. I am absolutely not falling in love."

"Bet you he kisses you when he drops you home tonight after dinner. And I bet you kiss him back."

"Stop it. It's not like that. We're just friends."

"Of course you are."

With that he went to pick up the mail, which had just

come through the door. "By the way," he said as he returned to the counter, "I spoke to somebody at the Citizens Advice Bureau about getting access to Debbie Harry. He put me on to this woman solicitor, who thinks she might be able to help. God knows what it's going to cost, though."

"I know. It's bound to be expensive, but it's worth having a chat with her."

Martin agreed that it probably was. "I have to do something," he said, putting the envelopes down on the counter. "I can't just sit back and let Christian steal her away from me." He pointed to the return address on a brown envelope lying on top of the pile. "Hold on to yer hat, that one's from Islington Council."

Abby snatched the letter and started to tear it open. "God, I bet Christian's convinced them to make me stop displaying flowers on the pavement." She unfolded the letter and scanned the first paragraph. She couldn't have been more wrong.

"Omigod, this is amazing," she cried. "Get this: *Dear Ms. Crompton, we have received a complaint about potential hazard occasioned to pedestrians by your pavement floral displays. We recognize that outdoor presentations considerably enhance the atmosphere and ambience of the surrounding neighborhood and are reluctant to ask you to desist from displaying your wares on the pavement. We would advise you, however, to exercise caution and good sense when it comes to use of pavement space. We would also refer you to paragraph five, subsection nine, of the local government health and safety regulations, which clearly states that a full five feet must be left between any display and the edge of the pavement in order to facilitate pedestrian locomotion. Failure to comply with this may result in prosecution. Meanwhile, we will be taking no action against yourself at this particular moment in time. Yours, I. Strutt, brackets Missus.*"

"Well, good old I. Strutt brackets Missus," Martin cried. "For once common sense has prevailed."

Abby shook her head with disbelief. "Yes, but Christian must be apoplectic."

"I know. Great, isn't it? I bet at this very moment he's lying on the floor, chewing the carpet and kicking his feet." Martin clapped his hands with glee and went out to buy apricot danishes to celebrate.

After he had closed the door, Abby found herself wondering how on earth Toby had managed to end up with a creature like Christian. She wondered if they would stay together.

SINCE THIS was her first proper date with Dan, she took her time choosing what to wear and getting ready.

She picked out a teal-colored gypsy skirt and a long, slightly paler top with sleeves that flared at the wrist. She finished off the outfit with a string of small brown glass beads, which came down to her waist, and a wide chocolate-brown belt, which she fastened at her hips.

Instead of straightening her shoulder-length hair, she decided to scrunch-dry it. She did this because a) natural waves were back in fashion and b) Toby had hated this look on her. He said it made her look unkempt and disheveled.

When she finally looked at herself in the full-length mirror, she decided she looked utterly kempt and perfectly sheveled and—even if she did say so herself—rather sexy.

She was even more cheered up when Dan not only told her how lovely she looked but was particularly complimentary about her hair. She, in turn, complimented him on his suit, which was navy, beautifully cut and set off by a sparkling white open-necked shirt. For some reason—maybe because over breakfast she'd read part of a biography of Tony Curtis, which was being serialized in the *Daily Mail*— that quaint, old-fashioned word *dreamboat* came to mind.

He took her to an Italian place in Belsize Park. She hadn't been anywhere like it in years. Franco's was one of those traditional, family-run eateries with red-check table-cloths and Chianti bottles hanging from the ceiling. Toby never took her anywhere that wasn't minimalist and edgy, in all the posh food guides, and cost a fortune. She could just see him turning his nose up at this place and dismissing it as an appalling, Disneyesque cliché.

Here—had she the mind—she could have tucked the corner of her napkin down her top and worn it like a bib, stuck her elbows in the air, got pasta sauce round her mouth and nobody would have given her a second glance.

While they waited for their food to arrive, they munched on bread sticks and drank the house Chianti. After a couple of glasses of wine, Abby found herself talking about Toby.

"Abby, we really don't have to discuss the breakup. You've already said it makes you feel uncomfortable, and it really is none of my business. You don't owe me any kind of explanation."

"I know, but I feel ready to talk about it now...if that's OK."

"Of course it's OK."

Just then the waitress came over and placed steaming bowls of spaghetti vongole in front of them. Abby waited until the waitress was out of earshot. The she began twisting her fork in the mountain of pasta. "Toby's gay," she announced.

She was waiting for his look of surprise, his cry of astonishment, but there was none. He simply nodded.

She looked at him. "You guessed, didn't you?" she said. "You worked it out that night in the elevator when I told you how bad our sex life was."

"I have to admit that the thought did occur to me."

She was shaking her head. "How come everybody was able to see it so quickly? Don't get me wrong. I'm not that naive. It wasn't that I didn't suspect Toby was gay, but I could never be certain. I feel so stupid."

"You mustn't. If he told you outright that he wasn't gay, what reason would you have not to believe him? He stuck to his story that he was too exhausted for sex. You loved him and had no reason to think he was being dishonest."

"Maybe. But to think he started an affair with Christian..."

"What? The guy you told me about? Martin's ex—the one who won't let him have access to their dog?"

"The very same."

Dan topped up her glass with wine. "So, what was your role meant to be in all this, to marry him and provide a smoke screen for his gay affairs?"

"Pretty much. I can't imagine the likes of Lady Penelope handing over the family estate to her gay son."

Dan's face had darkened. "What he tried to do to you is unforgivable. Utterly and totally unforgivable. I can't imagine how you must have felt, discovering he wanted to use you."

She shrugged. "I'm not going to tell you I wasn't devastated, but you have to understand that Toby lives in fear of his mother. Plus, his friends and work colleagues are nearly all upper-class or minor aristocracy, and they're a pretty homophobic bunch." She lowered her voice. "Clearly they all choose to forget what they got up to at boarding school."

Dan let out a soft laugh. He put his wineglass to his lips. "It's commendable the way you make excuses for him, but I just want to thump him—or, even better, challenge the swine to a duel."

She burst out laughing. "Now, that would be something worth watching."

"You may mock, but when I was a kid I must have watched *The Three Musketeers* at least a dozen times, and I reckon I picked up several rather cunning and dastardly moves."

She was laughing again. She'd never met anybody who had the ability to lift her spirits the way this man did.

"Toby's sexuality aside," Abby went on, "the class issue would always have been a problem between us. His friends thought it was hysterical that he was engaged to a girl from Croydon." She told him about the country-house weekend in Dorset and how she'd been made to look a fool when she got dressed up for dinner.

He winced. "It really beats me how people can be so cruel."

"It didn't do much for my confidence, I can tell you. It was the same with his mother. She clearly expected him to marry a well-bred filly from the shires, and I was never going to be that. I would never have been good enough for her—particularly as I didn't hunt. Lady P was master of her local hunt, 'doncha know.' " She put her wineglass to her lips. "I think if I know one thing for certain, it's that I never want to become involved with another rich, posh bloke. I just want to be with somebody ordinary and down to earth." She wanted to add "like you," but she didn't, because she didn't want him to think she was being pushy and trying to take their relationship to the next level.

"I totally understand. I'd feel the same if I were you."

She drank some more wine. "Look, if I gave you the impression I'm a terrible inverted snob, I'm sorry. I'm really not. It's just that Toby's friends are a bunch of racist homophobic bullies. I think it's going to be a while before I make my peace with the upper classes." She put her wineglass back on the table. "OK, that's enough of me and my prejudices. How's the film going?"

"Oh, you know . . . coming along."

She accused him of being modest, and after some gentle persuasion she got him to admit that he was rather pleased with the rushes he and his editor had looked at the other night.

Neither of them could manage a whole dessert, so they decided to share a panettone-bread-and-butter pudding. "Thanks for listening to me prattle on about Toby," she said, scooping up a spoonful of rich, creamy custard.

"It was no effort, honestly."

"Well, thanks anyway."

His hand moved across the table and gently squeezed hers. It felt warm and strong and she didn't want him to let go.

"My pleasure," he said.

After dinner he drove her home. As they pulled up outside the shop, she thanked him for another wonderful evening. "I've had such a great time."

"Me, too. Abby?"

"Yes."

"You know how I said this would just be dinner and there was no pressure?"

She nodded.

"Well, I was wondering if this would feel like too much pressure."

"If what would feel like too much pressure?"

"This."

With that he leaned across and kissed her very gently on the lips.

Afterward, she was smiling. "No," she said, "that didn't feel like too much pressure at all."

"Good." He moved even closer. "How's about this?" He kissed her again.

"No, that's fine."

He began playing with her hair. Then his fingers moved over her lips and down her neck. Her entire body was prickling with delight and desire. Finally he cupped her face in his hands and kissed her a third time. In a moment they were in each other's arms, her lips parted, his tongue frantically seeking and then finding hers. He tasted faintly of red wine. She could feel the moisture seeping from between her legs. If he'd suggested coming up to the flat, she wasn't sure she would have had the strength to say no.

As they pulled away, she was aware that a single tear was falling down her cheek.

"Oh, God, I came on too strong. I'm so sorry. Please forgive me."

She shook her head and smiled. "No. No, you didn't. I think I just feel a bit overwhelmed, that's all."

He wiped away her tear. "I'm sorry this is such bloody bad timing. If you think us seeing each other is going to be too much for you, we should end it here and—"

"No. I want to carry on. I really do."

"That's great, because I do, too."

They kissed again and then again and a few more times after that.

They stopped only when a gang of teenagers in hoods appeared and hung around making *wurrgh* noises.

After a bit the kids disappeared. Nevertheless, he insisted on seeing her to her front door, where they kissed again.

She watched him drive off. Then she let herself into the shop and switched on the light. Her eyes went to the counter and the vase containing Dan's feeble attempt at a flower arrangement, which she hadn't had the heart to throw away. She smiled to herself. Then she went over to one of the zinc vases and helped herself to a purple stem of scented stock. As she climbed the stairs to her flat, she breathed in the sweet, heady aroma.

Chapter 11

ON SUNDAY, ABBY HAD lunch with Soph. Lamar was attending a World Health Organization conference in Luxembourg, where he was presenting a paper on infant malnutrition in the Third World.

The two women met at a café on Hampstead Heath. They ordered cappuccino and toasted paninis with sundried tomatoes, salami and mozzarella.

"Lamar is such a good person," Soph said. "He really cares about the world—particularly children. It's one of the reasons I'm crazy about him."

"I take it he wants loads?"

"Children? Yeah, half a dozen at least." Soph laughed and took a bite of panini. "Still, what the hell. I never had a figure to start with." She paused. "So, come on, dish. You haven't told me about your date with Dan. What did you wear? Where did he take you? What did you eat? Did he pay? Did he kiss you? How was it?"

"That gypsy skirt and top I got in Whistles. A lovely Italian place called Franco's. Spaghetti vongole. Yes, he paid, although I tried to persuade him to go halves because

I know he doesn't have a lot of money. Yes, he kissed me and, yes, it was great. In fact, it was more than great. It was bliss. Scozz hasn't stopped teasing me about it, because I had told him our relationship wasn't like that and there was no way Dan would kiss me."

Soph laughed. Then she lowered her voice. "So, come on," she said. "When are you going to—you know—do the deed?"

Abby suddenly realized her friend must have asked a dozen questions in the last two minutes. She decided to tease her a little. "Always with the questions already. What am I, a mind reader? I should know when I'm going to sleep with him?"

Soph got the joke and started to giggle. "God, you sound exactly like my great-aunt Yetta. But, come on, surely you've thought about it."

"What am I? A nymphomaniac?"

"Abby, stop messing around. I'm being serious. You do want to sleep with him, right?"

"Of course I do. The truth is, it was as much as I could do not to invite him up to the flat last night."

"God, you've really got it bad."

Abby nodded. "You might be right, but I'm so worried about rushing into something I might regret."

"On the other hand, Dan might be the best thing that has ever happened to you." Soph spooned up some cappuccino froth. "By the way, I finally told my parents about Lamar."

"You did? How did they take it?"

"Brilliantly."

"See, I told you they would."

"In fact, they were both pretty upset with me when I

explained how nervous I'd been about telling them." Soph picked up her napkin and dabbed her lips. She looked troubled. "There's something you should know."

"Sounds ominous—God, you're not pregnant, are you?"

"No," Soph said with a half smile, "I'm not pregnant. I'm engaged."

"Omigod! Soph! That's amazing."

"Isn't it? I have to say it was an unconventional proposal. Lamar rang me last night from Luxembourg and we ended up talking for ages. All the time, I could just tell he had something on his mind. You know me. I kept nagging him about what it was. I just wouldn't back off. In the end I must have worn him down, because he came straight out with it. He just said: 'I love you and I want us to get married.' At that point, I think I screamed. He said, 'Is that a yes?' I said it was most definitely a yes, and then we agreed to pretend he hadn't mentioned the M word. That way he can still take me to dinner when he gets back and go down on one knee."

"Oh, sweetie. I am so happy for both of you." Abby stood up and put her arms round her friend.

"You OK with this?" Soph said. "I've been really nervous about telling you. After Toby and everything, I thought you might be a bit…you know…"

"Bitter, jealous and resentful?"

Soph nodded.

Abby returned to her seat. "Look, I'm not going to pretend the Toby thing hasn't been hard. And, yes, part of me wishes you and I were both planning weddings and that we could go shopping for dresses together. How fabulous would that be? But you are my best friend. I love you and I want you to be happy. I couldn't be more delighted that you've found Lamar. He's good-looking, kind, intelligent.

He even has a social conscience. He's perfect for you. I just know the pair of you are going to grow old together."

"Thanks, Abby." Soph reached across the table and took her friend's hand. "That means so much to me."

Abby was smiling. "Good, because I meant every word of it."

"So, Mum and Dad want Lamar to come to dinner on Friday night."

"Fantastic."

"And I thought you and Scozza could come, too. To be quite honest, I'd be happier if you were there. You know how my mum and dad bicker. You and Martin could help keep the atmosphere light." She broke off. It was clear another thought had occurred to her. "Hey, why don't you bring the gorgeous Dan, as well?"

Abby said she was happy to come and was sure Scozza would be, too, but she wasn't sure she felt right inviting Dan. "I haven't known him that long. I'm not sure taking him to meet my best friend and her bickering parents is the best idea. Plus, Friday night is going to be a family occasion. He might feel like a fish out of water."

Soph made the point that Scozza was coming and he wasn't family. Nor had he met her parents before. "And although my parents and I love you to bits, technically you're not family, either. Oh, go on, just ask him. I'm desperate to meet him. If it's a no, I'll understand."

Eventually, after much badgering, Abby gave in and agreed to invite him.

DAN RANG the following evening, just after ten. He was in Devon filming and had only just finished for the day.

"I'm going to be down here all week," he said, "but how about I drive back to London one evening and we go out again?"

Abby said that although she would love to see him, she wouldn't hear of him driving two hundred miles for the sake of one evening. Not that she didn't appreciate the thought. "OK, I'm back Friday," Dan said. "How about dinner?"

"Ah, speaking of Friday . . ." She explained about the engagement dinner. "Soph's dying to meet you, but you really don't have to come. An evening with my best friend's eccentric, elderly parents who are meeting their daughter's fiancé for the first time isn't going to be the most riveting occasion. And Soph's mum and dad are always arguing. You're bound to feel awkward. I'll totally understand if you say no."

"Will there be chopped liver?" he said.

Abby giggled. "Definitely."

"And chicken soup?"

"Yes."

"With matzo balls?"

"Are you kidding? Soph's mum is a great cook. Her chicken soup always includes the fluffiest matzo balls."

"I don't suppose she does stuffed chicken neck?"

"Actually, she does."

"Really?"

"Really."

"OK, count me in. I adore Jewish food. I haven't had homemade chopped liver or stuffed chicken neck since Jonathan Lieberman from school invited me to his house for Friday night dinner."

"But I'm worried you might find the evening a bit too much. You don't know Soph. You don't know her parents. I don't want you feeling uncomfortable."

"Don't worry, I'll be fine. Nearly all my Jewish friends from school had parents who bickered. I used to think it was part of the religion. You know, the eleventh commandment: thou shalt constantly shout and scream in front of thy son's school friends, thereby causing him excruciating embarrassment. Anyway, how could I possibly feel uncomfortable? You'll be there."

SINCE DAN would be battling through the Friday night traffic to get back to London, they had agreed it made little sense for Abby to wait for him to pick her up. They would each make their own way to the Weintraubs' flat in Croydon.

Abby took Martin with her in the van. He was spectacularly bad company, since he spent the entire journey on the phone to Ichiro. Their first date had been a triumph. Martin must have described it to Abby a dozen times, and by now she knew the order of events by heart. First they'd had drinks at the Met Bar. Then they went to eat at Nobu. Martin had the black cod. Ichiro ordered the ceviche. Afterward they shared a chocolate bento box. They had talked nonstop.

Conversationwise, tonight had been the same. Ichiro had phoned Martin on his mobile just as they were leaving the shop. Their dialogue had focused on two subjects: Martin's fight to get custody of Debbie Harry and Ichiro's search for a new job. It seemed that Martin had persuaded Ichiro he couldn't carry on working for an employer who treated him like something the dog had brought in. An hour later their conversation was just about drawing to a reluctant end. "No, you have to hang up first," Martin cooed.

"I can't say good-bye.... No, you ... no, you ... I can't. Oh, please don't make me. OK, how about this—we'll do it together on my count. One ... two ... three ... You still there? Me, too. Look, you have to be the one to hang up.... No, I can't.... See you tomorrow, then." A giggle. "I can't wait, either.... No, I'll miss you the most. You can't possibly miss me as much as I'll miss you. I'll be counting every second—"

"I think we're here," Abby announced.

Martin pressed end and practically fell into a swoon. "I am in love. I am so totally, utterly and completely in love."

If Abby had heard this once in the last few days, she had heard it fifty times.

"That's great, Scozz, and I really am happy for you, but meanwhile, what did you do with the strudel we bought for Soph's mum and dad?"

"He's just so perfect. I mean, he's gorgeous and sexy. He's into the environment. And he's really deep. He bought me this amazing book about angels. He's also into self-improvement. Did I tell you that his aim is to fully integrate his inner and outer life in order to achieve spiritual peace?"

"Yes, I think you may have mentioned it once or twice. Scozz, I don't mean to be rude, but could you possibly break off from your reverie for just one second to consider my inner peace? I gave you the strudel to look after. I queued up in the Jewish baker's for half an hour this afternoon. Please tell me you didn't forget it."

"Strudel? Oh, yeah, it's in the back of the van."

Abby had retrieved the precious strudel and was locking the van when Dan pulled up alongside her. He wound down his window.

"Hey, well done. You made it right on time," she said.

"For once the traffic wasn't too bad. I even had time to pick up a strudel."

Faye Weintraub seemed delighted to receive two three-foot-long apple strudels. "So we'll have one later on with coffee," she said as they stood in the hall, with Sam taking coats, "and then there's one for the freezer."

"Excuse my wife, she thinks of the freezer as another mouth to feed."

"Sam, don't start," Faye said through a rictus smile. "We have company."

"Who's starting? I am merely pointing out—"

"Well, don't."

The Weintraubs—she in navy slacks and a belted stripy cardigan, he in fawn slacks and velour carpet slippers—were in their mid-seventies. As Faye would tell anybody prepared to listen, they had spent twenty years trying for a baby. Then, when they were approaching middle age and had long given up thoughts of becoming parents, along came their miracle baby, their beloved Sophie.

As a child, Abby often used to go round to Soph's for tea after school. There could be no doubt how much Soph's parents adored their daughter. They called her Sophie Sunshine and always greeted her when she came home from school with the kind of embrace most parents reserved for a child who had just returned from fighting in a war zone.

Sam was always fretting about his daughter going out in the cold. Even when she was eighteen, on the pill and sleeping with Josh Abrahams from school, he would beg her to wear a vest.

In the early days, Abby had been frightened by the way Faye and Sam sparred with each other. It was hardly surprising, since her own parents never argued—at least not in front of her. Every so often she was aware of Jean and Hugh conducting a strained, wordless dance around each other, but that was about as far as it went, and it never lasted more than a few hours.

It was years before she realized that Faye and Sam didn't hate each other. According to Soph, they had both come from volatile backgrounds and this was the only way they knew how to communicate—at least with each other. It was different with Soph. They would reprimand her, even ground her from time to time, but Abby never once heard them raise their voices in anger to her. Instead, they sat her down, explained what she had done wrong and why they were punishing her.

Faye and Sam didn't bicker all the time. At mealtimes their sniping gave way to intelligent discussion. Soph—and Abby, if she happened to be visiting—were expected to take part.

Chez Crompton, mealtimes were spent discussing what was—at least to Abby's teenage mind—utter trivia: a loose patio tile that needed repairing, a neighbor's overflowing trash can that was starting to smell, whether the chops they were eating were slightly less fatty than the chops they had eaten last week. Elbows were kept off the table. Abby knew not to speak with her mouth full.

The Weintraubs, on the other hand, debated politics while shoveling food into their mouths. If they kept their elbows off the table it was only because they were busy gesticulating.

Faye and Sam weren't learned people, but they were thoughtful, intelligent souls who took a liberal worldview that the teenage Abby had come across in few adults. She had certainly never encountered it in people as old as the

Weintraubs. Back in the early nineties, before it became a respectable view, Sam was saying that all drugs should be legalized. "That would get rid of the dealers and stop people stealing to feed their habit."

They frequently discussed God. The Weintraubs believed in a divine creator; Soph didn't. At fifteen she had declared herself to be a Jewish atheist Darwinist. (Nearly two decades later, she hadn't shifted from that position.)

"Faith is simply belief without evidence," she would argue. "How can you believe in something for which there is no evidence?"

"But that's the whole point," Sam would reply, waving a fork or soup spoon. "Faith involves the suspension of reason. Wasn't it Martin Luther King who said reason is the enemy of faith?"

"I just don't understand," Soph would come back, red of face by now, "how you can respect Christians—for example—who believe, in the absence of any evidence, that a man was born to a virgin without a biological father being involved or that this same fatherless man came alive after being dead and buried for three days."

Argument would be followed by counterargument. Counterarguments would be examined and rejected and new hypotheses proposed.

It went on like this for hour after hour. By the time Abby got home, her head would be spinning. Usually her mum and dad were to be found in the living room. Hugh would be reading the paper. Jean might be knitting or watching a wildlife documentary on BBC2 with the volume turned down, so as not to disturb Hugh. Abby would snuggle up next to her mum on the sofa, close her eyes and listen to the soft, steady tick of the grandfather clock in the hall.

BY NOW Soph had appeared, looking gorgeous in a burgundy wrap dress. She gave her parents a good-natured ticking-off for leaving everybody standing in the hall for so long. Her eyes immediately alighted on Dan.

"So, you must be Dan," she gushed, taking his hand and holding on to it for fractionally too long. "Abby's been telling me all about your film." She turned to Abby. "God, he really is gorgeous," she said in an excited stage whisper.

"Soph, how much have you had to drink?"

"Nothing... OK, maybe a couple of thimbles of Mum and Dad's sweet sherry to calm my nerves."

Faye led everybody into the living room. Lamar, who had been sitting on the sofa, stood up as everybody came in.

Abby was suddenly aware of music playing softly in the background. *What we need is a great big melting pot...*"

"Oh, my God," Abby whispered to Soph. "Is that..."

"...and turn out coffee-colored people by the score."

"'Melting Pot'?" Soph said. "Yep. It's Dad's attempt to put Lamar at ease. Before that he was playing 'Israelites.'"

The two women looked at Lamar, who was fiddling with his gold signet ring and giving the impression of being considerably less than at ease.

Soph started making the necessary introductions while Sam brought round tiny glasses of sweet sherry on a silver gallery tray. Faye directed people to the nibbles on the coffee table and then disappeared into the kitchen to check on dinner.

"Careful as you sit down, everybody," Sam said. "My wife Windexed the seat covers in your honor, so they might be a bit slippery." He put the empty tray down on the sideboard. "Anyway, as I was saying to Lamar before you all arrived, there have been several prominent black Jews—especially in the U.S. I looked them up on Wikipedia." He produced a scrap of paper and began reading. "There are the obvious ones like Sammy Davis, Jr. and Whoopi Goldberg. Then there's that American musician Lenny Kravitz and some basketball player I've never heard of.... What's his name? I can't read my writing..." He was squinting at the paper.

"Don't worry, Mr. Weintraub," Lamar said. "It really doesn't matter."

"Yes, it does." Sam was squinting at the piece of paper. "This is going to bother me all evening." He excused himself and went in search of his reading glasses.

With Sam and his list of prominent black Jews temporarily out of the way, the atmosphere eased and everybody started to relax. Dan got chatting to Lamar about child malnutrition.

"Jordan Farmar," Sam exclaimed, walking back into the room.

"Dad, what are you on about?"

"The name I couldn't read. The black Jewish basketball player—his name is Jordan Farmar. Born November thirtieth, 1986. He plays for the Los Angeles Lakers—"

Suddenly Faye bustled in. "Right, why don't we all sit down?" With that she placed a large oval serving plate in the middle of the table and began directing people to their places.

"Chopped liver OK for everybody?" she asked once everybody had sat down.

"Omigod," Soph cried. She had noticed, as had everybody else, that the chopped liver was fashioned into the shape of a man. Sticking out of one hand was a tiny black, green and yellow ANC flag. "Mum, what have you done?"

"What do you mean what have I done? It's Nelson Mandela."

"You have carved the chopped liver into the shape of Nelson Mandela?"

"Yes, your father and I thought it would make Lamar feel at home."

"But how could you possibly think something like this—" Soph spluttered.

Before she had a chance to finish, Lamar took her hand and gently shushed her. "Faye, I think it's a wonderful touch," he said, biting his lip to stifle his laughter. He reached across, picked up the plate and helped himself to a portion of Nelson Mandela's livery head. He passed the plate to Martin, who had turned as pale as veal. "Actually, I'm not very keen on offal. If you don't mind, I think I'll wait for the soup."

Faye told him not to worry and that she appreciated that liver was an acquired taste. "To make up for it, I'll make sure you get the boiled chicken foot in your soup. You'll like that."

Martin looked like he might pass out.

"So, Mrs. Weintraub," Dan said, relieving Martin of the plate of liver, "how long have you and Mr. Weintraub been married?"

"Oh, only since 1485."

Sam opened his mouth to offer a caustic response, but Soph glared at him as if to say, "Don't even try."

"Wow, this chopped liver is gorgeous," Dan persevered. "Tell me, Mrs. Weintraub, do you make it with fried onions or raw?"

"Oh, fried. You don't get the same flavor with raw. The secret is to fry them very slowly, so that they caramelize. Then you add the liver. If you like I can give you my recipe."

Dan said he would love to have the recipe.

"So," she said, "why don't you tell us about this film you're making."

"Well, it's a romantic comedy—"

"Of course, it was my wife's idea to get married on April twentieth," Sam said, apparently unaware that Dan was in mid-sentence. "Turns out it was Hitler's birthday."

Nobody seemed to know whether to laugh or offer condolences.

"Sam got me a mood ring," Faye said. "When I'm in a bad mood it leaves a big red mark on his head." She let out a loud cackle. "So, Martin, Sophie tells me you're gay. Mazel tov."

"Omigod! Mum! Please."

"What? I shouldn't congratulate the man on his sexuality?"

"No. Would you sit eating chopped liver and congratulate a person for being straight?"

"But being straight is nothing to be proud of. Martin will have struggled to come out. He will have fought hostility and prejudice. The fact that he has survived is something to be celebrated."

"I agree," Sam said.

"See, for once in his life, even your father agrees with me. That's something else we should be celebrating."

"But you've embarrassed Martin," Soph said. "Can't you see that?"

"Of course she hasn't," Martin broke in. "Your mum was trying to be kind, and you've no idea how much I appreciate that. . . . Thanks, Mrs. W."

"My pleasure, darling."

And to show her precisely how much he appreciated her gesture, Martin chewed and sucked on his boiled chicken foot without so much as a murmur.

By the time everyone had a couple of glasses of wine in them, the atmosphere lightened considerably. So much so that nobody was remotely embarrassed when Sam asked if anyone could explain why blacks had rhythm and Jews didn't. And everybody hooted with laughter when Lamar suggested that during the war black Jews would have been in hiding and picking cotton.

Eventually, Sam stood up and made a speech in which he welcomed Lamar into the family and said how delighted he and Faye were that their little Sophie Sunshine, whose face hadn't changed since she was five, was marrying a Jewish doctor.

While they drank coffee and ate apple strudel, Sam asked if anybody would mind if he put on the nine o'clock news. There were rumors of an imminent cabinet reshuffle, and he was anxious to find out who had been fired. Nobody raised any objections. After five minutes spent looking for the remote and blaming Faye for tidying it away, Sam finally found it under a cushion.

"*. . . And our top story this evening. Two hundred British passengers aboard the Irish cruise liner the* Bantry, *which docked in Buenos Aires a week ago, are refusing to disembark.*"

Sam wasn't concentrating, as this wasn't the item he was interested in. Everybody else was chatting—apart from

Soph, who was on her way to the kitchen to refill the cafetière. "Hey, Abby. Aren't your parents on the *Bantry*? They seem to be staging some kind of protest."

"Omigod," Abby cried. "It's actually happened."

"What has?" Dan said.

Abby quickly explained about her parents' "Antarctic expedition" that had turned into disease-ridden chaos. Soph grabbed the remote and turned up the volume on the TV. By now everybody was glued to the screen. "They've been in Buenos Aires a week?" Abby said. "How come Mum hasn't been in touch?"

"The vacationers, who insisted their three-week Antarctic cruise be cut short, are said to be suffering from severe gastroenteritis. They claim this has been caused by appalling hygiene standards on board and are calling for compensation. The ship's owners, McGinty Maritime, are refusing to accept liability and say there will be no payouts. A short while ago I spoke to the company's lawyer in Dublin . . ."

An interview followed, in which a haughty woman lawyer claimed that the passengers had been infected by a fellow traveler and the outbreak had nothing to do with poor hygiene standards on the ship.

"What a load of old crap," Abby snapped. "My mum was cleaning sewage out of her sink from day one. It's a wonder they haven't all got typhoid."

"Oooh, look," Soph said. "There's your mum."

"Where? Where?"

There must have been over a hundred people gathered on the deck, most of them waving banners with *PEOPLE POWER* or *SHITTERS BUT NOT QUITTERS* written across them in thick, wobbly felt tip.

"What do we want?" Jean was shouting into a megaphone. God knew where she'd gotten it from, Abby wondered—maybe one of the lifeboats.

"Justice," the protesters roared back.

"When do we want it?"

"Now! Now! Now!"

Abby could see her dad standing just behind Jean. His hand was resting on her shoulder in an almost paternal gesture. He looked tired and like he'd lost a bit of weight, but his face was beaming with pride.

"Gimme a J." Jean was punching the air, rousing her troops like some kind of Marxist revolutionary. Abby wouldn't have been a bit surprised to hear her calling for workers of the world to unite and join the armed struggle.

"J!!!"

"Gimme a U."

"U!!!"

"Gimme an S . . ."

"Blimey," Abby mumbled, "My mum's turned into Che Guevara."

"Aren't you proud of her?" Soph said.

Abby sat down on the sofa. By now her mother was leading the protesters in "We Will Overcome." "I have to say, I am rather," she said, grinning.

At that moment Abby's mobile rang.

"Abby it's me, Mum."

"Mum! Why haven't you been in touch? We've just been watching you on the news. You were brilliant. I'm at Soph's. There's a crowd of us here and we all watched it."

"Tell your mum," Faye broke in, "that Sam and Faye Weintraub say good luck and power to the people." She raised her arm and made a fist.

Abby relayed the message. "So, Mum, are you sure you're all right?"

"Darling, do stop fussing. Dad and I have been a bit poorly. That's why we've been out of touch. A few people who were really ill have been taken to the hospital, but the rest of us are on the mend. We've all still got the trots, but it's nothing like it was."

"You sure?"

"Positive. And fresh food and water have been smuggled on board by some of the locals who saw us on the TV. To tell you the truth, your father and I are really rather enjoying ourselves. Having a cause at our age is so invigorating. I'd go so far as to say we're having the time of our lives."

SOPH EVENTUALLY made it to the kitchen, where she made a fresh pot of coffee and cut up more strudel. By the time she returned to the living room, the TV had been switched off and everybody was wondering how long the protest would be allowed to go on before the police got involved. Abby said she had visions of armed Argentinian police raiding the ship, dragging off all the passengers and throwing them into some hellhole of a prison to await trial.

"For what?" Soph said, pouring coffee. "All they've done is refuse to get off the ship. If you ask me, the worst that can happen is that they get thrown out of the country."

Everybody else agreed. Abby calmed down, but at the back of her mind she still had images of poor Jean and Hugh rotting in an Argentinian jail for the next twenty years.

By ten o'clock Sam and Faye were beginning to flag. Despite the coffee, Sam had fallen asleep—mouth open—

in one of the armchairs, and Faye was making noises about having to be up early for her aqua aerobics class.

"You know what," Abby said to Dan, "it's getting late. I think it's time we let these people get to bed." She turned to Faye and thanked her for a wonderful evening.

Sam stirred himself to say his good-byes—helped along by a sharp dig in the ribs from Faye. After her parents had taken their leave, Soph hugged Abby and Martin and told them how grateful she was that they had come and how she couldn't have gotten through the evening without them. "And, Dan, it's been great meeting you. Sorry if my mum and dad were a bit much."

Dan reassured her that Faye and Sam were delightful and that he had a great evening.

"Gorgeous and a diplomat," Soph giggled to Abby.

As Abby and Dan stood on the pavement waiting for Martin, who'd run back up to the flat to get his scarf, Dan suggested that, since it wasn't late, she come back to his place to watch a movie. Abby said she would love to but couldn't since she had to give Martin a lift home.

"Why not let Martin take the van?"

"Then how would I get home?"

"I'll give you a lift."

"But I can't expect you to come out again late at night when you've just driven all the way from Devon."

"I wasn't thinking of driving out again—at least not tonight."

"Right. I suppose I could always get a cab."

"Abby, I don't want you to get a cab, a bus, a train, a tram or even a rickshaw."

She felt herself blush. "You don't?"

He was shaking his head and smiling.

"So, you're saying that I could...I mean, you're suggesting that I...stay over?"

"Yes. But I'm aware that we agreed no pressure, so it's entirely up to you."

She thought about it for all of half a second. "I'd love to," she said.

Chapter 12

"YOU'RE QUIET ALL OF a sudden," Dan said to Abby as he started the car engine. "Look, I really understand if coming back to my place feels like too much, too soon."

She smiled. "It's not that."

"What, then?"

"I keep thinking about my parents—Mum in particular. This *Bantry* thing is just so out of character. The nearest my mother ever got to making a public protest was when the local Women's Institute held a home-baking competition and Mum pointed out to the judges that somebody had entered a bought cake. She was rather proud of herself, until my aunty Gwen convinced her that whistle-blowers always come to a sticky end. For the next six months she was sure that Bought-Cake Woman was out to get her. She couldn't walk down the high street without looking over her shoulder every five minutes."

"What are you saying? That she's never been much of a role model?"

"No. She's been a great role model. All the time I was growing up, she was there. She was kind, loving, patient, a great listener. As a child I felt so safe and loved. I think the problem is that she feels she's been a poor role model because she stayed at home to raise me instead of having a career. I just hope a bit of her isn't waging this war on the *Bantry* to impress me."

"Well, maybe that's part of it, but I'd say this incident on the ship has stirred up an energy and passion in your mum that may have lain dormant for years."

"You're right. It was my first thought when this whole thing started. And in many ways, seeing this other side of her is brilliant, but at the same time the whole thing feels weird. It's like I hardly know her—or my dad, come to that." She opened the window a crack to let in some air. "I wish they weren't so far away."

Dan rested a reassuring hand on her knee. "I'm sure they'll be fine," he said.

"Yeah, you're right. I've got to stop letting my imagination run away with me." She managed a smile. "So, what film are we going to watch?"

"How about *It's a Wonderful Life*?"

"Great. It had occurred to me that you were going to force me to sit through *The Godfather*. I'm not sure I could take three hours of mumbling."

"Here we go again," he said, shaking his head in mock despair. "Look, there's absolutely no mumbling in *The Godfather*."

"Of course there is. It's all mumbling."

"No, it isn't."

"Is."

"Isn't."

"Is."

"OK, now we absolutely have to watch it," he said. "Just so that I can prove to you I'm right."

"You're on."

FROM THE outside, Dan's flat was pretty much as she'd imagined: a basement in a white stucco house on one of Camden Town's slightly less desirable streets. Inside, it smelled of fresh paint and new carpet. "Only been here a couple of months," he explained. "Did all the decorating myself."

She took in the white walls and light gray carpet, which gave the place a cool, contemporary feel.

"Of course, the furniture is all Ikea. Keep it simple, I thought. Can't go wrong with black ash."

She smiled to herself. With the exception of Martin and Toby—whose tastes in interior design were much more expensive and in Toby's case distinctly "Byronic Man"— every man she knew decorated by going to Ikea with a rented van and coming home with umpteen flat packs of black ash furniture. This they considered to be suitably un-fussy and masculine. Dan was clearly of the same mind. The coffee table, dining table, desk and bookshelves were all black ash.

The man theme didn't stop there. Surfaces were littered with old newspapers, car magazines and books. Then there were boy toys all over the place: an iPhone here, a Black-Berry there, a digital camera half buried behind a sofa cushion.

"Oh, this is great," she said. Even though the place wasn't to her taste, she really did love it. Toby's flat had been full of Persian rugs, heavy satin drapes, fainting couches and spectacularly expensive "objets," which looked like they had been arranged with the aid of a T square. It had been stylish to the point of intimidation. By contrast, Dan's place was so refreshingly blokey.

He took a packet of matches out of a *Santos for President* coffee mug that was sitting on the desk and knelt down in front of the pretty marble fireplace. She noticed that a fire had already been laid. He struck a match and waved the flame over a waxy fire-lighter cube, which lit up in an instant. Moments later the paper and wood began to spit and crackle.

Once the fire got going, he made his way to the bookcase. Three shelves were packed with DVDs. His fingers began sliding over the top row. When he couldn't find *The Godfather*, they moved down to the middle shelf. Finally he turned to face her. "Found it," he declared, waving the box in the air.

He put the DVD into the machine and disappeared into the kitchen. He came back with a bottle of wine and two glasses.

"OK, for ten bonus points," he said, sitting down next to her on the black leather sofa, "do you know what word is never mentioned in this film?"

"Easy. Mafia."

"Is the correct answer! Blimey, for somebody who hates this film, you're not bad on the related trivia."

She said she remembered it only because the week before it had been a question on *Who Wants to be a Millionaire?*

He poured them each a glass of rioja. Finally the titles ended and the action began. A few minutes went by. They sat sipping their wine in silence.

"Hear OK?" he asked her eventually. "No mumbling yet?"

"Not as such. I'm already bored, though."

"Can I remind you that boredom is not the point at issue. We are here to consider whether or not mumbling occurs."

"Ooh, sorry, Mr. Prosecuting Attorney, sir," she said, giving him a gentle poke in the ribs. "I stand corrected."

Another five minutes passed. In the background the fire spat and hissed.

"Anybody mumbled yet?" he asked.

"It's all mumbling."

"What do you mean? Who can't you hear? What can't you understand?"

"Marlon Brando sounds like he's got a mouthful of marbles."

"Yes, but can you hear him? Can you make out what he's saying?"

"I suppose...but that's not what I meant by mumbling."

"It isn't? You don't define mumbling as quiet, indistinct speech?"

"Usually, yes. But to me, a mumbling film is one where the baddies sit around smoking cigars, drinking and scheming in the semidarkness and you have no idea what they're talking about."

"So, you're having trouble following the plot?"

"You mean there's an actual plot?" she teased.

"Your sarcasm displeases me," he said, doing a perfect impression of Marlon Brando.

She started to giggle. "I love it when you make me laugh."

"So, you're laughing at me?" he said, still very much in character. "This offends me and it offends my family. I may have to teach you a lesson."

"Really?"

"I am afraid so." He put his wineglass down on the coffee table. Then he took hers and put it down, too.

The next thing she knew, he was kissing her.

"You know, I'm a very slow learner," she said as they finally pulled away. "You might have to try that again."

He held her face in his hands, drew her gently toward him. This time their kissing was harder, more urgent. Their mouths opened and his tongue found hers. At one point his hand went to her breast. She heard herself let out a soft murmur of desire, felt the moisture between her legs. Somewhere, far away, guests at the Corleone wedding were singing in Italian.

They carried on kissing intermittently as he undid the buttons on her blouse and eased it out of the waistband of her skirt. Finally his lips moved to the tops of her breasts. She placed her hand on his crotch and pressed. He was hard against her hand.

Still kissing, they moved onto the rug in front of the fire. As they went, Dan somehow managed to reach out and switch off the film. She trembled as his hand slid over her thigh and up toward her panties. "Open your legs," he whispered. Her eyes were closed now and her breathing had become heavy. Helpless, she let her knees fall open. As he pulled the crotch of her panties to one side, she let out a soft whimper. His fingers traced the edges of her labia. Every so often he would plant a kiss on her breast.

"OK," he said eventually, "let's get these off." She lifted her bottom and he pulled off her panties. She was aware that it was a strange time to start being modest, but her knees were back together again. "Hey, come on, relax. It's OK. Just let go."

Her legs fell open. His fingers were teasing her labia again. Then, suddenly, he parted her. She gasped. His touch was frustratingly light. For the time being, he seemed to be avoiding her swollen, throbbing clitoris. By now she was practically weeping with frustration. "Touch me. Please."

"Ssh. What's your hurry?" The gentle grazing continued. When he did finally touch her, she let out a low, almost animal sound that she hardly recognized. He moved over her clitoris in a firm, circular motion. Once or twice he stopped and thrust two or maybe three fingers inside her. Each time he did this, it took her breath away and she cried out in startled pleasure.

She reached for his fly, yanked it down in one smooth movement. She caressed the tip of his penis, which had emerged from his underpants. A pearl of semen had formed there. She rubbed it gently with her finger. A few moments later he had taken off his jeans. His thick, hard penis sprang from his boxers.

He flipped her over onto her stomach. She felt his penis brush her buttocks. Soon she was on her knees, a cushion supporting her stomach.

"Oh, God, that's amazing," she whispered as he began spreading her moisture over her buttocks. Then he reached underneath her and did the same to her vulva. His strokes were firmer now. He was working on her, clearly determined to make her come. Just as she felt she might be about to, he pushed hard into her vagina. Again he had taken her by surprise, and she let out a whimper. His thrusts were fast and deep, almost painful, but he never stopped the circular motions over her clitoris. Her breathing was slower and she felt herself drifting and floating. She was aware of nothing apart from the sensation between her legs. Finally his thrusts became faster, his grip on her shoulders tightened. Then the quivering inside her began and started to grow stronger.

Afterward, as they lay in each other's arms, watching the flames dance in the fire, she felt her eyes filling with tears.

"Hey, what's up?" Dan said, wiping her cheek. "Did I do something wrong?"

"No. You did absolutely nothing wrong. That was fantastic." She began staring up at the ceiling. "It's just that, all the time I was with Toby, I forgot what it feels like to really want somebody..."

"...and have them really want you back?"

She turned her face toward him and nodded.

"I know." He kissed her wet cheek.

They made love twice more in front of the fire before they went to bed—to sleep. They spent the night nestled like spoons in Dan's black ash bed.

SHE GOT up just after seven, put the kettle on for coffee and had a shower. When she came back to the bedroom, Dan was lying on his back, still fast asleep. The duvet was down by his waist, exposing his chest and stomach. In the daylight, she could see that his torso was firm and toned—he clearly worked out. He moved in his sleep. The duvet slipped to reveal the line of dark hair that led down from his navel. She wanted him all over again. She let her towel drop. Then she burrowed under the duvet and ran her tongue along the length of his penis. Still half asleep, he let out a murmur of pleasure. She did it again. His penis began to harden.

"Umm, Abby, that you?"

She poked her head up from under the cover. "Of course it's me. Who else were you expecting?"

"Just checking I wasn't dreaming," he said, still groggy with sleep. "I thought I was doing something kinky with a wet dog."

She told him she'd just had a shower and her hair was wet.

"In that case feel free to carry on." She did, until his erection was quite rigid.

"Come up here," he said eventually.

As she emerged from under the duvet, he rolled on top of her and kissed her. His body smelled deliciously of sweat and sleep. Suddenly his fingers were deep inside her, pushing and probing. After a little while, he maneuvered himself off the bed. Standing on the floor, he pulled her toward him. He bent her legs and gently forced them back onto her chest. The next thing she knew his tongue was all over her vulva, flicking, stroking, caressing. She was letting out tiny moans of delight. Then his fingers were inside her again. When he stopped, he began tantalizing her with his tongue all over again. By now she wanted to feel his penis inside her. She took hold of it and guided it toward her vagina. He pushed himself inside her. "Harder," she pleaded. "Harder." He obliged, all the time flicking her clitoris with his fingers. She could feel he was about to come, but he withdrew and gently but thoroughly worked on her until he was sure she was ready. He entered her again and they came together.

"I never ever thought that was possible," she said, as

they lay breathless and sweaty in each other's arms. "I always thought it was some fantasy cooked up by Hollywood."

"Just takes supreme skill." He grinned.

She bashed him playfully on the arm and he kissed her.

WHILE ABBY got dressed, Dan went into the kitchen to finish making coffee. "Don't suppose you own a hair dryer?" she called out.

"Bedside cabinet. Second drawer down."

There were two bedside cabinets. The hair dryer turned out to be in the one on his side. She was closing the drawer when a magazine that had been lying on top of the cabinet slipped to the floor. She picked it up. It was called *Counter Intelligence* and appeared to be the S&M in-house magazine. She found herself flicking through the pages, her eyes coming to rest on photographs of new staff members, retirees receiving giant floral tributes, or grinning employees-of-the-month popping champagne corks.

"Coffee," Dan announced, coming into the bedroom, carrying two steaming mugs and wearing nothing but his boxers. "Good, you found the hair dryer. Hope it still works. Haven't used it since I had long hair. That has to be ten years ago."

"Bet you looked gorgeous with long hair," she said, taking a mug of coffee from him.

"I thought so, but my girlfriend at the time kept telling me I looked like Celine Dion." He paused. "Maybe I should test out the dryer before you use it."

"Oh, I'm sure it'll be fine."

"Probably, but you never know." He picked up the dryer and pushed the plug into the wall socket.

"So," she said, "how come you get the S&M staff mag?"

"Sorry?" He couldn't hear her because he'd just switched on the hair dryer, which was now making a tremendous and distinctly unhealthy racket.

"I said—"

Just then there was a blue flash and a bang, followed by a *phut*. The hair dryer had stopped blasting out air.

"Well," Dan began, "if you want my considered diagnosis, I'd say it's knackered."

"I'm inclined to agree," Abby giggled. She told him not to worry. She had a scrunchy in her bag. She would pull her hair back. As she went rummaging for the scrunchy, she forgot all about the S&M magazine.

Chapter 13

DAN INSISTED ON GIVING her a lift to work.

"Bet you wish you hadn't now," she said, looking at her watch. In the last ten minutes, they had moved no more than a few yards. There was construction on Camden Road, and the traffic was down to a crawl. Abby rang Martin to tell him she was going to be late for work. He said not to panic and that he'd already opened up. "By the way," he purred, "I can't wait to hear how last night went. Was it totally fabulous?"

"OK, Scozz, if you could make a start on those orders, that would be great."

"Oops. Silly me. Dan's there and you can't speak—right?"

"Pretty much."

"OK, see you in a bit."

For the next hour, the traffic inched through North London. Abby was anxious for news from Buenos Aires, so they kept the radio on. There was nothing other than the briefest of reports saying that the protest was continuing. It was past eleven by the time Abby and Dan reached Upper

Street. After ten minutes spent driving around looking for a parking space, Dan finally got lucky and found a spot a few doors down from Fabulous Flowers. As they got out of the car, Abby saw a figure she recognized coming out of the shop. It belonged to Christian. She felt herself flush with anger.

"See that bloke over there in the green vest?" she said to Dan. "It's Christian. Bet you anything he's been upsetting Scozza again. You know, for two cents, I'd get hold of him and—"

"If you like, I could set him straight, tell him a few home truths."

Abby's eyes remained fixed on Christian, who was walking in their direction but appeared not to have seen them.

"Thanks, but this isn't your fight. I'm not sure Scozza would appreciate it."

"But it's not just about Scozza. Christian has hurt and bullied you, too. He also stole your boyfriend."

"I know, but I don't want to make a scene. I think the best thing would be to ignore him."

"I could try out my fencing moves on him." Dan smiled, assuming the pose of a musketeer about to skewer one of Cardinal Richelieu's dastardly scoundrels. "*En garde*, Christian, you worm." With that, he played air sword for a few moments, parrying and counterparrying before finally lunging at a lamppost, which was closer than he thought, and bashing his hand. He let out a yelp and began rubbing his knuckles.

"See," Abby giggled. "You're nothing without Aramis and d'Artagnan."

She watched Christian pass them, his eyes self-consciously focused on the pavement. It was clear to her that he had finally noticed them but was too embarrassed to make eye contact. It was then that she realized she couldn't let him go by without a confrontation. Before she knew what she was doing, she was striding out to catch up with Christian. She overtook him, positioned herself in front of him and blocked his path. "Look, Christian, if you've been to the shop and upset Martin again—"

"Let me pass," he said. It had occurred to her that, since he'd stolen Toby from her, he might have the grace to be just a little shamefaced, but Christian appeared as arrogant and haughty as ever.

"Just leave Martin alone, that's all. Or I'll—"

"Or you'll what?"

She glared at him. "You'll see."

"You seem to forget that I am in a relationship with an exceedingly high-powered lawyer. If I were you, I'd think twice before I started threatening people."

"So, how are you and Toby?" The question came out with a curled-lip sneer that was so unlike her.

"My relationship with Toby is none of your business. Get out of my way."

By now Dan was at her side. "He's right. Come on, let's go."

Christian looked Dan up and down in that snooty way of his. Then he turned back to Abby. "I'd take your friend's advice if I were you."

Dan took Abby's arm and steered her away. He had been steering her for a few seconds when he suddenly let go. "Shit. Look at my car. I'm getting a ticket."

"Go, go," Abby cried. "Sort it out. I've said all I'm going to say to Christian. I'll meet you back at the shop."

Dan started running to his car and Abby headed toward Fabulous Flowers.

"Oh, by the way," Christian called after her. "I think you should know that I am appealing the council's decision allowing you to continue with your pavement displays."

"Right! That's it! I've had it." Flushed, Abby ran back over to Christian. "Why are you doing this?"

"Doing what?"

"Constantly persecuting me. What have I ever done to you?"

Christian wasn't about to be drawn into an argument, and he attempted to walk away. She grabbed his shirtsleeve. A few passersby noticed and slowed down to take in the action.

"Take your hands off me," he snarled. Her hand remained attached to his sleeve.

"I said, take your hands off me." She did as he instructed, not least of all because more people were staring now.

"Do you know what, Christian? You are a nasty, spiteful, vindictive, jealous bully. God only knows what Toby sees in you."

"More than he saw in you, if I'm not mistaken."

"Only because he's gay! I mean it, Christian, if you don't stop harassing me, I will take action."

Christian had opened his mouth to reply when Toby appeared, a bulging Sainsbury's carrier bag in each hand. "Would the pair of you mind telling me what on earth's going on?" he barked, placing the carriers on the pavement. "You may not be aware, but you are causing a public spectacle."

Christian looked down at the ground. Now that Toby had turned up, he appeared—for the moment, at least—embarrassed.

Toby turned to Abby. "What's all this about?"

Abby put her hands on her hips. "Blimey, is that the greeting I get? What about 'Hi, Abby, how are you? Long time no see. How's life since I left you for another man?'"

"God, Abby, please don't start."

"I'm not starting. I'm just making a point, that's all."

He smiled. "On your high horse as ever, I see." His words weren't without affection. "So, how are you?"

"Fine, thanks. You?"

"Fine, too."

"Good."

"Bloody hell," Christian butted in. "Now that we've established that the two of you are fine, can we please go?"

"No, you most definitely can't," Abby cried. "Not until you promise to stop threatening Martin and me."

Toby turned on Christian. "Christ. Don't tell me you have been in the shop terrorizing Martin again. You told me you were going to the drugstore for shaving cream."

Christian ignored Toby and continued to glare at Abby. "I am threatening you and Martin? If anybody is being threatened, it's me. Toby, can't you see that this woman is mad?"

"Don't be ridiculous. Abby is not mad. The only mad person around here is you."

Christian blushed. Abby couldn't believe he was taking this admonishment from Toby without fighting back. When Toby suddenly remembered he'd forgotten to buy bok choy, he dispatched Christian back to the supermarket to fetch it. The man obeyed without so much as a murmur.

Abby was astonished. "My God, he's like a pussycat around you," Abby said. "Do you have some kind of magical hold over him?"

Toby shrugged. "When Christian detects even the faintest fear in people, he's in there like a Rottweiler. But he doesn't scare me. Never has. I think it's because I'm one of the few people who understand how vulnerable he is."

"Oh, please. Christian is about as vulnerable as Goebbels."

"Abby, he had a lousy childhood."

"Yeah, yeah, I know. Scozza told me—his mother died and his dad was a drunk."

"Right, and my father was a drunk, too, if you remember. I can sympathize with many of Christian's issues."

Abby was in no mood to engage in a sympathetic analysis of Christian's psyche. She decided to change the subject. "So, how's your mother?"

"Ah—well, she still scares the pants off me, if that's what you mean, but I've been getting some therapy. My shrink pretends to be my mother and I have to shout at her and tell her how bullying and cruel she is. It's going OK, but it'll be ages before I get up the courage to confront Mother for real."

Abby assured him that he would get there.

He didn't seem convinced. "Actually, I haven't seen her in ages. She's involved in some media project. Telly thing, apparently. Won't tell me anything. Deeply hush-hush by all accounts." He paused. "Anyway, I'd better go and catch up with Christian. Great to see you, Abby."

"Toby," she said. "Before you go—I've started seeing somebody."

"Wow, that's great news."

"That's him over there." She nodded toward Dan, who

was remonstrating with a traffic warden. "It's Dan—you know, the film director I got stranded with in the elevator."

Toby made no attempt to look in Dan's direction. Instead, he gave a thoughtful nod. "From the way you talked about him, it did occur to me that the two of you had a connection. I'm pleased for you, Abby. I really am."

He started to move off. Then he stopped. "I want you to know," he began, his voice soft and hesitant, "that you are a wonderful person and that I really did have feelings for you. I did love you. If I wasn't gay, you would have..."

"...been the one?" She was grinning now.

"No question." He took Abby's hand and squeezed it. "I just want to say again how sorry I am for what I put you through."

"I know you are. And hearing it really helps."

"I'm glad."

Just then Christian reappeared, carrying a bag of bok choy. "My God, the madwoman's still here."

"Come on, calm down," Toby said firmly, taking Christian's arm.

"I will not calm down," Christian hissed.

"Yes, you bloody will. Now come on."

Christian allowed himself to be led down the street. "But the woman is mad. She's ill. You know that as well as I do."

"I'm not the one who's mad," Abby cried, getting angry again. "It's you. You're round the bloody bend. You need help—"

By now Dan had returned. "C'mon," he said, endeavoring to calm her down. "Let Christian go. You've made your point." He paused. "So that's Toby. Good-looking bloke."

Abby blinked. "Omigod, you're jealous! You're jealous of a gay man."

"Abby, how can I possibly be jealous of a man who by virtue of his genetic makeup has no romantic interest in you?"

She thought for a moment and said she didn't know, but jealousy often defied logic.

"Well, not in my case it doesn't."

Toby continued to drag Christian down the street. Judging that they were still within earshot, Abby couldn't resist calling out to Christian one last time. "For your information, my boyfriend Dan here fences. For England. If you come near me or Martin again, I'll set him on you. He has some brilliant moves. You should see him! He can parry... and thrust... and leap from one chandelier to the next. Just you wait."

Abby had succeeded in causing another scene, and passersby were giggling and smirking. Dan took hold of Abby's arm again and practically pulled her toward the shop. She knew he was going to be furious with her for claiming he was some kind of fencing master, but she'd gotten so worked up that she hadn't been able to stop herself. She waited for him to tell her off, but all he did was grin. "So, I'm officially your boyfriend, then, am I?"

Her hand went to her mouth. "Oh, God. I'm sorry. I shouldn't have said that. It was way too forward."

"Not at all. I couldn't be more pleased. But just so we're absolutely clear—that would appear to make you my girlfriend."

"I guess it does." She smiled.

"And you're sure this is what you want? It's not too soon after Toby?"

She paused and looked directly into Dan's eyes. "Look, maybe you and I getting together so soon after my relationship with Toby is a bit risky, but I can't help what I'm feeling."

"And what are you feeling?"

"That we have a real connection and I want to see where it takes us."

He was beaming. "Me, too."

She planted a kiss on his lips. "Ooh, by the way, what happened with the traffic warden? Please tell me you didn't get a ticket."

"Actually, I didn't. I was parked in a residents' bay, but when I pointed out the commotion going on across the street and that I was with you, he let me off."

"He didn't!"

"He did. Honest."

"Well, that has to be a first...So, you hungry?" She suddenly realized that they hadn't had any food since the night before.

"Starving."

She invited him into the shop and said that after she'd touched base with Martin, she would nip down the road to get coffee and pastries.

AS THEY walked in, Martin was finishing serving a rather greasy, clueless-looking lad wearing a T-shirt bearing the slogan: *I do my own calculus stunts.* Martin was being polite but barely saying a word. His usual energy and sparkle seemed to have vanished.

"I hope your mum enjoys them," he said to the teenager, offering him the weakest of smiles. He handed him a bouquet of blue and white hyacinths.

The boy grunted his thanks and turned to go. Since the shop was so narrow, Dan had to move to one side to let him pass. Abby held the door open for the lad. "See you again," she said with a smile. The boy offered another grunt and stepped onto the pavement. Abby let go of the door and headed toward the counter. "Christian's been in here threatening you again, hasn't he?" she said. "I just had words with him outside."

"He's being so evil and vicious," Martin said, his eyes suddenly glassy with tears. "I'm not sure I can cope anymore." Apparently Christian had found out through mutual friends that Martin was planning to see a lawyer; he'd come charging into the shop, ranting and raving about how he would rather give Debbie Harry away than let Martin share custody.

"I wasn't about to mention that suing him would cost thousands and was out of the question for anybody on an ordinary income. I dunno, maybe I should just give up and let Debbie go."

By now Abby was on the other side of the counter, hugging Martin. "Not on my watch, you don't. You adore that dog. We will sort this thing out. I don't know how exactly, but we will." She opened her bag and took out a tissue, which she handed to Martin. He started dabbing at his eyes.

Dan, who had been hovering uneasily, clearly searching

for something useful to say, suddenly offered to go out and fetch the coffee.

"Sure you don't mind?" Abby said.

"More than happy."

"Come on, Scozz," Abby said after Dan had gone, "it's going to be OK. I promise."

Abby decided that as they were both pretty fired up, she would close the shop for twenty minutes so that they could get their breath back.

They went upstairs to the flat to drink their coffee and eat the pains au chocolat Dan had bought. With some caffeine and sugar inside him, Martin began to cheer up.

"Don't you just love what Abby's done with this space?" he said to Dan. "See how she's used white as her neutral background color and then added in color with her accessories—flowers, fruit, the apple-green sofa and fuchsia cushions. I think it looks fab. Her talents don't end with flowers. She's got a real gift for color and design."

Abby felt herself blush. "Oh, stoppit," she said to Martin.

"No, Scozz is right," Dan said. "The place is stunning. Makes me a bit embarrassed about all my safe black ash."

Martin made a face and turned to Abby. "I'll tell you one thing for certain," he whispered. "This one ain't gay."

"DINNER TONIGHT?" Dan said to Abby as he was leaving.

"That'd be great."

"Pick you up at eight."

Abby and Martin were just about to reopen the shop when Martin's mobile rang. It was Ichiro. "Hi, Ichicoo..."

I'm at work, babe, so I'll need to be quick. What is it?...Of course I miss you....No, I miss you more....I can't wait until tonight, either...."

"Look, Scozz," Abby said, once Martin had ended the call. "You've had a rotten morning. Why don't you take the rest of the day off? Go and spend some time with Ichiro."

Martin seemed horrified by the suggestion. "What? No way. You've had a lousy morning, too, and you pay me to work Saturdays. End of discussion, OK?"

"OK. But I really don't mind you taking some time off."

"Maybe you don't, but I do. Plus, I love working here. This is the first job I've had where I wake up in the morning and can't wait to get to work."

"You've no idea how much I appreciate hearing that," she said. "Your loyalty means so much to me."

She knew now probably wasn't the time to tell him, because she wasn't certain where the business was heading, but she couldn't help herself. "You know, if and when the time comes to expand Fabulous Flowers, I want us to become partners."

Martin looked stunned. "You're kidding."

"Why would I kid you? You are intelligent, keen, energetic, loyal. You know the business inside out. You have a wonderful sense of design and you're a great mate. What more could I want in a business partner?"

"I don't know what to say."

" 'Yes' would be a start."

"That goes without saying. I'd give my right arm for an opportunity like this."

"Brilliant. Let's agree that we'll see how the business pans out over the next few months and take it from there."

He nodded. "Abby?"

"What?"

"Thank you. From the bottom of my heart. I won't let you down."

"I know," she said, and she planted a kiss on his cheek.

"So," he said, once the shock had worn off, "you haven't told me how last night went. What happened to 'I'm not remotely ready to start a new relationship'?"

She shrugged. "I guess I changed my mind."

"Good for you, girlfriend. So, was it fabulous? I mean...did you?"

She put her hands on her hips. "Martin Scoredaisy, if you are standing there hoping for details, you are going to have a long wait."

"But you did do it...right?"

"Yes, we did it. It was bloody fantastic. And we've decided to carry on seeing each other.... That's all you're getting."

"You mean you're officially *stepping out* together?"

Abby smiled at the quaint choice of words. "Yep, we are *stepping out.*"

Martin squealed and flapped his hands in delight. "Right, I have to tell Soph."

"Hey, don't you dare. This is my news. I want to be the one to tell Soph."

"OK, but be quick, 'cause if she phones I won't be able to control myself. I'll blurt. I just know it."

IN FACT, an hour or so later, Soph rang Abby. "Just wanted to say thank you again for being there last night. Honestly, I don't know what I'd have done without you lot. And Dan is gorgeous."

In the end it was Abby who blurted. "We did it."

"Did what?"

"Oh, come on! You know . . . it . . . Sex."

"No!"

"Yes."

"When?"

"Last night, after we left you."

"At his or yours?"

"His."

"So, what's his place like?"

"Nice. Rather a lot of black ash, though. But I can't tell you how much I prefer it to that French salon thing Toby had going on. I always liked his taste in clothes, but his ideas on interior design were way over the top."

"So what does he look like naked, our Dan?"

"*My* Dan looks amazing naked. And before you ask, it was fabulous. The best orgasm I've ever had. Correction— make that orgasms, plural. OK, no more questions. You've got plenty to be getting on with."

Abby looked up to see an elderly, prim-looking woman in a green quilted jacket and silk head scarf. "Omigod," Abby muttered, her face turning crimson. "Speak to you later," she hissed to Soph, before pressing end.

She performed some nervous throat-clearing before asking the woman how she could be of assistance.

"You didn't have to end your conversation on my be-half," the woman said eagerly, eyes lit up. "When you haven't had sex with a man in thirty-seven years, you rather enjoy living vicariously. That's not to say I don't do it, you understand, but it's all so predictable, what with it being just me and Dildo Baggins."

While Abby groped for a suitable response, the woman

looked wistful, as if summoning the exquisite memory of some long-lost lover. She must have spent several seconds staring into the middle distance before finally snapping out of her reverie to inquire about the price of a narcissus-and-hyacinth centerpiece.

Chapter 14

DAN BOOKED A TABLE at a posh French place in Kensington, to celebrate their new status of girlfriend and boyfriend. They ate steak tartare infused with herbs and garlic, followed by moules in butter and more garlic.

"I'm assuming," he said, "that etiquettewise it's permissible to make love if we both smell of garlic."

"Totally." She grinned, reaching out under the table to rub his leg with her foot. "When you've both eaten it, I don't think you smell it. You sort of cancel each other out."

Afterward they went back to her flat and made love until dawn. They carried on so long partly because they couldn't keep their hands off each other and partly because of the game Abby had devised. This involved thinking of a film and guessing how many stars Roger Ebert, the eminent *Chicago Sun-Times* film critic, had given it. Abby would check their estimations on the *Sun-Times* Web site. The one who got closest was rewarded with an orgasm.

With Dan's superior film knowledge, it came as no surprise to Abby that his guesstimates were far more accurate than hers. This meant that orgasmwise she started to lose out. The balance soon turned in her favor, though. It was pretty obvious that Dan was letting her win on purpose. When she challenged him, he denied it categorically, and since having Dan go down on her for twenty minutes at a time was an experience she had no intention of forfeiting, she decided not to press the point.

They woke just after nine, made love again and demolished fried egg sandwiches. What little was left of the morning, they spent rug shopping. Abby had explained how drafty the flat became in winter and that somehow she had never gotten round to buying rugs. "Any reason we shouldn't do it today?" he said.

She shrugged. "None, I guess."

They schlepped from Habitat to Heal's to Conran and back to Habitat, where Abby bought two huge shaggy white rugs for less than three hundred pounds—plus thirty pounds delivery since they wouldn't fit in Dan's car. They had a late lunch at Babushka in Primrose Hill. Abby had a bowl of thick, steaming borscht, and Dan had a chopped-liver bagel, which he said was nice but not as good as Mrs. Weintraub's.

After lunch they strolled along the main drag, stopping to look round the expensive, arty shops.

"I was thinking over lunch," she said, as they browsed in a jewelry shop where all the pieces were made out of fluorescent Perspex, "that you hardly ever mention your parents." She pushed a chunky bubble-gum-pink ring onto her finger and took it off again when she saw the hundred-fifty-pound price tag.

"Not a lot to say," he said. "They're both lovely people. Warm, generous, supportive. I know it sounds boring, but we've always gotten along. I gave them a few hairy moments when I was a teenager, but apart from that..."

"You've never told me what they do."

"Mum's never really worked. She studied art history and then got married."

"Didn't she have to go out to work after your dad died?"

"No. There were various insurances. She was pretty well provided for."

Abby nodded.

"And my stepdad still runs his own business."

"What sort of business?"

"He's in the rag trade."

She looked up at him. "Aha...that makes sense now. God, all the color has drained from your face. You OK?"

He swallowed. "Yes, I'm fine. Bit of indigestion from the chopped liver. You know, it really wasn't that good."

"All I was going to say was, now I understand how you manage to put your own clothes together so effortlessly. Even though you say it bores you, style seems to be in your blood."

He thanked her for the compliment but said style wasn't something he thought about. "Certainly not consciously."

They carried on up the hill, hand in hand, toward the park. At one point Abby stopped to look at the Whistles window.

"Abby."

"Mmm."

"Look, there's something I really ought to tell you."

" 'K." She was only half listening. A black minidress

with short puffed sleeves and a sixties Peter Pan collar had caught her eye. "That is gor-geous. I'd love to try that on."

"You see, the thing is—" Dan went on.

"Mm? . . . ? I wonder if they've got it in my size."

"It's about my dad. There's something I need to tell you. You see, when I said he was in the rag trade—"

"I wonder if it comes in any other colors." She turned to face him. "Sorry, I was being rude. I got a bit carried away. You were talking about your dad."

"What? No. I was just saying that dress is very Twiggy and that you'd be *mad* not to try it on."

"You won't be bored waiting?" She explained how it always took her ages to make up her mind and how there might be other stuff she would want to try on, as well.

"How's about we make a deal?" he said. "I wait while you try on the dress, and afterward I get to go into that camera shop across the street and look at the vintage Leicas."

She said it seemed a fair exchange.

The young assistant, who had a dolphin tattoo on her upper arm and a blue-black Amy Winehouse beehive, found the dress in Abby's size and led her to a cubicle. "Cool," she said, apropos nothing in particular. "Shout if you need another size."

For some reason—probably because people were still in the restaurants, lingering over Sunday lunch—the shop was empty. As Abby got undressed, she heard Dan and the assistant chatting. At one point she asked him to excuse her while she went downstairs to fetch some new items from the stockroom.

Abby was standing in front of the mirror, admiring the

dress. It fit perfectly. All she needed to complete the Swinging London effect were some lace tights and a pair of round-toed granny shoes.

"Wow, that looks amazing," Dan said, pulling back the curtain. "I hope you're going to take it."

"I think I might." She smiled.

"Makes you look dead sexy."

"Really?" she said, turning to look at her profile in the mirror.

"Really."

The next thing she knew, he was running his hand up her thigh. She clamped her hand onto his to stop him. "Dan, for Chrissake, anybody could come in."

"There are no customers, and the clerk has gone to the stockroom."

"But she'll be back any second. What if she comes in to check how I'm getting on?"

"I'm prepared to risk it." He pulled the curtain across. Then he pressed his body against hers so that she was forced back against the cubicle wall.

"We can't," she whispered.

"Of course we can." His hand was moving up her thigh again.

"No, we can't," she giggled. "Now, stoppit."

Suddenly his lips were on hers. After a couple of seconds of futile struggle, she gave in and kissed him back. As his tongue probed hers, she began grappling with the buckle of his jeans belt.

His hand had reached the crotch of her panties. She started letting out little whimpers of delight, which were clearly louder than she thought.

He shushed her gently and began tugging at her panties. She stepped out of them and felt him part her. Her stomach quivered. This time there was no time for teasing. He spread her moisture with a touch that was firm and rhythmic. Sometimes he broke off to push his fingers deep into her. The pleasure was so intense, she felt her legs might buckle. She carried on fumbling with his belt. Finally it was loose. She tugged at his fly buttons and eased his jeans and boxers to his hips. His erection sprang out. She took hold of it and began pumping. This time it was her turn to shush him. He continued to work on her—his fingers going from her clitoris to her vagina and back again.

"I'm going to try it on," a female voice said. "You stay with Daddy...Honey, please don't let him out of the stroller."

Abby stared at Dan, her eyes wide with panic. His hand froze. They were barely breathing as they heard the footsteps get closer. Finally there was the rattle of metal rings on the curtain pole as the woman went into the cubicle opposite theirs.

Abby was about to pull up her panties, but Dan grabbed her arm. "No you don't," he whispered into her ear. There was something daring, almost reckless about this man, and she found it irresistible. The next thing she knew, he was kissing her and she was kissing him back. Ever so gently, he parted her again. She trembled with delight. His fingers found the spot. There was something about the hugely increased danger that was driving her faster toward orgasm. She took hold of Dan's erection and guided it into her. His face looked a question, as if to say: "You sure you're ready?"

She nodded and let out a tiny gasp. He pushed himself inside her. His thrusts were slow and deep.

"Mummy, Mummy," a tiny voice cried out from his stroller, "are you coming?"

"In a minute, sweetie," came the voice from the changing cubicle opposite.

Dan worked on her clitoris, thrust harder and faster. At one point a hanger fell to the floor with a clatter. They were barely aware of it.

"But, Mummy, are you coming yet?" Dan and Abby could hear the child bouncing in his stroller.

"Almost, darling. Won't be long."

Abby could feel the tiny tremors growing inside her.

"What about now. Are you coming now?"

"Aaah!"

"Ssh." Dan placed his hand across Abby's mouth as he pushed inside her one last time. She felt his body tense for a few seconds, then relax.

"Now. Are you coming now?"

Abby was lost in the gigantic, curling waves of her orgasm. Finally she gave a low grunt of delight from behind Dan's hand.

"All done now," the woman called out. Abby and Dan heard her pull back the curtain to her cubicle and walk back into the shop.

The pair dissolved into silent, hysterical laughter. She smoothed the skirt of the dress. He did up his jeans belt. Finally they pulled the curtain aside. Dan stepped into the narrow passageway between the two rows of cubicles. "I love it," he said, referring to the dress in an ostentatiously loud voice, almost inviting the sales assistant to approach and witness the lack of hanky-panky that had gone on. The girl ambled up just as Abby was admiring herself in the communal mirror at the end of the passageway. "Cool. I mean, that is so totally random." Abby couldn't be certain, but she assumed the girl was trying to communicate her liking for the dress. Suddenly the girl's eyes seemed to be focused on the floor. Curious, Abby looked down. It was then that she noticed her ankle and the panties caught round it. Her face probably along with several of her internal organs, turned scarlet. She had forgotten to pull up her knickers. How could she not have pulled up her knickers?

For a moment, the shop assistant looked confused. Her eyes went from Abby to Dan, whose faces were positively engraved with embarrassment. The penny dropped and the girl screwed up her face. "Eeeuuuwww. That is just so gross." With that, she turned and strode back into the shop.

"Come on, let's get out of here," Dan said.

"OK, but I want the dress. I love it." She also felt it would be extremely bad form to leave the shop without paying for a dress in which she had just had sex.

Abby made her way to the till. "Really sorry," she mumbled to the salesgirl. "Don't know what came over us. It was very wrong. I do apologize."

The girl wrinkled her face. "You two are really sad, yeah? I mean, you have to be like easily as old as my mum and dad."

"What?" Abby said, more than a little hurt. She wasn't vain, but this was the first time she had been taken for middle-aged. "I'm thirty-four."

"Yeah, same age as my mum."

"SO SHE wasn't disgusted by us having sex, per se," Abby said to Dan. They were in her kitchen, loading the dishwasher after dinner. "She was disgusted because we were apparently such old farts."

Dan shrugged. "You know what teenagers are like. Everybody over the age of twenty-five is ancient." He asked where she kept the dishwasher tablets. She directed him to the cupboard under the sink. "I'm sorry to eat and run," he said, bending down and rooting around in the cupboard. "I'm going to miss you." He was going back to Devon tonight and wouldn't be back until they started filming in the shop on Wednesday morning.

"I'm going to miss you, too."

Dan was on his feet now, dishwasher tablet in hand. She took it from him, placed it in the dispenser and hit the on switch. As the machine began to fill with water, he brought her toward him and kissed her. His kiss was warm and tender and she wanted it to last forever. Afterward, they stood holding each other, her head on his shoulder.

"I'm so glad I found you, Abby Crompton."

She looked up at him and smiled. "Ditto."

Before he left he gave her a final rundown on how Wednesday morning was likely to pan out. The crew, plus Lucinda Wallace and her leading man, a relatively unknown named Ed MacIntosh, would be there by seven. All being well, they would be gone by mid-morning. There would be cables running over the pavement and a couple of large vans parked outside on yellow lines, but all the relevant permissions had been granted by the local council, so Christian wasn't likely to bother them.

"That's OK. Scozz and I can open up an hour later and stay open another hour at the end of the day. Doesn't make much difference, there's plenty of trade well into the evening."

She walked downstairs with him, into the shop. "Right, then," she said, as they reached the front door. "See you Wednesday." They kissed again.

"See you Wednesday." He smiled, and she opened the door for him. "By the way, Lucinda's great and pretty unstarry as they go, but I should warn you that she does have this tendency to think of herself as the fairy on top of her own Christmas tree."

"I have a couple of rich women clients like that," Abby said. "I'm used to it. Don't worry. I'm sure we'll all get along."

She watched him walk the few paces to his car. As he climbed in, he turned to wave. A few moments later the engine started. It was several seconds before a gap formed in the traffic and he was able to pull away. She stood waving in the doorway as the car's taillights merged into all the others and disappeared.

Chapter 15

AT HALF PAST FIVE on Wednesday morning, Abby's phone rang.

"Hello, darling. It's me, Mum. Are you watching the news?"

Abby rubbed the sleep from her eyes and attempted to focus on the face of her alarm clock. "Mum, it's practically the middle of the night. Why would I be watching the news?"

"It's over! We won!" Jean was practically squealing with excitement. "The owners of the *Bantry* have caved in. They've agreed to pay all the passengers compensation. The publicity has been awful for them, and I think they just wanted to put an end to it."

Abby sat up in bed. "Oh, my God! Mum, that's fantastic news. I am so proud of you. Dad must be, too." She could hear a kerfuffle in the background as Hugh grabbed the phone from Jean.

"What a girl your mother is, eh? She even persuaded the shipping company to put everybody up in a five-star hotel for a few days so that we could recover. The passengers have organized a party in her honor tonight. Your mum is quite the star. I've lost count of how many newspaper and TV interviews she's done. And you'll never guess who she just had on the phone."

Abby could hear Jean begging Hugh not to "spoil it" and saying that she wanted to "be the one to tell Abby." The next moment her mother was back on the line.

"OK, guess who I've just been speaking to."

"Oh, I dunno—the Queen."

"Funny you should say that, because this person is a queen in a manner of speaking."

"How can you be a queen in a manner of speaking?... Oh, hang on, I geddit. It's somebody gay. I dunno—Elton John."

"Why on earth would Elton John phone me?"

"I don't know. You said you'd been talking to somebody who was a sort of queen, and Elton John fits the bill."

"It's not somebody gay. Now be serious. Guess again."

"OK, Nelson Mandela."

"Abby, I said be serious."

"What's not serious about Nelson Mandela?... OK, that bloke you like from *Antiques Roadshow*—the one who wears the stripy blazers."

"Nope. Guess again."

"I can't, Mum. It's half past five in the morning. I give up."

"Opera!"

"Opera? Hang on. I'm confused. What's me guessing who you just spoke to got to do with the opera?"

"No. No. You don't understand. I've just been speaking to Opera."

Abby switched the phone to her other ear. Suddenly what her mother was saying started to make sense. "Mum, are you telling me that *O-prah* Winfrey, the Queen of Talk, just phoned you?"

"Opera, yes. Well, it wasn't her at first. It was one of her researchers. Apparently the *Bantry* story is huge in the States because of all the American passengers on board. They're even calling it the *Mutiny on the Bantry* over there—isn't that clever? Anyway, they want me to go on the show...you know, ordinary housewife takes on corporate giant."

"No! You're kidding."

"I'm not."

"That's amazing. I can't believe it."

"Neither could I. In fact, I still can't. Anyway, the researcher was about to ring off when Opera comes on the line. She said I was an inspiration to ordinary women all over the world. Me? An inspiration? Can you believe it? When I said I was just a housewife from Croydon, she said something so wise. Now, let me get this right...how did it go? Oh, yes—she said that people can't become what they need to be by remaining what they are and that the greatest discovery of all time is that a person can change his future by changing his attitude. Isn't that brilliant?"

Abby's instinct was to say: "She should try telling that to the single mother living in a housing project and working for less than the minimum wage." Instead, because she hadn't the remotest wish to rain on Jean's parade, she agreed that *Opera's* wisdom was indeed brilliant.

"She really is a wonderful woman. She's so positive. Opera says that every day brings a chance for you to draw breath, kick off your shoes and dance."

"Good for Opera. So will you be going on the show?"

"You bet. Opera says: the biggest adventure you can take is to live the life of your dreams."

A COUPLE of hours later, Abby, Soph and Martin were in the shop, drinking tea, waiting for Lucinda Wallace to arrive. Around them, Dan and the film crew were lugging in lights, cameras, cables and huge metal boxes full of electronic equipment. "I just can't get my head round it," Abby was saying to Martin and Soph. "My mother is going on *Oprah*. It's surreal. She'd better bring home a DVD."

Dan, who was keeping half an ear on the conversation while he schlepped around, made the point that the media interest would be just as intense once Jean got home. "Her face is going to be in every newspaper, on every chat show."

"You know, in many ways," Martin mused, "me mam's not unlike Oprah. She's got some wonderful pearls of wisdom. The wisest thing she ever said was, 'Never fry bacon in the nude.' And to this day, whenever I cook a full breakfast, I make sure my bits are covered." He chuckled at his own joke. "She also said that by the time you can make ends meet, they've changed the ends, and that if everything is coming your way, you're in the wrong lane."

With that, he sashayed over to the window. He wanted to be the first to spot Lucinda.

The next second, he was clapping his hands with excitement. "Ooh, she's here, she's here," he squealed. "Quick, come and look." He beckoned Abby and Soph without taking his eyes off the young woman getting out of the black cab.

By now Martin's nose was practically pressed against the window. Suddenly he was oblivious to the noise and chaos going on around him. He paid no heed to the electric cable being laid inches from his feet or to the guy hauling a silver camera case trying to squeeze past him. He ignored the near-collisions, the good-natured banter and occasional effing as the film crew attempted to go about their business in the few square feet that made up Fabulous Flowers.

A real live film star was about to make her entrance. Admittedly, Lucinda Wallace wasn't quite up there with Kate Winslet or Julia Roberts. But having been named Best Newcomer at last year's British Film Awards for her role in *The Forgotten Hills,* she was clearly well on her way. Martin had made no secret of the fact that he was in awe, not only of Lucinda's celebrity but of the illustrious show-business circles in which she moved. These days, Lucinda spent much of her time in L.A. Judging by the photographs of her that appeared regularly in *Hello!,* she hung out with the greats. She regularly air-kissed—and, for all he knew, French-kissed—Hollywood royalty. And he was about to meet her, thereby acquiring his own bit of glamour-by-association. "It reminds me of that song my old gran used to sing," he had said to Abby a few days ago. A far-off, wistful expression on his face, he had picked up a bunch of white roses and begun waltzing round the shop: *"I danced with a man, who danced with a girl, who danced with the Prince of Wales."*

Abby, who until now had been keen to give the impression that she was unfazed by the prospect of a famous movie star in her midst, suddenly found it impossible to contain her curiosity. Even Soph, who could speak with great eloquence on how the deification of celebrities was taking over from religion as the opiate of the people, had set her alarm for six A.M. in order to be at the shop for Ms. Wallace's arrival.

Tripping over themselves with excitement and barely avoiding a collision with a particularly blubbery and irritable lighting man, who had lost a lead, the two women made their way over to the window.

"That's her," Martin pointed, "getting out of the black cab."

"What, no limo?" Abby remarked, taking in the tall blonde woman in jeans and Ugg boots. From a distance, at least, she looked perfectly ordinary.

"She doesn't go in for all that stuff. She—and I'm quoting from *Hello!* here—*famously eschews the trappings of celebrity.*"

"Not sure I'd *eschew* them," Soph said. "I'd love some of her trappings. Not that I don't have trappings of my own. I do. It's just that mine are the wrong kind. I was born with the wrong kind of trappings."

As Lucinda got nearer, Abby's eyes focused on the star's greasy, scraped-back hair. "My guess is she also eschews hair-washing."

Martin shrugged. "Why bother, when there's a hair and makeup artist waiting?" He paused. "You know, that powder-blue coat she's wearing is so perfect for her coloring. Makes her skin look like cream satin."

"Yeah, yeah, and her farts smell of gardenias," Soph said, clearly deciding it was time Martin stopped stargazing and got a grip.

"I will have you know," Martin said, full of indignation, "that the divine Ms. W does not fart!"

"Course she doesn't," Soph came back. "Famous movie

stars come minus a digestive tract and, like the Queen, they
give birth sidesaddle."

At this point, Dan joined them, looking flustered.
Somehow a camera lens had gotten scratched and he had
been outside on his mobile, frantically trying to organize
the rental of a replacement. This wasn't easy at seven-thirty
in the morning, but he'd finally found a facilities house that
was open and they were biking over a new lens. "Should be
here in twenty minutes or so. Then we can get going." He
looked at his watch. "Where's our star? She should have
been here half an hour ago."

The door opened.

"Dan, I am *so* sorry," Lucinda gushed, with a voice that
you could have poured on a waffle. "Please forgive me.
Hope I haven't held things up too much." Despite the
scraped-back hair, lack of makeup and what turned out to
be rather grubby jeans, Lucinda Wallace had made a movie-
star entrance. This was partly due to her beauty. On close
inspection her eyes were perfect almonds, their soft gray-
blue setting off her pale caramel (albeit unwashed) locks.
Her plump, girlish cheeks had a rose blush that gave her
face an old-fashioned prettiness and innocence. She reminded Abby of a Jane Austen heroine: a Dashwood sister
in Ugg boots. There was also something about the way she
held herself that contributed to her entrance. Her height—
Abby was guessing five nine or ten—gave her considerable
presence. She stood erect and confident, owning the space
around her. Nobody was left in any doubt that the world
was Lucinda's stage and that her place was resolutely in the
center.

She greeted Dan with a double kiss and then proceeded
to remove some lint from his lapel. "That's better," she

soothed, smoothing the fabric. Abby felt a sudden surge of adrenaline and wasn't sure why.

Dan performed the introductions.

"Abby," Lucinda cooed, almond eyes lit up, hand outstretched, "I have heard so much about you from Dan. I just know we're going to be great friends."

"I'm sure we will." Abby smiled.

Lucinda shook hands with Soph next, leaving Martin hovering in the background, still desperate to be introduced. In the end he couldn't wait any longer. "Miss Wallace—"

"Oh, Cinders, please. It's what all my friends call me."

Soph let out a snort at this. Nobody seemed to hear apart from Abby, who gave her friend a discreet but firm dig in the ribs.

"May I say," Martin went on, sounding like Uriah Heep with performance anxiety, "that you are . . . I mean, I am . . . my greatest fan and I've seen all your films. It's such a pleasure for you to be here in our little shop, and if there's anything at all I can do to make your life more comfortable . . . anything. Just name it."

"Think of him as a veritable Buttons," Soph murmured. Abby's elbow made contact with her friend's rib cage a second time.

"Thank you," Lucinda said, removing her coat. She looked round for somewhere to put it. When *Buttons*—who appeared to be lost in a reverie, which may or may not have involved him single-handedly rescuing the Divine Miss W from a raging inferno—failed to take it from her, she handed the coat to Abby.

"So why *are* you late?" Dan asked her good-humoredly.

"Night job ran over. Couldn't get away. There was so much cleaning up to do this morning and I didn't have time to go home, shower and change. Hence the filthy jeans and ghastly hair, I'm afraid."

Dan turned to the others. "Cinders volunteers at a homeless shelter."

"Oh, only a couple of nights a week," she said, with an expression that Abby took for genuine modesty and diffidence but Soph would later describe as "bloomin' self-righteous and smug, if you ask me."

"You must be totally exhausted," Martin said, snapping out of his daydream and hurriedly relieving Abby of Lucinda's coat. "Why don't I get you some coffee?"

"That's very sweet of you," Cinders purred, "but I'll be fine. I find I don't need stimulants. I get such a buzz from charity work. I'll be on a high all day. Helping the underprivileged does that. It seems to boost my energy levels rather than deplete them."

"Funny you should say that," Martin said. "The same thing happens to me."

Soph started laughing. "What, you get a high when you dump your old clothes outside the Oxfam shop?"

"Yes, actually, I do," he said, indignant at her challenge.

"I feel it's so very important to give something back," Lucinda pronounced, turning to Abby. "Do you volunteer, Abby?"

"Er...um, not really," Abby said, suddenly feeling guilty, not to say intimidated by this beautiful, talented, hugely successful woman who also found time to give to others less fortunate. "I'm so busy building up the business, I don't have time."

"Oh, I'm sure you could make time," Cinders said. "Letting go of the need to control, that's the secret. You have to learn to delegate. It is so freeing."

"Really?" Abby replied, her lips forming a thin smile. Her guilt had suddenly turned to irritation. She felt the need to change the subject. "Anybody hungry?"

Soph said thanks but she had to get to work, and Dan said he'd picked up a bacon and egg sandwich on the way over.

"Actually, I missed breakfast," Cinders said. "I could manage *un petit quelque chose.*"

Martin offered to go out and fetch whatever she wanted. Then he remembered he had this morning's orders to deliver. Abby felt she had little choice but to volunteer. "Why don't I go?" she said.

"Oh, darling, would you?" Cinders gushed. "That is so kind. So, what places are good round here?"

Abby explained that there was *Paul,* the excellent French patisserie, as well as a greasy spoon a couple of blocks away or an organic place a bit farther down the road.

"Sweetie, if it wouldn't be too much trouble, do you think you could get the menus from all three and then I can decide?"

"I guess," Abby said, looking out the window and noticing the heavy clouds that had formed.

She'd made it halfway down the road when it started pouring. She cursed herself for not bothering to bring an umbrella. She got menus from Paul and Simply Organic. Not surprisingly, Stefanos at the greasy spoon hooted at her request for a menu. "You want bloodeey menu, you go to bloodeey Savoy."

Abby arrived back at the shop, her hair soaking and plastered to her head. By now, Lucinda's romantic lead, Ed MacIntosh, had arrived and was chatting to one of the film crew. The thirty-something actor had made his name on the stage but as yet was unknown in the film world. With his dark chocolate eyes and magnificent jaw that gave every impression of having been carved to order, he had what Abby's mother would have described as matinee-idol good looks.

"Gay," the voice whispered directly into her ear. It was Martin on his way out, his arms cradling half a dozen bunches of flowers. "He's seeing an interior-designer friend of Ichiro's." Suddenly Martin's eyes were on Abby's hair. "It's a look, I guess, but I'm not sure it's quite you." Then he winked at her and was gone.

Abby introduced herself to Ed MacIntosh, who, on seeing the rain dripping down her face, reached into his pocket and handed her a freshly ironed handkerchief. Then he said how grateful everybody was that she had been prepared to lend them Fabulous Flowers. "Dan's on such a tight budget. I don't know what he would have done without you."

"Oh, it's my pleasure. So far I'm rather enjoying it."

"Quick word of advice," Ed said, lowering his voice. "Cinders has this knack of getting people to run round after her. If she tries it on you, just make up an excuse and refuse. Once she has a willing slave, she doesn't let go."

"Oh, I'm far too busy to start running round after her," Abby said, shoving the menus into her jacket pocket.

Just then, Cinders appeared on the stairs leading down from the flat.

"Oh, darling, there you are. I wondered what had happened to you. Did you manage to get the menus?"

Abby caught Ed's expression. He was rolling his eyes. "Too late. I'm telling you—you have to watch her. She'll have you filling her bath with ass's milk next."

She offered him an embarrassed smile.

"Would you mind bringing the menus up to the flat?" Cinders continued. As part of her business arrangement with Dan, Abby had agreed to allow her living room to be turned into a makeshift dressing room. Clearly Cinders had wasted no time moving in.

"Sweetie, you look like a drowned rat," Cinders said as they walked into the flat. "This is all my fault, sending you out. You'll catch pneumonia. Now, then, we must find you a towel and dry you off. Where do you keep them?"

Abby said not to worry, but Lucinda insisted she direct her to the linen closet.

She returned a few moments later. "Sorry, darling, I could only find this." She was holding an ancient, frayed tea towel.

Abby took it from her. She could feel water trickling down her neck toward her shoulder blades. "The towels are on the next shelf up," she said, making her way to the linen closet.

"Sorry, didn't think to look."

When Abby came back into the living room, her head was wrapped in a towel turban.

"Now, then, what do you recommend?" Cinders said, perusing the menus. "I could manage a jambon and salad baguette. Or the smoked chicken sounds nice. Tell you what, why don't we get both? And I'd like a jasmine tea. Oh, and could you get me some wheat-grass juice from the organic place? I loathe the stuff, but it's supposed to be so cleansing. Look, I'd offer to go and fetch everything, but I must have a shower before the hair and makeup people arrive."

Abby knew she should probably heed Ed's warning, but

she didn't want to make a fuss or cause any ill feeling. Since the rain had eased off, she quickly blow-dried her hair and went back out.

When she returned, Lucinda was out of the shower and was sitting on the sofa, wearing Abby's beloved jade silk kimono. "Found this hanging in the bathroom. Hope you don't mind."

"No, not at all." Actually, Abby did mind. She minded rather a lot. She adored the kimono, not so much because it had been a birthday present from Toby but because it made her feel wondrously glamorous whenever she put it on. Now Lucinda was wearing it. Not only did it make her look glamorous in a way that Abby could only dream of, but she had clearly put it on immediately after spraying herself with deodorant, and now the underarms were covered in white marks.

On seeing the two baguettes, Lucinda's face fell. "Oh, darling, I'm not sure there's enough here. It just occurred to me that when the hair and makeup people finally get here, they are bound to be starving. And one has to feed the troops, I always feel. I know it's a dreadful bore, but you couldn't possibly go back, could you, and get some more supplies?"

This time Abby stood her ground. "Actually, Cinders, I can't. I've got stacks of invoices to do, not to mention umpteen calls to make. I really must make a start. I'm sure the *troops* can take care of themselves." She went over to the kitchen and picked up her mobile and her laptop. "If you need me, I'll be working in the bedroom."

Lucinda didn't appear angry at being refused, just taken aback. It occurred to Abby that it wasn't often that people dared to say no to the Divine Miss W.

No sooner had Abby settled herself on the bed, propped up by pillows, than the phone rang. It was Soph.

"So, what do you think of our Cinders? Talk about a self-obsessed luvvie."

"I know, but at least there's no marcrobiotic chef or trainer in tow. And, so far, she hasn't asked me to put rose petals down the loo."

"Give her time. I don't get it. She's an actress, for Chrissake—a performer, a court jester. These actors are all the same. They acquire a bit of fame and they expect to be treated like blinkin' gods. And the media plays along, running round after them, taking their opinions seriously. I mean, who cares what bloody actors think about the state of the world? I certainly don't..."

AFTER AN hour or so spent typing invoices and sending e-mails, Abby decided to make a cup of coffee. As she opened the door into the living room, she saw Dan and Cinders huddled together at one end of the sofa. The star's arm was draped round his neck. Her head was resting on his shoulder. Abby was aware of her heart rate picking up and her stomach muscles tightening. Cinders was still in the kimono but looking even more stunning. The hair and makeup artists had clearly come and gone, leaving her with smoldering, smoky eyes and lustrous, meticulously turned curls that tumbled down her back. Abby almost expected her to announce that she was "ready for my close-up, Mr. DeMille." A script, from which they were both reading, lay open on Dan's lap. "Oh, darling, please don't make me say that," Cinders pleaded. "In real life, when a man asks a woman for a date, no woman actually replies, 'I'd like that.' And yet it's a phrase practically every screenwriter uses."

"I have to say, I agree," Abby volunteered, flicking the switch on the electric kettle.

"See, even Abby agrees, and she knows nothing." Before Abby had a chance to respond to the comment, Cinders turned to Abby and corrected herself. "Omigod, I am so sorry. That came out all wrong. What I meant to say is that you know nothing about scriptwriting. I'm sure you know lots and lots about other things . . . you know, flower arranging and plants and whatnot."

Abby couldn't work out if Cinders was being bitchy or whether she was genuinely making a mess of apologizing for her original remark. She decided to give the woman the benefit of the doubt and say nothing.

Dan hadn't heard Cinders's comments. He was deep in thought, his pen hovering over the script. "OK," he piped up suddenly. "Maybe it would be sexier if she simply smiled and said, 'Pick me up at eight.'"

"Brilliant," Lucinda exclaimed, drawing him toward her and planting a kiss on his cheek. "Darling, you are so clever." Now she was ruffling his hair. He seemed mildly irritated by this and gently but firmly removed her hand from his head.

Abby asked if Dan and Cinders fancied a cuppa. Dan said he would love one. Cinders asked if Abby had any Earl Grey or jasmine tea.

"Sorry, only your basic builder's brew, I'm afraid."

Cinders said in that case she would pass. Then she got up and disappeared to the loo.

Abby poured boiling water into her coffee cup. "We still on for lunch?" she said to Dan.

"I'd love to, but I can't. There are quite a few more problems with the script. Cinders and I have to sort them out. We'll probably have lunch together."

"What about dinner? I could cook us something."

"Fantastic. I'll pick up some wine."

By now Cinders had returned. "Oh, darling, you said we were spending this evening at your place going over rushes." Her spoiled-child pout wasn't lost on Abby.

Dan looked at Abby. "Actually, Cinders is right. I did say we'd go over rushes."

"But you're more than welcome to join us," Cinders cooed.

"That's kind of you, but I'm sure you've got loads to discuss." Abby turned to Dan. "Tomorrow night, then?"

"It's a date."

"Ooh, don't you remember, darling?" Cinders butted in again, barely disguising her glee. "We've got dinner with that chap from the National Lottery."

Dan ran his fingers through his hair in frustration. "Bugger . . . Abby, I'm truly sorry, but nearly half our funding came from lottery money. If I want more for future projects, I really need to stick close to this guy."

Abby told him not to worry. She knew how vital meetings like this were. The bit she found disconcerting was the delight with which Lucinda announced Dan's lack of availability.

It wasn't until Saturday that Abby and Dan got an evening together. Abby decided to cook Jamie Oliver's roast venison with potato, celeriac and parmesan bake.

While Abby stood at the kitchen worktop, grating parmesan, Dan uncorked a bottle of wine. "It's so good to have some time on our own." He put the wine bottle down, came up behind her and began kissing the back of her neck.

She rolled her head in appreciation. "I know. Even though you've been around, I've really missed you."

"Me, too. Do you realize, we haven't even had time for a snog?"

It hadn't been for the want of trying, though. They'd tried sneaking a few minutes in the bedroom, the back room downstairs and even the bathroom, but every time, somebody had started calling for Dan. They hadn't had any sleepovers, because Dan was at home viewing rushes into the small hours.

By now her arm was tired from all the cheese-grating. "I haven't weighed it, but that must be enough," she said. With that, she began sprinkling cheese over the layers of sliced potato and celeriac.

"So when are your mum and dad coming home?" he said, pouring wine into glasses.

"Not for a while. Since she appeared on *Oprah*, she's become quite a celebrity across the pond. Now all the talk shows want her." According to Hugh, Jean's performance on *Oprah* had been magnificent. She hadn't displayed even a hint of nerves. Instead, she had spoken with a power and conviction that had clearly inspired the women in the audience, because at the end of the show they all rose to their feet and chanted, *"We love Jeanie."*

"Women are stopping me in the street and calling me a feminist role model," Jean had told Abby on the phone. "Can you believe it? Me? A feminist role model. You do have to giggle."

Baffled as Jean was by her newfound fame, Abby had

been left in no doubt that her mother was loving every minute of it.

They had just taken their wine into the living room and were snuggled up on the sofa when Dan's mobile rang. He took his phone out of his pocket, looked at the caller display and groaned. "It's Cinders. Whatever the problem is, I'm not dealing with it tonight. She can leave a message." With that he switched the phone off and put it back in his pocket.

"I think Cinders has got a thing for you," Abby said, immediately wishing she hadn't. Now he was going to think she was jealous and needy. Great.

Dan didn't seem remotely perturbed by her statement. Instead, his face broke into a smile. "No more than she has a thing for every other man on the set. Haven't you noticed the way she drapes herself over the crew? It's just a luvvie thing. Like a lot of stars, she's hugely insecure and desperate for attention."

This was precisely what Soph and Martin had said when she confided her fears to them. Abby decided she really had to loosen up and let the matter drop.

"So, she's not after you, then?" she heard herself say. So much for loosening up.

"What? God, no. What you have to understand is that her behavior has nothing whatever to do with romance and everything to do with control. Cinders needs to have all eyes permanently focused on her. Believe it or not, it's the only way she feels good about herself. She's petrified that my relationship with you takes my focus off her. It makes her feel insecure. The reality is, she's on the verge of becoming an A-list Hollywood star. She's not remotely interested in a relationship with a struggling director like me."

"And what if she were?"

He took her wineglass from her and put it down on the coffee table. "OK," he said, cupping her face in his hands, "first, I am one hundred percent committed to our relationship, and even if I weren't, there is no way on earth that I could ever take on a woman who was that self-centered and needy. Does that answer your question?"

Before she had a chance to say anything, he was kissing her in a way that left no doubt that her question had been well and truly answered.

Chapter 16

FILMING WAS MEANT TO last a week but ran into a second. Abby didn't mind. In fact, she almost welcomed it. The early starts meant she was at her laptop by eight, replying to e-mails and sending invoices. She couldn't remember the last time she had been so on top of her paperwork.

Most nights, Dan stayed for dinner. If neither of them felt like cooking, they would order in and eat on the sofa, watching the TV news or some daft soap. Usually Dan had to rush home as soon as they'd eaten. He was now working with a film editor. Even though *Bouquet* wasn't quite finished—he had been working on it for three months—they were trying to get a rough cut ready as soon as possible to show film distributors.

By now Abby was making the final plans for Mr. Takahashi's daughter's engagement party, which was less than two weeks away. Everything had been bought. The ornamental Asian bridge, the miniature pagoda and fountain had all come from a swanky garden center in Chelsea, which specialized in creating Eastern gardens.

Once the "scenery" had been delivered to Mr. T's

apartment, Abby went over one afternoon to put everything into position. She marveled at the red painted fretwork on the arched black bridge. She oohed and aahed over the intricate carving on the roof of the miniature gold pagoda, which had turned out to be not quite as *miniature* as she had imagined. It stood a full seven feet high. She started to panic that it was going to dominate the room.

It took Ichiro to reassure her. "Abby, calm down. The ceiling is twelve feet high and the room is sixty feet long. Believe me, we have plenty of space to play with."

He was right. Once they had found the perfect spot for the pagoda and bridge, they turned their attention to the indoor fountain. They were still struggling to hook it up to the main water supply on the terrace when Mr. T and his daughter arrived. The diminutive, giggling Miss T wore a gray business suit and pearls. She spoke no English, but it was clear from her excited exchange with her father that she was delighted by the Asian idyll Abby had created.

"Now then, Miss Crompton," Mr. T barked, waving a chubby forefinger, "promise me you not forget my peen-is."

Ichiro turned scarlet. "His what?" he mouthed at Abby, straining not to laugh. "Is there something I should know about?"

Abby hissed at Ichiro to behave and turned to Mr. T. "Don't worry, Mr. Takahashi, the"—she paused for Ichiro's benefit—"*peonies* are all on order."

"Big ones? I want very big peen-is."

By now Ichiro could barely contain himself.

"You understand? Very big peen-is."

Abby said that wasn't going to be a problem.

"You also get me lavender. For terrace."

"Lavender?" Abby's face fell. "Ooh, Mr. Takahashi, it's

far too early in the year for lavender. English lavender doesn't flower until July. And it's not very Japanese, is it? I mean, it's not exactly in keeping with our theme."

"Maybe not, but it smells good. You find! Money no object!"

Abby practically saluted.

SHE SPENT the next few days trying to source spring lavender. Occasionally, Dan would sneak up behind her while she was sitting at her laptop and start massaging her shoulders and kissing the back of her neck. "Why don't we lock the bedroom door and do it now? Surely you can spare a couple of minutes?"

She would burst out laughing. "Is that what we're reduced to? A couple of minutes?"

"That works for me. Thirty seconds would work for me!"

"God, you so know how to woo a girl."

Then she would shoo him away, telling him she was waiting for an important call from a lavender supplier in Devon or Norfolk.

She spoke to several suppliers of Spanish lavender. It had a more piney smell than the English variety, but since it flowered much earlier, she knew it was her only option. None of the British growers had any in full bloom. They blamed it on spring coming a couple of weeks late this year. One said that if money really was no object, her best bet was to find a supplier in Spain and have it flown in. After spending hours Googling and phoning Spanish lavender growers who spoke no English, Abby eventually found a British woman who grew lavender commercially on the is-

land of Majorca. She said it would be no problem to supply
Abby with two dozen tubs.

"We're talking thousands of pounds to have it flown in
from the Med," Abby told Ichiro over the phone. "I know
Mr. T said he wasn't worried about the bill, but you'd better
double-check that he's up for spending this kind of
money."

Ichiro phoned back a few minutes later to confirm that
Mr. T was more than happy to pay.

IF MARTIN wasn't too busy and Soph felt able to play
hooky from the office for half an hour or so, they would
meet in the shop to watch the filming. One morning
Ichiro—who was just as starstruck as Martin—joined
them. He'd managed to steal a couple of hours off work
because Mr. T was out of town. They watched a couple of
scenes being filmed, and all agreed that the most memorable
was the one where Ed kisses Cinders for the first time.

"It's so real," Martin had whispered between takes. "I
was totally carried away."

"I know," said Ichiro. "The two of them are totally
awesome. You'd never think Ed was gay. I mean, it really
looks like they've got the hots for each other. How do they
do that? And with all these people watching."

Abby gave a shrug. "They are both extremely good actors."

Before Ichiro left, Abby asked him how the job hunting
was going.

He said that he wasn't looking for a job anymore.
Instead, he was thinking about doing a course in interior
design.

"Oh, Ichiro, that's so up your street. I can just see you on the phone to Madonna discussing throw cushions."

Ichiro laughed. "That is so sweet of yeeeeuuww, but the problem is how I'm going to pay for the course and support myself and my grandparents back in Japan. Part of me knows the universe will provide and that I need to reach for the stars, live life without fear and surrender to the strength of the earth, but I have to admit that I'm struggling."

ABBY WAS aware that, as well as being a fine actor, Cinders had incredible stamina and dedication. There were times when half a dozen or more takes were required. Ed would occasionally get ratty and snap at Dan or one of the crew, but Lucinda never lost her temper or threw a hissy fit. No matter what she was asked to do or how long it took to set up lighting and camera angles, she remained calm, good humored and utterly professional. Apart from that first morning, she was never late arriving on set, and when filming was over for the day, she never rushed off. Instead, she hung around chatting to the crew, which clearly endeared her to them.

Having become aware of Cinders's good points, Abby did her best to like her, but it still wasn't easy. For a start, she was forever kidnapping Martin. Cinders called it "borrowing," as in: "Oh, Abby, you don't mind me borrowing Martin for a few ticks, do you?" No sooner had he finished his deliveries each morning than she would send him out to collect her dry cleaning or detox herbs from her Chinese healer. "A few ticks" inevitably turned into an hour or more.

On returning from a mission—if Cinders was between takes—Martin would make them both jasmine tea and the pair would spend a few minutes chatting in the living room. Abby could hear them from the bedroom. Cinders seemed to have a genuine affection for Martin, judging by the time she spent listening to him singing Ichiro's praises or tearfully lamenting the loss of Debbie Harry. It turned out that she, too, owned a pooch that was the love of her life.

"You poor darling. I just don't know what I'd do if I were separated from Princess Coco."

"I thought about hiring a lawyer and taking Christian to court, but I can't afford it."

"Of course you can't. It would cost thousands." She paused. "There just has to be something I can do to help you get her back."

Then one day Christian turned up—with Debbie Harry in tow—to complain that the film trucks were blocking the road and holding up the traffic. Dan was very calm and tactful and showed Christian the letters he had received from the council, giving the crew permission to park outside the shop. Christian snorted. There was clearly nothing he could do to challenge the council's decision.

By now Martin had seen Debbie Harry and rushed outside. On seeing him, the dog strained on her lead and began to yelp in delight.

Martin cried out to her. "Hi, Debbie...how have you been? Who loves you, baby?"

"Don't come any nearer," Christian warned, raising an open palm.

"You can't tell me what to do. I have every right to pet my own dog."

Christian began pulling on Debbie's lead, but she refused to budge. Then she began rearing up, trying desperately to get closer to Martin. Christian yanked the lead hard. The dog began barking. He yelled at her to shut up and pulled the lead again.

"Stop it," Martin cried. "You're hurting her!"

Martin could contain himself no longer. He lunged forward and made a grab for Debbie Harry's lead. But Christian was too quick for him and managed to sidestep the attempt. Martin lost his balance and fell flat on his face. Christian merely smirked, yanked Debbie Harry's lead and led the poor yelping animal away.

By now a shaken Cinders was helping Martin up off the pavement. "My God, you OK?"

He brushed some dirt off his sweater and the knees of his jeans. "Yeah. I'm fine. It's that poor dog I'm worried about. Christian has a vicious temper, but I've never seen him take it out on an animal, least of all Debbie. I'm really scared."

"Me, too. I saw how he treated her. What a horrible, horrible man. Right, we have to do something about this. I don't know what, but I promise, I will come up with something."

MARTIN WAS only too aware that by being at Cinders's constant beck and call, he was deserting his post at Fabulous Flowers. He kept apologizing to Abby for letting her down. "I just don't know what to do. I do try saying no to her, but then she starts looking pathetic and I give in. Plus, she's really taken an interest in Debbie Harry and wants to help me get her back. I feel guilty refusing her when she's been so kind."

Abby could see he was in a quandary. She told him not

to worry and that she would have a quiet word with Cinders
and sort things out.

In the end she didn't need to. Katie Shaw, Dan's location
finder, reappeared and came to the rescue. It turned out that
Katie wasn't so much a location finder as Dan's occasional,
ad hoc girl Friday. Frantic as he was with filming, Dan had
noticed what was going on between Martin and Cinders
and had taken time out to deal with the situation. "She's
meant to be working at my flat doing all the paperwork on
the film, but I think we really need her here to relieve
Martin and nurse our star," he told Abby.

Abby couldn't have been more impressed or grateful.
"Oh, darling, you are so totally brilliant," she said one
morning, doing a perfect impersonation of Cinders, which
had Dan hooting with laughter and dragging her into the
back room for a quick snog.

A jolly, easygoing soul, Katie took Cinders's demands in
stride. One morning, when she was on her way out to run
some errand or other, she took Abby aside: "I just wanted
to say how utterly fab it is that you and the Deejster have
got it together. When his last relationship broke up, he
turned into a dreadful old crosspatch, but now he's totally
transformed and back to his old self."

"You really think that's due to me?"

"Of course. Who else?"

If Abby had known Katie better, she would have
taken the woman into her confidence and admitted that she
wasn't convinced. For a few days after her "big" conversation with Dan, during which he had reassured her that
Cinders's absurd, overly demonstrative behavior toward him
and all the other men on the set was nothing more than

luvvie insecurity, she felt as if a massive weight had lifted from her. Then the doubts had started to creep back.

Try as she might, Abby couldn't get over the fact that whenever she saw Dan and Cinders together, the woman's hands were all over him. If she wasn't straightening his shirt collar, then she was smoothing his hair or resting her hand on his knee. Despite what Dan had said about her draping herself over all the men on set, Abby was in no doubt that Cinders was far more touchy-feely with him than she was with the other men, whose clothes and hair she tended to leave alone.

Cinders also continued to make claims on Dan's time. Since he was now spending most evenings with his film editor, this was usually in the afternoons, when they had finished filming. Abby knew there were justifiable and often urgent script-related reasons for them to spend time together, but she couldn't prevent her mind from filling with fantasies—involving silk negligees, champagne and chocolate-dipped strawberries—in which Cinders finally managed to seduce Dan.

One morning, she was working in her bedroom and thinking about going for a walk and picking up a lunchtime sandwich when Martin came bursting in.

"Hey, ever thought of knocking before you enter a lady's boudoir? I could have been naked."

Ignoring Abby's protest, he perched himself on the edge of her bed. "I have news," he cried, clapping his hands in glee. "And I got this straight from the horse's mouth. Our Cinders has a secret boyfriend back in L.A. Some mega movie star, apparently. That was all she'd tell me."

"You're kidding."

"Nope. And he sounds gorgeous. Tall, dark, fabulous

body . . . By the time she'd finished describing him, I was getting quite hot under the collar, I can tell you."

"I'm gobsmacked. I don't know what to say."

"Oh, it was OK. I managed to control myself—"

"Not about you getting turned on, you dope—about Cinders having a boyfriend. It never occurred to me."

"So now will you stop fretting? Dan, Soph and I have been right all along. Cinders wants Dan's attention, not his body."

The relief Abby felt at the news was instantaneous. It shot through her and warmed her like malt whiskey on a freezing day.

She soon found herself mellowing toward Cinders. Not only did the woman appear to be no threat, but she had also kept her promise to help Martin get custody of Debbie Harry. It turned out that Cinders had a TV-producer friend who had just received a commission to make an English version of *Judge Judy*, which would be given the tacky imitative title *Judge Trudy*. The producer was on the lookout for suitable cases that Judge Trudy could preside over.

"Anyway, when Rollo—that's the producer—heard about my dispute with Christian, he said it would be perfect for the show," Martin told Abby.

"And Christian's agreed to this? I don't believe it. Why on earth would he risk losing Debbie Harry? It makes no sense."

"Au contraire. It makes perfect sense. Christian is so arrogant and deluded that it won't have occurred to him for a second he could lose."

"And you've both agreed to abide by the judge's decision?"

"Absolutely," Martin said. "That's the deal."

"But has it occurred to you that you could lose?"

"Of course it has, but since I can't afford to hire a lawyer and take Christian to proper court, what choice do I have?"

Abby was quick to thank Cinders for helping Martin.

"My pleasure," Cinders said. "That awful Christian creature needs to be taught a lesson."

Abby had warmed to Cinders so much now that once or twice, when Katie wasn't around to run errands, she even offered to go out and fetch her an herb tea. When Cinders took to watching films on her iPhone between takes, Abby found herself saying that Cinders was more than welcome to watch movies on her big-screen TV. Cinders seemed genuinely touched by the offer but insisted she was fine with her iPhone. She gave every impression of thoroughly enjoying being curled up in one of Abby's armchairs with her headphones on, lost in her own world. Afterward, she never volunteered the name of the movie she had been watching. Stranger still, if anybody inquired, she would pretend not to have heard and change the subject.

WHEN THE final day of filming arrived, Abby felt quite sad. She was going to miss the film crew and their banter. Even though they hadn't spent much quality time together, she was going to miss having Dan around. It occurred to her that she might even miss Cinders. Getting back to "normal" seemed a rather dull prospect.

She'd told Dan that she was going to cook a celebratory end-of-filming dinner. She promised candles, champagne and tiramisu, and he promised to stay the night.

At lunchtime she popped into S&M to pick up a couple of individual racks of lamb.

No sooner had the store's automatic doors parted than she noticed a crowd of women gathered round one of the long checkout counters. An S&M assistant was handing out leaflets. Assuming she was promoting some kind of special offer, Abby went over to investigate.

A middle-aged woman in a business suit finished scanning her leaflet and looked up at Abby. "About time, too," she said. "I've been saying for years that the customers are the best people to canvass about what's going wrong at S&M."

"I wrote to them ages ago," another woman was saying, "with a list of complaints and suggestions of ways they could turn the store around, but I didn't even get a reply. Now they actually want to know what I think. Can you believe it?"

Abby blinked. What? The powers that be at S&M were actively seeking customer opinion— just as she'd suggested to Dan? She took a leaflet from the assistant and began reading. Customers were being asked to give their views on the cut, color, quality and style of clothes. *Would you say S&M garments are a) enhanced by the occasional motif or b) spoiled by the look of the motifs?*

Would you say that S&M a) always keeps up with fashion trends, b) usually keeps up, c) rarely keeps up and needs to improve?

She read to the end. Every subject raised by the questionnaire was one she had previously discussed with Dan.

What was more, it turned out that as part of a general modernization scheme, the company was about to revamp every one of its eight hundred stores. They were taking on

Trevor Monk, the award-winning designer who had just "interiored" the Hotel Bristol in Park Lane.

Abby put the leaflet in her bag and carried on toward the food hall. How weird was this? She had suggested every one of these changes to Dan. What had he been doing—passing them on to the powers that be at the company without telling her? She laughed at the ridiculousness of the idea. He had no "in" at S&M—at least none he'd mentioned. Then suddenly her mind flew back to when she'd found the S&M in-house magazine in Dan's flat. Maybe he did have some connection with the company. And if he did, why hadn't he said something? What could he possibly have to hide?

When she got back to Fabulous Flowers, she was still puzzling and fretting. She went up to the flat to put her shopping in the fridge. Cinders was curled up in an armchair, glued to the screen of her iPhone. She was moving her head in time to whatever music she was listening to. Abby watched her for a second or two. Eventually Cinders started singing. At first Abby couldn't make out the words, but as she got more carried away, her singing got louder and Abby finally realized that she was singing along to Hank Reno's "Cherokee Lou, Don't Let Me Die in the Jailhouse."

Abby went over and waved her hand in front of Cinders's face, just to let her know she was there. Cinders looked up, took the white buds out of her ears and said hi.

"I thought you went to the pub with Dan and the crew," Abby said.

"I did, but then I realized that I'd left my iPhone here. I just came back to get it. I guess I started watching a movie."

"*Tumble Down?*"

"Yes." She reddened, clearly embarrassed at being found out.

"Biopics can be a bit so-so," Abby said, "but this has to be one of my top films. Liam Heggarty and Geneva Raine couldn't have been better cast—and I just adore the music, don't you?"

"God, yes," Cinders said. A wistful look came over her. "'Cheatin' Woman, Gonna Drive My Truck Right over You' is my all-time favorite."

"In fact—and don't say I said this, because it's absolute heresy, but sometimes I think Liam Heggarty does Hank Reno's songs better than he did. The man is an absolute genius."

Cinders's face broke into a smile. "I think so, too," she said.

"And the onscreen chemistry between him and Geneva Raine was amazing."

"I guess so." Cinders seemed less taken with this remark.

Abby began loading the fridge.

"So, you're serious about Dan, then?" Cinders said, putting her phone in her handbag.

The out-of-the-blueness not to say the intimacy of the question threw Abby. Until now their conversations had been fairly superficial. Maybe Cinders had detected that Abby was warming toward her, and asking about Dan was her way of reaching out.

"It's early," Abby said, "but, yes, I think I am serious about him."

"And it's obvious to anybody who sees you two together that he feels the same way. I saw the pair of you the other day, giggling like a pair of kids as he dragged you into the back room for a quick snog."

Abby could feel her cheeks turning pink. "All I'd say is that we've got a long way to go. I've only just come out of a relationship—so it's a bit complicated."

"It's funny," Cinders said, "I'd always thought that with his background Dan would have fallen for somebody a bit more..."

She was clearly groping for words.

"A bit more what?" Abby prompted, closing the fridge door.

"Gosh, how can I put this?"

"Cinders, what on earth are you trying to say?"

"It's just that with his background, I rather thought that once he'd finished playing the field, he would end up with somebody—you know—of a similar pedigree, as it were...."

"Dan has a pedigree? You make him sound like a Labrador. I don't understand."

Now it was Cinders's turn to look perplexed. "You mean you don't know? Dan hasn't told you who his mother and stepfather are?"

"All I know is that his mother was a widow before she remarried and his stepfather is in the rag trade." As she heard those last two words come out of her mouth, everything started to make sense.

Cinders smiled. "The rag trade? Well, I guess that's one way of putting it." She paused. "Look, I've said too much. This is none of my business. You need to talk to Dan. I really should get going." With that she stood up, swung her Mulberry tote over her shoulder and headed toward the door.

Abby made no attempt to stop her. She was too caught up in her own thoughts.

So Dan had a "pedigree" and his stepfather was in the "rag trade." Abby didn't need to talk to Dan. She was pretty certain she knew who he was. How on earth could she have been so stupid?

Abby's laptop was sitting on the coffee table in front of her. She lifted the lid and clicked on Google. Then she typed in *S&M, Dan Chipault*.

Chapter 17

ABBY WAS ABOUT TO hit search when she heard foot-steps on the stairs. "That you, Scozz?" She assumed that Martin was about to go to lunch and was coming upstairs to ask if she would take over in the shop. Instead, when she looked up, she saw Dan coming through the door. His face was pale and taut with anxiety.

"Abby, could you stop whatever it is you're doing?" His voice sounded positively grave. "There's something I need to tell you. I've been trying to do it for weeks, but I couldn't get up the courage until now. So will you just sit down and let me get it out?"

"Dan, I am sitting down."

"Ah. Right. So you are."

"And looking at you, it occurs to me that maybe you should be sitting down, too."

"Good idea." He lowered himself into an armchair. "OK...here goes." He cleared his throat. "Right...well... you see, the thing is, I haven't been entirely honest with you about my background. You need to know that my family is far from ordinary. The truth is that we have aristocratic connections and are rather wealthy."

"Rather?"

"OK, very wealthy. No, that's not true. We are, in fact, positively rolling in dough. The other thing you don't know is that my stepfather is Sir Malcolm Grant, the chairman of S&M. He is paid a salary by the company, but he also inherited his own vast private fortune, as did my mother. You should also know that I have been telling him about your ideas of ways to improve S&M."

He sat waiting for her to react, but she didn't.

"You don't seem surprised."

"I'm not."

"You've already seen it, haven't you?"

"The S&M leaflet? With all my ideas in it? Yes."

"Shit. I was hoping to talk to you before that happened."

"Well, you're too late. I picked one up about an hour ago. It didn't take me long to put two and two together—especially after Lucinda started talking about your *pedigree*. You were clearly relaying my suggestions to somebody very senior in the company. I'm assuming it was your stepfather. When you said he was in the rag trade, I didn't realize you were using the term quite so broadly."

He winced. Her sarcasm wasn't lost on him.

"I don't know what to say, other than I am so sorry for being dishonest about my background and that I should have been up front with you from the beginning."

"Damn right you should have."

"It was also unforgivable that I passed your ideas to my stepfather without telling you. The thing is, I couldn't not tell him."

"So, did you pass the ideas off as your own?"

"What? No! Of course I didn't . . . Look, what you don't know is that things have been going from bad to worse at S&M. In the last few weeks my stepdad has been under massive pressure from the shareholders to resign. I have huge respect for Malcolm, but he would be the first to admit that, as far as S&M goes, he has made some poor judgment calls. I think he realizes now that, like the rest of the board, he's one of those middle-aged, Middle England dinosaurs you keep going on about. He was so scared of losing the company's conservative customer base that he became paralyzed. He just couldn't find it in himself to fire the accountants he was surrounded with and take the creative leap he needed. They've done so much damage, insisting he keep cutting prices rather than modernize. Then I told him about you and Fabulous Flowers. I found the piece about you in the *Sunday Times* 'Style' section—where you were placed number twelve in the 'Hundred Hottest Shops' list. I told him you'd been voted Boutique Retailer of the Year. I went on and on about how you'd built up your business from nothing and how you had all these big hotshot clients. I told him how clever and creative you are—not just with flowers—and that you were passionate about S&M and what it needed to do to improve. He must have been impressed, because finally the stubborn old bugger started listening. But at the same time, I didn't dare let you know about him. I realize now that in every respect I behaved like a complete and total ass. My only excuse is that I was scared."

"Scared? Of what?"

"Of you walking out on our relationship. I know how Toby and his mother treated you—the extent to which they made you feel socially inferior. I know what you went through with his dreadful friends. And you kept telling me how you just wanted to be with somebody from an ordinary background."

She was managing to stay calm, but inside she was raging. She was furious with him for believing that she couldn't have coped with the truth. "Do you really think I am that weak and narrow-minded? Didn't it occur to you that we could have worked through this problem together?"

His eyes were fixed on hers now. "I think that if you had discovered who I was, you would have made all kinds of assumptions about my friends and family and run a mile."

She was starting to lose her temper. "How dare you presume to know what I would have thought or done?"

"But you'd already admitted to me that you were an inverted snob."

"That was just me sounding off because I was upset. I didn't mean it."

"Well, thanks for telling me."

They fell into silence. Dan was looking down at the floor. "I'm sorry," he eventually said again. "I panicked."

She nodded. "I understand that, but it means that from now on I am going to find it hard to trust that you will be honest with me. How do I know you won't make a habit of censoring information because you think me knowing the whole truth wouldn't be good for me? Dishonesty aside, that kind of behavior is patronizing in the extreme."

"I know. I know. I will never ever lie to you again. Please believe me. It's going to be hard, but I want you to start trusting me again."

"In the end I couldn't trust Toby."

"But I'm not going to have a clandestine affair with another man!"

She managed a smile. "I know. But I'm talking about secrets in general. It's secrets that damage a relationship."

He began rubbing his forehead. "Can you forgive me?"

"Forgiving is the easy part," she said gently. "Like I said, the big question is whether I can trust you again. I'm going to need some time to think things through."

He nodded. "If it helps, I'm not actually loaded. Well, not yet, anyway. There's money in trust for me, but I don't get a penny until I'm forty. And I didn't lie to you about how I financed the film. Mum and Dad would have helped if I'd asked, but I was determined to raise the money on my own."

That impressed her and she told him so.

"Anyway, Malcolm's so grateful to you, he can't wait to meet you. He keeps asking me to set up a lunch and can't figure out why I've been holding out on him. It wouldn't surprise me if he's starting to think you don't exist."

"I think after everything that's happened, now wouldn't be a good time to meet him. There are things we need to sort out first."

"I agree."

Another silence followed. Once again it was Dan who broke it. "There's something else you need to know about my parentage." He took another deep breath. "My mother is a French countess whose family are direct descendants of Marie Antoinette."

"Marie Antoinette?" Despite being furious with Dan, it was as much as she could do to stop herself from laughing. "Oh, come on. You *are* kidding."

"No. I can show you the family tree."

"Blimey."

"Mum's full title is La Comtesse Marie Joseph d'Anjou Jonelle Bergerac Chipault."

Now Abby laughed. "So, does that make you…"

"Le Compte d'Anjou Jonelle Bergerac Chipault? Embarrassingly enough, it does. Except I don't assume the title until her death. And of course I haven't the remotest intention of ever using it." He paused. "Like Toby, I went to posh schools with other rich kids. I met Cinders when we were both at Millfield, but none of my friends are obnoxious, champagne-swilling toffs. And neither are my parents. Mum isn't a pompous old windbag like Lady Penelope. She's down-to-earth, kind, irreverent and has a filthy sense of humor. I just know you'd love her. You'd like my dad, too. They're both really good fun."

Abby let out a sigh. "In that case, you really should have had the courage to tell me the truth."

"You're right. I should have." He stood up. "I'll go now. Take some time to think. Take as long as you need, but you should know that I have never felt sorrier for anything in my life and that, more than anything, I want to carry on seeing you."

She managed a weak smile.

As she watched him go, she thought about the champagne, the two lamb racks, the ingredients for the tiramisu she was going to make…the celebration that wasn't going to happen now.

Her appetite gone, Abby went into the kitchen and poured herself a glass of wine from a bottle of merlot that she'd started a couple of days ago. She took a sizable gulp, ignored the sour taste and topped up her glass.

Back in the living room, she sat on the sofa, her legs curled underneath her. She reached for the remote and tried to watch the TV news, but she couldn't even begin to concentrate. She channel-surfed for a few minutes before switching off the TV.

Finally deciding that the merlot was undrinkable, she went back into the kitchen and opened a fresh bottle. It wasn't until she was two glasses in that she admitted what was on her mind. Angry as she was with Dan for lying to her, he did have a point. Had he told her about his background earlier, she might well have walked away without even attempting to get to know him.

The affair with Christian aside, Abby had come away from her relationship with Toby more bruised and angry than she cared to admit. Despite the success she had made of her business, despite her high-profile clients, not to mention the press plaudits Fabulous Flowers had received in recent months, Toby, his mother and his friends had succeeded in making her feel socially inferior. Dan had picked up on this and panicked.

Of course he should have been honest with her. He had behaved badly. On the other hand, it was a measure of his feelings for her, and it was important not to lose sight of that. Did this one mistake—albeit a pretty serious one—have to be a deal breaker? He was contrite and racked with guilt. Surely she could forgive him and find the courage to trust him again.

On the other hand, were there other things he had been dishonest about? Despite her having a boyfriend back in L.A., perhaps Dan did have feelings for Cinders after all. But that made no sense. If he wanted Cinders, why would he be begging Abby not to end their relationship? Then again, life had taught her that where matters of the heart were concerned, things often made no logical sense.

Confused and uneasy, she decided to sleep on it. There was no point to making a rash, impetuous decision that she might come to regret.

She slept on it for two nights. For once she kept her own counsel and didn't go running to Martin or Soph for help and advice. She knew what they'd say, that she had to put Dan's mistake behind her and believe him when he said he would never lie to her again. She had to start trusting again. That was the hard bit. She wasn't sure that she could.

On the third evening, she decided to go late-night clothes shopping in Hampstead. She thought a new top or a pair of jeans might cheer her up. On the drive over, she found herself thinking about Dan. It was getting near dinnertime, and she imagined him home alone, about to shove a frozen meal in the microwave. She felt her eyes starting to fill up. In an instant she made the decision to go there, tell him she was taking him out to dinner and that they were going to have a long talk about trust issues. But basically her message would be that all was forgiven.

SHE WAS just about to press the buzzer to Dan's flat when the street door opened and Katie appeared. "God," Abby said, "you only just leaving? It's past seven. Dan is such a slave driver."

Katie laughed. "The man is an absolute poppet and you know it. It's just that with the filming over, there was a mass of administrative odds and ends to tidy up. We've both been working like lunatics. Dan only stopped an hour or so ago, when Cinders arrived."

"Cinders is here?" Abby heard herself say, aware of her heart rate picking up.

"Yes, and she seemed to be in a bit of a state. She was desperate to talk to Dan. He whisked her into the living room and they've been there ever since. Haven't got a clue what's going on." She paused. "Was Dan expecting you?"

"No, I thought I'd surprise him."

"Well, I'm sure he'll be more than grateful. You might be able to help him cheer Cinders up."

Abby's smile belied her anxiety.

It was then that Katie remembered she had left a pile of letters in Dan's study. "I was planning to address them at home and put them in the mail first thing tomorrow." She rooted round in her handbag for her door keys. "Thank the Lord Dan let me have a set of keys. I'm always forgetting something." Eventually she found them and let them both into the flat. While Katie scuttled off down the hall toward the study, Abby hovered in the main doorway. Part of her couldn't face stepping into the flat and hearing what she feared she might hear.

There wasn't a sound coming from the living room, which pretty much ruled out the scenes of wild debauchery she had begun to imagine. In the end she managed to convince herself that Cinders was merely having some kind of emotional episode or other and Dan was trying to help. She started down the hall, waving good-bye to Katie, who was by now coming back in the opposite direction, looking at her watch. "Be a miracle if I make my bus," she said, picking up her pace.

Abby crept toward the living-room door, which was ajar. She peered inside. Dan was sitting in a black leather armchair. Abby could see only Cinders's profile. She was standing by the window, her back to Dan. Neither of them was saying a word. Several seconds passed before Cinders broke the silence.

"Darling, you really have to tell her," she was saying. "In the end it's the kindest thing. Of course, it will be a blow, but she'll get over it. You've been promising to do it for weeks. I simply can't wait any longer. I love you and I want us to be together. I want us to create our own perfect nest. We can't do that until this thing is sorted out....Right now it's all such a mess. I need order in my life. I can't bear the way everything is all over the place. Look, if you won't tell her, then I will."

Abby thought she might be sick. Tears rolling down her face, she turned on her heel and ran toward the front door. A draft must have caught it, and it slammed loudly behind her.

She ran down the path, shaking with shock and disbelief. It was Toby and Christian all over again. This was becoming a habit. Was she ever going to stop finding lovers cheating on her? Three days ago Dan had been practically on his knees, apologizing for not being honest about his background and saying how much he wanted to be with her. Now this. How could he do this to her? How could he?

She was several yards along the pavement when she heard Dan's voice. "Katie! Hey, hang on. Did you remember those letters?" It was obvious that in the dark he couldn't see who she was. Abby ignored him and carried on toward her car. She could hear footsteps jogging behind her. "Abby," he cried, finally making her out. "Slow down. What on earth's the matter? Was that you in the flat just now? How did you get in?"

She kept running.

"Christ!" The lightbulb had come on. "Katie must have let you in and you heard Cinders. Abby, please come back. That wasn't what you think..."

Weeping and breathless, Abby reached her car. She climbed in and locked the doors. Dan had caught up and was tugging on the driver's door handle and banging on the window. "Abby! Please! You have to listen."

She turned the key in the ignition and started to pull away. Dan let go of the handle. She drove to the end of the road and turned left. She had no idea where she was heading.

Chapter 18

BY NOW ABBY'S EYES were so full of tears that she couldn't see and had to pull over. No sooner had she turned off the engine than her mobile rang. She wiped her eyes with the back of her hand and took the phone out of her bag. When she saw Dan's number, she switched off the phone. She sat for a full fifteen minutes, her body racked with heaving sobs. She couldn't work out who she was more angry with—Dan, for betraying her, or herself, for being naive enough to believe that Dan would be able to resist Cinders in the end. Given the choice between the beautiful, posh actress who was about to become a Hollywood A-lister and the florist from Croydon, who was he going to choose?

And of course Cinders didn't have a boyfriend back in the States. That was something she'd concocted to keep Abby off the scent.

Overwhelming as her anger was, more than anything she felt bereft. She had known Dan for such a short time, but losing him felt like losing part of herself. Without him she was hollow, incomplete. She hadn't dared admit it to herself until now, but she had fallen in love with Dan.

Two hours later, having hit the M1 and driven practically to Luton and back, she arrived home.

She lay on the bed, fully clothed and staring at the moon shadows on the ceiling. The ache she felt inside was almost physical. She was certain that she would never ever find love again. She was one of those people whom love tantalized and teased but finally evaded. She fell into a dreamless sleep and was woken the next morning by somebody banging on the door to the flat.

The previous evening's events hit her with the force of a wrecker's ball. Tears started to well up in her eyes. "Who is it?"

"Me." It was Martin. "It's past nine. You OK?"

She lowered her feet onto the floor. Her head throbbed. Her mouth and tongue were as dry as felt. She stood up and went to the front door.

"Hey," she mumbled, rubbing her head.

"Hiya. Bloody hell, you look terrible."

"Cheers."

"Did you sleep in your clothes?"

Abby looked down. "Seems like it."

"What happened? Judging by the swollen eyes and the smudged mascara, I'm guessing an extremely boozy night?"

"You could say that." Then she burst into tears.

He immediately put his arms round her. "Hey, Abby, what on earth is it? Come on, tell your aunty Scozza. Surely it can't be that bad."

"It is," she wailed. "Dan's in love with Cinders."

Martin was stroking her back. "OK, that sounds pretty bad. Look, you go back to bed and I'll bring you a nice cuppa. Then we'll talk."

She plodded to her room and collapsed onto the bed. A few minutes later Martin was back with sweet tea and jam toast.

"I've phoned Soph. She's on her way."

"But she's got a business to run. You shouldn't have bothered her."

"Oh, please. Here's you in the midst of some terrible emotional trauma and looking like death. Can you imagine the bollocking I'd get if I didn't call her?"

"I guess." Abby sipped the hot tea, but when she tried the toast she simply couldn't get it down.

By the time Soph arrived, Abby was sobbing into her pillow. Soph sat down on the bed beside her and began stroking her friend's hair. "Sweetie, you have to tell us what's been going on. Now, come on...take a deep breath."

"I've fallen in love with Dan," she cried into the pillow.

"All right."

"No, it's not bloody all right. It's all wrong. He loves Cinders."

"How do you know? What happened exactly?"

After some cajoling, Abby turned over to face them. "I caught them last night at Dan's flat. She was begging him to tell me the truth about their relationship. I knew I couldn't trust him. I've been such an idiot." She looked at Martin. "Cinders never had a boyfriend in L.A. That was just a line she spun you. She knew you'd tell me and that it would stop me becoming suspicious."

The rest of the story—about Dan being the son of the S&M chairman and a megawealthy French countess—came out in fits and starts.

"It feels like my life's turned into a bad fairy tale," Abby said, wiping the snot from her nose. "I mean, how many girls manage to get swept off their feet by not one handsome prince but two and then have both of them cheat on her?"

For a few moments, Martin and Soph seemed lost for words.

"So," Martin said eventually, "Dan's a toff. Who'd have thought it? I mean, he seems so ordinary. How you pull that off when your mam's related to Marie Antoinette, I have no idea."

Like Abby, they both understood why Dan had panicked and felt he had to keep his background a secret. Like her, they even understood why he had relayed Abby's ideas about how to improve S&M to his stepfather without telling her. What they couldn't get their heads round was Dan cheating on her. "I just can't believe Dan would do this," Soph said. "He's such a lovely, genuine sort of a bloke. I didn't have him down as the two-timing type."

"My guess," Abby began, "is that Cinders has been working on him ever since they started filming. I think he fought her off for a while, but in the end he couldn't resist her. And sometime in the last three days she finally managed to seduce him. She's one of those beautiful, manipulative women who are used to getting anything they want. Most important of all, she's posh. Toby admitted that he always wanted to be with somebody of his own class, and I think that deep down, despite claiming the opposite, Dan does, too."

Soph and Martin listened to her, hugged her and commiserated with her until Abby finally decided Soph should get back to work. "And I can't sit around moping. I have to open the shop."

"No way," Martin said. "I'll manage the shop on my own today. You are staying in bed. No arguments."

She didn't attempt to raise an objection. She remembered how Martin had made her rest after she found out about Toby and Christian. She laughed a quiet, bitter laugh. It was almost becoming a routine.

After Soph and Martin had gone, she fell asleep immediately. It was four o'clock when she woke. She knew it wasn't a good idea, but something made her switch on her phone and check her voice mail. There were twelve calls, all showing Dan's number. She had no intention of listening to them. Instead, she sat on the edge of the bed, her thumb pressing delete over and over again.

It took all her energy and willpower, but afterward she put a brush through her hair, washed her face and went downstairs. The shop was empty. Martin appeared to be coming to the end of a phone call.

"Thank you for letting us know.... Yes, I'll be sure to tell her."

"Tell who what?" Abby said.

"Gosh, you're up," Martin said, his face etched with anxiety, which Abby took for concern about her.

"I thought I'd come down . . . you know, see what's going on." She managed a pale smile.

"That was the lady in Majorca—you know, the one who's supplying the lavender for Mr. T's party."

"Right. When's it arriving? One of us will need to go to Heathrow in the van and pick it up."

"It's not."

"Not what?"

"It's not arriving. The Spanish baggage and cargo handlers have just gone on strike. No planes are taking off or landing on the mainland or any of the islands."

Abby swallowed hard. "You have to be kidding."

"I wish I was."

"But today's Wednesday. The party is on Sunday. What am I supposed to do?" She fell onto one of the stools in front of the counter. She could feel herself starting to shake.

"Abby, calm down. It's only the lavender for the terrace. I mean, it's not as if we can't get the cherry blossom or peonies. Mr. T won't mind."

"Of course he'll bloody mind," Abby cried, her temper flaring in a way it never would normally. "You know what he's like. You've seen how he is when he gets angry. He's a perfectionist and a control freak. He'll go ballistic."

"Abby, you have been through enough stress in the last twenty-four hours. You have to take it easy. I'm frightened you're going to lose it completely. Let me sort this out. I'll tell Ichiro and he'll speak to Mr. T."

"Don't you dare! If Mr. T finds out I can't get the lavender, he will sack me. Once news gets out that I let him down, I could lose all my corporate clients."

"That's ridiculous. All your clients know how reliable you are. Plus, they like you. Nobody would ditch you over one slipup that isn't even your fault."

"It doesn't work like that. Liking me has got nothing to do with it. People will see that I can't be trusted. Nobody will be interested in the details. They simply won't risk employing me anymore. And it doesn't end there. London is such a village. Everybody knows everybody else; you know how fast gossip spreads and how facts get distorted in the telling. Eventually it could filter down to street level that Fabulous Flowers isn't what it was and, hey presto, all the wedding and party orders dry up. That is our bread and butter. Without them, I would be finished. There would be no Fabulous Flowers." She took a deep breath. "OK, we have to stay focused. There has to be something we can do. But what? What?"

Martin seemed to be at a loss for words. "By the way, Dan called in earlier," he ventured. "I told him you were asleep."

"Well done. I can't face him. I don't want to hear one of those 'it's me not you' speeches—particularly not with all this chaos going on."

It was odd, but Abby almost cheered up. She had lost the love of her life, but she wasn't about to lose her business in the bargain. She was going to come out fighting and solve this problem.

She began by phoning her contact in Majorca, just to confirm what Martin had told her. There was no mistake. Then she hit the phones, calling all the lavender suppliers she could find in other Mediterranean countries. The story was the same everywhere. Yes, they could get the plants to her, but not at such short notice. The problem appeared to be the official paperwork involved in exporting plants.

At one point she phoned Toby, on the off chance that somebody in his law firm might know somebody who might possibly have a contact in the French Civil Service who could speed up the official paperwork. "There's no one I can think of," he said. "Have you considered bribery? You could always bribe some Greek official a few hundred quid to forget about the paperwork."

"And end up in the Sparta State Pen. Not exactly on my list of things to do before I die."

Toby said he was really sorry he couldn't help. She told him not to worry. She decided it would be rude to hang up without engaging him in some chitchat, so she asked him how work was going.

"Oh, you know, much the same. Busy as ever."

"And your mother? I'm assuming she's in fine fettle?"

He gave a soft laugh. "You assume correctly. She's still involved in this media project I was telling you about the other day. No idea what it is. She says she won't tell me a thing until it's a done deal. I can't think what it could be."

Abby asked him to let her know, particularly if it turned out to be something exciting. Then she said she had to go, because a customer had just walked in.

"OK," he said. "So I guess I'll see you on Friday."

"Friday?"

"The court case. Remember?"

"God, yes, I'd forgotten. . . . So you're going to be there to support Christian?"

He said he was. "And you'll be there with Scozza."

"Yes."

"Right."

It was clear from the sudden awkwardness between them that they had both realized this wasn't going to be the easiest of occasions.

"OK," she said. "I guess I'll see you in court."

"Yes. See you in court."

MARTIN AND Christian didn't have a day in court so much as an evening. The one thing the pair had been able to agree on was that they needed to be at work during the day. Since there were ten cases to get through during the day, the producer hadn't taken much persuading to put Roberts vs Sitwell at the bottom of his list. Filming would start at eight.

On Friday morning, Martin arrived at the shop looking anxious and pale and carrying two suit carriers.

"What do you think?" he said to Abby. "The gunmetal Armani or the navy Hugo Boss? And which shirt? The white looks fresh, but I'm thinking pale pink could work. And what about a tie? A bit OTT, maybe?"

Abby said the whole suit thing was OTT, because it looked like he was making a special effort to impress and that the judge might see it as a ploy. "Just go as you are. Let Christian wear a suit. You'll see how greasy and smarmy it makes him look."

Martin considered for a moment or two. "You might be right." He hung the suit carriers in the back room. "OK, I thought we could go over the speech I've written for the judge. You know, my opening remarks." He pulled a thick wad of paper from his back pocket. "If your lordship pleases," he began.

"If your lordship pleases?"

"Yes. What's wrong with that?"

"Scozz. This is cable TV, not the Central Criminal Court."

"Too much?"

"Maybe just a smidge."

"OK, how about this?" He cleared his throat. "Members of the jury, I would like to draw your attention to the words of the great Roman thinker Marcus Aurelius, which I think are apt in this case: *Does the lantern's flame shine with undimmed brilliance until it is quenched—*"

It was as much as Abby could do not to burst out laughing. "Scozz, you sound like you've swallowed an entire *Frasier* episode."

Martin's crest couldn't have fallen any further. "Five hours I spent in the library last night, trawling through philosophy books..."

"Oh, God. Scozz, I'm sorry. I don't mean to make fun, but you're trying too hard. All you have to do is answer the judge's questions truthfully and sincerely. That's what's going to win you the case."

He nodded. "I know, but somehow it doesn't feel like it's going to be enough. You sure you don't want to hear my summing up? I refer to the Stoic philosopher Claudius Maximus."

Somehow they got through the day. If Martin wasn't obsessing about whether or not to get a haircut, he was practicing his courtroom "voice," which he had decided should sound sufficiently baritone on account of all British judges being homophobes.

As they were leaving for the TV studio, Dan texted Abby to say he was out of town until late Saturday night. *Please let's talk Sunday. I need to explain.* She felt a lump form in the back of her throat as she deleted the message. Cinders had texted Martin earlier on to say she couldn't make the court case because she was away for a few days. Abby had said that it didn't take a great leap of imagination to work out who she was out of town with. Martin offered to phone Cinders and ask her outright if she was having an affair with Dan, but Abby said she had all the evidence she needed and really couldn't see the point in Martin getting involved.

THE FILM studio was on a large industrial estate in Neasden, behind Ikea. Martin gave his name to a young woman wearing a headset. "Martin Roberts. She ran her pen over the list on her clipboard. "Oh, yes, the dog-custody dispute—Roberts versus Sitwell. You're on in an hour." She directed them to the canteen and said they would be called just before eight o'clock.

Theirs was the last case of the day, so the canteen was empty. They ordered coffee and sat down on metal chairs, which were meant to look industrial and edgy but were just cold and hard. "God, Abby, I'm so nervous. I mean, what if the case goes against me and I never see Debbie again? I don't think I could bear that."

She reached out and took his hand. "It won't. Don't worry."

Just then an agitated-looking and breathless Ichiro appeared. He was wearing a very fitted canary-yellow military jacket with a mandarin collar. "My God, the journey took me forever. I thought I wasn't going to make it in all that traffic." He pulled a chair out from under the table and sat down. "So, Marty, how you doing? You're not wearing a suit. I thought we agreed you should wear the Armani or the Hugo Boss."

"Abby and I decided it might be a bit OTT."

"You could be right. So, are you nervous? You need to stay focused. Have you been practicing your opening remarks? And did you try those yoga exercises I mentioned? And what about the mantra? You really have to try and stay calm."

"I'm perfectly calm. It's you who sounds like you need a chill pill."

Ichiro began fanning his face with his hand. "Tell me about it," he said. "I've already taken six herbal tranquilizers. I'm just so wired about this whole thing and I don't know why—after all, it's you taking the stand on national TV, not me."

Abby offered to get him a cup of tea. "No, I'm good, thanks. So ... Abby, how are you? Marty told me all about you and Dan. What can I say? The man is clearly a complete jerk. But don't you worry about a thing. Leave it to Ichiro. I will talk to all my girlfriends, and between us we will find you a god." He turned to Martin. "Shall I tell Abby my news?"

"Sure."

"I've told Mr. T I'm quitting! I've given a month's notice."

"No! How did he take it? I bet he went mad."

"Mad doesn't begin to describe it. He went totally apoplectic. He ranted and raved about how it had taken years to 'break me in,' that I alone understood all his quirks and foibles, that he couldn't face training somebody else. He even offered me a brand-new BMW to stay. I'm ashamed to say that I was tempted. When I said no, he threatened to have a heart attack, but I just ignored him."

When Abby asked him if he'd found an interior-design course, he said that he had.

"Wow, that's brilliant news. So have you worked out how you're going to fund it? Did the universe provide?"

"It most certainly did. Didier, my hairdresser, was blow-drying me the other day and happened to mention that he was looking for a part-time receptionist. I offered my services and he accepted. But that's not all." Ichiro looked at Martin as if to say, "Is it all right to tell her?" Martin nodded. "OK ... wait for it—Marty and I are moving in together. OK, I admit that it's partly to save money, but it's mainly because we're in love and we absolutely want to be together."

Even though it did occur to her that the two of them had known each other for only five minutes, Abby could feel her eyes welling up. She reached out and took one of their hands in each of hers. "Omigod, that's fantastic. I'm so happy for you. I can't say I'm exactly surprised, though. You guys are so right for each other—"

She stopped in mid-sentence, distracted by the arrival of Christian and Toby. "He's here," she hissed.

Christian had forsaken his trademark turtleneck sweater and quilted jacket for loud Mr. Toad tweeds and a green woolen tie. He glared at Martin, who met his glare and raised him an eyebrow. Martin's bravado belied his true emotions. "I'm just not sure I can go through with this," he whispered.

"Come on, you've made it this far," Abby said. "Of course you can."

At one point she caught Toby's eye and they exchanged awkward smiles.

THE COURTROOM was small and packed with film crew tending their equipment. "I feel rather at home," Abby quipped. In front of the judge's raised bench were two lecterns, one for the plaintiff and another for the defendant. There were half a dozen leather-covered pews for spectators.

They were greeted by the female court usher. She was wearing a wig and black gown. She directed Martin and Christian to the lecterns. The rest of them—including Toby—were directed to the front pew. "This feels a bit awkward," he said to Abby, who was sitting next to him. "You know, bearing in mind we're on opposite sides. Maybe

I should move seats." But the usher shooed him back and said they were about to start filming.

"By the way," Toby said to Abby, "I think you ought to know that the council turned down Christian's appeal to stop your pavement displays."

"Really? That's a relief."

"For you, maybe. He's been giving me hell over it for the last two days."

"All rise," the usher announced. "Her Honor Judge Trudy Kenwood presiding."

Ichiro, Abby and Toby rose. "Kenwood?" Abby mouthed to Toby. "Strange coincidence."

The next moment, a very large bewigged and gowned figure heaved into view and took her place behind the bench.

"Bloody hell!" Toby hissed. "It's my mother!"

"You are not wrong," Abby said. "And, look, she's had her teeth whitened."

"This must be the secret TV project she was going on about."

"But her name's not Trudy."

"It's her middle name. Guess they thought Judge Penelope was a bit of a mouthful." He covered his face with his hand.

"Too late. She's seen you."

"Oh, God. How does she look?"

"So far, I'd say she seems rather confused. I strongly suspect that she's wondering what the dickens you've got to do with this case."

"I'm leaving. I can't face this. She's bound to find out I'm in a relationship with Christian." He stood up. Abby grabbed his arm and yanked him down again. "Oh, no, you don't. At some stage you need to tell your mother you are gay. Now's as good a time as any."

She didn't have a chance to continue her lecture, because Ichiro had piped up. "Did I hear right? Are you telling me that the judge is Toby's mother? How could that happen? Toby, did you know about this? Jeez, did you arrange it? Marty can't possibly get a fair hearing if the judge is biased. I'm going to put a stop to this right now."

"Please don't," Abby pleaded. "I promise you, Toby knew nothing about this. His mother is a real-life magistrate. I've met her, and I know for a fact that she's too stubborn to allow family loyalty to influence her decision."

"She's right," Toby said. "Given the choice, my mother would always support the side I'm not on."

"I'm not sure that's entirely true," Abby said.

"Bloody is. You don't know her like I do."

Much to Abby's surprise, Ichiro seemed satisfied with their defense of Lady Penelope and made no further threat to interrupt the proceedings.

"But I'm not ready," Toby whispered.

"Not ready for what?"

"To tell her I'm gay. I need time to prepare my speech, to get myself into the right frame of mind. I need to let Christian know that I'm going to tell her. He's standing over there. He has no idea who she is. Oh, God, this is such a mess." Toby looked as if he might burst into tears.

At this point the usher came over and told them to be quiet. Abby apologized.

Lady Penelope, aka Judge Trudy, carried on reading her notes. From time to time she would look up and peer at Martin and Christian over her pince-nez.

"Now then," she said finally, "it would appear that Mr

Roberts and Mr. Sitwell were in a relationship for five years.
When that broke down, a dispute arose over who should
care for their pet dog, a St. Bernard named—do I have this
right?—Debbie Harry." She turned to the usher. "Is this
some kind of joke? Is this Debbie Harry some person I
should have heard of?"

"I think you'll find that Debbie Harry was a famous
eighties pop star."

"I see," Lady Penelope grunted. "Never heard of her."
She looked at Martin. "Mr. Johnson, since you are the
plaintiff in this case, I will hear from you first."

"As your lordship pleases—"

"Mr. Roberts, I am not a lordship. I would thank you
not to address me as such."

Christian sniggered.

"Sorry," Martin said.

"Now, then, Mr. Roberts, the facts of the case, if you
please."

"Well, Mr. Sitwell and I bought Debbie Harry two years
ago when she was a puppy. She was the cutest little thing. I
fell in love with her immediately. She had these big brown
eyes and the cutest little nose. Christian wanted to call her
Brandy, but I thought that was such a cliché for a St. Bernard,
bearing in mind they carry barrels of brandy round their
necks. Anyway, I've loved the real Debbie Harry since forever.
I mean, her *Def, Dumb & Blonde* album was sheer genius."

"Mr. Roberts," Lady Penelope broke in, rolling her
eyes. "Will you please confine yourself to the relevant facts
or we will be here until midnight."

"Yes, sorry, your worship."

Lady P was becoming exasperated. "I am not a lordship,
nor am I a worship. *Ma'am* will do nicely, thank you."

Christian was looking positively smug by now, as if he had already won.

"Ma'am, if I might interject at this point," he said with a weasellike charm, "the facts of the case are very simple—"

The judge turned on Christian. "No, Mr. Sitwell, you may not interject. Might I remind you that Mr. Roberts is giving his evidence? You will have your turn in due course. For now please be quiet."

Christian blushed scarlet. "Of course." He squirmed. "I do apologize, ma'am."

The judge turned back to Martin and instructed him to continue.

"Anyway, we brought Debbie Harry home to live with us. I got her a kennel with her name on it and one of those fleecy things to sleep on. Not that she slept at first. I was up with her most nights because she was missing her mum. I used to bring her into the living room and we'd watch old movies together. She seemed to like that."

"Mr. Roberts, I must ask you to keep your evidence more concise."

"Sorry... Anyway, everything was fine until my relationship with Mr. Sitwell broke up. I caught him having an affair with this transvestite who performs in one of the gay bars in Soho. I can't remember which one——"

"Even more concise, please."

"Right."

Eventually Martin told the story of how Christian refused to let him see Debbie Harry after the breakup, how he came into the shop to threaten and harass him. "My boss, Miss Abby Crompton, can confirm this."

The judge asked if Abby was present. "She is, ma'am," Martin said, pointing her out.

"Miss Crompton, please approach the bench."

Abby stood up and crossed the courtroom.

Lady Penelope looked at her over her glasses. She clearly recognized Abby, but her stern expression and demeanor left Abby in no doubt that this was neither the time nor place to exchange pleasantries. "So, Miss Crompton, you are Mr. Roberts's employer?"

Abby nodded. "Yes, ma'am."

"What can you tell the court about Mr. Sitwell's behavior?"

Abby didn't hold back. She told the judge about the scenes she had witnessed in the shop, where Christian had shouted and bullied Martin. She even managed to describe how Christian had bullied and harassed her. Lady P said this was completely irrelevant, but it was clear she would take it into account.

When Abby had finished, Lady P thanked her and turned to Christian. "Mr. Sitwell, what do you have to say in response to these allegations?"

"Ma'am, the plaintiff and Miss Crompton are somewhat deranged."

"Is that so?"

"Absolutely, ma'am. The point is that, whenever Mr. Roberts looked after Debbie, he didn't feed her properly or give her the vitamins she needs."

"You have evidence of this? Did she lose weight?"

"Well, no, but she got three colds last winter."

"And so you took her to the vet?"

"Yes."

"Did the vet advise you that the colds came about as a result of the animal not having been fed properly?"

"Not as such."

"What do you mean, 'not as such'? Did he or didn't he?"

"No," Christian mumbled.

"I see. So, let's recap. The dog didn't lose weight. Nor did the vet suggest that her colds had been caused by poor nutrition. I would put it to you that you have no evidence whatsoever that Mr. Roberts was abusing the animal."

For once Christian was at a loss for words. In desperation, he turned toward Toby. "Toby," he cried out, his tone close to panic, "tell the judge that we're together and that we would provide a wonderful, loving and caring home for Debbie Harry."

Lady Penelope brought her gavel down onto its block. "I will have silence in my court," she bellowed. She looked directly at Toby. He averted his gaze. It was several seconds before she turned back to Christian. "Mr. Sitwell, are you telling me that you and this gentleman are living together— as a couple?"

"Indeed."

"I see." Lady Penelope took a few sips of water from the glass on the bench. "I see," she repeated. Her eyes went back briefly to Toby, who was still refusing to look at her. She gazed in his direction for several seconds. Finally she returned to the case before her. "Mr. Sitwell, have you heard of the actress Lucinda Wallace?"

"Of course."

"Well, I can assure you that she isn't deranged, and she has issued this court a sworn affidavit saying she saw you shouting and bullying Mr. Roberts. She also said you tugged so hard on the dog's lead that you caused her significant distress."

"That's a lie!"

"I don't think so." Lady Penelope arched her hands. "In

the case of Roberts versus Sitwell, I find for the plaintiff, Mr. Roberts, who will have sole custody of the dog Debbie Harry. The dog will be handed over to Mr. Roberts no later than ten A.M. tomorrow." She looked back at Christian. "Mr. Sitwell, I am prepared to review my judgment six months from now. That will be dependent upon you agreeing to go to an anger-management course and completing it successfully." For a second time, she brought her gavel down onto its block. "Case adjourned."

"This is ridiculous," Christian cried. "It's absurd. I demand a retrial. I demand a new judge. I will not accept this. I will not give up that dog."

"Oh, you will, Mr. Sitwell," Lady Penelope said, her calmness clearly belying her anger. "Believe me, you will. If you don't, I will recommend to the police that they prosecute you for harassment and animal cruelty. That way you will lose the dog and more than likely your position with the retailers' association."

Christian suddenly looked broken.

The cameras continued to roll as Abby and Ichiro hugged Martin. "Hey, what did I tell you?" Abby said. "I knew you'd win."

"Actually, if I remember rightly," Martin said with a grin, "you suggested I could lose."

"I did? Oh, well, what do I know? That'll teach you to never listen to me."

"Well, I knew we'd win," Ichiro said, opening his shoulder bag and taking out a fuchsia-pink dog bowl. Around it, written in fake diamonds, was the name *Debbie Harry.* "Isn't it just awesome!"

Everybody agreed that it was.

While Abby, Martin and Ichiro continued to revel in

their victory, Toby approached Christian and put his arm round his shoulder. "Come on," he said gently. "Let's go home."

"I do not need effing anger management," Christian snarled, making two fists.

"You know what?" Toby said. "You do. And what's more, you've needed it for a very long time."

He was leading Christian out of the courtroom when Lady Penelope appeared, still in her judge's regalia.

This time Toby looked her directly in the eye. He was silent for a few moments, clearly summoning every ounce of his courage. "OK, Mother, now you know I'm gay. If you want to shout at me and humiliate me, then go ahead. Get it off your chest. Tell me what a disgusting pervert I am and how I've sullied the family name. Disinherit me. Disown me if you want. I don't bloody care. I've had a lifetime of your hectoring and bullying. It ends now. If you can't accept me for who I am, then sod it. I don't care."

"Good for you."

Abby, who was standing several feet away with Ichiro and Martin and pretending not to listen, smiled. "Wow, he's finally done it."

"I will not be treated like an idiot," Toby carried on, oblivious to his mother's comment. "I am one of this country's top corporate lawyers. I don't care if you're not proud of me. I don't need your approval anymore and I don't need your money. I'm proud of me, and that's all that matters."

"But I am proud of you."

"And I will not put up with your endless interfering in my life—like when you demanded that Abby see a gynecologist to check that she's fertile."

"Quite right! Bravo!"

"What? You're agreeing with me?"

"Yes."

"Well, that has to be a first."

"I admit that I can be a trifle domineering on occasion and that I need somebody to tell me to mind my own business. Your father used to do it when he was sober. Thirty-four years I have been waiting for you to stand up for yourself, and it's finally happened. About bloody time."

Toby blinked in disbelief. "There's no cure for being gay, you know. No posh head doctor you can send me to. This is it. This is who I am."

"Don't be a complete ass, Toby. I don't give a flying fig if you're gay."

"You don't?"

"Of course not." She removed her wig and began scratching her head. "Our family has a proud tradition of stately homos. Apparently, my father had a long-standing affair with Noël Coward. Although I wouldn't have minded you telling me."

"I'm sorry. I thought you'd fly into an almighty rage, and I couldn't face it."

"Well, you've managed to face me now. I'd say that's a step in the right direction." At this point, Lady Penelope turned to Abby and beckoned her into the group. "Come here, my dear." Abby took a few steps forward. "I'm sorry you and Toby didn't make it. I rather took to you, Abby. I admire a girl with spirit."

"You remembered my name," Abby said.

"Having to make more of an effort these days," she harrumphed. "Frightful nuisance. Doesn't matter so much when I'm being a regular magistrate back home and there are other people in court to remind me, but one simply can't be a TV judge and forget people's names. Got myself one of those invisible hearing-aid whatnots, too. Producer insisted."

Christian took her attention next. "As you may have guessed, I am Toby's mother."

"How do you do?" Christian said with a snarl. He wasn't about to forgive her for what he saw as a cruel, unreasonable judgment simply because she was the mother of the man he lived with.

"Oh, I do very well, as it happens. I am just wondering why my son has gotten himself involved with a man who has anger-management issues." She turned to Toby. "Have you any idea what you're taking on? Not your best move, if you ask me...."

"I am not asking you. I don't give a damn what you think and I am not asking your permission. Christian needs help, and I'm going to be there to support him, because I love him." He turned to Christian. "Come on. Let's go."

The pair had gone no more than a couple of paces when Lady Penelope called out to Toby. He turned. "Point taken," she barked. "Right...well, then...good luck...to both of you." She attempted—possibly for the first time in her life—an expression of motherly concern.

Toby appeared to note it and smiled back. "Thanks," he said.

Chapter 19

ABBY HAD INSISTED THAT Martin take Saturday off to get reacquainted with Debbie Harry.

By now it was almost lunchtime and the shop wasn't too busy. She decided to use the time to change the water in her display vases and check out blooms that were past their best. She had just removed some drooping orange ranunculus when she heard the door open. A paunchy, gray-haired man dressed in a rugby shirt and jeans was coming toward her, smiling.

"Can I help you?" she said, returning the smile.

"You must be Abby." He held out his hand.

She found herself taking it. "Yes...sorry...and you are?..."

"Malcolm Grant. Dan's stepdad."

"Goodness." She was taken aback. The last thing she'd expected was the chairman of S&M to walk into her shop unannounced, wearing jeans and a rugby shirt.

"I am so pleased to meet you at last." His manner was easy and avuncular. She took to him immediately. "I can't tell you how many times I've asked Dan to set up a lunch or at least bring you into the office so that I can meet you and thank you for everything in person, but he keeps putting me off. Says you're both too busy or some such rot."

"Well, Dan has been very busy with this film." She became uneasy. She needed to get this out of the way before they went any further. "And I should tell you that something else has happened in the last few days. We're not actually seeing each other at the moment."

Sir Malcolm seemed taken aback. "Really? I'm sorry about that. He seemed so smitten. Every time we meet up or he comes home, he doesn't stop talking about you... and you seem so nice." He paused. "Anyway, your relationship is your private affair. I'm actually here to talk business."

"Business?"

"Absolutely. Look, I'm not going to beat around the bush. I want to invite you to meet the members of the S&M board. We want to offer you a consultancy post."

She frowned. "A consultancy post? I'm sorry, I don't understand."

"It means we'd like to use you—purely on an ad hoc basis—to take a look at what our fashion designers are coming up with each season. We want your advice on style, cut and color. We'd like you to supervise the redesign of our shop interiors."

"Sir Malcolm—"

"Malcolm, please. The *sir* makes me sound like such an old fart."

She laughed. "Malcolm... I'm very flattered, but I'm not a fashion or interior-design expert. I was only telling Dan the things that most of your customers have been saying for ages. It wasn't rocket science."

"That may be, but it's you we have to thank for giving

us our wake-up call. All of us on the S&M board have been resting on our laurels for too long. We became arrogant and complacent—not to say stubborn. As chairman I should have taken the lead, but I admit I was too scared to modernize and change. We surrounded ourselves with accountants when we needed designers. Even when our share price began to tumble, we refused to listen to criticism and take advice—that is, until Dan started talking about you. He was so fired up. You should have heard him. When he talked about your creativity, your energy, your passion for S&M, he got so carried away. He told me how you took him round the stores, critiquing all the clothes. He said in particular you singled out the dreadful floral motifs. His enthusiasm for you and yours for S&M were catching, and finally—almost too late in the day—I took notice. I can't begin to tell you how grateful we all are. It wouldn't be putting it too strongly to say you've pretty much saved our bacon at S&M. And we want to show you how much we value what you've done."

"Thank you, but I was more than happy to offer you my suggestions about how to improve S&M. I wouldn't dream of taking any kind of reward, and although your offer of a consultancy post is incredibly generous, I really am committed full time to my business."

"But we would require your services only once a month or so, and the financial package we have in mind for you is extremely generous."

"I don't doubt it, but as I say, I am trying to build a business and I really must stay focused."

Sir Malcolm smiled. "I respect that. Look, maybe we could come to some other financial arrangement? A one-time payment, maybe?"

"What? No. I wouldn't think of taking money."

"It would be our gift. A thank-you present."

"That is very kind, but I really don't want anything."

He chuckled. "You know, Abby, I'm not sure you have quite grasped how much value you have been to S&M. We are not some struggling charity, you know. We can afford to pay you."

"I know. But that really is my final word."

"Never say that in business. In any negotiation, you always need to leave yourself room to maneuver. I suggest you sleep on it." He looked at his watch. "I'm sorry, but I have to get going. I've got a plane to catch. I'm having dinner with one of our suppliers in Seville."

"Malcolm," Abby said, biting her bottom lip, "I don't want to be the bearer of bad tidings, but haven't you heard? The Spanish baggage handlers are on strike. There are no Spanish flights taking off or landing."

He looked distinctly awkward. "Yes, I have heard about the strike, but it doesn't really affect me. I . . . you see, Dan's mother and I . . . we . . . we have our own private jet. We take off and land at small airports and tend to be able to bypass strikes."

"Wow, that is amazing. I'd love to have my own private plane. Imagine, jetting off to Cannes when you feel like it, or Rome or Istanbul—" She didn't so much stop in mid-sentence as screech to a halt. "Omigod! Hang on, if you have a private plane and you are able to bypass strikes, then that means . . ."

"Yes?"

"Oh, God . . . no, this is awfully nervy . . . I'm not sure I can even ask. OK, there is one thing you could do for me."

"Name it."

"Well, you see, there are these lavender plants sitting in a garden center in Majorca..."

She explained about the stranded lavender, Mr. T, and how tomorrow's party might just make her career, if it weren't for the Spanish baggage handlers' strike.

"Consider it done. Fudo Takahashi is such an old tyrant—did some business with him years ago, before I came to S&M. Impossible man. You definitely don't want to let him down. I'll send my pilot over to Majorca to pick up the lavender. We're leaving Spain first thing in the morning. The plants will be in the country by lunchtime. We land at a small airport in the Cotswolds. I will see that the plants are put in a van and delivered to Mr. Takahashi by mid-afternoon."

"I don't know what to say. Thank you. Thank you so much." The next thing she knew, she was on the other side of the counter, hugging Sir Malcolm.

"My pleasure," he chortled. "It's the very least I can do." He handed her his business card. "E-mail me the addresses of the garden center in Majorca and old Takahashi's place in London."

ABBY GOT straight on the phone to Martin. "Omigod," he cried. "I don't believe it. This is fantastic news. What an amazing coincidence, Sir Malcolm going to Spain. I'll tell Ichi to expect the plants tomorrow afternoon. You do realize that this is the second wonderful thing to have happened. First I get Debbie Harry back, and now Fabulous Flowers is going to live on to fight another day. They say things always happen in threes. Maybe you and Dan will work this thing out and get back together."

"After the way he has behaved, I really can't see that happening."

"No, maybe you're right."

No sooner had Abby gotten off the phone than her mobile started ringing. She assumed it was Dan and ignored it. When she went to check on who had called, the message turned out to be from her mother. "Darling, we are leaving New York tonight. Flight gets in Sunday at lunchtime. Please, don't worry about meeting us. We'll be fine with a cab."

Abby phoned straight back to say that of course she was meeting them and how could they even think of taking a cab. "I've missed you both so much. I can't wait to see you."

"We've missed you, too, poppet. There's so much to tell you. I don't know where to start. And I can't wait to catch up with your news. How's Toby?"

Abby had been dreading this question. "Yeah...he's... fine."

"And we really do need to finalize all the wedding plans. Maybe Dad and I should invite Toby and Lady Penelope for dinner next week."

"Tell you what, Mum, why don't we talk about everything tomorrow?"

"All right. You seem a bit down. Everything OK?"

"I'm fine, just a bit preoccupied. I'm doing the flowers for this huge A-list party tomorrow night."

"Ok, darling. See you tomorrow."

That night, Abby couldn't sleep. She tossed and turned in bed, convinced that something would go wrong and the lavender wouldn't make it to Mr. T on time. Then she started worrying about the rest of the flowers. What if some disaster befell them on the way to Mr. T's? Eventually she fell into a restless sleep, her dreams filled with images of crushed cherry blossoms and limp, drooping peonies.

She woke around nine and found herself thinking about Dan. Despite her restless night, things had clarified in her mind. Until now, speaking to him was the last thing she wanted to do, but her thoughts had performed a complete U-turn. "Dan wants to talk. OK, let's talk." Her emotional strength had returned. Suddenly she was fired up and filled with the overwhelming need to tell Le Compte d'Anjou Jonelle Bergerac Chipault precisely what she thought of him. What was more, she wanted to do it in person. She decided to pay him a call.

On the drive over to Camden, Abby rehearsed everything she was going to say. She would tell Dan what a cruel two-timing bastard he was. Then she would tell Cinders—assuming she was there, too—that she was a selfish, spoiled, predatory beast whose only interest was satisfying her own needs and to hell with anybody else's happiness. She would leave them rendered speechless by the power of her rhetoric, her dignity intact, her point well and truly made.

When she rang the buzzer, there was no answer. She assumed the pair were still asleep and tried twice more. Nothing. There was only one other place he could be. If Cinders hadn't stayed here, then he had slept at her place. Abby had no trouble remembering the address. She must have heard Katie telling umpteen deliverymen where to send various orders of detox herbs.

The Notting Hill house was exactly as she'd imagined, a white rendered Victorian villa with pretty arched windows and ornate black wrought-iron balconies. Abby parked the car in a resident's bay. To hell with it if she got a ticket, she thought. She walked toward the house. Somebody was opening the living-room curtains. It was Cinders. Her hair was tied back and she was wearing a black silk kimono. A man appeared behind her briefly. She didn't get a good look at him, but it could only be Dan. This time Abby wasn't about to run away. Instead, she marched up the steps and picked up the heavy brass knocker.

A Filipino maid came to the door. "I've come to see Cinders," Abby said, marching past the poor woman, who couldn't have been more than four foot ten. She threw open the door to the living room. Cinders and Dan were standing in front of a huge roaring fire, locked in an embrace. Dan was wearing a white terry-cloth dressing gown. For some reason he looked taller than usual.

Cinders jumped and pulled away. "Oh, my God!"

"Not so blinkin' cocky now, are we, Miss I-can-have-whoever-I-like-and-sod-the-rest-of-the-world."

"Abby, please—"

Abby turned to Dan. "So, let's have it. You're the one who's been wanting to talk. What have you got to say for yourself?"

She stood looking at him. She blinked. She even rubbed her eyes like some cartoon character, hoping the man in front of her would morph into the person she was expecting. Her stomach lurched. She felt sick.

"Omigod, it's you!"

The exquisite dark-haired man cleared his throat with embarrassment. He turned to Cinders. "This is Abby? The woman you told me about who owns the flower store?" He spoke with a strong American accent.

Cinders nodded.

"Hi, Abby. Good to meet you." Then, to Cinders: "I think maybe I should go upstairs and take a shower."

Abby wanted the ground to swallow her up and deposit her at the earth's core. "Omigod...Liam...I mean, Mr. Heggarty...sir...what have I done? This is awful. I thought you were somebody else. What can I say?"

"It's fine." He smiled. "No harm done." He walked toward the door.

"I love all your films," she called after him. "And if you ask me, you actually do Hank Reno's songs better than he does."

He closed the door behind him. Abby turned to Cinders. "I don't understand. How did I get it all wrong?..." Then a dastardly thought occurred to her. "Unless, of course, you're seeing Liam and Dan."

"Oh, for God's sake, Abby, of course I'm not. I've never been interested in Dan. He and I are friends. Nothing more. Without putting too fine a point on it, darling, I don't think he's quite in my league."

"But the other night I overheard you telling him how much you wanted to be with him and how he should tell me about his relationship with you."

"What you couldn't see from outside the room was that I was on the phone. I wasn't speaking to Dan. I was speaking to Liam in California. We've just bought a house in the Hollywood Hills, and the woman we hired to oversee the renovation work has turned out to be hopeless. I was trying to persuade him to sack her."

Abby lowered herself onto a velvet fainting couch and suspected it might be about to be used for the purpose it was intended.

"Bloody hell! What have I done?"

"Quite a lot, actually. For a start, Dan is inconsolable. I've kept on and on at him, offering to phone you, but he insists on sorting this mess out for himself. You could at least have taken his calls."

"I was too angry...I'm so sorry, Cinders. I've made a total ass of myself. Will you apologize to Liam for me?"

"Of course I will, but he'll be fine. It's Dan you need to speak to."

Abby explained how she'd already been round to his flat and there was no answer.

"Well, he told me he would be home Saturday night. Maybe he popped out to get the Sunday papers."

ABBY TRIED calling him on his mobile, but it seemed to be switched off. She looked at her watch. Her parents were due at Heathrow at twelve. She would head out to the airport and try him again when she got there.

Construction meant the traffic heading onto the M4 was bumper to bumper. It eased up once she hit the motorway, but she was still more than half an hour late. She parked the car in the short-term parking lot and ran to the arrivals hall. She stopped to look at the arrivals board and, to her relief, discovered that the plane had been late and had only landed twenty minutes ago. Jean and Hugh would probably still be at the carousel, waiting for their luggage.

She carried on toward the barrier. There were three camera crews waiting, along with dozens of photographers and journalists. She shook her head in amused disbelief. Part of her wanted to turn to the rest of the people waiting for their friends and relatives and cry: "Do you know who the TV crews and journalists are waiting for? My mum! That's who."

The trickle of people coming through the barrier became heavier. Abby spotted her dad first. He was wearing a check sports jacket and a Chicago White Sox baseball cap. Perched on top of the trolley he was pushing was a three-foot-high, inflatable pink Empire State Building. Jean was a couple of paces behind. She was wearing a navy blazer over tailored beige trousers. Her hair and makeup were immaculate. She looked cool and poised—less like Jean Crompton, Croydon housewife, and more like a senior business executive.

"That's her," shouted one of the cameramen. The press pack surged forward. "Jean, how does it feel to be home?" "Hugh, you must be very proud of your wife." "Jean, there are rumors that you might be considering a career in politics."

Abby tried to fight her way through, but in all the commotion she didn't stand a hope. She stood waving her arms. "Dad! Mum! Over here." But Jean and Hugh couldn't see or hear her. Jean smiled for the cameras. "OK," she said brightly, giving the impression she had been dealing with the press for years. "If you can all hang on, we have a press conference arranged in the first-floor conference room in half an hour. You will all have your chance to ask questions then. Right now we would like some private time to say hello to our daughter, who we believe is here somewhere."

"Mum! I'm here."

The cameras and the reporters turned toward Abby. "How does it feel to have your parents back?"

"Fantastic!"

"Did you see your mother on *Oprah*?"

"No, but I can't wait to watch the DVD."

"Did you fear for your parents' health during the Mutiny on the *Bantry*?"

"All the time. I never stopped worrying."

As Abby hugged first Jean and then Hugh, cameras whirred and clacked around them. Abby was crying. Jean was crying. Even Hugh had a tear in his eye.

"Oh, Abby, it is so good to see you," Jean said through her tears. "We've missed you so much."

"I've missed you, too."

At this point, an airport executive appeared and introduced himself. He offered to escort them to the conference room where the press conference was due to be held. Abby looked at her watch. "Thing is, Dad, you didn't tell me about this press conference. I'm not sure I've got time to hang on. I thought I was taking you straight home. I'm doing the flowers for this party tonight and I really need to be there in a couple of hours. It's going to take ages to get everything done."

Jean explained that they didn't know about the press conference until their London publicist called them at JFK to say it had been arranged.

"You have a publicist?"

"Actually, she has two." Hugh grinned. "One in London and one in New York. It's like being married to Madonna."

"Oh, stoppit," Jean giggled, digging her husband in the ribs. She turned to Abby. "He's so proud," she said.

"And with good reason," Hugh added.

By now the airport executive was trying to hide his impatience behind a thin smile. Jean picked up on this. She shooed Hugh off to the conference room, barely giving

Abby a chance to kiss him good-bye, and said she would join him in fifteen minutes. "Come on," she said to Abby. "Surely you've got time for a quick cuppa."

Abby detected something different about her mother's manner and tone. It wasn't brusque or bossy so much as assertive.

Abby smiled. "Course I have."

Jean put her arm through Abby's and they headed toward the airport Starbucks. Jean's pace was brisk. She held her body erect, her chin forward.

Abby ordered a tall cappuccino. Her mother asked for a half soy half low-fat java-chip Frappuccino with an extra shot. "Ooh, and could I have some whipped cream on that?"

"My God, America's really rubbed off on you."

Jean shook her head. "Maybe a bit," Jean said as they sat down. "But it has more to do with what happened on the *Bantry*. Since then I have no problem asking for what I want. Do you remember that story I used to read you when you were little, about the mouse that roared? Well, I feel like that."

Abby nodded. "You've changed. Your body language is different. You look so poised and in control. I've never seen you like this before."

Jean took her daughter's hand. "Don't panic, poppet. I'm still the old me, deep down. It's just that I feel I've tapped into something that has been wanting to come out for a long time." She paused. "I don't want to go on about it, but my father really damaged me when I was growing up. He left me a frightened, cowering wreck, too frightened to say boo to a goose. Over the years, with your dad's help, I gained a bit of confidence, but I never realized quite how angry I was and how much I needed to let it out. The *Bantry* was the catalyst. When the owners wouldn't give in and pay us compensation, I suddenly became this erupting volcano."

"I thought perhaps that's what had happened," Abby said.

"And there's something else."

"What?" Abby could sense what was coming.

"I've never felt I was a good role model for you."

"Oh, Mum, stop. Please. You've been a fantastic role model—"

"How could I have been when I was at home all day, cooking and cleaning? I suppose I went to the Women's Institute, but that was about it. I never *did* anything. I've never achieved anything."

"You achieved me."

Jean took her daughter's hand and patted it. "I know. And I'm so proud of you, but at the same time I've always wanted to do something to make you proud of me."

Abby's eyes started to fill up. "Oh, Mum, I've always been proud of you. After all, you stayed at home to take care of me. I can't think of a time when you weren't there. Remember when I first started school and was really nervous every day and we'd sing 'One Hundred Bottles of Beer on the Wall' all the way there? And then when I was a bit older, you'd test me on my tables? Whenever there was a school play, I'd have the best costume. When we did that dramatized version of the Three Little Pigs and I was grass, you spent weeks sticking green raffia onto that cube of foam. And when that awful Hayley Saunders told me she didn't want to be my friend anymore, you scared her half to death with your lecture about karma. She told me years later she thought karma was some bloke who was out to get her. You've been the best mum."

"Thank you. That means so much to me." Jean picked up a spoon and began toying with the whipped cream on top of her coffee. "But when I started to lead the protest on the ship, I couldn't help thinking that I was doing something to make you *really* proud."

"You know something, Mum—this isn't about what I feel. This is about you. For the first time in your life, you feel proud of yourself, and that's what counts."

Jean nodded and let out a half laugh. "You're right. In a strange way, I was standing up to your grandfather."

"I think you were," Abby said. "So, what's next?"

"I'm doing the *Richard & Judy* show tomorrow, plus various newspaper and magazine interviews. A couple of publishers have approached me about writing a book about what happened on the *Bantry*. Then there are the requests for after-dinner speeches. But I thought when all the fuss finally dies down, I might set myself up as an assertiveness trainer."

Abby clapped her hands. "Brilliant. You'd be fantastic, Mum, just fantastic."

"You know what? I think so, too."

When they'd finished laughing, a look of concern came over Jean's face. "Abby, what's the matter? I've been looking at you and you seem preoccupied."

"Well, it's a long story, and I wasn't going to tell you until we got home." She took a breath. "Toby and I broke up."

Jean looked at Abby in amazement. "Good grief. Why?"

"Mum . . . Toby is gay."

"Gay? I don't understand."

"Toby is homosexual. He left me for a man."

"Abby, I know what gay means. What I don't understand is what he was doing getting engaged to you if he knew he was gay."

"He was too scared to come out."

"You mean he used you as a sort of smoke screen?"

Abby nodded.

"The bastard! How dare he?"

"Mum! You've never sworn like that in your life."

"I know. I'm only just getting the hang of it. The stress of the *Bantry* drove me to it. Your father doesn't approve of women swearing, but I have to say it's great fun. So liberating."

"Anyway, I've been seeing somebody else, but we've had a falling-out, which was sort of my fault and I need to fix it."

Just then Jean got a text on her mobile. "They're waiting for me in the conference room," Jean said. "I have to go."

The two women stood up. Jean put her arms round her daughter. "I am so sorry this happened to you. It must have been dreadful and I hate it that I wasn't there for you."

"It was OK. I had Scozz and Soph. Look, you go. We'll talk again tomorrow."

"Yes...and good luck fixing things with this new chap."

"Thanks, Mum. And, by the way, I'm really, really proud of you." She put her arms round her mother and held her tight.

AS ABBY made her way back to her car, she tried Dan again on his house phone and on his mobile, but he was answering neither.

When she arrived at Mr. T's flat, Ichiro was waiting for

her. He was wearing a silver lamé tunic over skinny jeans. He planted a kiss on each of her cheeks. "All the flowers are here and everything is totally awesome." He led her into the enormous living room. "I put all the flowers in buckets and vases like you said. We didn't have enough, so I borrowed from the neighbors."

Ichiro had lined the containers full of blooms against the wall. She went over to look at them. The lotus flowers and baby pink peonies were open and perfect. The cherry blossom branches were covered in exquisite pink and white tissue-fine flowers. Her suppliers had done an excellent job. From outside, the divine fragrance of English lavender came wafting in.

Abby couldn't wait to get her hands on the flowers and start working. While Ichiro hung paper lanterns from the ceiling, she arranged the cherry blossoms so that they seemed to spill out of the giant floor vases she had rented. When she had finished with the blossoms, she turned her attention to the peonies. She arranged them in clear glass vases, each one a different size and shape, and stood them on Mr. T's Steinway. Bonsai trees were dotted on sideboards and occasional tables.

Two hours later, the fountain was bubbling gently next to the pagoda and filling a tiny brook. Abby looked heavenward and prayed none of the water would leak.

Ichiro couldn't contain himself. "Omigod, this is so totally awesome."

"I agree." The booming voice came from nowhere and made them both jump.

Mr. T had come into the flat and was now coming toward them. He ignored Ichiro. It was obvious he was still

furious with him for handing in his notice. "Miss Crompton, this is very good work. Very good work indeed. I shall
recommend you to all my friends. I love big penis. I tell all
my friends you give me very big penis."

"Oh, Mr. Takahashi, I'm not sure that is such a good
idea. You see—"

His face suddenly broke into a broad, mischievous grin.
"OK, maybe not." Then he winked at her. He turned to
Ichiro, barked some orders in Japanese and then disap-
peared.

No sooner had Mr. T left than the intercom buzzer
went off. Ichiro answered it.

"Dan? Look, I don't know how you found out Abby was
here, but I'm pretty sure she doesn't want to see you."

Abby ran over and grabbed the intercom phone from
Ichiro: "Yes, yes, I do. Dan, come up." She pressed the door
release.

"I don't geddit. That evening when we were in the court
canteen, we all agreed the man was a total jerk. Now you
want to see him? I'm telling you, Abby, you're in denial. So
many abused women are. You have to walk away, the way I
am walking away from Mr. T. He isn't going to change."

"Don't worry, Ichiro. You don't understand. Things
have changed. There's been a huge mistake. It was all my
fault."

"Sweetie, it's what all abused women say. I used to think
like that. I thought it was me who made Mr. T mad. Now I
know that I'm not to blame for his behavior, and you're not
to blame for how Dan treats you. His behavior is his responsibility, not yours. You poor deluded girl. Now, when
he gets here, I'm not going to let him in."

"But you have to. I'll explain later. I promise. You have to believe me. There really has been a mistake. Dan never cheated on me. Really, he didn't."

"Abby, there is no mistake. The man is a two-timing bastard. He will never be faithful. I know it's painful, but you have to face up to it. Get angry if you want. Cry if you need to. Lash out and scream. We could even chant if that helps."

The doorbell rang.

"Please, Ichiro. Please let him in. I'm begging you."

Ichiro sighed. "OK, if you say so."

He opened the door and greeted Dan with a face like stone. Not that Dan noticed. He ran toward Abby and took her in his arms.

When they started kissing, it was breathless and frantic.

Ichiro grimaced and tutted with disapproval and made no effort to move. Abby decided that he was either desperate to find out what had been going on or he had gotten it into his head that Dan could turn violent. She wasn't about to ask which it was. Neither was she going to waste more time trying to convince Ichiro that Dan wasn't the bastard he thought he was. Instead, she led Dan out onto the terrace and closed the sliding door behind them.

It was dark now and the air was cold. Dan took off his jacket and put it round Abby's shoulders.

"I just spoke to Cinders. She said you'd stopped by."

Abby nodded. "Burst in, more like. Liam looked as if he wanted the ground to swallow him up. Then Cinders explained everything and how I'd gotten the wrong impression. I don't know what to say. I've behaved so badly and made such a fool of myself."

"You were angry. When you came round to my flat the

other night and found us, it must have looked awful—Toby and Christian all over again. I just wish you'd given me a chance to explain."

"I know. I should have taken your calls, but I pretty much hated you by then." She paused. "How did you know I was here?"

"I phoned Scozz. Don't worry, he didn't betray you on purpose. He just let it out by accident. I think it's all this excitement at getting Debbie Harry back."

"Well, I'm glad he told you. I've been trying to get you, but your phone's been off."

"No battery. I forgot to put it on charge when I got back last night." He rearranged the jacket so that it fit more securely on her shoulders. "You know, it was only after you said you never wanted to see me again that I realized..."

"Realized what?"

He moved forward. She was aware that they were standing with their foreheads and noses practically touching. "That I have fallen in love with you."

"I love you, too."

"You do?"

She nodded.

"I think I fell in love with you in the elevator when you hyperventilated into that paper bag."

"And I fell in love with you when I discovered you'd been winding me up about Bialystock joints and Ulla oscillators."

"I was so proud of that," he chuckled. "So, do you think you can cope with me being rich?"

"Dan, you need to understand that my problem with Toby wasn't that he was rich per se; it was his snobbishness and all his dreadful friends. You are the kindest, most unaffected person I've ever met. And your dad's great, too. Of course I can cope with you being rich."

"Dad told me he popped in to see you and all you wanted by way of reward was for his pilot to pop over to Majorca to pick up the lavender for tonight's party."

"Yes, but your dad saved my bacon. If I'd let down Mr. T, he'd have bad-mouthed me to all his friends and my business would have been severely up a creek."

"I know. God, you must have been bloody petrified. I'm sorry you had to go through all that on top of everything else."

"It's OK. It all worked out in the end."

"Anyway, talking of business, I have news."

"Good or bad?"

"I have secured nationwide distribution for *Bouquet*."

"Omigod. That is sensational." She threw her arms round him. "Dan, I am so proud of you."

"You know how we've been rushing like mad to get a rough cut together—well, we finally finished and I was able to send it to this distribution company. That's why I was away. I was meeting with their chairman at his place in the Cotswolds. Anyway, he loved it."

"That means it has to be a hit, right?"

"It's not guaranteed by any means, but I think we could be well on the way. Having Cinders helped. I couldn't have done it without her."

"God, I really do have to make it up to her."

"Don't worry. She's pretty thick-skinned, and, anyway, I think she's got other things on her mind just now."

"I guess."

"So, getting back to me being rich, I take it you'd have

no problem flying to Rome next weekend in my dad's private jet?"

"Blimey. You get to use that?"

"Actually, I get to fly it."

"What? You're a pilot?"

"I am. That is my final ever secret. Promise."

"Cross your heart and hope to die?" She grinned.

"Absolutely."

"You know," she said, "I find pilots rather sexy."

"I was hoping you might." He pulled her toward him.

Surrounded by twinkling Japanese lanterns and candles, breathing in the heady aroma of lavender, they kissed again. Beyond them, the city sparkled like a box of jewels.

Inside, Ichiro was on the phone, pacing frantically, his words spilling over one another:

"Marty, whaddaya you mean, you don't know what's going on? I'm telling you, things are crazy here—Abby and Dan are on the terrace making out like it's their final chance before their plane goes down—I can't believe she is doing this after the way that asshole has treated her—the poor thing is so in denial—she needs help—I'm thinking we need to stage a full-on intervention here—you know what, maybe I should put in a call to my shrink back in Santa Monica...."